HIGH STAKES

"We have nothing to say to each other." Anne's eyes blazed with a blend of pain and rage. "You went out with me because of what you thought I could do for you," she challenged with contempt.

"No," Glenn denied. "Maybe at first I figured it wouldn't hurt my chances for advancement in the company, but that was only in the beginning. We had something great."

"I noticed!" she jeered, tears stinging her eyes.

"That isn't enough to make it in the world," he continued. "When Felicia phoned and asked me to take her to that benefit, I realized what she could do for me. Felicia won't be hampered by your brand of ethics. She'll do whatever is to her advantage and to hell with everybody else. When it comes to a showdown, she'll win over you."

"We'll see who wins!" Defiance lent sharpness to Anne's voice. Eventually either *she* would control the company, or Felicia would. They could never rule jointly.

LOYALTIES

JULIE ELLIS

ZEBRA BOOKS
KENSINGTON PUBLISHING CORP.

ZEBRA BOOKS

are published by

Kensington Publishing Corp.
475 Park Avenue South
New York, NY 10016

First Zebra Books printing: December, 1990

Printed in the United States of America

For Susie and Richie,
who believe with me that the world
can be made a better place in which to live

If a man walks in the woods for love of them . . . for half his days, he is esteemed a loafer, but if he spends his whole day as a speculator, shearing off those woods, he is esteemed industrious and enterprising—making earth bald before its time.

Henry David Thoreau

Prologue

BADEN-BADEN was discovered by the Roman Emperor Caracalla in A.D. 211, and he personally designed its first baths, still to be seen in the catacombs beneath the Römerplatz. In 1541 medical practitioner Theophrastus Paracelsus declared the hot springs of Baden-Baden the most perfect in the world. The internationally famous spa—visited in season by royalty, the diplomatic set, and those simply very rich—lies midway between Paris and Vienna, on the east bank of the Rhine, with the Black Forest as an awesome backdrop.

In this July of 1855, Baden-Baden took pride in its reputation as the "Queen of the Black Forest." No one loved the Black Forest more than fifteen-year-old Annie Sudermann. She expected to spend her life in her hillside village overlooking the immaculate white town of Baden-Baden, with the Black Forest forever there for her. On this late afternoon she had no inkling of the upheaval her life was about to undergo.

Today Annie walked swiftly from the Hotel zum Hirsch—where she worked as a chambermaid—along the wide, immaculate streets that led away from the hotels and the homes of the wealthy to the modest village where she lived now with her sister Hannah and her brother-in-law Ernst. This was the day on which she received her wages, religiously handed over to Hannah each week.

The heat diminished as she left the town behind her. A shimmering mist hung over the broad, clear river. She was thankful that tomorrow she would not go to the hotel. When she was done helping Hannah in the house, she would walk deep into the forest, where the air was always crisp and the towering dark firs and pines, the moorland tarns, the lush green moss made this a special private place, the centuries-old trees her friends. At the rustic cottage built by Ernst with his own hands when Hannah was a bride, Annie pulled the door wide and walked inside. She stopped short, her pretty face etched with astonishment as she watched Hannah smooth a white crocheted tablecloth across the kitchen table. This tablecloth was used only on special occasions—when the other three sisters and their husbands came from nearby villages to celebrate a family wedding or to mourn a recent death.

All at once Annie's heart was pounding. She remembered with fresh anguish the last such occasion. Eleven months ago the sisters had gathered here to grieve for their father. Their mother had died when Annie was born, twenty-eight years after Hannah's birth. Annie knew the villagers had viewed her late arrival with superstition-tainted distrust. They whispered that Annie—so unlike her four older sisters—was a changeling.

"You're late," Hannah said querulously, extending a hand for Annie's wages. "You went into the forest instead of coming straight home from the hotel."

"No, Hannah. I'm early today." Though Hannah always sought to conceal her impatience at Annie's presence in the cottage, Annie knew she was an intruder. The last of Hannah's own children had married and moved away a year ago. "I came straight home."

"Go wash your hands and face and put on your good dress. Tonight Herr Sachs, who lives near Sophie, is coming for supper."

"Why?" Annie asked curiously.

"Because." Hannah was terse. And then her face softened. "Sophie and I worry about your future. You're not like the other young girls in the village. You frighten away the young men with your ways. But now something wonderful is hap-

10

pening. Only if you please Herr Sachs," she stipulated. "He's worked for years in the Black Forest. He's saved his money. Now he wants a wife." She paused dramatically. "To go with him to America."

"Me?" Annie gasped, pale with shock.

"If you please him. He hears that in America a woodsman can buy timberland for almost nothing. With what he has saved, Herr Sachs can have his own sawmill. Think of it, Annie! If Willi Sachs agrees to marry you, you'll have a husband with a business. You'll live in America!"

"I don't want to marry him," Annie said with rare defiance, her face suddenly hot. "I don't want to go to America!" A strange country, far from the Black Forest.

"If Willi agrees, you'll marry him," Hannah decreed. "He's considered Bertha, the butcher's daughter in Sophie's village. But you speak some English," she pointed out in triumph. Annie had learned English from visitors to the hotel. "That will be useful to him in America. Now go and change into your good dress."

Willi was thirty-eight years old, burned dark from the sun, brawny and with a belly that revealed an addiction to lager beer. Trembling, Annie stood before him when they had been introduced and geared herself for the comments about to be uttered.

"Pretty enough," he conceded, "but skinny. A strong wind would blow her away." But Annie saw the heat in his eyes.

"She's strong," Hannah said quickly. "These small, thin ones are deceiving. Annie works twelve hours every day at the hotel. Then she comes home and helps me with the house and the sewing. In the village school the teacher said she was the smartest child he'd ever taught."

Three days later Annie was married to Willi Sachs. The following morning—after a night of submission to Willi's crude, rough passion, which she tried to erase from her mind—they began the first lap of their trip to America. Each night Annie gritted her teeth and told herself it was a wife's obligation to submit to her husband. Embarrassed but determined, Hannah had been blunt about this.

In America Willi and Annie traveled north to a town in New York called Albany, known as the "timber capital of the world." As Willi anticipated, he was able to buy from the state for twelve and a half cents an acre a tract of four hundred acres a few miles up the Hudson. Annie's homesickness for Baden-Baden and the Black Forest lessened as she walked in awe through the pristine forest, lush with white pines, that now belonged to her husband. Some of the blue-green needled pines grew to a height of more than two hundred feet. Willi boasted the Eastern white pines were the most important trees in North America.

But Annie was sick with shock when she realized that all of these fine, tall trees would be cut down to be fed to the sawmill Willi would set up in the spring when the logging was done.

"Not just a few acres here and there," Willi gloated. "Every tree means money! In Albany the lumber business is booming. I can sell every foot of board I bring in!"

Here in America timbermen were clear-cutting the forests—cutting down all the trees in a stand—and then moving on to virgin timberland in another area. In the Black Forest there were strict rules about which trees might be cut.

"I'm going to be rich, Annie," Willi boasted while they walked together through his newly acquired timberland, and he slapped her on the rump. "It's all there for me to take!"

Willi set up the most primitive of lumber camps along the Hudson. A log bunkhouse with straw-filled bunks in tiers and an area where the lumberjacks sat around in the evenings to drink, smoke, chew tobacco, and swap stories. For Annie and himself he'd built a crude hut that was also the workmen's kitchen.

Annie cooked for the men. Their meals of necessity reduced to beans and salt pork, bread and molasses, and strong bitter tea. Willi had haggled over wages, hiring as cheaply as possi-

12

ble. He forced Annie to account for every scrap of food she put on the table.

"Give the bastards enough to eat, but don't let 'em eat us out of my profits," he exhorted. "Stretch the salt pork. Don't make the tea so strong."

And each night that he was not too exhausted for the effort, he exercised his brutish lust on her. First sullen, then furious and reproachful as the months sped past without her becoming pregnant.

"What kind of a wife are you who can't give me a son?" he railed in shame.

Annie knew the men taunted Willi in ribald humor about the continued flatness of her belly. And they looked at her with barely concealed desire. Theirs was a lonely, isolated world—Annie the only woman the men in their lumber camp saw for weeks at a time. They were rough, tough, hard-drinking, but they knew they'd best not try to dally with the boss's woman.

Annie loathed the bitter winter—the below-zero weather, the blizzards, in painful contrast to the less severe weather of Baden-Baden. She was relieved when spring arrived and the logging was done. Now the logs were driven downriver to Willi's new sawmill. She and Willi would spend the spring and summer in more civilized quarters in Albany.

Her life settled into a pattern of lumber camp in winter, sawmill in spring and summer. The years raced past. The country was torn apart by the Civil War, but this hardly touched their lives. On March 3, 1863, Congress empowered President Lincoln to draft men between the ages of twenty and forty-five. Willi had just reached his forty-sixth birthday. Willi's bitterness grew uglier when, despite his efforts, Annie did not conceive. She was relieved when at last he abandoned hope of giving her a child and only on rare occasions wrestled with her under the blankets.

Annie watched in futile despair while Willi and his lumber-jacks pillaged their forestland. Willi was smug in the knowl-edge that by owning both forestland and sawmill he was amassing more money than he had dreamt was possible—but they continued to live as though poverty-stricken.

In the fall of '72—after more than seventeen years of marriage—Annie realized in astonishment that she was carrying a child. Willi strutted with gross pride that at the age of fifty-five he would soon be a father. Now he plotted a new life for them. With a son on the way he was greedy for wealth. Their forests were almost barren, but Willi reminded Annie that there was always more timberland to be had in this enormous country, though a few people—stricken by the sight of stark, barren land where once there had been thick stands of trees—cried out in concern. In this same year the first national step to conserve scenic resources was taken. Yellowstone National Park, the first national park in the world, was established.

"We're moving out," Willi decided when Annie was in her eighth month. "To Saginaw. I hear a man can buy timberland in Michigan dirt cheap. I'll go ahead and buy, then come back for you and the boy."

But the son Willi was convinced Annie carried was a daughter. Still—after a few days of initial disappointment—Willi was proud of having sired a child. All the affection he had never shown his wife was bestowed on tiny Naomi.

Willi was pleased also by the passage of the new Timber Culture Act, which provided 160 free acres to anyone who agreed to cultivate trees on a quarter of those acres. It was a simple matter for cagey loggers to cut down the trees on 120 of these acres and then make a pretense of "cultivating" the 40 acres left untouched.

"The government made me a present," he gloated to Annie when the 160 free acres were added to those he had bought at a pittance.

Now—not for Annie or himself but for his tiny daughter—Willi built an ostentatiously large house in the new Victorian style, dark and foreboding inside and adorned with an excess of stained and varnished woodwork. He sent Annie out to buy furniture, then humiliated her by sending back the classically beautiful designs she chose and replacing them with awkward, distastefully ornate pieces, all the while complaining "we're bein' robbed blind by those vultures."

But except for the house and its ugly, expensive furnishings, Willi was tighter than ever. Annie was forbidden to buy new clothes for herself; he bought nothing for himself. Annie must mend every garment. She must account for every penny spent on the table. But regularly he ordered Annie to buy new dresses, new bonnets for Naomi.

Now Annie remained in Saginaw when Willi went to the lumber camp in the winter months. He complained about having to hire a cook. He predicted poverty for them in the face of the current financial panic and the shocking political scandals erupting in the nation involving five cabinet officers and a group of congressmen—though in truth they were not affected. At intervals he left the lumber camp—when the weather permitted—to come home to see his daughter and occasionally to exert his husbandly privileges, though Annie knew he was visiting the plushier whorehouses when he was in Saginaw.

Two years later Annie gave birth to a second child. Willi—again convinced he had given his wife a son—stalked from the house in rage when the midwife informed him that he had a second daughter. He ignored Rachel—"Rae" to her mother almost from birth—and squandered all his attentions on strong-willed, tempestuous little Naomi. Nor did he ever return to his wife's bed again. He was satisfied to dally in the whorehouses of Saginaw, now a booming lumber town.

Willi spoke to his wife and younger daughter only when it was essential to his comfort. Annie devoted herself to the children, socializing little because she knew that local residents disliked Willi for his arrogance, his crudity, his often shady business practices. She read all that was written by the new conservationists. She worried about the raping of American forests.

She read about Senator Carl Schurz of Missouri, who labeled the timber barons "thieves who steal whole forests." He pleaded for forest preserves, pointing to the millions of acres of American forests that were now wastelands, their soil destroyed by erosion. She applauded when President Hayes—in 1877—appointed Senator Schurz Secretary of the Interior.

"The goddamn bastard!" Willi yelled. "Schurz is tryin' to ruin us! Can't he see we got enough forests in this country to last us forever? We cut down, and they grow back. Folks in this country need lumber to build. How's this country gonna grow with crazy men like Schurz tryin' to tell us what to do?"

Willi joined with other Michigan timbermen to press for retaliation by their congressmen. These efforts were duplicated throughout the country. Carl Schurz—himself once a German immigrant—was labeled "outrageous, un-American." The programs he recommended would destroy "honest enterprisers who form the solid backbone of the Republic." The timber barons were triumphant when the pressures they exerted were successful.

Annie gritted her teeth and refrained from expressing her own opinions. Her job, she told herself, was to raise her two daughters and to keep Willi's house. Physically, Naomi and Rae were striking replicas of their still-lovely mother, but Naomi had inherited her father's explosive temper, his unpredictable moods. Naomi loved to go with her father to see the trees chopped down; Rae cried at the sight of a tree falling to the ground. It worried Annie that Rae would so often capitulate to Naomi's demands rather than fight back.

While often Naomi was an enigma to her, Annie could understand affectionate, warm, quietly intense Rae. She felt Rae's bewilderment, her hurt that her father ignored her but doted on Naomi. She was recurrently distressed that her own efforts to change Willi's attitude toward his younger daughter were futile. In truth, she and Rae were little more than inanimate objects in Willi's daily life.

16

In 1883, when Naomi was ten and Rachel eight, Willi died of a stroke in a whorehouse bed. In addition to his wife and daughters, only a sprinkling of business acquaintances attended his funeral—eager to buy the business from his widow at a distress price. Willi had no friends.

Annie listened with strained politeness to the offers made, her fury growing that these men dared to try to buy at such ridiculous prices. *Because she was a woman.* Her bright mind grappled with her options. Suddenly she determined to take over the company herself. Despite her role as housewife and mother, she had assimilated much about the inner workings of the timber business. She amazed their competitors by rejecting all offers. Henceforth Annie Sachs would run Sachs Timber Company.

She knew their acquaintances were shocked that she would dare to enter the business world. It was unwomanly. She had two daughters to raise. Her place was in the home. But buoyed by the new freedom provided by Willi's death, Annie was determined to run the company. She would provide for her daughters. They would lack for nothing despite the loss of their father.

To the astonishment of the town, quiet and gentle Annie proved an excellent business woman. Sachs Timber prospered during the coming years. Annie raised her daughters with a firm hand, though often her battles with headstrong Naomi were secretly unnerving. She acquired friends, entertained at small dinner parties designed to expand her daughters' social lives. Though there were eligible men who looked upon her with interest, Annie never once thought of marrying again. Her children were her life.

On Naomi's sixteenth birthday Annie and the girls moved into a beautiful new house overlooking the river. During the past two years Annie had discarded the ugly furniture Willi had chosen and replaced it with tasteful pieces. The time was coming to look seriously for suitable husbands for her daughters. Annie was confident in the knowledge that they were

17

eminently marriagable, their mother's financial status being sure to appeal to the best families in town.

But Naomi, ever willful, rejected suitor after suitor. She flirted outrageously, gave each hope of success, and then moved on to another eager young man. By the time Naomi was eighteen—her girlfriends either wives or engaged, or humiliated at the prospect of becoming "old maids"—Annie was fearful of her older daughter's future.

A bright student, Rae graduated at sixteen from Miss Simpson's School for Young Ladies in a garden ceremony in early June of 1891. She was elated at the prospect of going in the fall to Cornell University in Ithaca, New York.

"Mama, you're letting Rae go to a coeducational college?" Naomi shrieked, and Rae sensed an undertone of outraged envy. Neither of the Sachs girls had ever shared a classroom with a boy. "A thousand miles away from home?"

"Rae will be fine," Annie Sachs insisted. "She's been well brought up."

Annie was proud of Rae's decision. Naomi had not once considered higher education. Still, Annie was wistful at the prospect of Rae's living in Cornell's Sage dormitory, far away from home. But they'd write each other twice a week, she comforted herself.

Three days after graduation Rae met handsome young Joseph Mueller at a soda fountain run by his uncle. Over chocolate ice cream sodas Rae and her friend Delia listened while Joseph's uncle explained that his nephew was only in America five months and that he had come to Saginaw to open an office as a consulting forester.

"It's a new thing in America, this being a forester," Mr. Mueller explained, beaming at his nephew. "Joseph went to a forestry school in Germany and then in France. He speaks three languages," he added with pride.

"Two and a quarter," Joseph chuckled, his eyes betraying his interest in Rae. "My English so far is not good."

"Oh, but it is," Rae said with admiring intensity.

"Tell your mama about Joseph," Mr. Mueller encouraged.

18

"In America we don't have men trained like this. Maybe one or two," he shrugged. "But your mama should hear what he has to say about managing the forests."

Annie was pleased to invite Joseph Mueller to dinner along with his uncle. Naomi was away at the Grand Hotel at Mackinac Island with a girlfriend and her mother. Rae and Annie sat at the Duncan Phyfe table in the Sachs's elegant dining room and listened to Joseph talk ebulliently about his growing-up years in Freudenstadt, high in the Black Forest mountains and close to Baden-Baden, while his uncle beamed that he and his nephew were being entertained by such a prominent family. At intervals Rae's eyes left Joseph's face to rest tenderly on her mother, caught up in nostalgic memory of her childhood.

Though his uncle was not a member of Saginaw's upper social circle, Joseph became part of the Saginaw group that included the wealthy young ladies and gentlemen of the town. They went on exuberant cycling outings, picnics in the nearby woods, attended parties at one another's houses, watched the Fourth of July parade together, and the fireworks display afterward.

Joseph acquired an assignment for the summer as consultant to Sachs Timber Company and anticipated another job in Saginaw in the fall. He talked openly to Rae about his towering ambitions. Born into a modest home, he had envied the wealthy guests who came to the Black Forest resort towns.

"One day I mean to live in the fashion of men like J. Pierpont Morgan and Andrew Carnegie and John D. Rockefeller," he said with a mesmerizing intensity.

Rae understood. Mama was rich in the eyes of folks in Saginaw, but Joseph spoke of another world. A world he meant for her to share. Still, for propriety's sake they strove to conceal their true feelings from others, since they had known each other only a few weeks. Not even Delia—her best friend—had been told. But secretly Joseph had declared his intentions. She exhorted him not to talk to her mother yet about a formal engagement. Mama was so pleased about her going off to Cornell that she must attend college for a year before she and Joseph were to marry.

"Rae, it'll be so awful with you away at college," Joseph sighed.

"I'll be home for Christmas," she comforted. "The railroads are making such wonderful time. My goodness, you can go all the way from New York City to San Francisco in seven days!"

"At Christmas let me talk to your mother," he pleaded. "And when you finish your freshman year at Cornell, you'll come home and we'll be married."

"Yes," Rae promised, her face radiant. "Oh, Joseph, I do love you."

Naomi came home from the Grand Hotel only a week before Rae was to leave for Cornell. With a flurry of self-consciousness Rae introduced her sister to Joseph at a party at Delia's house. Naomi knew instantly that they were interested in each other, Rae guessed. She recognized Naomi's wise little smile.

Late that evening Naomi charged into her bedroom. "Rae, you've got a beau! You're such a sly little kitten—you didn't say a word." She was looking at Rae as though she had never truly seen her before.

"Naomi, don't tell Mama," Rae pleaded. "Not yet." Why couldn't she ever keep anything secret from Naomi?

On a steamy Saturday morning a few minutes past eight Naomi watched stealthily from a bedroom window while Rae and their mother climbed into the stylish family landau for the trip to the railroad station. She'd said good-bye to Rae the night before, since she never left her bed before ten in the morning. She frowned in irritation. It was disgusting the way everybody made a fuss because Rae was going off to college.

Girls of their "means and quality" in big cities never went off to school or even thought about having a profession. They were supposed to marry rich men and take their place in society. How would *she* ever marry rich here in Saginaw? Mama had only allowed her to go to the Grand Hotel with Eleanor and her mother because Eleanor's mother insisted places like the Grand Hotel were fine for "husband hunting."

Naomi left the window and settled herself on the bed again. She wished she was still at the Grand Hotel. It was so dull here. At the Grand Hotel you never knew who would show up. Famous people like the Marshall Fields and the Swifts and the Armours visited the hotel. *Really* rich people.

Everybody in Saginaw thought Mama was rich. If they were rich, they wouldn't live in Saginaw. They'd live in Detroit or maybe New York. They'd travel to Europe every year and buy their clothes in Paris.

If Mama was smart, they'd be rich. She leaned back against the pillows and thought about how Mama was so stupidly concerned about their timberland. Other timber owners didn't waste time—and money—letting whole stands of trees just stay there earning nothing. Papa had been dead eight years, but she still remembered him saying, *"Every tree is money in the bank. When we run out of forests here, we'll move west. Plenty more for the taking."*

Papa would have kicked Joseph out of his office instead of listening—the way Mama did—to his fancy ideas about managing their timber. Mama invited Joseph to dinner all the time because she liked to talk to him about Baden-Baden and the Black Forest. Didn't Mama know Rae was just wild about Joseph? No. All Mama thought about was running the business. Now Rae was on her way to Cornell University halfway across the country. Did she expect Joseph to wait around for her to come home?

A secretive smile lighted Naomi's face, lent a provocative glint to her eyes. It was time Joseph Mueller realized Rae had a sister. He had hardly looked at her so far, though he'd been here for dinner twice since she came home. All the girls thought he was so good-looking. If she wanted to, she could take him away from Rae. It just might be fun to do that.

21

Annie was at first disturbed when Naomi began to give a succession of parties at the house—always inviting Joseph and singling him out for special attention. She had expected Joseph to approach her about marrying Rae. But, she considered, Rae had gone off to college. If she were in love with Joseph, she would have fretted at such a long separation.

It was a compulsion with her to see her daughters *happily* married—not for Naomi and Rae the bitter, painful marriage their mother had endured. While Joseph did not represent himself as Naomi's suitor, Annie knew Naomi was in pursuit.

Tonight, closeted in the room that served as her office at home, Annie enjoyed the gay laughter of the young people in the drawing room, the sound of Naomi's untrained but pleasing voice singing the popular "After the Ball" while one of the young men played the piano.

Annie was conscious of a pain in her chest. She frowned in annoyance. Heartburn again. She must tell Mattie not to serve fried food so often. She glanced at the clock on her desk. Naomi's guests would be leaving soon. That meant it was time for her to make a brief appearance as their official chaperone.

On impulse she asked Joseph to remain a few moments when the others left. She knew he was now working as a consultant for another company, but it would not be unseemly to ask him what he was hearing about two other firms pulling out of Saginaw. Rumor was that they'd cut out their holdings of white pines in the Great Lakes area and were moving west.

Annie realized that her own lands were not inexhaustible. How much longer could she continue to operate here? She clung to her decision to leave one acre untouched for each five cut. Still, another three or four years and she'd be running out of timberland. It was disturbing to consider pulling up stakes and moving.

Annie sat with Joseph and Naomi before a blazing fire in the cozy family sitting room. Joseph was disarmingly eager to talk shop.

"I hear that out west—in California and Oregon and Washington—there are huge stands of timber that can cut thirty thousand feet to the tree," he confided. "Can you imagine the possibilities, Mrs. Sachs?"

"A lot of that talk may be bunkhouse myths," she cautioned.

"If it's true, and I suspect it is, from the way important timber people are beginning to set up out there, there are unbelievable fortunes to be made." Joseph glowed with ambition.

"Mama, you look tired," Naomi said, ingratiatingly solicitous. "Enough of timber talk. You go on upstairs to bed, and I'll see Joseph to the door."

While her mother walked up the graceful winding staircase that led to the second-floor bedrooms, Naomi strolled down the hall with Joseph to the front door—her mind conjuring up a future that a smart man like Joseph Mueller could make reality.

"Why don't you like me, Joe?" She stood before him, her eyes contriving to be both accusing and inviting.

"Naomi, of course I like you," he stammered.

"You don't act like it," she pouted. "You act as though I don't exist." She dropped a hand on his arm, lifted her face to his. "I think you're the most fascinating man I've ever met."

"Naomi, I . . . " He seemed to be involved in some inner struggle. "I think you're beautiful."

"Then show it," she commanded, lifting her face to his. "Joe," she purred, "don't you want to kiss me?"

His mouth came down on hers as though he were mesmerized. Her arms closed in about his shoulders, and she thrust her slim body against his. All at once the awkward kiss was passionate and knowing. They clung together for heated moments until Joseph pulled his mouth from hers.

"Naomi, I'm sorry," Joseph apologized, shaken by his temerity.

"I'm not," Naomi said with deceptive sweetness.

Naomi was amused by the way Joseph tried to avoid her in the coming days and was triumphant at her effect on him.

He was dying to kiss her again, she gloated. He wanted to do everything with her—like if they were married. Then all at once this wasn't a game anymore, just to prove she could take him away from Rae. Listening to him talk to Mama, she realized how ambitious he was—and how smart. Joseph would be rich someday. Detroit-rich, not like Mama.

With Christmas approaching, and Rae due home from college in ten days, Naomi was determined to reel-in Joseph for keeps. She gave a surprise birthday party for Eleanor and contrived for Joseph to remain afterward to talk to her mother about how yet another timberman was pulling up stakes to head westward.

"Here in America we can't control forestry the way we have in Europe," Joseph explained to Mrs. Sachs, and Naomi listened in absorbed attention. "Most of the woodland in this country is in the hands of private owners. The government can't tell them what to do. And what they want," he said with a mixture of unease and envy, "is to wring every dollar they can from their timberland."

"But the time will come when we'll have no more trees to cut," Annie worried. "This country will face a timber famine."

"Mama, enough business talk," Naomi decreed. "You're looking so tired. Go on upstairs to bed. I'll see Joseph to the door." She remembered with a surge of excitement the last time she had said this. Tonight would wind up her little campaign.

"I've stayed too long." Joseph smiled apologetically as he rose to his feet.

"I always enjoy talking with you about the timber business," Annie told him. "And about home."

Annie left the drawing room to go upstairs while Joseph paused at Naomi's instructions to bank the fire in the grate.

"Joe, I think it's wonderful that you know so much about the trees," Naomi said softly when he rose to his feet and deposited the shovel he'd been using on the hearth. "Someday you're going to be very important in the lumber business."

24

Her eyes glowed admiringly as she leaned toward him, the neckline of her dress revealing a sliver of curvaceous breasts. "And very rich," she predicted.

"I aim to be." He cleared his throat, his eyes involuntarily fastened to the delectable view she provided.

"Why do you keep running away from me?" she reproached. "Don't you want to kiss me again?"

"Yes." It was an anguished admission. "Oh, God, yes!"

She lifted her mouth to his in provocative invitation. Her arms tightened about his shoulders while their mouths clung. And then one hand moved to find his and bring it to the neckline of her dress. She heard the low groan of excitement well in his throat while his hand found its way to the rich spill of a breast and fondled. She was conscious of the hard mass that pressed against her pelvis.

"Let's go into the little sitting room," she whispered. "Nobody will bother us there."

"Naomi!" Joseph gasped, but she knew he couldn't wait.

"It'll be wonderful, Joe," she promised and reached for the doorknob.

After tonight, Naomi reminded herself—while Joseph hovered over her on the absurdly uncomfortable sofa and labored to enter where no man had been before—he would have to ask her to marry him.

Later, when he had kissed her good night at the door, Naomi whispered sweetly in his ear.

"Joe, talk to Mama about us tomorrow. Tell her we want to be married in June."

Pale with disbelief but determined not to show it, Rae sat beside her mother in the landau and listened to the report of Naomi's engagement to Joseph. In his last letter he had seemed as ardent as ever. He'd mentioned parties in town, dinner at the house on Thanksgiving. *How could Naomi do this to her?* No doubt in her mind that this was of Naomi's doing.

"They'll have a big church wedding in June," Annie went

on, glowing with maternal pleasure. "You'll be Naomi's maid of honor."

"No!" Rae recoiled from the vision of herself standing at the altar while Naomi was being married to Joseph.

"Rae, why not?" Her mother stared in dismay. "Naomi will be hurt."

"I hate fancy weddings." Rae struggled for composure. "I mean, everybody sitting there and staring. I'd just die, Mama." Naomi *knew* she and Joe were secretly engaged. All their lives Naomi enjoyed taking things away from her. Every time she'd won a prize in school, Naomi always managed to break it. Last year when Delia's mother took Delia and her to Detroit and bought them each a beautiful ball dress, Naomi had been furious. When Delia's father gallantly said she looked like Rowena in *Ivanhoe* in that dress, Naomi managed to spill fruit punch down the front the second time she wore it.

"Rae, people will think it so strange that you're not your sister's maid of honor. However will I explain it to them?"

"All right," Rae capitulated. She'd stand up there while the minister married Naomi and Joseph and pretend she didn't care one bit. But inside she'd be dying a little.

Rae spent most of her school vacation with Delia. She contrived never to be alone with Naomi for one minute, but at intervals she was conscious of the glint of triumph in Naomi's eyes—and of Joseph's discomfort. When she'd congratulated him on his engagement to Naomi, he had turned crimson. And she sensed a wariness in him. He was scared to death she'd show his letters to Mama, she suddenly realized. Never! She had too much pride for that. Let Naomi have him if she wanted him so bad.

As soon as Joseph completed his current assignment, he was coming into Sachs Timber Company to work for Mama. Rae understood. Ambitious Joseph Mueller was visualizing himself as head of Sachs Timber Company one day. It would have been the same if he had waited for her, she thought in anguish. But he was too impatient to wait.

Rae was relieved when the time to return to college arrived. Though she dreaded the prospect of yet three more years away from home after this one, she vowed to stay at Cornell until she earned her degree. That way she would be away from Naomi and Joseph for long stretches of time.

Rae dreaded the fancy wedding, steeled herself to play maid of honor. After the church ceremony and the lavish wedding dinner attended by Saginaw's socially prominent residents, Naomi and Joseph left for a two-week honeymoon at the Grand Hotel, where they would occupy the honeymoon suite. Naomi had gone into a temper tantrum when her mother rejected a month-long European honeymoon, but Joseph had sided with his future mother-in-law. His presence was needed at the lumber company.

Rae knew it would be painful to live under the same roof with Naomi and Joseph. But the evening her sister and Joseph returned to the Saginaw house was the most anguished Rae had ever experienced. Long after everyone had retired for the night, she lay sleepless—painfully conscious that Naomi and Joseph shared a bed in a room just across the hall.

In the days ahead Rae comforted herself with the reminder that she'd soon be going back to school. But disquieting suspicions tugged at her. *Mama wasn't well.* She was pale. Often she seemed out of breath. She brushed aside Rae's anxious questions, but Rae was aware that she was shortening her hours at the office.

"I don't have to work so hard with Joseph in the business," Annie alibied. "It's time I relaxed a bit."

Rae secretly consulted with their family doctor. His evasiveness—no doubt at her mother's insistence—alarmed her even more. She refused to return to Cornell. She was terrified at the possibility of losing her mother.

Astonishingly, Naomi was displaying an interest in the lumber business. Rae knew her mother was pleased, once Joseph made it clear he offered no husbandly objections. Now it was Naomi who went into the office each morning with Joseph while her mother lingered in bed an extra two or three

27

hours. Soon it was obvious that even a few hours a day in the business exhausted Annie Sachs.

Though ordered to bed by her doctor, Annie insisted on making all major business decisions. Each night Rae stood at the foot of the bed, anxious that her mother not become over-tired from discussions with Joseph, with frequent contributions from Naomi, about the day's activities at Sachs Timber Company.

On Christmas Eve Annie insisted on coming downstairs while her two daughters and son-in-law decorated the tree— all of them aware that this might be her last Christmas. After an hour Joseph carried his mother-in-law upstairs to her bed. She would never leave it again.

Rae clung to her mother's bedside in the grueling days and nights ahead. Mama was only fifty-two. She should have many years ahead of her. But as the new year approached, the family realized that Annie Sachs had only days left of life. Rae slept in a chair across the room from her mother's bed. Mattie tiptoed into the room at intervals with a tray, urging Rae to eat.

On New Year's Eve Naomi and Joseph came into the room with Annie's attorney.

"Mama has to sign some papers for Mr. Leavitt so Joseph can take over the business," Naomi explained. "Go downstairs and tell Mattie to send up coffee for us. We might be here for a while."

Before 1893 rolled in, Annie Sachs was dead. Desolate— and fearful of a future without her mother—Rae lay across her bed and gave way to solitary grief. Naomi and Joseph, along with Mr. Leavitt, were making funeral arrangements.

After Annie's funeral, attended by a multitude of friends and business associates, her daughters and son-in-law returned to the house. Rae flinched as she walked into the foyer. *Mama would never be in this house again.*

"Rae, go tell Mattie to make us coffee," Naomi ordered imperiously. "Mr. Leavitt will be here in a few minutes to read Mama's will." Rae stared uncomprehendingly. "It's something the law requires. He has to read Mama's will to us."

Half an hour later Rae sat beside her sister on their mother's beloved Chippendale sofa and tried to assimilate what Mr. Leavitt was saying.

"Those are the formal terms," he said when he'd finished reading the will—clearly ill at ease. "What it means is that Naomi, as the older sister, inherits the business, the house, and the furnishings. She will, of course, look after your welfare, Rae. Those were your mother's wishes."

Despite her grief, her shock, Rae's mind was alert. She remembered Mr. Leavitt coming into her mother's bedroom only hours before she died. With papers to be signed. *Mama didn't know what she was signing.* Naomi had stolen her share of Mama's estate. But she wouldn't fight over Mama's belongings. It would be degrading to Mama to do that.

"I'd like to have the cameo Mama used to wear on special occasions." Rae fought for composure. "For sentimental reasons."

Within days after her mother's death, Naomi was fighting with Joseph about selling their timberland, the mill, and the house and moving out west. Sitting alone in her room after dinner one night, Rae heard them. Their strident voices carrying across the hall.

"Joseph, you've said yourself that people will be making unbelievable fortunes out west. Let's go out there while the timberland is for the taking!"

"Naomi, it's a big decision," he hedged. "We have to think this out carefully."

"You've told me that our sales are dropping off because we're running so much low-grade material," Naomi pushed.

"Not just us," Joseph said defensively. "Everybody in the Lake States is in trouble. Your mother was aware of that. Log supplies are dropping in quality."

"That's what I'm saying. Let's sell out and move west before we're caught in a situation we can't handle. Joe, everybody is saying the country's heading into a depression. Let's sell be-

29

fore prices drop to the bottom! Then buy land in California. We can buy tremendous acreage. Mama left a fortune in her bank accounts."

Naomi sounded like Mama, Rae thought. Mama had always been so smart about running the business. But Naomi wasn't concerned about conserving the forests the way Mama had been. Naomi was greedy. She wanted money and power.

By spring Annie Sachs's holdings had been sold—a fortunate move because the economic situation was causing much anxiety. The lumber market was showing signs of collapse. Some substantial timber people were wiped out.

Naomi, Joseph, and Rae headed for San Francisco. Naomi and Joseph meant to buy as much timberland in Mendocino County as Naomi's extensive funds would allow, after setting aside money for the construction of a sawmill. Funds that rightly should have been divided between the two sisters.

Still caught up in grief, Rae allowed her sister and brother-in-law to shape her life. Where could she go without money? What kind of job could she find that would take her away from this hateful household? The future seemed bleak and frightening.

The three moved into a rented, gingerbread-trimmed house on Lombard Street, in a quiet, genteel neighborhood. Later, Naomi said, she would buy a house. Naomi hired a housekeeper. Joseph rented a small downtown office at Kearny and California streets, which would be their San Francisco sales and marketing headquarters.

"You'll work at the office," Naomi told Rae. "All you have to do is receive phone calls and take messages. You should be able to do that," she said with familiar arrogance.

Rae spent lonely days in the office of the new Miller Timber Company. Naomi had insisted that in cosmopolitan San Francisco—where fine opera, theater, and concerts were part of daily life—she and Joseph would be known as Miller. It was more American than Mueller. In the evenings Rae sat alone and read. Naomi and Joseph were seldom home. They were dashing about Sonoma and Mendocino counties in search

30

of available Douglas fir timberlands plus a strategic locale for a sawmill. The huge Douglas firs—towering two hundred feet or more, their trunks fifteen feet in diameter and bark a foot thick—provided strong and knotfree lumber.

Because of the shakey economy Naomi was buying up timberland at far less than Joseph had predicted. Always friendly with people who called the office, Rae picked up valuable bits of information. She urged Naomi to extend her search to Humboldt County in the northern part of the state and to buy coast redwood tracts. She fought to make Naomi understand the difference between the Sierra redwoods—so difficult and wasteful to log—and the coast redwoods. The coast redwoods—their lesser girth more manageable—provided the most beautiful and useful of American woods. Their potential was awesome.

"Naomi, she's right," Joseph at last conceded. "Let's go up to Humboldt County."

Naomi and Joseph traveled north and bought huge tracts of coast redwoods. Though Naomi was still dubious about the efficiency of cutting down redwoods, she listened to Joseph's exhortation to buy.

While Naomi and Joseph were struggling to locate a mill within their price range, Rae learned in conversation with a bank clerk that a mill was to be sold at a sheriff's sale within the next week. Naomi connived with the bank officer to publish the wrong date for the sale, so that she and Joseph walked off with an incredible bargain. Because of the painful state of the economy Naomi was able to hire prospective loggers at shockingly low wages. The mill, she plotted, would run around the clock. Two twelve-hour shifts, rather than the normal ten-hour shifts.

Rae was enthralled at her first sight of the giant coast redwoods, that thrived in cool sea air and Pacific fogs. The huge trees, towering almost three-hundred feet in height and with trunks as much as twelve feet in diameter, grew astonishingly close together, as though fighting for space in the forest. How

Mama would have loved the redwoods, Rae thought wistfully. As she had loved the trees in the Black Forest.

"The world's largest trees," Joseph told Naomi and Rae with infinite respect, and for an instant Rae caught a glimpse of the old Joseph—before Naomi and ambition took charge of his soul. "Some of these were here before the birth of Christ."

"And they're going to make me one of the richest women in this country," Naomi prophesied. "You'll see."

Rae was pleased when Naomi and Joseph brought Marshall Lazarus, a gentle Southerner, to work in the office. He was knowledgeable about the lumber business, conscientious, and tireless. And it was good to have another person to share the long hours of each day.

A warm, intelligent young man, Marshall lived in a furnished room. He talked pensively of his hometown in South Carolina, though since the death of his parents he had roamed from place to place. Like Rae he loved the woods.

"I have a tree outside my window. Every morning," he said with wry humor, "I lean out and tell it 'good morning.'"

He had acquired no friends since arriving in San Francisco a few weeks earlier. Rae realized that, like herself, he was lonely. When he summoned up courage to invite her to go with him to the theater, she accepted. Mama would have approved, she comforted herself. And when she was with Marshall, she could brush away her feelings for her sister's husband.

Naomi was furious when she discovered that Rae was being courted by Marshall Lazarus.

"He's an employee of the company!" Naomi shrieked. "How dare he pursue my sister!"

"Marshall is a fine person." Color flooded Rae's face. "Mama would have liked him very much."

"He's a Jew. Let him find a girl of his own kind."

"Marshall didn't ask what church I attend," Rae shot back. In truth, they attended no church since Mama died. "I didn't ask his faith. He's a fine person," she reiterated.

"He's an unemployed person." Naomi's face was tight with rage. "I'm firing him tomorrow morning."

"You can't run my life anymore, Naomi." All at once Rae felt an exhilarating infusion of strength. She wasn't alone anymore—she had Marshall. "I won't stop seeing him."

"As long as you live under my roof," Naomi decreed with deliberate calm, "you won't see Marshall Lazarus."

Three days later Rae and Marshall were married by a justice of the peace. Despite the civil ceremony, Rae promised Marshall that she would observe his faith.

Rae promised herself that in time she would learn to love her husband. The morning after their wedding night—spent grandly at the Palace Hotel—they began the long trek to Belleville, Georgia, where Marshall had decided they would live.

"I have enough saved up to take us to Belleville and to set up a small sawmill. That doesn't cost much. And one day, my darling," he said tenderly, "we'll own a mountaintop of Georgia pine that would have made your mother proud. And we won't be clear-cutting, the way your sister and her husband are doing. We've got too much respect for the trees for that."

Tears blurred Rae's vision as their train chugged eastward through the night. She remembered Naomi as a little girl, even then trying to rule her sister's life. How could two sisters—sharing the same mother and father—part in rage this way?

Instinctively Rae knew she would never see Naomi again.

One

ONCE a sleepy town sitting on the banks of the clay-red Chattahoochee in northern Georgia, Belleville had mushroomed into a bustling city since the end of World War II. Most of its more affluent residents had moved away from downtown—a mixture of antebellum grandeur and urban blight—into beautifully laid out suburbs of pseudocolonials, Cape Cods, or "California" ranch houses, with picturesque curving streets and young landscaping. Occasionally a wise homeowner contrived to save a century-old magnolia or towering evergreen from destruction by builders, but most sprawling lawns featured only young saplings incapable of providing even meager shade.

Belleville's expansion was due to its dramatic emergence as a paper mill center, utilizing Georgia's second growth of pines. While the West Coast and western forests were dominating the timber industry, experts were predicting that in fifteen years the vast southern pines would take the lead. But as in much of America, some of its family lumber companies were being driven out of business by postwar competitiveness and the need for increased capitalization—at a time when bank interest rates were soaring to 12 percent. Lazarus Timber Company, founded by Marshall and Rae Lazarus seventy years ago, was fighting for survival.

On this Monday, November 25, 1963, Belleville's paper mills, its offices, its stores, its schools were closed. Since the terrible news had flashed around the world on the previous Friday afternoon, its residents, along with those of the rest of the nation, had clung to their television sets, shutting out of their lives everything except the drama of burying their assassinated president.

In the Lazarus family house, situated on one of Belleville's still-stately downtown avenues, the living room television set had been on since 7:00 A.M. In jeans and gray oxford-cloth shirt Anne Forrest, Rae's twenty-one-year-old grandaughter, sat on a Persian rug with slim legs tucked beneath her small frame, shoulders hunched in tension, blue-green eyes somber. The president who had mesmerized the younger generation with his commitment to a "New Frontier" was dead.

Anne's father leaned forward from a sage-green damask-upholstered lounge chair, his lean, patrician face reflecting his sense of loss—though he had never been a Kennedy admirer. The action on the television screen commanded his attention. John F. Kennedy was about to leave the White House for the last time.

"How much longer is this going on?" Denise Forrest shifted in impatience at one corner of the richly carved Empire sofa. Anne knew her mother was furious that her afternoon bridge party—like social events around the world—had been cancelled because of the tragedy. "It's all so morbid."

"Denise, shut up!" Kevin Forrest ordered without moving his eyes from the television screen. Anne was startled to hear her quiet, genteel father speak to her mother in such a tone. Sometimes she rebelled at his patient acceptance of her mother's petty tyrannies.

A year ago today, Anne remembered with fresh anguish, they had buried Grandma. And she remembered the hordes of people who had come to pay their last respects to Rae Lazarus. Everybody in Belleville had admired her, even those who bitterly opposed her in business. Despite advancing age, until that fatal heart attack, she had been at her office every day. Always fighting for the timber industry against greedy forest owners daring to clear-cut, against the illiterates who considered periodic burning of the woods a necessary ritual. She'd fought for ways to prevent and control forest fires, still a serious menace.

Her dark eyes red from crying, her generously padded shoulders drooping, Mary Lou came into the living room with a tray of coffee.

"Stay with us, Mary Lou," Kevin said gently. "Sit down and watch."

Mary Lou had first been Mother's nursemaid and then their housekeeper. She was like a member of the family, Anne thought tenderly. And President Kennedy had been somebody special to her because he was putting Negroes in top government jobs.

"Kevin, turn that thing off now," Denise demanded, although her daughter and husband were still engulfed in the tragedy that gripped the world. Denise's close friend, Avis Moore, whose husband was one of the wealthiest men in the South, was leaving in ten days for Maine Chance.

"I'm going to be just desolate here without Avis," Denise sulked, though in truth Avis was away from Belleville for at least seven months out of every year. "It would do me so much good to relax out there. Not that I need to take off weight, like Avis." She gazed complacently at her slim torso, perfect legs.

Still a beautiful woman at forty-eight, Denise relished the knowledge that strangers took her for fifteen years younger. She liked to believe that people thought she might be Anne's slightly older sister—though physically they bore little resemblance. Denise had inherited the Lazarus features, Anne those of her great-grandmother, Annie Sachs.

Mother knew how hard Dad was fighting to keep the business competitive, Anne protested silently. He'd had to borrow heavily from the banks, and each monthly payment was another crisis. How could Mother expect him to hand over money for her to lie around in a posh beauty spa? Wasn't it enough that she's be at the Moores' Palm Beach house for two weeks in January?

36

Mother didn't even remember that it was a year ago today that they buried Grandma. Dad remembered. He had been closer to Grandma than her only child. Grandma loved Dad like a son—because he was so much like Grandpa. Anne had only faint recall of her grandfather. He had died when she was seven.

She didn't honestly know what she wanted to do with her life, Anne reflected. She had come out of Barnard in June with a B.A. in English lit—not much she could do with that. Conscience told her she ought to be with others of her generation who were involved in sit-ins against segregation or working for voter registration or with the Peace Corps. She was hiding from guilt by working with Dad at Lazarus Timber. He'd said he needed her—"You think like your grandmother when it comes to the business."

The four years at Barnard had opened her eyes to so much. The civil rights movement, America's growing involvement in Vietnam, the new feminism. Living in a dorm in Manhattan had been culture shock—but she was glad for it. Whatever she was to do with her life, she vowed, she wouldn't become a carbon copy of her social-butterfly mother.

"Anne, I hear Ted will be coming home from Paris at Christmas," Denise said archly, puncturing her introspection. Ted was Avis's son, at the moment professing a commitment to art. A year earlier it had been writing. Anne interpreted her father's frown: He wanted her to marry Jewish. *"It saves a lot of trouble when you marry into your own faith."*

"Ted sounds as though he's coming home to stay this time," Denise continued. "Of course, we all know he'll eventually take over his father's business."

"Mother, I don't care what Ted Moore decides to do." Anne jiggled one foot in annoyance, ran a hand through her shoulder-length near-black hair. Mother was forever trying to throw her at Ted because of the Moore money. "There's lots more to think about in this world than getting married."

"You are the most impractical girl I've ever encountered!" Denise rose to her feet with an accusing glance at her husband.

37

"I knew she never should have gone to school up in New York. She's come back with a mess of weird ideas. Folks up north are just looking to make trouble for us. And that crazy talk about 'women's rights.' Southern women know from the day they're born how to take care of themselves. Kevin, can't you talk some sense into her?"

"Anne's a grown woman, Denise. And a bright one." He smiled affectionately at his daughter, though his eyes were somber. "She can see what a lot of folks here in town don't want to see."

"No matter what I say, Kevin, you always take Anne's side. Sometimes the two of you make me feel a stranger in my own house. I'm going upstairs to lie down for a while. These last four days have been just too much for my nerves."

Aboard the Miller Timber Company's private jet, beginning its descent to Belleville Airport, Arthur Blumberg geared himself for the task ahead. Only for Naomi Miller would he have allowed himself to be sucked into this weird mission, he thought grimly. Not because of the astronomical yearly retainer Miller Timber Company paid Blumberg, Marconi, and Stern, the law firm founded by his father. Because a dozen years ago, when his son Josh was a twelve-year-old at camp and badly injured by a hit-and-run driver, Naomi Miller had sent her private plane across the country to bring him home to San Francisco.

There were a lot of people who hated Naomi Miller. Some because of her sharp business dealings. Some out of jealousy. Others were obsequiously in awe of her because she was one of the richest, most powerful women in America. At ninety she still commanded enormous respect. A reluctant chuckle escaped him. At ninety she was shrewd enough to know how to control her empire even from the grave.

She'd looked so vulnerable lying there in her bed. Her elegant bedroom transformed into a hospital room. For the past eight days he had spent hours daily at her bedside, working to draw up the rash of documents that would assure her empire would continue according to her dictates even after her death. Two highly respected psychiatrists had examined her to attest that she was of sound mind at the time her new will was drawn up and signed.

Then last night she had sent her son, Doug, to ferret Blumberg out of a temple affair and bring him back to the house. "Nothing's changed in the will," she emphasized, her voice raspy with the effort to speak. The nurse shaking her head in disapproval at this effort. "But I want to see Rae's granddaughter. Make her think that her inheritance depends upon her coming out here. I want you to fly to Belleville, Georgia—Doug's alerted the crew. Tell her whatever you have to, but before I leave this world, I want to see my only grandniece. Artie, bring her home to me."

As though mesmerized by the events of the day, Anne and her father sat before the television screen watching a newscaster recap the happenings. On the sofa Denise sipped at a cup of Earl Grey tea and flipped through the current issue of *Town & Country*. She glanced up with a frown at the intrusion of the doorbell.

"Who has come calling on a day like this?"

Mary Lou was already hurrying down the hall to the front door.

"It's not Avis," Denise continued. "She and Herb flew up to Washington, D.C., yesterday to pay their respects. They can't be back yet."

Mary Lou appeared at the living room entrance.

"Hit's a gennamun to see Miss Anne," she reported hesitantly. "Mist' Blumberg from San Francisco."

"Show him in, Mary Lou," Denise ordered, shooting a questioning glance at her daughter. Anne shrugged in bewilderment.

"Yes'um."

A well-tailored man of about fifty, clutching an expensive

leather briefcase, walked into the room. Anne rose to her feet and smiled politely. *Why had he asked to see her?*

"I'm sorry to intrude on a day like this," he apologized, "but I'm here on an urgent matter. I'm an attorney with Blumberg, Marconi, and Stern of San Francisco. We represent Mrs. Naomi Miller." He paused, as though anticipating the shock this announcement would create.

Anne heard her mother's involuntary gasp. They knew, of course that Naomi Miller was Grandma's long-estranged sister. The internationally known "timber baroness." Though Grandma had never meant it to be that way, Naomi Miller was always an invisible presence in their lives.

Blumberg's eyes settled on Anne. "Your great-aunt, I believe."

"Yes." Anne managed a startled admission. Her mind charged back to the hot, humid night fifteen months ago, when her grandmother confided what she had kept locked inside for seventy years: that she and her sister Naomi had not fought over "some trivial disagreement" as always professed. First, Naomi had contrived to marry the man she loved—and then to steal her inheritance. Money that helped to lay the foundation of the Miller fortune. But only when Naomi tried to prevent her marriage to Marshall Lazarus—the real love of her life—did Rae break up with her sister. *"I've told this to no one, Anne—only to you."*

"Please sit down, Mr. Blumberg," Kevin said while Denise gaped in astonishment. "I'm Kevin Forrest, Anne's father, and—"

"I'm Denise Forrest," she interrupted. Bristling. "Naomi Miller is my aunt." Her implication was unmistakable. A niece should take precedence over a grandniece. The atmosphere in the living room was suddenly electric. *"If Mother and her sister had not behaved like two small brats, we'd be living in the lap of luxury,"* Anne remembered Denise fuming at regular intervals. "What is this all about, Mr. Blumberg?" Denise asked.

"Mrs. Miller is very ill," the attorney explained, sitting on the sofa beside Denise. "In truth, she's not expected to survive. She's very eager to see her sister's grandchild before she dies."

"What about her sister's *child?*" Denise demanded, her color high. "Does my aunt believe I'm dead?"

"Mrs. Miller has closely followed the progress of her sister and her family through the years, despite their long estrangement," he said evasively. His discomfort obvious. "At great expense, I might add. She knows about the Lazarus Timber Company." *So insignificant beside the Miller timber empire,* Anne thought. "About your marriage to Kevin Forrest," Blumberg told Denise. "About your attendance at Barnard," he smiled at Anne. "She was pleased to learn that you've spent your summers working with your grandmother at Lazarus Timber."

"My grandmother died a year ago." Anne struggled to keep back the surge of recriminations that assaulted her. "Not once in all the years did her sister make any effort to contact her. Or my mother or me." But Grandma kept secret scrapbooks containing newspaper reports of every major event in Naomi Miller's life, cut painstakingly from her subscription to the *San Francisco Chronicle.* Grandma knew about family births and marriages and about Naomi Miller's triumphs in business. She knew that Naomi's husband—whom she had once loved and had presumably loved her—died at forty-six in a tragic accident. She could hear Grandma's voice now, her anguish still fresh, revealing her efforts almost seventy years ago to mend the breach between herself and her sister: *"When I read in the* San Francisco Chronicle *that Naomi had given birth to a daughter, I was so excited. I wrote a long letter, sent a sterling silver cup for the baby. Naomi never replied."*

"Why does my great-aunt suddenly want to see *me?*" Anne's eyes challenged his.

"Mrs. Miller has only days ahead of her." Apprehension lent a sharpness to the attorney's voice. "She's clinging to life in the hope of seeing you."

"But not *me?*" Denise was shrill in indignation.

"I'm sorry, Mrs. Forrest. At this point in her life Mrs. Miller is concerned only about the future of the company she's spent

41

so many years building. It remains a private company—she's long refused to go public. She's convinced that her great-granddaughter and her grandniece are the two members of her family who are capable of continuing her empire. Under proper guidance, of course. Under certain circumstances," he turned to Anne, "you and her great-granddaughter, Felicia Harris, your cousin, will inherit ninety percent of the Miller Timber Company stock, divided equally between you."

Denise was rigid with rage. "Why am I being ignored?"

"Upon your aunt's death, Mrs. Forrest, you will receive an inheritance of ten thousand dollars," the attorney told her with a hint of reproof. "Your presence will not be required at the reading of the will. You will receive a certified check in that amount from the estate."

"My aunt is one of the richest women in the world!" Denise trembled with indignation. "And she deigns to will me ten thousand dollars?"

"Denise, that's ten thousand more than you ever expected," Kevin said with acrid humor.

For the rest of her life, Anne thought, Mother would be the outraged martyr. She'd talk about this endlessly at bridge parties and luncheons and charity affairs. How unlike Grandma, she told herself with a fresh sense of loss. Grandma had never once considered fighting for what was rightfully hers. *"I could never fight Naomi over Mama's money. It would be tarnishing her memory. Mama didn't mean it to be that way— I understood."* Grandma always said she was "Annie Sachs's child, Naomi was Willi Sachs's child."

"I'll take this to court!" Her mother's shrill voice punctured Anne's introspection. "You'll hear from our attorney!"

"No, Denise." Kevin was terse. "You'd spend more in legal fees than the ten thousand willed you."

"Anyone who contests the will automatically loses whatever has been left to him or her," the attorney cautioned.

"You said that Anne would be a major heir under certain circumstances," her father pinpointed. "Would you please tell us what these are?"

"First, Anne must agree to fly to San Francisco to see her great-aunt. Then—"

"Kevin, we're being so inhospitable," Denise broke in. With chameleon swiftness she became the charming Southern hostess, reluctantly accepting the role of mother of an heiress. "I'll ask Mary Lou to bring us coffee. And nobody can leave this house without trying Mary Lou's superb pecan pie."

Over whipped-cream–heaped pecan pie and chicory-laced coffee—in the Georgian dining room used only on formal occasions—Arthur Blumberg explained first the basic conditions of the will. Naomi's son, Douglas—with forty years experience behind him—was to train Anne and Felicia to run the Miller lumber business. Naomi had set up an elaborate working schedule: a twenty-year "internship," with 90 percent of the stock held in escrow for Anne and Felicia provided they fulfilled the terms of the will.

"I must explain that if either of the two young women fails to follow the terms of the will, then the ninety percent of Miller Timber Company stock held in escrow for them will go to the Naomi Miller Museum of Art in San Francisco," Mr. Blumberg said.

"Then it's Russian roulette." Anne clutched at a reason to reject Naomi Miller's dictates.

"Hardly." Mr. Blumberg's smile was gently reproachful. "When you consider the stakes, you must realize that it would be a rare person who won't follow through. Douglas will hold the deciding vote when there's an impasse in any major decision." Unexpectedly Blumberg smiled. "Mrs. Miller is sure her sixty-seven-year-old son will survive for the next twenty years. But provisions have been made in the event of his death."

While the attorney continued to explain in dizzying detail the conditions of the will, Anne tried to assimilate the situation. If she accepted the terms of the will, she'd be a millionaire many times over at the end of twenty years. In the meantime she would earn a starting salary of fifty thousand dollars a year, to be increased in increments of five thousand each year. Her

43

salary at Lazarus Timber—in difficult weeks unpaid—was fifty dollars a week. But could she survive in the framework Naomi Miller had devised?

"We'll be puppets on a string!" Anne said accusingly when Blumberg paused. "Indentured servants! And how can she expect me to learn to run a company as enormous as Miller Timber?" She was startled to feel a flicker of excitement at the prospect.

"Anne, you grew up in the timber business," her mother scolded. "All your life you've sat at the dinner table and listened to your grandmother and your father rehash the day's activities at our company. You've worked there during summers since you were fourteen. You soak up business details like a sponge—Dad's always saying that."

"Mrs. Miller is one of the shrewdest business women in this country." Blumberg's voice deepened in respect. "Doug has been an important asset, but *she* runs Miller Timber. She figures Doug can keep things on an even keel for four or five years; but then, she insists, fresh blood must come to the helm." He focused intently on Anne. "She's plotted your business education, and Felicia's, to spread over those four or five years. It'll be rigorous and demanding. Doug will be your instructor. Aside from her son, Mrs. Miller has only contempt for the business instincts of other family members—except for you, Anne, and Felicia. She's convinced you two have inherited her shrewdness and imagination." Blumberg smiled faintly. "She was quite impressed by that fire-control system you devised for the Lazarus timberlands last year."

"So was I." Kevin chuckled reminiscently.

"How did she know about that?" Anne felt oddly exposed. Someone she knew not at all knew so much about her.

"Your Aunt Naomi hires expensive detectives," Kevin surmised. "And Mrs. Miller is correct. Anne has a real feeling for the business. Like her grandmother and her great-grandmother."

"And like Felicia." Blumberg nodded. "Off the top of her head she made a suggestion that Mrs. Miller adopted for the

44

business. But this situation will come as a great shock to her. Felicia is more concerned with jet-set activities than with the lumber field. And I understand what a tremendous shock this is to all of you," he added compassionately. "I realize you need time to digest what you've learned. I'm registered at the Hilton. The company jet is at the Belleville airport. We're standing by to fly you to San Francisco," he told Anne, and Denise gasped. This was a world she yearned to share. "If all this sounds terribly unreal, remember that Naomi Miller is a larger-than-life woman—a legend in her own time. I've been instructed to stand by with the flight crew until noon tomorrow."

"Mr. Blumberg, just how much money are we discussing?" Denise asked, faintly breathless. "Other than Anne's annual salary." Staggering in itself.

"Conservatively I'd say Anne's share of the estate will come to around sixty million dollars. Providing, of course, that the business continues on an even keel. The company is privately owned," he reminded. "Mrs. Miller's son, Douglas, will inherit ten percent of the stock. The other ninety percent will be held in escrow, as I explained, for twenty years after Mrs. Miller's death when it will be divided equally between Anne and Felicia—provided both young women have remained with the company for those twenty years. If either defects," he reiterated, "their ninety percent of stock goes to the Naomi Miller Museum."

"She'll be running my life until I'm almost forty-two years old," Anne protested again. *She'd have to live in San Francisco.* Already she felt a sense of loss. College in New York had been a temporary situation—this was a twenty-year commitment. Yet how could she reject that kind of money? Even with just her salary she could help Dad keep the company running. For Grandma that was so important. A kind of immortality, she'd said once. And with all that money, she reminded herself in youthful idealism, she could contribute to important causes. Yet she hedged. "I'll need some time to think about it," she said, parroting Blumberg's formal manner.

"Anne, of course you'll go!" her mother said. Anne heard her father's grunt of reproach. "After all, Mother loved her sister despite the old feud. She talked about her often," Denise told the attorney. "Always sad at their separation." Now she exuded a pseudomessianic glow. "Isn't it time, Mr. Blumberg, that this family was brought together again?"

"What about Mrs. Miller's children and grandchildren?" Kevin asked quietly. "I would expect them to contest the will."

"If they contest, they'll lose the trust funds to be set up for them. I've mentioned that clause," Blumberg reminded. "The document will stand up in court. We've left no loopholes." He rose to his feet. "I'll be at the Hilton awaiting your call," he told Anne. "Please remember, Mrs. Miller's hold on life is very fragile."

Two

HER mind in turmoil, Anne stood at a window and watched Arthur Blumberg climb into the waiting rented limousine. She was scarcely aware of her mother's verbal assault as the Cadillac pulled away from the curb and headed for the attorney's hotel. On a day when life in America appeared to have been put on hold, Arthur Blumberg had arrived to throw her own life into chaos.

"Denise, stop this tirade," her father interrupted in exasperation. "This is Anne's decision to make. We can't make it for her."

"This is the kind of opportunity that comes to one person in a hundred million!" Denise shrieked. "Anne can't afford to let it get away from her. And the lawyer said it loud and clear—the old lady can die at any time."

Anne swung away from the window. "I'm going, Mother." She managed a shaky smile. "This is absolutely unreal, but I'm sucked in by the prospect of all that money." She would be taking back what had belonged to Grandma. What Naomi Miller had stolen from her. All at once it was terribly important to do that.

"Then get on the phone and call Mr. Blumberg," her mother ordered.

"Denise, give the man time to return to his hotel."

Dad seemed ambivalent about her decision. He knew it meant they'd be living on opposite sides of the country, Anne thought, and shared his distaste for this. Yet for once Mother was the realistic member of the family. She couldn't walk out on all that money, and what it could accomplish.

"I'll fly home often," she promised. "And you'll both come out to San Francisco." Anne paused. "If I can see this thing through—"

"It isn't a prison sentence," her father emphasized. "You don't have to see it through if conditions are unbearable. You can always come home."

"Kevin, how can you be so negative? Mr. Blumberg talked about an inheritance of sixty million dollars." All at once Denise appeared distraught. "Oh, God, suppose the old lady dies before Anne arrives? Anne's coming to her bedside is one of the conditions of the will."

"I doubt that." Kevin squinted in reflection. "I'm sure the will is set, and the requirement for Anne's presence was a sudden whim on Mrs. Miller's part."

"Anne can't take a chance," Denise said sharply. "Wait another five minutes and call. We're not more than five minutes by car from the Hilton."

Anne heard the tension in Arthur Blumberg's voice when he answered his hotel phone. He was anxious to bring her home to her great-aunt. She heard his relief when she agreed to fly out to San Francisco with him at seven-thirty the following morning. He explained that she need not concern herself with extensive packing. Later she could fly back to Belleville and make the necessary arrangements.

"The car will pick you up at a quarter past to bring you to the airport. You'll be making a remarkable old lady very happy."

"I'll be ready," she assured him, even while bitterness surged in her because the attorney referred to her great-aunt with such respect. He didn't know how she had mistreated her own sister. For Grandma, as much as for herself and the family, she meant to secure what was willed to her.

Dad, too, had suffered through financial struggles that would not have occurred if Grandma had not been cheated of her inheritance. Deep inside, she thought in rare candor, Dad must have often regretted marrying Mother. Grandma worried about him. *"Your mother could be so charming in those days—six weeks after they met she married him. He deserves better than he's got from Denise."*

Because of her mother's demands Dad had given up thoughts of teaching and had gone into Lazarus Timber. He should have been a college professor—or perhaps editor of some literary magazine. If the business was successful, he'd be less harried, have more time for himself.

Tenderness welled in her as she thought about his cabin in the woods, where he escaped at intervals for two or three days at a time. If she had all that money, she could give him a whole island for himself.

After dinner—wrapped in a haze of unreality—Anne packed one of the valises that had made the trek between Belleville and New York during her Barnard years.

"Take along at least one gown, Anne." Her mother hovered in the doorway, radiating a blend of excitement and resentment.

"Whatever for?" Anne brushed this aside. "This isn't a social visit."

"With all their money they probably dress for dinner," Denise surmised.

"I won't. Mother, Naomi Miller is dying. I don't have to worry about dressing."

Early morning sunlight spilled over the colonnaded white colonial built sixty-two years ago by Rae and Marshall Lazarus, as Anne joined her mother on the rear seat of the limousine and her father handed over her valise to the chauffeur. The air was cool and invigorating. When the car began to move, Anne leaned forward for a final glance at the tall, lush, velvet-leaved magnolia on the front lawn, at the splash of chrysanthemums in late bloom. When she returned, she would be somebody else, her mind taunted.

49

"Phone when you can," her father urged gently, sliding beside her on the seat. "If just to let us know you arrived safely."

"I'll probably be back home in a week or two," she said and felt her mother stiffen. "To make arrangements about my clothes and books—" Her voice trailed off. This separation was too sudden, she thought in simmering panic. It wasn't like going off to school.

As soon as the car turned off the road into the airport, they saw the private jet—capable of flying nonstop to San Francisco—waiting on the runway. Arthur Blumberg emerged to welcome Anne aboard. Careful not to disturb Denise's bouffant coiffeur—popularized by Jackie Kennedy—Anne kissed her mother good-bye, moved into her father's warm embrace.

"Give 'em hell, Annie," he said, his eyes bright with love and pride. "You can handle this deal."

The Miller plane, designed to provide Naomi Miller with the ultimate in comfort, reflected the kind of life-style Anne had never experienced. The forward section was wood paneled, furnished as an airborne sitting room and dining area with galley concealed close by. Arthur Blumberg showed off the bedroom and bath that comprised the rear section.

"This plane has seen a lot of mileage," he said nostalgically while they settled themselves in beige leather-upholstered lounge chairs in the forward section. "My father always hated to fly. He delegated me to travel with Mrs. Miller when it was required. She couldn't bear to waste a minute. In-flight we used to work." He hesitated. "Try not to be put off by the family, Anne. They're naturally going to be upset by the will—and they're an outspoken bunch."

"Do they know I'm coming?" Anne asked.

"Yes." Blumberg smiled understandingly. "Doug told them of his mother's wish to see her only grandniece. That's all they've been told," he emphasized.

"Could you tell me a little about them?" Anne asked, fighting self-consciousness. She dreaded the confrontation with a great-aunt and generations of cousins who were strangers to her. Grandma had been forty years old when Mother was born. She had left a daughter and one grandchild. Naomi Miller had two children, two grandchildren, and three great-grandchildren.

"Douglas is close to his mother," Arthur began. "He's not innovative in the business, but conscientious and hardworking. His real interest is the Naomi Miller Art Museum. He studied art in Paris as a young man. His widowed sister Eva, two years older than he, has never gotten along with their mother. She travels a great deal. Eva has two sons, Bruce and Leon. Bruce is an attorney and Leon an accountant, both on staff at the company, though Bruce and Edwina, his wife, are away from San Francisco more than they're there. Felicia is their daughter. The image of Mrs. Miller as a girl. Very much like you," he said in sudden recognition. "Except that she's a blonde—this year. And she nurses a perennial California tan."

Anne smiled up at the steward who brought them coffee. This was *weird,* being aboard a private plane en route to San Francisco. Every minute carrying her miles from home.

"Felicia's worked in the company?" Anne asked.

"Felicia has never worked a day in her life. She dropped out of Radcliffe near the end of her sophomore year and has played the jet-set scene ever since, thanks to her great-grandmother's spoiling. She's a few months older than you. But she's bright, and Mrs. Miller respects brains. And she's the only one in the family who ever opposed the old lady." He chuckled in recall. "I think one of Mrs. Miller's happiest moments was the morning after Columbus Day of last year. We had a terrible windstorm that blew down thousands of trees along the Pacific Coast—far more than the regional mills could handle—and Felicia said, 'salvage the timber and export it.' That's exactly what the smart timber people did."

"Is Felicia an only child?" Like her father before her, Anne had often wished for a sister or brother. But now she was discovering a bunch of cousins and was intimidated because they lived in that rarified world of the ultra-rich.

"Felicia has a brother. Todd's seventeen and away at boarding school. Leon and Consuelo have a fifteen-year-old son, Adrian. I understand he's quite a handful. Pity, because Leon and Consuelo are fine people."

"You expect Felicia to go along with the terms of the will?"

"Felicia is shrewd, and she's accustomed to high living," he reassured her. "She'll go along with the will."

Later the steward brought them a luncheon tray. Anne was surprised that she ate with such relish. Over roast beef sandwiches and a salad Arthur Blumberg talked about his own family. His wife was involved in local charities. His younger son, Bert, was a junior at the University of California at Berkeley and scheduled to go on to law school. The older son, Josh, was teaching at Berkeley while earning his Ph.D. in European history.

"Bert, I understand. Right now he's basically interested in football and girls, in that order. But Josh—" Blumberg spread his hands. "He's bright and warm and compassionate. But I don't understand him. He spent most of the summer on some crusade for the grape-pickers. He went to Washington in August for Martin Luther King's 'Freedom March.' All through high school he wanted to be a lawyer, then halfway through college he decided law was a dirty word." But Blumberg's love for both of his sons was obvious.

After they had eaten and Anne was suppressing yawns, Blumberg urged her to stretch out on the sofa for a nap.

"You probably slept little last night," he guessed sympathetically, and she nodded. She had been too tense and apprehensive to sleep. "I'll go visit with the crew for a while."

Shortly before two o'clock California time the plane began its descent to San Francisco International, twelve miles south of the city. Anne was only vaguely conscious of the dramatic San Francisco skyline. Her heart was pounding. Questions darted across her brain.

The cousins knew she was arriving. Wouldn't they suspect she was here for more than a deathbed visit to the aunt she'd never seen? Was her black suit—a Chanel copy bought last year at a fabulous sale at B. Altman in New York—"right" for the occasion? Her checkerboard Mary Quant minishifts, which she adored because they were "fun" clothes, seemed too frivolous. As though it were a precious amulet, she touched the delicate cameo at the throat of her white overblouse. Grandma had given it to her on her eighteenth birthday. It had belonged to Great-grandmother Annie, for whom she was named.

A gleaming maroon Mercedes limousine was waiting for them. The longtime family chauffeur, Walter, leapt from behind the wheel to open the door for them. Anne felt his curiosity when Mr. Blumberg introduced them.

Mr. Blumberg pointed out special places of interest as they drove toward the city. He talked with civic pride about the city's growth.

"You see those houses there?" He pointed to a cluster of pleasant, modest row houses. "Fifteen years ago they sold for around twelve thousand dollars—today they go for seventy-five thousand."

Anne managed a pretense of interest. In truth, she was aware only of the sea-scented fog that seemed to stretch in every direction and of the bursts of saffron yellow blossoms on the acacia trees that appeared at frequent intervals. And of foghorns blaring, mournful and eerie, in the distance.

Then they were in the city proper, climbing and descending hills. The fog gave way now to a delicate winter sunlight. Anne was conscious of ostentatious bay-windowed Victorian houses, small, vari-colored row houses seeming to hover precariously on perpendicular patches of earth. Here and there a display of modern architecture.

"This is Washington Street," Mr. Blumberg told her. "The house is just ahead, at the top of the hill." In addition to the San Francisco house, Mr. Blumberg had told her, Naomi Miller owned houses in Squaw Valley, Lake Tahoe, Acapulco, and a ranch in Wyoming. She also maintained an apartment in Washington, D.C.

Walter pulled up before a four-story, white-limestone,

neo–Renaissance castle with tiled turrets and stone chimneys rising from its multi–level rooftop. She was to live here for at least two years. An intimidating prospect. After two years, according to the terms of Naomi Miller's will, she could live wherever she chose.

"The house offers some of the most spectacular views in San Francisco," Blumberg told Anne as he held the car door open for her. "Just look below before we go inside."

Anne stepped out onto the curb and turned around to gaze down in rapt wonder at much of San Francisco. Though the weather was sunny up here on the hill, the bay below was drenched in fog, with the towers of the bridges piercing the fog like minarets of ancient Moslem mosques.

"All this sunshine up here," Anne marveled, "and that fascinating fog down there."

"We have a saying around here," Blumberg reminisced. "If you don't like the weather, take a short walk."

Now they crossed the sidewalk and approached the massive oak entrance. Moments later a uniformed maid opened the door to admit them. Anne felt the small, slim maid's curiosity while she exchanged greetings with Mr. Blumberg, then acknowledged his introduction. Clearly, even the staff knew that Naomi Miller's grandniece was coming to the house. Everyone must understand that meant she would share in the estate, she reasoned. They just didn't know to what extent.

"We'll go directly up to Mrs. Miller," Mr. Blumberg told the maid while they crossed into the huge, green Carrara marble-floored, oak-paneled entrance hall. The walls were lined with fine tapestries. A Waterford crystal chandelier of asymmetrical design hung from the ceiling.

The sound of feminine voices drifted from a room off the entrance hall. "Everything was all arranged!" a young voice complained. "I'd found some marvelous clothes at Courrèges in Paris. I . . ."

"Felicia, stop bitching about missing a week at Gstaad. Mother didn't choose this time to die." The husky-voiced older woman would be Eva, Anne pinpointed. Felicia's grandmother.

"Let's go upstairs," Mr. Blumberg reiterated and prodded Anne toward the hand-carved, polished oak staircase.

Anne walked slowly up the stairs beside Mr. Blumberg, her throat tight, her hands cold. She felt herself suffocated into silence—it would be unthinkable, when Naomi Miller lay dying, to say what was in her heart. At the head of the stairs she paused for an instant to brace herself for the encounter ahead.

A tall, lean, impassive-faced woman in her sixties appeared to be waiting for them.

"Mrs. Morrison, this is Anne Forrest," Mr. Blumberg said. "Mrs. Morrison has been your great-aunt's housekeeper for almost forty years."

"She keeps asking for you," Mrs. Morrison said with an air of reproof, and Anne was conscious of a disapproving scrutiny. "She expected you hours ago."

"We did our best," Mr. Blumberg said dryly.

"I've had a room prepared for Miss Forrest," the housekeeper said. "Please ring for me after she's seen Mrs. Miller."

"Thank you, Mrs. Morrison." Mr. Blumberg indicated to Anne that their destination was farther down the hall.

"Mrs. Morrison is devoted to Mrs. Miller. She was a twenty-six-year-old widow with a small child when she was hired to join the domestic staff. It was one of Mrs. Miller's many acts of kindness through the years."

To strangers Naomi Miller might have been kind, Anne mocked inwardly while she walked beside Mr. Blumberg to a room at the end of the burgandy carpeted hall. She waited beside him at the door while he knocked lightly. Again, she felt an invisible hand at her throat, commanding silence. She hated the greedy, powerful woman who had hurt her grandmother so deeply. Why hadn't she tried to mend the breach years ago, when it would have meant so much to Grandma? Guilt, Anne surmised with contempt, that came with the approach of death brought about this effort at retribution.

55

The door was opened. A white-uniformed nurse gestured to them to come inside.

"She's awake, Mr. Blumberg," the nurse reported. "But don't stay more than a few minutes."

"Nonsense," a voice called from the bed with an authority that belied its owner's fragile hold on life. "I want to see my grandniece."

Slowly Anne walked into the large, high-ceilinged bedroom, furnished with magnificent Chinese antiques. Heavy gold damask drapes shut out the afternoon sunlight. Naomi Miller lay against a mound of pillows in an exquisitely carved Ming dynasty bed.

"Closer," Naomi Miller commanded. "Miss Paterson, open those bloody drapes."

Obediently Anne moved to the side of the bed. Now sunlight filled the room, highlighting the features of the imperious old lady. For an instant Anne froze in shock. She had not expected her great-aunt to look so much like her grandmother. The years had marked her more heavily, but the resemblance was astonishing.

"You're wearing Mama's cameo—" Naomi seemed shaken by this discovery. Did she remember that it was all that Grandma received from her mother's estate?

"My grandmother gave it to me on my eighteenth birthday," Anne explained, for a moment oddly defensive. *The frail old lady lying there on the bed was Grandma's sister.*

"You're the image of Rae." The words seemed wrenched from Naomi. "The way she looked the last time I saw her." For an instant she closed her eyes and Anne turned to the nurse in alarm. "We wasted so many years." Naomi opened her eyes again. "Why couldn't Rae write to me? Why did I have to hire detectives to learn about my sister and her family?"

Anne bit back the words that threatened to tumble out. Grandma *had* written. She had sent a silver cup when her sister's first child was born. Naomi Miller preferred to forget.

"Grandma loved you," Anne forced herself to reply, struggling to mask her bitterness. "She kept hundreds of newspaper clippings about you."

Naomi's heavily lined face lighted. "There's a strain of strong women in this family. Rae had more backbone than I ever expected. We got that from our mother. You have it. Felicia has it." Her face tightened now. Her eyes glittered. "You and Felicia will carry on what I've created. Doug is a good son. He has his feet on the ground. But he has no real business sense—he knows only what he learned from me. You and Felicia have the gift." She sighed. "I thought I was invincible. That I'd live to a hundred and ten."

"You're tired," the nurse objected. "They should . . ."

"Oh, shut up, Paterson. Artie, call on the house phone and ask for Felicia to be sent up immediately." She gestured with one heavily veined hand to the pair of phones on the oriental lacquered table beside her bed, and Blumberg moved to obey. "You'll meet the rest of the clan at dinner," she told Anne with barely concealed disdain.

While they waited for Felicia to appear, Naomi asked Artie about his family. As the other two talked, Anne was conscious of her great-aunt's covert scrutiny. She had to play Naomi Miller's game, Anne told herself tersely, but she would be the winner.

"With children you always have trouble," Naomi said tiredly, when Arthur Blumberg paused. "With each decade comes fresh troubles. Even when my daughter is close to seventy, I worry about her."

Anne tensed at the knock on the door. Without waiting for a reply Felicia pushed open the door and walked inside. She was two or three inches taller than Anne, pencil-slim in a black knit shift that ended mid-thigh, with high black-suede boots. Her California tan was several shades darker than her geometrically cropped hair; her eyes the same blue-green as Anne's.

"You sent for me, Naomi?" Felicia ignored the others. Anne was startled that she called her great-grandmother by her given name. She suspected that no one else in the family would take this liberty.

"Look at them, Artie," Naomi said, gazing from Felicia to Anne. "Alike as two peas in a pod. Felicia, this is your cousin from Georgia. Anne, this is Felicia."

"Hi." Felicia's voice held an undertone of hostility.

"Hi, Felicia." Anne was polite, yet disconcerted by the recognition of a strong family resemblance between this arrogant blonde and herself.

"Anne will want to rest up until dinner," Naomi told Felicia. "Then you'll take her downstairs and introduce her to the others."

"Yes, Naomi," Felicia said softly. Anne could envision her erupting in rage when she heard the terms of the will.

"Felicia reminds me of myself at her age." Fleetingly, pride seemed to erase a dozen years from Naomi's face. "Strong-willed, spoiled, and a fighter. Don't let me down, Felicia. I could never count on the others. You're my only hope. You and Rae's granddaughter," she amplified. "You're true descendants of Annie Sachs."

But Grandma always said that she, Rae, was "Annie Sachs's child." That "Naomi was Willi Sachs's child."

Three

THOUGH she was exhausted from the emotional stress of the day, Anne knew it would be impossible to rest until dinner. She prowled about the square, high-ceilinged corner bedroom furnished in Chinese Chippendale, pausing at intervals at a window that provided an awesome view of the bay. The whole clan—as Naomi had referred to the family—would be at dinner, she warned herself.

From Mr. Blumberg she knew that Doug and widowed Eva lived here in the twenty-seven-room mansion with their mother. When she was in San Francisco, Felicia—Naomi's favorite—stayed here. The two grandsons and their families maintained lavish homes in the prestigious suburb of Hillsborough, sixteen miles south of the city, but Naomi Miller's mansion was their San Francisco pied-à-terre.

She was beset by doubts that she and Felicia would be able to carry out the terms of Naomi's will. Felicia knew nothing about the business—wanted to know nothing about it. She was more concerned about the growth of her fingernails than the growth of trees in the Miller timberlands. But now that she had agreed to be part of Naomi Miller's fantasy, Anne admitted to herself, she was determined to make it work.

Dinner would be served at seven because that was the time Naomi Miller preferred it, and as long as she remained alive, her preferences would be respected. At six Anne forced herself to shower and change for dinner. It seemed absurd to dress for dinner at the family house.

Before she went into her adjoining, totally modern bathroom, she laid out the two-piece lilac wool she had bought on sale at Rich's in Atlanta last month. It was casual but smart.

Showered and dressed, she waited nervously for Felicia to come for her. Expecting it, she nevertheless started at the brisk knock on her door and managed a tentative smile as she responded.

"Dinner's always served promptly at seven," Felicia reminded. She wore a daringly short, winter-white shift that Anne recognized from the pages of *Vogue* as a Courrèges. "Naomi can be a martinet about some things." She smiled faintly. "About most things."

While they walked downstairs, Felicia talked about Betty Friedan's recent book, *The Feminine Mystique,* which she was reading. "God, that woman talks sense!" Felicia said in fervent admiration. One point of common interest, Anne silently conceded.

Behind Felicia's conversation Anne was aware of her intense curiosity: *Why was this cousin from Georgia, whom they'd never seen before, suddenly here in this house?* But the family knew that Naomi Miller had sent for her. The implications in that must be fomenting unrest among them. All so greedy, Anne assumed, that they would resent even a small bequest.

Would Felicia and she be able to work together the way the old lady decreed? If they couldn't, then the Naomi Miller Art Museum would inherit one hundred and twenty million dollars worth of Miller Timber Company stock. Oh God, this was unreal!

"They'll be in the family sitting room until Wong announces dinner," Felicia told her when they arrived downstairs, and gestured to a room far down the wide hall.

Anne's heart was pounding when she walked with Felicia into the paneled, neoclassic family sitting room, its priceless French and Italian antiques attesting to the Miller wealth. Two men in expensively tailored suits sat on a pair of Louis XV chairs flanking the marble-faced fireplace and discussed the Kennedy assassination.

Across the room two women shared a gold silk-damask—covered settee while another, older, woman sat opposite them in a barrel-shaped chair in matching damask. The three women wore smart dinner dresses that Anne was sure were Paris originals. Mother had been right about dressing for dinner, though Felicia obviously considered that to be for older generations.

"Oh, I know it'd be absurd to pay twenty-five hundred dollars for a terry cloth bathrobe, even though it is lined with mink, but I just might do it," the eldest of the three said with brittle amusement. She was tall with bleached-blond hair and taut skin that hinted at a series of face-lifts. Eva, Felicia's grandmother, Anne pinpointed. The other two women would be Edwina and Consuelo.

"Naomi asked me to introduce you to our cousin," Felicia said briskly, and a barrage of eyes suddenly focused on Anne, the atmosphere super-charged now. "This is Anne Forrest, Naomi's grandniece from Georgia."

Anne's face was hot as she acknowledged each introduction. All of them wondering why she was here, she thought to herself. Suspicious and hostile, she surmised. All of them Grandma's family. *Her* cousins. Neither Eva nor her two sons bore any physical resemblance to Naomi Miller, though Eva and Bruce shared her aura of arrogance. On sight Anne liked Leon and his Brazilian-born wife, Consuelo.

"Anne, you and Felicia look so much alike," Consuelo said in gentle astonishment.

"Grandma must have looked like them when she was their age," Leon said. "Three beautiful women," he added gallantly and Eva bristled. No one would ever have called *his* mother beautiful, though through the years she had achieved a brittle attractiveness.

"Wong's waiting for Doug to arrive before he'll allow us to go in to dinner," Eva explained in irritation. Her eyes esti-

61

mated the price tag of Anne's lilac wool. "Doug is my brother."

"Doug's here," a tired voice intruded. "I stopped by to look in on Mama for a minute."

"I hope you didn't try to talk shop with Mother." Eva's eyes were antagonistic. Anne suspected that already Eva was concerned that her brother might inherit more of the family estate than she.

"You're Anne." Doug walked to her with one hand extended in welcome, then on impulse leaned forward to kiss her on the cheek. He was a tall, slender man with near-white hair and erect carriage. His blue-green eyes were compassionate and sensitive. Like Dad, Anne suspected in sudden sympathy, he had been pushed into the timber business. His mother would not have allowed him to do otherwise. "My mother's so pleased that you agreed to come." His eyes told her that he understood she had accepted the terms of the will. Instinctively, Anne knew that without Doug on her side she would never be able to survive this partnership with Felicia.

"Here's Wong." Eva rose to her feet as an elderly, dignified Chinese man appeared at the entrance. "Let's go in to dinner."

Dinner was to be served in the French Empire family dining room that adjoined the sitting room. Doug took his place at the foot of the table and seated Anne at his left. Felicia automatically sat at his right. Doug chuckled as Anne gazed compulsively at the fine painting of Naomi Miller—executed more than fifty years earlier—that hung over the mantel.

"That was Mama," he said with infinite sadness.

"It's like looking at a painting of my grandmother," Anne whispered. How could two sisters who looked so much alike be so different?

When Leon began to discuss with Doug the tragic events that had gripped the nation for the past few days, his sister-in-law ordered him to drop the subject.

"Leon, I can't bear to hear another word about the assassination," Edwina objected. "And the weather here has been just abominable. Under any other circumstances Bruce and I would be at the Acapulco house this time of year. We never go to Palm Beach until after New Year's."

"I'm annoyed as hell at Todd," Bruce frowned. "He should be here at a time like this."

"No reason to drag Todd home from boarding school," Felicia told her father. "You know Naomi and he have never got along. She won't ask to see him."

"She's his great-grandmother." Edwina was affronted by her daughter's remarks. "Todd ought to be here."

"Todd's seventeen and fiercely independent," Doug explained to Anne. "My mother and he have become mortal enemies."

"Mother knows Todd loves her," Eva hastened to defend him. No doubt she worried about his status as prospective heir, Anne thought, and remembered Mr. Blumberg's mentioning trust funds that had been set up under the will.

"We didn't send for Adrian," Consuelo apologized. "Fifteen is such a difficult age. And he's having problems at school. We . . . " she turned to Leon for encouragement, " . . . we thought it would be better to let him stay there." She hesitated. "For now."

Anne ate without tasting, ever-conscious of the tempest that was sure to erupt when Naomi Miller died and her will was read. At intervals her eyes strayed to the painting that hung over the mantel. Unaccountably, she felt close to her grandmother in its presence.

Dessert was being served when Mrs. Morrison appeared in the doorway. Pale and trembling.

"I'm sorry to interrupt you at dinner," she said, her voice hoarse, "but I thought you ought to know. Miss Paterson has sent for Dr. Weinstein. Mrs. Miller has lapsed into a coma."

"Oh God," Eva wailed. "It's come to that."

"Grandma's a tough old lady," Leon said, but his face was somber. "She just might come out of it."

His face drained of color, Doug rose to his feet.

"I'll go upstairs to stay with her. Please go on with your dinner." Anne detected a hint of irony. "We don't know how long she'll remain in a coma."

63

Feeling herself an intruder, Anne sat with the other women in the family sitting room, before the incongruously cheerful blaze in the fireplace grate. Almost immediately Leon had followed his uncle to his grandmother's bedside. Ten minutes later Bruce and Felicia had gone up to her room. Felicia had remained fleetingly, saying, "I can't bear to see her that way. That's not Naomi."

While the others reminisced about Naomi Miller's past triumphs, Anne struggled to cope with a towering unease. There would be an awful scene when the family discovered the terms of the will. And was the will as impregnable as Mr. Blumberg believed?

"Mother's had a marvelous life," Eva summed up. "And she's done it all on her own." *Plus an inheritance stolen from Grandma,* Anne silently accused. "My father died when she was only forty-one," Eva turned to Anne. "And he was the first to admit that she ran Miller Timber Company." Again, Anne was conscious of unspoken questions about her presence here.

"Will you be staying for the funeral?" Felicia asked.

"Felicia!" Consuelo stared incredulously. "Grandma is alive."

"That's a shell up there," Felicia lashed back. Despite her flippancy, she really loved the old lady, Anne realized. "Naomi's gone."

"Will you stop referring to Mother in that impertinent fashion?" Eva yelled at her. "It's so irritating!"

"Naomi liked it," Felicia shot back. "She told me about you, Anne," she said with a devious smile, and Anne tensed. *What had she told Felicia?* "When I dropped out of Radcliffe in my second year and refused to go back, she talked about how well you were doing at Barnard. She told me how you worked every summer at your grandmother's timber business down in Georgia."

"She never said a word to me." Eva was affronted. "Oh,

64

I knew Mother had a sister, and that they hadn't spoken to each other since they were girls. Is your grandmother alive, Anne?"

"No," Anne told her. "We buried her a year ago yesterday." She felt a fresh surge of grief. "I miss her very much."

"I wondered that she sent for you rather than her sister," Eva acknowledged. "Did your grandmother tell you about—" She stopped short. Flanked by his nephews, Doug stood at the entrance.

"Mama's gone," Doug said exhaustedly. "Send for Todd and Adrian. Mama would expect them to attend her funeral."

Of them all, Anne thought, only Doug genuinely mourned Naomi Miller. In some ways Eva was like Mother—too wrapped up in herself to feel deeply about anyone else. Dad and she had mourned for Grandma—Mother paid lip service. Her main concern had been what to wear to the funeral. *"Do you think pearls will be too much?"*

Rain—rare in San Francisco—threatened on the morning of Naomi Miller's funeral, though Doug insisted as they waited for the limousines to arrive that it was no more than a threat.

"It won't dare rain on the day of Naomi's funeral," Felicia said flippantly.

"Felicia, you really shouldn't wear that leopard coat," Edwina objected. Both she and her mother carried gleaming dark mink jackets. "It's too flamboyant."

"I'm not wearing it," Felicia contradicted. "I'm carrying it."

Like the other women Anne wore a simple black suit—the one in which she had arrived, though with a different blouse. The others wore Paris originals. Today Felicia had deserted Courrèges for Givenchy.

Anne was relieved when Doug indicated they were to ride in a limousine together with Leon, Consuelo, and Adrian. To the rest of the family she was an unwelcome intruder. She was grateful that Consuelo and Leon tried to make casual conversation. Adrian—lanky, smolderingly handsome, with his

65

mother's dark hair and eyes—sulked. Anne suspected he objected to being here.

It seemed to Anne that half of San Francisco turned out for Naomi Miller's funeral. The local florists had done a land-office business. At frequent intervals she was startled to recognize a famous face. This was a heady world in which she was moving.

Involuntarily, during the services at the funeral home and then at the cemetery, she found herself comparing this funeral to her grandmother's. The atmosphere here was that of an important business conference, she analyzed. People here came not to mourn Naomi Miller but to pay their respects to her wealth. Doug was fighting to retain his composure. Mrs. Morrison, the housekeeper, was tearful, genuinely grieving. But at Grandma's funeral, Anne remembered with pride, dozens of friends mourned for her. Rae Lazarus died a richer woman than her sister, Anne told herself. Richer in the way that counted.

From the cemetery limousines carried the family back to the Washington Street mansion. According to Naomi's dictates, the will was to be read in the library, immediately after her burial.

"No need for Todd and Adrian to go through this," Doug said when they assembled in the walnut-paneled library that had been Naomi's private domain, and Anne saw the two boys' relief. She had liked Todd on sight. His warmth, his rugged good looks, were appealing.

"Have Walter drive Todd and Adrian home," Eva ordered. "Now why isn't Arthur Blumberg here?"

Moments later Blumberg joined the family in the library. He took his place at Naomi's huge, leather-tooled desk and emptied his briefcase. Anne intercepted the apprehensive glance exchanged by Doug and the lawyer. They knew the bombshell that was about to be exploded.

In silence Leon and Bruce drew up several French Empire chairs to flank the sofa on which Eva and Felicia had settled themselves—both smoking, though in her lifetime Naomi had not permitted smoking in the library. Now the others took their places. Struggling with self-consciousness Anne sat on the most distant of the chairs.

Arthur Blumberg cleared his throat as he addressed the family.

"Mrs. Miller spent much time and effort in formulating her will. I must advise you that it is incontestable. Foreseeing some such efforts, she arranged to be examined by a pair of San Francisco's most eminent psychiatrists. And the will states that anyone who tries to contest her wishes will be cut off."

All at once the atmosphere was heavy with ominous overtones. They weren't a family anymore, Anne thought—they were a roomful of suspicious adversaries.

"Get on with it, Arthur," Bruce ordered tersely.

Arthur Blumberg and Doug were coexecutors, which was no surprise to anyone present. Now Blumberg read off the bequests to members of the household staff and of the business. Generous but not overwhelming. Charitable contributions, none of them impressive sums.

Her jewelry, except for her two separate strands of pearls, were to go to Eva. A strand of pearls to Edwina and to Consuelo. Her chinchilla coat was bequested to Eva, her sable to Felicia. Her mink was to be given to Mrs. Morrison.

Naomi Miller's homes and their furnishings—including her extensive art collection—were left in trust to Doug and Eva, to go after their death to the Naomi Miller Art Museum. A trust fund was set up to maintain the houses. Naomi stipulated that Bruce was to be relieved of his position—and salary—at the Miller Timber Company "since he regards it with such distaste." Now the attorney read off the list of the additional trust funds that had been set up: one million dollars each for her daughter, her son, and two grandsons.

"That's just part of it," Eva said shrilly while Bruce and his wife gaped in disbelief. "Mother wouldn't cut me off with a measly one million?"

"One million invested wisely will provide a comfortable

income," Doug told her. "After all, you'll continue to live here and . . ."

"What do you mean, a comfortable income?" Eva shrieked. "That won't cover my clothes and traveling expenses!"

"There has to be more," Bruce picked up. "We know what she was worth! This is insane!"

"Let Arthur continue," Doug said dryly. "And remember, if you try to contest it, you lose the trust funds."

"How could Mother do this to us?" Eva was white-faced, her eyes over-bright. "She was always a tyrant but . . ."

"Eva, shut up," Doug said through clenched teeth. "Please go on, Arthur."

The others listened in grim silence as Blumberg continued to read. Edwina gasped in outrage at Todd's bequest of ten thousand dollars, to be given to him when he reached twenty-one. Consuelo smiled faintly when a similar bequest was given to Adrian. Felicia sat ramrod stiff in her chair, her cigarette extinguished now while she waited to learn what had been left to her—her great-grandmother's favorite.

Blumberg paused, geared himself for the turbulence he was about to unleash. Slowly—one hand up in warning for silence—he read the heavily detailed main content of the will.

"What the hell does that all mean?" Felicia demanded, casting a momentary glance of hostility at Anne.

"I'll tell you," the attorney soothed. "Mrs. Miller was determined to provide her empire with the best possible management—but she meant to keep it within the family. She spent months working out this twenty-year arrangement which I've just read to you. Her daughter, her son, her two grandsons are to receive trust funds in the sum of one million dollars each, which are to go to the Naomi Miller Art Museum at the death of each trust-holder. Todd and Adrian are to receive ten thousand dollars each at the age of—"

"We know that," Felicia stopped him impatiently. "What is this nonsense about my working for the company? And how did she—" Felicia turned to Anne, "become a principal heir?"

"Felicia, I know this all comes as a shock to you," Doug

68

intervened. "Mama was a strong-willed woman—as we all know. She'll control her money even from the grave."

"I'm not going to work in the stupid timber company!" Felicia rejected contemptuously.

"You may have to, darling," her mother pointed out. "How else will you inherit all that money? Eventually," she conceded.

"I don't believe it's legal!" Felicia said defiantly to the attorney.

"It's legal, Felicia. It's Mama in her finest moment," Doug said with sardonic humor. "She was convinced that I could train you and Anne to carry on in her place. God knows, she had little respect for my own business judgment." A hint of bitterness seeped through.

"I know nothing about the bloody business. Why should I care what happens to it?" Felicia shot a malicious glance at Anne. "And why bring her into a family affair?"

"Because Anne *is* family," Doug said quietly. "Mama's sister's grandchild. Mama wanted Anne to share her empire with you. And there's nothing any of us can do to change that."

"And if I don't go along with this . . ." Felicia's eyes shot across the room again to Anne, ". . . along with her, then all the money goes to the Naomi Miller Art Museum?"

"That's right," Doug agreed.

"So you don't want us to make a go of it, dear Uncle Doug," Felicia drawled and Anne realized she was being sarcastic. Felicia had never thus far called him "Uncle." "You want to see all that money go to your precious museum. That's all you've ever really cared about in this world!"

"For Mama's sake I pray that you and Anne can continue her empire," Doug refuted. "She considered it her hold on immortality."

"We'll all sue!" Eva shrieked. "Bruce, you're a lawyer. Tell Arthur this insane will won't stand up in court!"

"It'll stand up," Bruce said with blistering rage. "Grandma has put us all in our place. The way she always has. Grandma will rule this family from the grave."

Four

FORTY minutes after stalking out of the Miller mansion library Felicia sat tense and impatient in one of a pair of black leather armchairs before the executive desk of Paul Emerson. He was studying a copy of the will, which she had thrown before him on her arrival.

"Paul, you have to see me—this is a crisis!" She'd been simultaneously imperious and beseeching on the phone. Jackie—Paul's sister and her long-time best-friend—had backed her up and agreed to join her at Paul's office.

Paul was two years out of Harvard Law and soon to be promoted to a partnership in his father's prestigious law firm. He was bright—and what he didn't know, Felicia reasoned, he would find out from his father. There had to be a way to break Naomi's will.

Two and a half years ago, at Paul's winter intersession from law school, Felicia had spent a heated weekend with him snowbound in a ski lodge at Sugar Bowl. They'd encountered each other occasionally since, but they'd both known it was a one-shot affair. Jackie had some creepy idea that Paul and she would eventually marry, but she had laughed this off. Outside of bed Paul was so square. *"Jackie, we can't spend twenty-four hours a day fucking,"* she'd said.

Paul sighed and laid aside the copy of the will.

"Felicia, it's useless," he conceded. "There's no way of taking this to court and winning. Arthur Blumberg is one of the sharpest attorneys in this country. He's drawn up a will that's unbreakable. Between him and your great-grandmother they've taken care of every possible contingency."

"How the hell could Naomi do this to me?" Felicia blazed. Rare tears—a blend of rage and reluctant grief—welled in her eyes. "She's thrown me into jail for twenty years!"

"Let's run off to Gstaad to ski for three or four days," Jackie cajoled. "You said your slave labor won't start for another week."

"Jackie, her great-grandmother was buried two hours ago!" Paul protested.

"So?" Jackie stared back defiantly and Felicia's eyes carried the same message. "She won't know if Felicia is sitting at home crying or schussing down the slopes at Gstaad."

"Naomi *did* say, 'no mourning period.' " Felicia's smile was flippant, yet inwardly she found it hard to accept that Naomi was gone. She didn't want to go back to the house, knowing Naomi would never be there again. "So why shouldn't I go skiing?"

"When?" Jackie pounced.

"Doug's warned me I can't charge anything to Naomi anymore. Damn!" Naomi had always been there to pay her bills. She might have complained sometimes, but she always came through. Felicia deliberated a moment, her eyes defiant. "I've got enough in my checking account to handle a long weekend. And my tan does need some fresh sun."

"We can fly to New York tonight, hole up at the Pierre until flight time to Geneva. We'll be on the slopes on Sunday morning," Jackie plotted exuberantly. "You've got those sensational ski clothes you bought at Courrèges. You can't let them go to waste."

"We'll miss the Saturday night gala," Felicia sighed. "We *will* get reservations at the Palace Hotel?"

"Keep your fingers crossed," Jackie bubbled. "There's usually somebody canceling at the last moment."

Felicia turned to Paul. "Last year we saw Louis Armstrong and Maurice Chevalier at the Palace."

"Not at the same time," Jackie giggled and the two girls exchanged amused looks in reaction to Paul, who seemed both outraged and fascinated by their flaunting of convention. Most people were so in awe of Naomi, Felicia remembered. It wouldn't surprise her if the flag at City Hall had been lowered to half-mast today.

"If you can make all the reservations at the last minute this way, I'll go, Jackie." Felicia sat upright, crossed her legs—sending her minidress to a height that elicited an involuntary grunt from Paul. "Paul, what about taking off time to make it a threesome?" Her eyes dared him to accept. How could he be settling for marriage to that insipid Eleanor Lansing? Pretty, Felicia conceded, but so dull and predictable. She couldn't be more than nineteen—she'd come out at last year's cotillion. "Dare you, Paul!" She might be in the mood to offer him a dress-rehearsal honeymoon.

"I'm a working attorney," Paul reminded them, but Felicia saw the glint of arousal in his eyes. She'd take any odds she could inveigle him into bed anytime she wanted. He was marrying Eleanor because of her family's political connections. Jackie said he had a mad ambition to become district attorney. For openers.

Felicia and Jackie headed for lunch at the elegant Blue Fox. Normally Felicia relished its offbeat locale—in a dark alley across from the City Morgue and next door to the Shore Patrol—as much as its superb food. Today she kept seeing Naomi's coffin being lowered into that ugly hole.

En route to the restaurant they stopped for a harried conference with Jackie's travel agent, accustomed to Jackie's sudden whims. By the time they had finished off the Blue Fox's baby boneless pheasant stuffed with wild rice and baked in clay, a call came from the travel agent. They had a night flight to New York, a flight to Geneva tomorrow evening. From Geneva they would take a train to Gstaad. At Gstaad a suite at the Palace Hotel was reserved for them.

"Great," Felicia approved when Jackie had relayed the vital statistics. "We'll collapse in the suite for three or four hours, have dinner in the Maxim Room, then go for some torchlight skiing. You never know whom you'll meet on the Gstaad ski slopes." The last time they were there they'd run into David Niven and Van Johnson and the young Aga Khan.

For a little while, Felicia promised herself, she'd forget the hell that lay ahead of her. How could Naomi expect her to work in the business? Still, she recognized that Naomi had singled her out over the rest of the family—even Doug—for the largest share of the Miller estate. Naomi had singled her out, and that bitchy grandniece, she thought resentfully. And she could lose everything if the two of them didn't learn to play ball. God, it was insane. In her old age Naomi had this fantasy about bringing her own family and her sister's family together. Why?

In skin-hugging Emilio Pucci white wool pants and sweater, her leopard coat draped about her, Felicia slept in her first-class seat for most of the flight to New York. Jackie woke her as the plane approached Idlewild. A limousine would be waiting to drive them to the Pierre, where they'd hole up until it was time to head back to the airport for their New York-to-Geneva flight.

"If Mother weren't insisting I be home for Christmas, we could run down to Nassau for Linda's houseparty," Jackie groused. "Sometimes she can be so conventional." *Like Naomi—when it came to major holidays,* Felicia remembered suddenly.

"I couldn't go, anyway," Felicia reminded. "I'm scheduled to be a workhorse." What did she know about the timber business, even though Naomi had kept taking her along on field trips since she was ten?

"Forget about the stupid job for now," Jackie ordered. "Remember that gorgeous ski instructor down in Chile last July? He said he'd probably be in Gstaad this winter."

"Gary North." Felicia's smile was dazzling. "Why do you think I agreed to Gstaad? Actually, I think Klosters has become much more chic—fewer Americans there. Even if Prince Rainier and Grace are forever showing up at Gstaad."

"You said Gary was out to marry some ultra-rich divorcée," Jackie recalled.

"I'm neither divorced nor ultra-rich," Felicia drawled. "At least, not yet. But for a couple of nights Gary North could be fun."

Fastening her seatbelt as the plane prepared to land at Atlanta's Hartsfield Airport, Anne was assaulted by conflicting emotions: relief that she could relax for a couple of days in comfortably familiar surroundings; joy that she would soon be able to remove painful financial pressure from her father's shoulders. And fear that either she or Felicia might make a wrong move. Could it be that she had left Belleville only a few days ago? It seemed as though she had been away half a lifetime.

As dictated by her new life-style, she was met by the chauffeur hired to drive her to Belleville. With the requisite low-keyed deference, he asked for her baggage check, collected her valise when she pointed it out, and escorted her to the waiting limousine. Leaning back against the red leather upholstery of the Cadillac, she realized at this moment the full impact of her new life. These past days she had felt herself an onlooker. Now, alone in the car with the chauffeur, she knew she was Anne Forrest, potential heiress to sixty million dollars.

She struggled to focus on what she had to accomplish by flight time Monday. She could pack her clothes, books, and records within hours, but she must gear herself for the separation from family and home. This wasn't college—this was a twenty-year term.

Mary Lou greeted her at the front door with an exuberant hug and unabashed awe.

"Your daddy'll be home in a few minutes," Mary Lou reported. "Your mama's on the phone in the living room."

"Anne?" her mother called.

"Yes, Mother." Anne steeled herself for the inevitable flood of questions.

74

"Avis, Anne just arrived," she heard her mother say.

Her father arrived as she was trying to make her mother understand that the will had to go into probate before the ten thousand Naomi had left to her only niece could be paid from the estate. While her mother erupted into indignation at this delay, Anne hungrily embraced her father. *Oh, she was going to miss him.*

Over dinner, to please Denise, Anne described the Miller mansion in minute detail. With her father she discussed what she knew thus far of the Miller Company operation.

"It's inconceivable that the old lady . . . " She could never bring herself to refer to Naomi Miller as "Aunt Naomi" even when she was so painfully conscious that this was Grandma's sister, " . . . that she could expect Felicia and me to run such a huge company."

"Annie, you'll be in training for years," Kevin reminded her. "Doug Miller isn't just handing over the reins tomorrow. You'll work your tail off," he predicted.

"She'll be paid gloriously," Denise snapped, and Anne felt her mother's resentment that she was inheriting so little in comparison to her daughter. "Fifty thousand dollars a year when she's just out of school! It's unbelievable. Oh, Anne," she added with a touch of smugness, "Avis is giving a dinner party for you tomorrow night."

"Whatever for?" Anne recoiled in distaste. She was in no mood for socializing.

"Darling, the whole town's buzzing about your inheritance." Denise's smile said that some of the celebrity was brushing off on her.

"Why did you have to tell people?" Anne tried to mask her exasperation. "Why couldn't you just say I was taking a job in San Francisco?"

"Anne, how could people not ask questions when you went dashing off in a private jet? Everybody in this town knows everything that's happening. You'll need something smart for Avis's dinner. We'll drive up to Atlanta in the morning to shop."

Anne promised herself she would spend as much time as possible at the office with her father. She felt self-conscious now in her own hometown. People wouldn't see Anne Forrest, who had been born and raised in Belleville. They'd look at her and see the heiress to an enormous fortune. Some would be pleased for her "great good luck," others resentful, jealous, or ridiculously in awe.

Felicia and Jackie spent the hours between flights in their suite at the Pierre. Felicia rejected Jackie's suggestion that they run down to Bergdorf's to shop.

"I'm practically a pauper," she said. "After this trip I can't spend a cent until I get my first salary check. After taxes there'll he practically nothing left." But her whole life-style wasn't going to change, she promised herself. She'd find time—and the means—to play now and then.

They slept their way through the New York-to-Geneva flight, talked animatedly on the train to Gstaad. Felicia felt a surge of exhilaration as they approached the quaint village in the hotel car. The air was exquisitely crisp and fresh. Lights shone from within the unostentatious chalets and the posh private schools that dotted the surrounding landscape. Then the elegant, turreted Palace Hotel, which, indeed, was once a royal palace, rose into view.

Wearing the dress-up loose blouses and matching tight pastel pants favored by the resort ladies at the moment for informal evenings, Felicia and Jackie were being seated at a choice table in the Maxim Room—where one wall was an exact reproduction of Maxim's in Paris—when Felicia spied Gary across the room.

"There's Gary," she whispered to Jackie when they were alone. "Who's that with him?"

"Alice Ransome," Jackie exclaimed. "God, she's had more plastic surgery. It's a chin build-up this time."

"Gary's thirty. He's getting anxious," Felicia surmised. "And Alice has all that money from her grandmother, not to mention what she'll inherit when her parents kick off." She ignored the menu, her mind zeroing in on the evening's possibilities. "Gary and I had a real ball in Portillo. Maybe I'll give him a whirl again."

"I'll stay out of the suite till one," Jackie said. "I'll find people we know at the bar."

"Involve Alice," Felicia ordered and suddenly raised a hand to wave at the table across the room. Gary had seen her. He seemed startled. Alice was pleased to be in the Maxim Room with such an attractive man. But she was no match for Felicia Harris.

"I have to be back downstairs before midnight," Gary told Felicia self-consciously while he unbuttoned his shirt.

"Midnight skiing?" Felicia mocked and pulled her sky-blue crepe blouse over her head with one swift gesture without waiting for a reply. She relished the way his eyes seemed to devour her small, huge-nippled breasts as she pulled away the fragile lace bra. "Or a private party at somebody's chalet?"

"Something like that," he hedged while he tossed his shirt on the floor and reached for the zipper of his trousers.

Her eyes holding his, her smile provocative, Felicia reached to thrust her tight pants—and simultaneously the strip of white lace beneath them—to the floor.

Her eyes fluttered shut as he brought his mouth to hers. His hands closed in about her breasts and his hips moved insinuatingly against her. She'd have an orgasm tonight, she thought in triumph. It didn't happen often but knowing she was getting what Alice hoped for later would help. She'd make him so tired that all Alice would get would be pallid leftovers.

"You are something, you know?" he said huskily when he hovered over her on the neatly turned-down bed and her fingers manipulated with skill.

"I'm the best," she drawled. Tonight she would be. Maybe

77

it would be great for her, too. Why were women always expected to lie and pretend it was?

She matched his frenzy while they moved together—knowing this was only the beginning. Tonight the only orgasm Alice could enjoy would be by herself.

Much later—when they lay tangled together in smug exhaustion—Gary sought his watch. He was worrying about Alice, Felicia imagined.

"I was sorry to hear about your great-grandmother," he said and sat up at the edge of the bed. He reached out to his mound of clothes on the floor. "That was a rotten deal about her will."

"Does the whole world know?" Felicia demanded.

"Things get around fast in our crowd," he said. "Everybody was shocked."

That explained his concern about the time. He wasn't about to discard Alice. Felicia Harris was not a great catch—not for another twenty years.

Naomi had won. She *had* to go through with this insane deal. If she didn't, she was nobody. She could handle that little bitch Anne. She could handle Doug. Naomi had known that, she realized with a surge of comprehension. Naomi meant for her to use them so she could get the hang of this business. Naomi meant for *her* to fill her shoes. That was the way it was going to be.

At eight sharp on Tuesday morning—hours before Eva would awaken—Anne left the house with Doug to begin her first day of employment at Miller Timber Company. Felicia had phoned from New York the day before to explain that she would not be home until Wednesday night. Anne had heard Doug's retort: *"Felicia, don't let it happen again. Miller Timber is a business, not a stop on the jet-set circuit."*

Company headquarters occupied six floors in the Naomi Miller Building in downtown San Francisco. The company owned five lumber mills and a pulp mill, scattered through

California, Oregon, and Washington. By contrast, Lazarus Timber Company offices occupied two thousand square feet within sight of its lumber mill, so close that the clamor of the machinery could be heard if the office windows were left open.

With the staff not yet arrived for the day, Doug led Anne on a tour of the various floors. Executives offices and the ornate, crystal-chandeliered conference room were located in the penthouse and furnished with handsome antiques. Naomi's suite of offices was furnished with a collection of fine Chinese antiques, the floors covered with Persian rugs. The desk in her inner office was a late seventeenth century French writing table decorated with brass inlay in a ground of tortoise shell. Anne remembered her grandmother's much-scratched, oak, rolltop desk that had served her from her twenty-seventh birthday to her death at eighty-seven. The other floors were utilitarian and modern; efficiency the key word everywhere.

Now in a spurt of activity the staff began to arrive for the day. Anne noted that even top-level executives were at their desks by nine. Naomi Miller would not have accepted anything less rigid.

Anne walked beside Doug with a fixed smile on her face as he introduced her to endless employees. Later she'd try to connect names with faces. Behind their polite words of welcome Anne was conscious of curiosity, resentment, and—in some cases, aborted ambitions. Every employee in the San Francisco headquarters must know that she and Felicia were being groomed to take over one day. With Naomi Miller growing old hope must have been deeply rooted in upper-echelon executives about their own advancement at her death. Not one expected Naomi Miller to retire until she was struck down, Anne surmised with reluctant respect. Like Grandma.

At last Doug led her to the penthouse office that was to be hers for the present. Compared to the executives offices on this floor, hers was extremely modest. She suspected it might once have been assigned to a secretary. He introduced her to

Shirley Madison, who had been one of three secretaries who reported to Naomi.

"Shirley is officially your assistant," he said with a glint of humor when he introduced her to the attractive young woman who occupied the adjoining office. "Actually, she'll be your guide in these early months."

"I'll need that," Anne laughed. On sight she liked Shirley.

"Shirley, you know what to do," Doug told her, all at once seeming tired. His mother's death had taken a tremendous toll on his strength, Anne thought in sympathy. "On Friday, Anne, you, and I and Felicia will fly up to Eureka to spend a few hours at our mill near there." In addition to the jet that had flown her to Naomi Miller's bedside, Anne had learned, the company maintained a smaller plane, and an additional pair of pilots, for short flights. Flying had been a way of life for Naomi and Doug.

The day sped past. Shirley—a twenty-eight-year-old divorcée with an "almost-seven-year-old" daughter—had been with the company for only three years, but Doug had been right when he said she knew more about the business than some employees who had been with Miller Timber for twenty years. Doug had chosen the perfect individual to help Anne understand the workings of the company.

Over lunch in the company cafeteria the two young women talked about their lives before joining Miller Timber Company. Anne learned that Shirley was a New Yorker who came to San Francisco with her new husband after graduating from Hunter College.

"I got pregnant practically on our honeymoon. The marriage was a disaster before Gerry was born," Shirley said in candor. "Hank's mother had spoiled him for any other woman. She died during his junior year at City College. I think he was in such a rush to get married so he'd have somebody to serve and pick up after him the way Mama did."

"How long have you been divorced?"

"Since Gerry was thirteen-months old. He just packed up and walked out. He said he was too young to be tied down as husband and father. Thank God, he cooperated on the divorce. He did that," she added bitterly, "on the grounds that I wouldn't ask for alimony or child support."

"It was rough on you," Anne said sympathetically.

"I went back to New York to live with my parents. That lasted about five months. In my mother's eyes everything I did for Gerry was wrong. I packed up and came back to San Francisco, and got a job here almost immediately."

As she paused, Shirley's eyes were appraising in a friendly fashion. "For somebody fresh out of school you know a lot about what goes on in this business."

"My grandmother had owned a timber company for over sixty years." All at once Anne felt self-conscious. Everybody here must know that Grandma and Naomi were sisters. And why she was here. "Our timber company was a tiny operation compared to this, but I grew up hearing business discussed at home every day. I worked with my grandmother during the summers—" Her voice trailed off.

"I was nervous about working with you," Shirley confessed. "I know Felicia." Her face was eloquent. "I was afraid you'd be the same type."

Anne laughed quietly.

"No two people could be more unlike. I was scared to death about meeting *you.* I expected some middle-aged woman who'd be so annoyed at having to put up with me."

Instinct told Anne it was good to have Shirley on her side. Already she sensed that there were those among the executive staff who would, reluctantly, support her, and others who resented her as a stranger and would support Naomi Miller's great-granddaughter as "family."

Anne recognized, too, that none of the top executives at the company were women. She was annoyed that Naomi Miller—herself a pioneer—had not seen fit to elevate women employees to key positions. Women weren't satisfied anymore to be second-class citizens.

Her first year at college had opened her eyes. She'd begun to see beyond the importance of making top grades and being

81

accepted by a great sorority—even though she was Jewish. The Barnard/Columbia world had changed her thinking. Living in Manhattan had changed her thinking.

She'd have to learn to take each day as it came, she exhorted herself. The twenty years ahead of her seemed a frightening hurdle.

Five

SINCE her return from Belleville, Anne was relieved that Eva had not put in an appearance at the dinner table. She had walked into the house on Monday just as Eva was sweeping off to a dinner party, but in those few moments she understood that Eva continued to regard her as an intruder. Doug had apologized painfully for his sister—both for her hostility and for her crassness at socializing so soon after their mother's death.

Tonight—over cream-of-broccoli soup followed by a fillet of pompano—Doug reminisced about the San Francisco earthquake.

"I was ten years old and Eva was twelve," he told Anne. "I remember all the details. Enmeshed, of course," he chuckled, "with all the legends and myths. It was on April eighteenth, 1906. About five in the morning the whole city began to shake. There was a terrible noise that woke everybody in the house. Right away we knew it was a terrible quake."

"I suspect my father's a little nervous about my living out here," Anne confided, her voice tender in recall. "But I suppose nobody ever thinks twice about another quake."

"Oh, we think about it," Doug admitted smilingly. "But always as an event in the distant future. Meanwhile we enjoy the city."

"The earthquake must have been frightening for a ten-year-old boy," she sympathized.

"Eva and I were sure it was the end of the world. Mama was outraged. To her the earthquake was a personal affront—we had just moved into a new house on Nob Hill." He winced in recall. "Our house miraculously escaped, but we saw the Fairmont burn. It wasn't the earthquake that destroyed San Francisco—it was the terrible fire that followed."

Anne knew that Doug was making an effort to put her at ease. She sensed, too, that he was coping with inner demons. He grieved for his mother, but he was deeply hurt that she had so bluntly indicated her lack of confidence in his ability to run the company. Strangely, Anne felt that he harbored no resentment over not inheriting a major portion of the company's stock. He had the use of the houses for his lifetime, his impressive salary, and his trust fund. For Doug this was sufficient.

While Anne was praising the brandied chocolate bavarian, she and Doug heard sounds in the foyer. Felicia had returned.

"Melissa, I'm starving," Felicia declared exuberantly. "Will you see what Agatha can scare up for me? I'll be in the family dining room. Walter's bringing in my luggage."

Anne managed a smile when Felicia appeared at the dining room entrance, dramatically attractive in a white wool suit and white fur boots that highlighted the golden glow of her skin.

"I'm back to join the salt mines," she flipped while she walked to the table. For an instant Felicia's eyes clung to the unoccupied seat at the head of the table, her desolation at Naomi Miller's death visual for that instant. "What time do I report for work?" The fleetingly painful mood was brushed aside.

"Anne and I are in the car at eight A.M.," Doug told her. For years he had been rising at six o'clock in order to enjoy a prebreakfast walk each morning. "Be there with us." He frowned as she grimaced. "Felicia, this is not a game," he warned.

"I'll be there." She sat across from Anne. "We have to play

on the team, don't we?" Her eyes were insolent as they met her cousin's.

"How was Gstaad?" Doug dismissed business talk.

"Cold and beautiful and expensive," Felicia shrugged, and Anne suspected it was the first time Felicia had ever considered costs.

"Since Christmas Eve falls on Tuesday, we'll be flying out to the Squaw Valley house on Sunday," Doug announced. "As usual," he emphasized to Felicia, anticipating her rejection of this tradition.

"I can't make it," Felicia told him.

"Felicia, the family always spends Christmas at the Squaw Valley house." He bristled at such crass disregard. "Be there." He turned to Anne. "The house is actually just outside of Squaw Valley," he told Anne. "You'll love it." But the others would not love having her there, she guessed instinctively "It's close enough to ski either at Squaw Valley or Sugar Bowl."

"I'll come out on Tuesday morning," Felicia capitulated.

"And we've decided to go ahead with the benefit at the museum on the twentieth. It's been on the drawing board for months. I expect you to be there, Felicia."

"If I'm not busy," Felicia shrugged.

"Be there," he ordered. "It'll end with a tribute to Mama. Everybody important in the state will be there. Probably even the governor."

"If I can find something to wear," Felicia drawled. "I'm short of funds, as you know."

"You'll have a paycheck on Friday," Doug said flatly. "I'm sure you'll manage."

A paycheck of almost a thousand dollars before taxes, Anne realized with a surge of anticipation. As much as she'd earned since graduation. How long before that tidbit of gossip circulated from the accounting department through the six floors of Miller Timber? How would the fifty-dollar-a-week receptionists and typists at Miller Timber react to that?

Most of her check would go home to Dad. She'd have to

hold out money to buy a dress for the black-tie benefit. Not a Paris original, but something far more expensive than she would ever have bought for a party in Belleville.

She'd die if Felicia pulled some crazy stunt that cost them this set-up. Even if they couldn't hold out for twenty years, let them stay with it for three or four years. Until Lazarus's giant bank loan was whittled down to something manageable.

Anne was relieved that she and Felicia saw nothing of each other at the office the next day. She concluded that for the present this would continue—except for those times when Doug would take them on what he called field trips. The first of these was scheduled for the following day.

On Friday morning Anne had breakfast with Doug in the airy breakfast room that provided a breathtaking view of the city. Felicia joined them in the foyer to wait for Walter to appear with the limousine. On the drive to the airport Doug talked about the tremendous changes that had taken place in the western timber industry in the past ten years.

"Once truck logging came in to replace railroad logging, we were able to move into stands that were previously inaccessible. Nobody was quicker to realize the potential this offered than Naomi Miller," he said with pride. "She shifted her thinking from emphasizing the volume of board-feet we turned out to focusing on the whole new range of products to be made from timber. That's when we opened our pulp mill."

"It seems to me," Felicia said with an elaborate casualness that captured Anne's attention, "that how much we turn out is far less important than how much we earn."

"Spoken like your great-grandmother." Doug beamed. For all Felicia's show of boredom with the job, she was out to score points, Anne interpreted. "Mama always said her concern was not in the amount of our annual sales but in the profits. We haven't always reached it," he reminisced, "but her goal was for a fifteen percent return on net earnings after taxes. We've hit over ten-point-two percent several times in the past ten years, and that's damn good."

86

At the airport they climbed aboard the plane used for short flights. Immediately, over coffee served from a thermos, they talked about the lumber mill at Eureka. Anne realized that Felicia had absorbed far more about the business than she admitted. Naomi Miller had seen to that. When Anne asked—almost shyly—if they would see one of the company's stands of redwoods, Doug's face lighted.

"We'll drive there," he promised. "We have trees that were growing when dinosaurs roamed the earth."

Four hours later Anne stood gazing up into the sky at the coast redwoods, growing so close together as to shut out the sunlight—the lowest branches eighty or ninety feet above the ground—their thick-ribbed, cinnamon-colored trunks, eight to a dozen feet in diameter. Anne could hear her grandmother's voice: *Annie, their beauty takes your breath away. That and knowing they've been there for over a thousand years. Some for over two thousand years.*

"These are the coast redwoods," Doug emphasized. "They're slightly younger and somewhat smaller in girth than the Sierra redwoods—but they're the tallest trees on earth. They thrive on the Pacific air and the moisture from the fogs. Usually they're found within thirty miles of the coastline—along the river banks and the lower slopes."

At intervals in the next few days Anne remembered the grandeur of the coast redwoods in Humboldt County. Somehow, having seen them she felt as though she had reached out and touched her grandmother for precious moments. She was grateful to be enmeshed in this learning process because that helped alleviate her bouts of aching loneliness. Shirley, too—so friendly and open—helped her fight off a powerful instinct to walk out on Miller Timber and return to Belleville.

Each day she and Felicia left with Doug for the office at eight sharp. She rarely saw Felicia until the next morning. After business hours, she gathered from Felicia's casual conversation on the drive to the office, Felicia went off to meet friends—who happened to be in town—at Amelio's or Ernie's or Trader Vic's.

On the Saturday afternoon before the museum gala, Anne left the office to take a cable car to Market Street to shop for a dress at I. Magnin. She was surprised to realize she was intrigued by the prospect of seeing the Naomi Miller Museum. One of her pleasurable discoveries about attending Barnard had been the accessibility of New York's great museums. And Doug had told her about San Francisco's range of first-rate museums.

At the marble-fronted department store—with elegant crystal chandeliers, imported pink-beige Rose de Brignoles marble walls, and high, silvered ceilings—Anne bought a beautifully draped turquoise chiffon with a price tag that elicited stabs of guilt, but she had just the coat to wear with it. She was sure the other women in the family would be expensively gowned. She harbored a quixotic determination to have Rae Lazarus's granddaughter appear equally well-dressed. Now she splurged on a white quilted parka and ski pants—to wear at the Squaw Valley house.

She left Magnin's and strolled down Post Street to Gump's, hesitating for a moment at the discovery of two entrances. On impulse she walked to the jewelry shop, knowing that she could hardly afford—at this point—the exquisite jade for which Gump's was famous but she was eager to choose a gift that her mother could display with pride. She settled on a brocaded evening bag with a crystal clasp that would be right for Denise's imminent trip to Palm Beach.

In the adjoining store her eyes lit up at the sight of a glowing pink Italian alabaster chess set. Her father was a dedicated chess player. She acknowledged to the cordial saleswoman that she understood the gifts might not be delivered by Christmas. They would be slightly delayed Hanukkah-Christmas gifts.

Leaving Gump's, Anne debated about how to handle the question of gifts for the family. She'd settle for books, she decided, a little tentatively. Doug had talked about Kenneth Rexroth Books on Union Street. She would choose books for everyone. Even Todd and Adrian, whom she had not yet met except briefly at the funeral, but who would be at the Squaw Valley house.

On the evening of the museum benefit Doug appeared in a rare festive mood; yet at intervals Anne sensed his discomfort at attending a gala so soon after his mother's death. Anne waited with him in the foyer while he sent a maid upstairs to tell Felicia that Walter was outside with the car.

"You're looking beautiful," he told Anne with an admiring smile. "That velvet coat has such regal lines."

"I inherited it from my mother," Anne confided. "She decided it was the wrong shade for her."

"Turquoise was my mother's favorite color," Doug said. "She knew how flattering it was to her."

"We're still terribly early, Doug," Felicia called as she descended the staircase, glitteringly attired in a long, dolman-sleeved dress of golden and silver paillettes that outlined her sleek figure. Around her neck was a triple strand of ginger-crystal beads. Over one arm she carried the sable coat that had been Naomi's.

"I'm the cochairman," Doug reminded. "I'm supposed to be there early."

Anne felt Felicia's eyes graze her dress and matching coat with barely concealed disdain.

"Where's Eva?" Felicia asked.

"She's over at Bruce's house—she's coming with Bruce and Edwina." He smiled wryly. "She said it would be too much to be one of three women escorted by me."

"I think we have a very distinguished, handsome escort," Anne said, in a convivial mood for the first time since her arrival in San Francisco.

"I hope the memorial to Naomi doesn't go on forever." Felicia lifted her eyebrows in a show of distaste. "I have a party later at The Other Room."

Walter drew up before the Naomi Miller Museum of Art—a classically simple three-story, white-stone structure, brilliantly lighted tonight. With a glow of anticipation Doug walked between Anne and Felicia to the entrance. He exchanged a few words with the attendants scheduled to handle the valet parking, then ushered the two young women inside. Anne was impressed by the airiness of the lower floor, the beautiful double staircase lined with clipped yews and topiary trees. Everywhere there were masses of exquisite pink and red roses.

"Doug, I'm so glad you're here." The woman who was his cochairman came forward with an eloquent sigh of relief.

Doug introduced her to Anne, then devoted himself for a few minutes to reassuring his cochairman that this year's benefit would live up to those of previous years. At a pantomimed command from Doug, Felicia led Anne away to show off the lower-floor exhibits.

Anne made the expected comments as Felicia pointed out the museum's special treasures, but her mind delved into her strange situation. Naomi Miller's will confined her to more than learning the business and working in tandem with Felicia. That two-year residency requirement threw her into a stifling closeness with the family.

Up till now she had seen little of anyone except Doug, but she sensed this was about to change. Tonight the family would be present en masse. According to Naomi's dictates—and Doug would fight to keep her traditions alive—they would all be together over the Christmas holidays. They would spend a long Easter weekend at the Acapulco house—and many summer weekends at Lake Tahoe. To her amazement she felt a growing resolution to become part of the family tapestry. In some odd fashion this would be bringing Grandma together with her sister.

"We'll have cocktails downstairs." Felicia's voice brought her back to the moment. "Among all of Doug's precious moderns," she mocked. "Dinner is always served in the eighteenth century and nineteenth century rooms, which open into each other. God, it's a drag."

Now guests were beginning to arrive. Strolling fiddlers in colorful costumes appeared about the lower floor. Waiters circulated with trays of champagne-filled glasses.

Photographers were snapping shots of the guests for tomorrow morning's newspapers. The women seemed so aware of the presence of the cameras—subconsciously, or perhaps consciously, Anne thought in sudden comprehension—holding flattering poses, heads lifted in the eternal gesture that detracted years from aging throats.

As at Naomi's funeral, Anne was taken aback to recognize a famous face here and there. She felt an unexpected stir of pleasurable expectation. The festive air was contagious.

Guests divided their attention between the paintings on loan from private collections, and newly arriving friends. Doug had told her that San Francisco society was often called provincial; but in truth, he said, it was to the West Coast what New York and Boston were to the East Coast. *"We're the cultural outpost of the western half of the country."*

Doug beckoned to Felicia to join them. Anne tried not to be self-conscious when a newspaper photographer snapped several shots of the three of them. No matter, she told herself—if the photos appeared in tomorrow morning's newspapers, she'd be listed simply as a guest. But she'd watch for them—Dad would enjoy seeing them. And Mother would show the photos around Belleville.

Wearing narrow bright-green satin trousers and a tunic of heavy gold embroidery, with ropes of pearls about her throat and diamond earrings dripping from her earlobes, Eva arrived with Edwina and Bruce. She smiled as she relinquished the chinchilla coat she had inherited from her mother, but her eyes were chunks of ice when they rested for a moment on Anne.

"Doug, you've done it again!" Eva effervesced girlishly as she moved toward him, ignoring Anne. "Everything looks so beautiful."

"We're oversubscribed," he said with pride.

"Where are we sitting?" Eva demanded. Without waiting for a reply she turned to Edwina, coldly attractive in an aubergine faille skirt and a top of muted green-and-coral brocade with chinchilla cuffs. "Let's go upstairs and check the place cards."

91

Anne's face brightened when she saw Consuelo and Leon arrive. Doug had introduced her to a stream of people, but she felt comfortable with no one in these monied surroundings. And she sensed the covert curiosity behind their smiles. Who was this "cousin from Georgia"—as Doug introduced her? Consuelo and Leon were the only ones among the San Francisco branch of the family who showed a genuine interest in the Georgia branch. Grandma had been their only aunt on their mother's side.

"You look lovely, Anne," Consuelo told her while Leon nodded in agreement. "I told Doug to be sure you were at our table."

"I'm glad." Anne began to relax. Like herself, Consuelo wore an elegantly simple dress. White crepe, with a narrow ruffle from the V of the neck down to encircle the hem, a jade pin at the front of the curved waist.

At dinner in the eighteenth century room Anne found herself seated between Doug and Leon. Consuelo and Leon were engrossed in conversation with a guest about the coming year's presidential election. Doug was reminiscing about his years in Paris, right after World War I.

"Mama was dead set against my studying painting, but I was headstrong at twenty-three. And rebellious," he confided to Anne. "Every generation has its young rebels. I stayed in Paris, living in a grubby attic studio, until my father died in a weird hunting accident and I had to come home. My mother insisted she couldn't run the business without me." *Doug knew that was just an excuse to drag him away from Paris, didn't he?* Anne thought. Doug's father had been Grandma's first love, Anne remembered. "I had to come home, also," he emphasized, "because my father had secretly kept me in money. But it's just as well that I did. I lacked the talent to be a great artist. It wasn't enough just to paint. I couldn't bear to be a bad painter."

After dinner several prominent San Franciscans offered glowing tributes to Naomi Miller. Anne sat at tense attention, resenting the tributes. The speakers weren't talking about

Naomi Miller, Anne thought in silent defiance. To her, they were talking about Rae Lazarus.

Anne sat at her desk, fighting yawns while she studied reports that Doug had given her this morning from their Eureka mill. Though it was past midnight when they left the museum and at least two hours later before she prodded herself to sleep, she had been at the breakfast table shortly past seven o'clock. Felicia ignored these morning breakfast conferences, but Anne realized how much she learned from Doug in what he called their "sunrise study group."

"Feel like coffee?" Shirley asked ebulliently from the doorway. "I just put up some water."

"Wow, do I!" Shirley knew about last night's gala. "I got about four hours sleep last night."

"I gather it was a terrific bash," Shirley teased and unfolded the morning's *San Francisco Chronicle* that had been tucked under one arm. "Photos all over the place." She flipped through until she located her quarry. "More photos earlier on in the paper, but this one on the business page should interest you."

"The business page?" Puzzled, Anne reached for the newspaper.

A three-column-wide photograph showed Doug flanked by Felicia and herself. Her mouth fell open in shock as she scanned the caption: TWO HEIRESSES TO NAOMI MILLER EMPIRE AT MUSEUM GALA WITH DOUGLAS MILLER.

"Oh, God, that's gross!"

"Don't knock it. You're a celebrity." Yet Shirley was sympathetic.

"I feel as though I'd . . ." Anne groped for a suitably strong description, settled on a variation of a New York cliché: "I feel as though I'd stripped to skin in an I. Magnin window."

"In this city you're big news," Shirley said matter-of-factly. "Nationwide you're news. If there hasn't already been a story in *The Wall Street Journal*, there will be." Shirley giggled.

"And here I'd been thinking about asking you over for dinner on Friday night to celebrate Gerry's birthday."

"Ask me," Anne coaxed. "It'll be such fun."

Instinctively she knew that Shirley would forever be her close friend. And she knew that she would need friends in the years ahead. Too much was happening too fast.

Six

EN route to the office on Saturday morning Doug reminded Anne that the following day the two of them would fly out to Reno. Squaw Valley was a short drive from there. Eva, her two sons, their wives, Todd, and Adrian were flying out this afternoon.

"It's a quick flight," Doug conceded, "but Edwina and Bruce will be bickering every mile. Adrian will be his usual obnoxious self. I'm getting old enough to try to protect myself from trivial annoyances. I told them we had a business meeting late this afternoon. We'll fly out in peace."

The Squaw Valley house, hidden among the magnificent slopes of the Sierra Nevada, Doug explained, actually was just outside of Squaw Valley, not a part of the famous resort. It was a replica of a Tyrolean chalet, set on a mountainside that was easily accessible not only to the amenities of Squaw Valley but to the lesser known but prestigious ski village called Sugar Bowl.

"The boys like to ski at Squaw Valley," Doug told her. To their uncle, Bruce and Leon—at fifty and forty-six—were still "the boys." "Felicia likes to ski at Sugar Bowl, which is far more difficult."

Of course, Felicia would be an accomplished skier. But, Anne consoled herself, at least she had a decent ski outfit, even if she had never skied. She had that pair of gorgeous sweaters she'd bought at Sak's fabulous after-Christmas sale last year, when she was still at Barnard—and the parka and ski pants from I. Magnin. Yet she felt gauche and unsophisticated beside Felicia. But Felicia would never know that, she promised herself.

Early the following morning—in her immensely becoming white parka and ski pants, ribbed red turtleneck rising high about her throat—Anne joined Doug in the limousine for the drive to the airport. Casually garbed in gray flannel slacks and burgandy cable-knit cashmere sweater, Doug appeared more relaxed than normal.

The smaller company plane was waiting for them. They took off immediately. At the Reno airport Jackson, the chauffeur-houseman from the Squaw Valley house, met them with a station wagon. They waited in the crisp golden sunlight while a multitude of Christmas-wrapped parcels was transferred from plane to station wagon.

All at once Doug seemed tense. He was dreading Christmas without his mother, Anne surmised sympathetically. Every holiday was painful that first year.

She remembered the first New Year's Day after her grandmother died. The first Passover seder when her grandmother had not sat there at the table with them. There had been no seder without Grandma.

In the station wagon, driving along the four-lane Reno-Truckee highway, Doug pointed out Squaw Valley in the distance and the surrounding snow-covered peaks that rose to awesome heights.

"My mother loved our weekend getaways—whether it was at Squaw Valley or Tahoe or Alcapulco. She always flew to the ranch for a week in October."

"All with gorgeous views." Anne visualized a montage of mountain peaks, Pacific Ocean, and stretches of autumn-hued ranch land.

"Oh, I doubt that Mama ever gave them more than superficial notice," Doug said dryly. "She enjoyed the isolation from the city disturbances. Our chunk of mountainside was her private kingdom. She said the air up there cleared her mind so she could plot her next venture." He paused. "Sometimes I would be very angry at Mama," he said softly, "and then she would do something so wonderfully sweet for me. She didn't really care much about the museum—" His smile was apologetic. *She cared that it bore her name,* Anne thought. *She cared a lot.* "But Mama knew that nothing in the world means more to me than that museum. And she gave to it with a generosity that staggered people. For me she did that."

They rode in silence for a few moments, then Doug talked again about his mother.

"You have to understand, Anne, that my mother was a very strong woman. She had all the strength in this family—except for Felicia, who's so like her. She was bright, stubborn, driving—and manipulative," he conceded. "I'm proud of her enormous success, but I feel so inadequate in comparison."

Deliberately Anne rerouted the conversation. Even with his mother dead Doug was controlled by Naomi Miller. What an awful legacy to leave him.

The magnificent Miller chalet—as Doug had described it to her—followed the lines of its Gstaad or St. Moritz counterpart. The peaked roof covered a three-leveled ten-bedroom mansion with wide balconies and shuttered windows. Despite its huge size, Anne fought against a sense of claustrophobia as she considered the four days ahead under one roof with so many of Naomi Miller's descendents.

Anne turned away from the chalet to gaze with awe at the spectacular sweep of mountains that rose on every side, the sky a dazzling blue, untouched by a single cloud—the air unbelievably fresh and invigorating.

"There's Todd up there on the deck. Hi, Todd!" Doug yelled with unfamiliar exuberance, and a face appeared above the railing.

"Hi ya, Unc!" Todd rose to his feet and leaned over a planter lush with red and pink geraniums. "Hi, Anne." She had met Todd at Naomi's funeral, though that had been no more than an introduction. "The skiing's great today."

"But you're lying on your rump in the sun," Doug scolded good-humoredly.

"I was on the slopes earlier. I came home when I got hungry."

"See you at lunch." Doug prodded Anne toward the entrance. "We're hungry, too. It's this marvelous air up here."

In the house—their weekenders carted off to upstairs bedrooms by Jackson—they found Eva, Edwina, and Consuelo lounging before a blazing fire in the floor-to-ceiling fieldstone fireplace. Consuelo was reading. Eva stopped short in the midst of conversation with Edwina. Anne suspected they had been discussing her.

"Bruce and Leon are on the slopes," Edwina reported. "Bruce is trying to get rid of his martini paunch before he has to climb into swimming trunks at Palm Beach next month. Adrian went for a bike ride into the village."

"In search of a junk-food lunch," Consuelo guessed. "Mandy told him we're having chicken-and-spinach crepes."

"How soon can we have lunch?" Doug asked. "Anne and I are famished. Must we wait for Bruce and Leon?"

"I'll tell Mandy to serve it right away." Eva rose to her feet. Again, she was making a point of ignoring Anne's presence.

"Did you have a pleasant flight?" Edwina asked Anne with unexpected cordiality.

"Lovely," Anne assured her—this new friendliness suspect.

Over chicken-and-spinach crepes and steamed baby carrots Eva and her daughters-in-law, with Anne listening politely, discussed having lunch the following day at Squaw Valley. Doug and Todd talked about the coming year's presidential election and Lyndon Johnson's promise of achieving the "Great Society." Both were oblivious to the women's conversation.

"You'll love the outdoor dining terrace." Consuelo turned to Anne and laughed at her astonishment. "It's radiant heated," she explained, "and that mountain sun is incredibly warm. People lie around the pool in swimsuits, with the snow shoveled back a few feet."

"I prefer Sugar Bowl," Eva said—her smile indicating she would forego this preference. "It's more exclusive. But then the world's changing," she sighed. "Look at the way people are pushing themselves into San Francisco society. Even some Jews have made their way into our *Social Register*."

"Mother, they've intermarried into our best families," Edwina said quickly, while Anne stared at her plate, her face hot. "Naturally they've been accepted."

"It's interesting that San Francisco has a *Social Register*," Anne said with calculated sweetness, "when nobody's been here for more than three generations."

"Doug said you went to school in New York, Anne," Consuelo intervened, stricken by the hostile undercurrents. "Did you enjoy living there?"

"It was exciting and different. So much to see and do." Anne struggled for poise. She must learn to ignore Eva. "And Barnard is a great school."

"Todd will go to Yale," Edwina told Anne. "My father and my grandfather both went there." But Todd was frowning at his mother.

"That doesn't mean I'll be accepted," Todd warned.

"Of course, you'll be accepted," his mother shot back in irritation.

"I'm not sure I want to go to Yale," Todd said, and Anne sympathized with the rebellion she sensed in him. "I'll be eighteen by the time I graduate. Maybe I'll just hitchhike around the country for a year before I go on to college."

"You will go to Yale, Todd," his mother said tightly. "Like my father and his father before him."

"What's for dessert?" Adrian demanded, sauntering into the dining room.

"What did you eat in town?" Consuelo asked.

"A pair of chili dogs and french fries," Todd guessed, grin-

99

ning, and Adrian nodded, settling himself into an empty chair opposite his grandmother.

"I can't stand the garbage Mandy hands out as food," he said arrogantly. Stiffening in alarm Eva gestured for quiet. Not that she was concerned for Mandy's feelings, Anne suspected—she was worried that a well-trained servant might walk out.

Adrian wasn't at all like either his mother or father, Anne decided. He was a throw-back to Willi Sachs.

Felicia arrived at dusk the following day. A day ahead of schedule. She was bored, she explained, because all Jackie had talked about was spending most of January at the Marbella Club on the Costa del Sol. She dropped her Hungarian suede greatcoat on the living room floor and sat on a sofa beside her mother.

"That's from St. Laurent's 'sport-de-luxe' collection," Edwina noted, admiring Felicia's honey-beige sealskin jerkin with knitted sleeves, worn with matching tights.

"The jerkin, not the tights," Felicia drawled, her eyes sweeping about the room. "I found the tights in a boutique in New York."

Anne and Todd sat hunched over a chess board on the walnut gaming table at the far end of the living room. Adrian was toasting marshmallows at the fireplace. At the other side of the room Consuelo was directing Doug and Leon in hanging decorations on the tall Douglas fir that had been brought in to serve as this year's Christmas tree. Felicia's father sprawled in a lounge chair with the martini shaker convenient for refills.

"Where's Eva?" Felicia asked.

"She went to a cocktail party at somebody's chalet at Squaw Valley," Edwina said. The angry glint in her mother's eyes told Felicia her grandmother had acquired another "handsome young protégé."

100

"When are you heading for Palm Beach?" Felicia asked. Damn! How was she going to survive in Naomi's straitjacket?

"The middle of January." Edwina's eyes swept across the room to Anne with the hostility she customarily managed to conceal. "I can't wait to get away. But your father says we won't be able to stay until spring with money as short as it is. We've *always* stayed until spring—"

They heard the sound of voices in the foyer. Eva was home.

"Darling, it was a superb party," Eva reproached Edwina as she strode into the room with the long strides she considered youthful. "Felicia, ski at Squaw Valley tomorrow morning. There are some absolutely gorgeous young men up for the holidays." She paused. "But don't come to the parties," she laughed. "You're such awful competition."

"Adrian, stop eating all those marshmallows," Consuelo called to him. "You'll spoil your dinner."

"That's not what spoils *my* dinner." Eva's superficial gaiety evaporated. Her voice dropped to a whisper. "How can I enjoy any meal when that little bitch is sitting at the table? Why does Doug insist on shoving her down our throats?"

"Because that's the way Naomi wanted it," Felicia said bitterly.

"Wouldn't you think she understood we don't like having her underfoot?" Eva demanded and smiled as Adrian sauntered toward them. "How's my precious grandson?" she cooed and lifted her cheek to be kissed. "I think it's just terrible the way Mother ignored him in her will." The ten-thousand dollar bequest was a joke, Felicia conceded. Were Leon and Connie as unconcerned about that as they pretended?

"I hope Anne goes out on the slopes tomorrow and breaks both legs," Felicia whispered viciously.

"She doesn't ski," Adrian told them. "Todd asked her."

"I still hope she breaks both legs," Felicia reiterated and tensed as she gazed up at Doug's grim face. He'd left the tree-trimming operation to court their admiration, she gathered. "Doug, the tree looks sensational," she said sweetly. "I'll have

Jackson bring down my presents and put them underneath later."

"I'll ask Mandy to serve dinner as soon as it's ready," he told them. "We're all up early out here."

"Felicia, don't start up with that girl," Edwina warned. "You need each other. I'd be terribly unhappy to see all that money go to the Museum."

"I'd be unhappy, too," Felicia said.

Anne came downstairs for an early breakfast with Doug, Leon, and Todd. She surmised that Bruce was sleeping off last night's heavy consumption of after-dinner Scotch. The women, she gathered, would emerge in time to leave for lunch at Squaw Valley.

Todd talked enthusiastically about the records of a new singer named Joan Baez. He was delighted to hear she was a favorite of Anne's as well, along with Bob Dylan. He talked reverently about a classmate's older brother who had been part of the August civil rights demonstration in Washington, D.C.—when two hundred thousand people heard Martin Luther King, Jr. make his eloquent "I have a dream" speech. Anne told the others about a Barnard friend who had just signed up with the Peace Corps.

Over coffee Leon and Todd decided to ski at Sugar Bowl.

"I may come home on a stretcher," Leon chuckled. "But Sugar Bowl's slopes are a real challenge. Right, Todd?"

"Right." Anne admired the camaraderie that ricocheted between Todd and Leon. "Sure you won't come with us, Uncle Doug?" Anne had made it clear earlier that she didn't ski.

"Sure. I'm settling myself on a chaise on the deck to read in that marvelous morning sun," Doug said with an air of anticipation.

"I'll walk down to the village," Anne decided. "Pick up some postcards."

"It's over half a mile," Leon cautioned. "And remember, coming back it's all uphill."

"Call the house from the village," Doug urged. "Have Jackson come down to pick you up."

"Thanks, but I doubt that'll be necessary. I became a walker when I was at school in New York. San Francisco and New York are the two cities where people walk. Everywhere else, people just jump into a car automatically." Not that this San Francisco family walked, Anne conceded in a corner of her mind. Except for Doug.

Twenty minutes later Anne emerged from the house into the brilliant morning sunlight, the snow crunching beneath her booted feet as she walked down the front steps. She paused a moment, reveling in the vista before her: pristine white mountain peaks rising into the radiant blue of the sky; the village nestled below a long, slow incline, spirals of smoke from chimneys visible in the distance.

With a sense of well-being absent in these past four weeks, Anne strolled down the path to the road, a center segment cleared earlier in the morning in anticipation of holiday travel. She was unaware that from the second-floor deck Doug followed her graceful progress between the snowbanks; unaware that at this moment Adrian was turning into the road astride his high-speed bicycle. She thought herself alone in this oasis of beauty. Then all at once the exquisite silence was shattered.

"Anne, watch out!" Doug shouted.

In a split-second of shock Anne saw the bicycle charging down the narrow road. As she dived into the snowbank on her right, while Adrian sped past, she saw the glint of rage in his eyes. *Because he had missed his target.*

"My brakes won't work!" he yelled belatedly.

"Anne, are you all right?" Doug hung perilously over the railing of the deck.

"I'm fine," she called back.

She heard Adrian cry out and swung about to see him flying off the bike and into a snowbank. He'd hit either a tree trunk or a boulder, she guessed.

"I'll be right down," Doug told her. "Don't move."

"I'm not hurt," she reassured him, impatient to escape this ugly scene. *Adrian had meant to run her down.*

"Doug, what is it?" Her voice harsh with alarm, Consuelo rushed from a door farther down the deck while tying the sash of her robe about her waist. But Doug was already hurrying downstairs.

"The brakes on my bike went!" Adrian yelled, his voice strident in the morning stillness. "I had to swerve into the snow to stop. I hit a big rock! I may have broken my shoulder—"

Anne stalled on pulling herself out of the snow. That little creep was lying—there had been nothing wrong with his brakes. Maybe now there was, from crashing into that rock, she guessed, as she struggled shakily to her feet. He'd have himself an alibi, but she knew to be on guard in Adrian's vicinity. She was grateful that most of the time he would be away at school or camp.

Doug stood beside Adrian's bed and stared down at his nephew in distaste. He hadn't believed that business about the brakes for an instant. Since he was three, Adrian had been a rotten little monster. Not little anymore—but still rotten.

"Doug, do you think we ought to drive him into Reno to the hospital?" Consuelo asked, pale and anxious.

"No," Doug said brusquely. "He's just shaken up. No broken bones. Not even a sprain. He'll have a few bruises."

"Oh God, Doug, he might have been badly injured."

"He wasn't." Doug's tone softened.

"Could I have some orange juice or something? My throat's so dry." Adrian tried to sound appealing.

"I'll tell Mandy to . . ." Doug began but Consuelo interrupted him.

"I'll go down for it," she soothed. "Doug, stay with him. He just might have a concussion. He shouldn't be left alone."

Doug waited until Consuelo was out of the room and beyond hearing.

"Adrian, if you ever try anything like that again, I'll make sure you're committed to a mental institution."

"I didn't try anything," Adrian said aggrievedly. "I told you . . ."

"I heard what Felicia said last night to you about hoping Anne broke both legs," Doug told him. Felicia and Adrian had always been close—both Mama's spoiled brats. Felicia and Todd tolerated each other. "But Anne might have been killed, and that wouldn't have helped Felicia. It would have cost her at least sixty million from your grandmother's estate." Why had Mama been so fond of Adrian? But he knew why—the little bastard knew how to butter her up. And Mama mistook his nastiness for strength.

"I just had an accident," Adrian sulked.

"Don't have another," Doug warned. He remembered with disgust that incident at Adrian's previous school, when the headmaster told them Adrian had been blackmailing a classmate with threats against his younger sister. "You've given your parents more than their share of ulcers." Consuelo had not wanted to send him off to boarding school. The therapists, three of them, had insisted on it. Felicia and Todd had gone to boarding school because their parents were seldom home.

"What's this about Adrian having an accident?" Eva burst into the room. "Connie's pale as a ghost."

"Nothing serious," Doug told her while Eva hurried to the bed. "Just a tumble off his bike."

Christmas was supposed to be a time of "peace on earth." There was little peace in this house, Doug thought grimly. In this *divided* house.

"Stay with him, Eva," he told his sister. "Consuelo will be back in a few minutes with his orange juice."

Anne had been so anxious to reassure him that she was all right. She'd insisted on going ahead with her walk to the village. He'd have Jackson drive him down. He needed to see for himself that she'd suffered no after-effects.

He'd have a talk with Felicia when she woke up. She'd have to learn to be careful what she said in front of that little bastard. How did people as fine as Leon and Consuelo produce a child as rotten as Adrian?

Seven

IMMEDIATELY after Christmas two high-level executives of Miller Timber handed in their resignations. Anne understood this was in retaliation for her arrival, along with Felicia's, on the company scene. Doug was unruffled. But he was unhappy when Leon announced at a family dinner on New Year's Day that he was retiring from the company in six months. Doug knew this would have infuriated his mother.

"Connie and I have given it a lot of thought." Leon spoke with confidence. "We can be comfortable on the income from the trust fund." Anne knew that their house and Bruce and Edwina's house had been wedding gifts from their grandmother. "I can play around with my painting again," he said with humorous self-mockery. "Nothing that I paint will ever hang in a museum, but I'll be happy." He exchanged a warm smile with his wife. "And I'm hardly irreplaceable."

Not only Doug but Leon had been pushed into the business by Naomi, Anne thought sympathetically. Why had it been so important for her to control everyone within reach?

Once word of Leon's imminent retirement circulated around the department, tensions developed there. Long-time key employees, philosophical about Leon's remaining forever, were suddenly avid to succeed him. The air crackled with their ambitions. Meanwhile, anticipating a shift in personnel, Doug ordered that another junior accountant be hired.

Like every other female at Miller Timber between the ages

of eighteen and sixty-eight, Anne was drawn to Glenn Rogers, the new junior accountant. When he walked into the company cafeteria, the room became electric. He wasn't handsome in a conventional fashion, Anne judged, but he had a potent charisma—a word that had become a part of the sixties vernacular with the presidential campaign of John F. Kennedy.

From office gossip Anne learned that Glenn was twenty-five, and that in addition to a bachelor's degree from the University of Pennsylvania he had an MBA from its Wharton School. He made it clear to all that he understood he was "low man on the totem pole" in Miller's accounting department and was willing to take on any irksome assignment. He was the first to arrive in the accounting department in the morning, the last to leave. Anne respected his work attitude.

Anne's life had settled into a pattern of engrossing hours at the office, where Shirley guided her through the maze of Miller Timber procedures. Usually she lunched with Shirley in the company cafeteria—never patronized by Felicia, unless she was summoned to a working lunch with Doug, sometimes in the executive dining room, more often a tray in Doug's office. Dinner was at the house with Doug, with after-dinner evening sessions about the business. Occasionally—at Doug's insistence—Felicia joined them for dinner and evening conferences. Except for these encounters she saw little of Felicia. She was ever awed—and sometimes intimidated—by all there was to learn about Miller Timber operations.

She phoned her father regularly on Sunday afternoons. Despite her hectic work schedule she missed him. Her mother's two weeks in Palm Beach were to extend to the month of January. She had phoned from Avis Moore's beach house there to say she had encountered Eva at a party.

"Darling, I couldn't believe it," Denise gushed. "My first cousin, whom I've never met. She hadn't the faintest idea who I was," she continued scornfully, "until I mentioned you. What a nasty, arrogant woman!"

Anne was surprised and intrigued when Glenn Rogers—on his second Friday in the office—asked her to have dinner with him on Sunday evening. Fleetingly, she suspected Glenn's motive. Every employee in the San Francisco office knew her status at Miller Timber.

"I don't know a soul in this town," he pursued, "and I hear you're new here, too."

"Oh, yes." He was lonely, too.

"Let's explore San Francisco together." He made it seem a glorious adventure. "Starting with dinner Sunday. Have you seen Fisherman's Wharf yet?"

"No," she confessed and laughed. "I know—that's a disgraceful admission."

"We'll have dinner there," Glenn decreed. "At a great restaurant with an awesome view of the Bay."

Anne was surprised to discover that Shirley disliked Glenn. Everybody else seemed to admire him.

"He's already figuring how soon he'll be running the department," Shirley said dryly.

"Shirley, you're antimale," Anne joshed. "That's what comes of devouring *The Feminine Mystique* over one weekend."

"I think Colton's already on to him." Joe Colton was the front-runner for Leon's position.

"Glenn's no competition for Mr. Colton," Anne protested.

"Not now. But young hotshots like Glenn Rogers have a way of pushing ahead awfully fast. Maybe it couldn't happen here when Naomi Miller was alive, but it's open season now."

Anne began to see Glenn two or three evenings a week, anticipating these occasions with increasing pleasure. She felt herself in touch with reality again. Like avid tourists they strolled along the pedestrian walk of the Golden Gate Bridge and marveled at the mesmerizing views from both sides. They explored the haunts of the Beats, roamed about the Berkeley campus—where students traditionally manned fund-raising and membership recruiting tables and gave speeches on political and social action in the sidewalk area in front of the campus. These were worlds she could understand. She couldn't understand Naomi Miller's world.

109

She made a point of not talking with Shirley about her evenings with Glenn. At disconcerting intervals she asked herself if Glenn's pursuit was motivated by her position. Each time she reproached herself for such cynicism. Like herself Glenn was lonely in San Francisco.

Glenn had grown up in a small coal mining town in Pennsylvania. His father had died in a mine cave-in when he was eleven. His mother died when he was seventeen. Bright and determined, he had fought to put himself through school. After graduation he had tried living in Chicago and then Dallas before coming out to San Francisco.

"I won't live and die the way my parents did," Glenn vowed impassionedly in a moment of soul-baring. "My father went down into a mine he knew was unsafe because he needed the money to support his family. My mother died because she had no money for decent medical attention. I'll make it big, Anne. I'm a driven man. I don't care how hard I have to work, I'll be a success in business. I know I have what it takes."

For the last two weeks Glenn had been pressing her to come up to his apartment, but each time she evaded this. For all her talk with Shirley about the New Woman, she wasn't ready to sleep with Glenn. She couldn't deal with that. Yet she would die, she thought, if Glenn walked out of her life.

At Barnard her roommate, Heidi Thomas, had bragged in their junior year that she'd slept with half a frat house at Columbia and was working on the second half. *"Annie, we're free! We're not slaves to men anymore!"* They'd all talked a lot about women's rights and sex but they didn't *do.* A few girls on campus, like Heidi, flaunted all the old conventions and boasted about what a sensational time they were having. The rest of them just talked.

On a Sunday evening in March Anne insisted that Glenn drop her off at her door instead of seeing her into the house as usual, because the earlier drizzle was threatening to become a downpour. Despite the weather they had driven up to Grizzly Peak and made love in what Glenn dubbed "the 1950s

110

fashion"—when it was acceptable to do "everything but" have sex.

"You might just make it home before the storm breaks," Anne cajoled and reached for the door on her side. "I'll make a dash for the house."

Mrs. Morrison herself responded to the bell. She seemed tense and angry. Anne immediately understood. Behind the closed door of the library Felicia was shrieking at Doug in fury. Mrs. Morrison had been devoted to Naomi Miller, but she had to force herself to tolerate Felicia.

"Doug, I have worked insane hours for weeks on end! You have no right to say I can't take three days' leave!"

"You can live without flying to London next weekend," Doug shot back. "We'll be going to the Acapulco house for four days next month."

"I am not talking as a member of the family." All at once Felicia's voice was Arctic cold. "I'm talking as an employee. One of the typists or a bookkeeper would get off with some trumped-up excuse—it happens all the time. *They* don't have to go to you. I want to take leave on Monday, Tuesday, and Wednesday of next week. Just consider me one of the employees."

"You're not a minor employee." Doug refused to be ruffled. "You're being trained to succeed Naomi Miller. That is not a nine-to-five occupation. I expect you to be on the job as required."

"I'm taking those days off. I'm telling you right now." Her voice followed Anne and Mrs. Morrison as they hurried up the stairs. "Next Saturday afternoon I'll be on a plane bound for New York. I'll be back on the job on Thursday morning. I will have used up three days of my vacation time. And if you want to go to court and declare the will invalid, be my guest!"

"Young people today have no respect," Mrs. Morrison whispered, slightly breathless from their precipitous rush up the stairs. "And Mrs. Miller spoiled that one something awful."

Anne was trembling as she opened the door to her room and walked inside. *Could everything—her inheritance, her fabulous weekly salary—be lost because of Felicia's ridiculous whim to spend a long weekend in London?* Would she change her mind and apologize to Doug?

Felicia wanted that money, too, Anne reasoned. What had she said that morning of the funeral, when they'd heard the contents of the will? *"How could Naomi do this to me? All I have are a few great clothes and my car!"*

Anne knew she'd sleep little tonight. The dream could be over already. For Grandma she wanted it to work. And for Dad, who was fighting so desperately to save Lazarus Timber.

Felicia charged into her room and slammed the door behind her. Her face glowed with triumph. She was betting Doug wouldn't allow her to walk out on the deal. He'd cave in. Even though his precious museum would benefit if she walked out, he was obsessed to see this thing through. Naomi hovered over his head every minute.

Felicia dropped herself across the bed and reached for the phone. She'd leave with Jackie on Saturday, be at Idlewild—now known as John F. Kennedy International—in time for the night flight to London. Jackie's travel agent had already made their reservations. It would be so comfortable to use the company plane for the flight to New York, but Naomi always insisted both planes be used only for business or family group travel.

It would be great. The trip would cost practically nothing. Jackie's mother had reserved a suite at the Savoy and found out at the last minute that she had to be in San Francisco. Jackie said they could sign tabs at the hotel for everything. And clothes in the Chelsea boutiques were smashing and cheap.

"All clear!" she reported when Jackie picked up on the other end. "I'll go in to the office on Saturday morning and cut out early."

112

"Doug okayed your taking the time off?" Jackie squealed exuberantly.

"He didn't okay it," Felicia conceded. "I'm going anyway."

"Felicia, you think you should?" Jackie was all at once anxious.

"Look, either I'm able to handle Doug, or I'm cutting out. I'm betting he'll knuckle under."

"You're playing games with a lot of loot," Jackie worried.

"I'm playing it the way Naomi would," Felicia said. "Do you want to go to London, or don't you?"

When her alarm went off in the morning, Felicia reached over to shut it off with her usual spurt of irritation. But she was instantly awake. Her mind focused on the encounter with Doug last night. She wouldn't have her routine juice and coffee on a tray this morning. She'd dress and go downstairs to the breakfast table. Before they left for the office, she would know where she stood with Doug.

Now doubts replaced last night's confidence. Was she wrong about Doug? Was he just waiting for the first real chance to dump her? With her and Anne out of the way he could sell the company and turn over the assets to the museum. Damn, she wasn't ready to see most of Naomi's money in the hands of that shitty museum!

She left the bed and hurried into the bathroom to shower. Under the steaming spray she replayed in her mind the heated confrontation with Doug. She wasn't going to crawl, she decided defiantly. Then he'd know he could make her jump through hoops.

This morning she ordered herself to brush aside her great outfits that earned such envious stares from the younger women employees. She chose a gray cashmere sweater and a simple skirt that, she thought with a touch of humor, shrieked "Radcliffe." She dressed quickly, intent on being at the breakfast table moments after Doug arrived there. She'd play it cool—and see what happened.

She paused with one hand on her bedroom door when she heard Doug in conversation with Mrs. Morrison. Wait a few minutes. Let him get settled in the breakfast room. She listened to the brief exchange between the two. Now he was going downstairs.

She frowned in annoyance when she heard Anne's voice in the hall. Mrs. Morrison liked Anne. If she had *her* way, she'd fire the old bitch tomorrow. It was weird, the way Morrison was wearing black for Naomi. It was as though she was reproaching the rest of the family.

Now Felicia left her bedroom and headed downstairs. She could hear voices in the breakfast room. God, Doug was already talking business with Anne.

"You have to understand," Doug was explaining, "that Douglas fir can't reproduce from seedlings without sunlight getting through. Selective cutting leaves too much shade."

He was arguing with Anne again about the need for clear-cutting. Why didn't Anne stop forever quoting her grandmother and her father? Rae Lazarus owned a small-time operation; Naomi built an empire.

Felicia strolled casually into the breakfast room. Doug and Anne glanced up in greeting. They both looked so somber. Felicia's throat tightened. Had Doug told Anne she was on her way out? Don't let him know she was upset. Play it cool.

"My car's in the shop," she lied. After the first couple of weeks she had elected to drive herself to the office. "I'll catch a ride downtown with you two." She'd already told Melissa she'd have juice and coffee when she came downstairs. Now Melissa was coming forward with this.

"Fine." Doug's voice was strained. He cleared his throat. His eyes were opaque. "Anne, if you're in the mood for a short trip home, you're free to take off two or three days of your vacation time and tack them on to a weekend. Felicia's running off next week, but any time after that will be all right."

"Early May?" Anne asked eagerly. "Since we're going to the Acapulco house at Easter."

Felicia dropped her eyes to the table to hide their glow of triumph. Doug had backed down. Naomi had trained him to follow orders—and his orders were to train her to step into Naomi's shoes.

Eight

IN the week ahead Felicia pushed herself to be cooperative with the woman who was overseeing her early training, though she considered her both patronizing and envious. She was attentive at a midweek evening meeting with Doug and Anne and bit back a sarcastic retort when Doug scheduled a Friday evening session. Couldn't he understand she needed that time to pack for her trip?

Lingering at the dinner table rather than retiring to the library as customary, they discussed a hypothetical situation. Earlier Doug had asked Felicia and Anne each to come up with a solution.

"You hit it right on the head, Felicia," Doug said approvingly when Felicia presented her solution. "You're thinking the way Naomi Miller thought."

"But all those miles of temporary roads would cause soil erosion and send damaging sediment down to the river," Anne argued. "It would be inviting disaster."

"Those roads would enable us to take out timber in the most efficient way possible," Doug pointed out. "With good designing there would be no trouble."

Felicia went up to her room with a sense of elation. Doug said she'd been "thinking like Naomi Miller." That was the reason behind all this crazy training. To prove which one of them was the logical successor to Naomi. She had to put up

115

with Anne along the road, but *she*—Felicia Harris—would call the shots.

Felicia packed one valise to capacity, tossed only lingerie in the other. She was leaving room for purchases in the Chelsea boutiques. Belatedly she remembered she'd need more cash. No problem. She'd go up to Accounting in the morning and have them cash a check for her.

In the morning she hurried downstairs to join Doug and Anne in the limo for the drive to the office. While Walter stashed her Mark Cross luggage in the trunk, she talked ebulliently about the plays she and Jackie expected to see in London.

Felicia kept her leopard coat wrapped closely about her, concealing her Courrèges minidress. Courrèges was selling the shortest dresses in Paris, and Doug had made blunt remarks about her wearing these at the office.

In her mind she planned the day's activities. Jackie would pick her up with a car for the ride to the airport. Doug would never know she was cutting out two hours earlier than usual. He was isolated up there in his penthouse office. And what could he do if he found out? *He was not about to dump her.*

She waited until past 10:00 A.M. before taking the elevator up to the top floor. She emerged from the elevator and turned to the left, down the long, narrow hall that led to Accounting. It annoyed her that Anne had an office—minute though it was—on the prestigious executive floor. But it had been a secretary's office, she reminded herself.

Approaching Anne's office she subconsciously slowed her pace. How could people say they resembled each other? She couldn't see it at all. At Anne's open door she paused an instant in curiosity. Who was the good-looking man so absorbed in conversation with her? They weren't discussing business. Not the way they were looking at each other.

So Anne had landed herself a guy, she mocked silently. He probably knew all about the will. He probably knew Anne was earning almost a thousand dollars a week. What was he making? Seventy-five? A hundred? Her mouth tightened in

116

fresh anger. Last year she'd spent close to fifty thousand on clothes and perfume.

In Accounting she wrote out a check and gave it to the cashier. The woman's eyes widened. Felicia gathered she was unaccustomed to cashing thousand dollar checks.

"It's good. You can call my uncle if you like." But Felicia's eyes dared the cashier to do this.

"I'll have to go into the safe," the cashier said. "It'll take just a moment." Now she was conciliatory.

While she drummed on the counter with one crimson fingernail, she saw the young man who'd been in Anne's office walk into the large open area of Accounting. He paused to chat for a moment with a girl at one of the desks, then crossed to where Felicia stood waiting.

"Hi." Her smile was meant to be dazzling. It succeeded.

"Hi." He sounded warm and outgoing.

"Are you new here?" she asked. She rarely came up to this floor.

"This is my tenth week with the company," he told her, his eyes appraising. She saw the glint of recognition. He realized she was Felicia Harris. "It's an exciting place to work."

The cashier returned and handed over crisp fifty dollar bills to Felicia. Now she turned to the man beside Felicia. "You're here for your expense loot," she guessed. "I'll have it in a few minutes."

"I'm driving up to the Eureka office for a few days," he explained to Felicia while she shoved the roll of fifties into a pocket of her jacket. "I hear it's great country up there."

"I'm Felicia Harris," she said. "Who're you?"

"Glenn Rogers. The newest accountant," he told her.

"Fresh out of school. Where?"

"University of Pennsylvania. And I've been out a while."

"I put in two years at Radcliffe, then cut out." *U. of P. was Ivy League, wasn't it?* "I'm not the college type. Right now I'm off to London for a few days." Her eyes swept over him. "See you soon."

At Heathrow Felicia and Jackie were met by one of the Savoy Hotel couriers on duty at the airport. With the internationally known Savoy courtesy and efficiency he guided them to the closest immigration booth, through customs, and out to a waiting hotel car, their luggage already being stowed away in the trunk. Fighting yawns the two young women leaned back against the rear seat and contemplated the days ahead.

"I've never stayed at the Savoy," Felicia remarked. "It's usually Claridge's or the Connaught."

"Mother and Dad always stay there. Dad because he says the Savoy is the only place in London where the drinks are cold and the bathtubs are six feet long. Mother because they always remember she adores yellow roses and have linen sheets on the beds." Jackie giggled reminiscently. "Dad loves to tell Savoy Hotel stories. About how when Quentin Reynolds stayed there, he kept three gold fish in the bidet—and how Gene Autry was allowed to ride his horse right into the ballroom."

"I'm dying to see Chelsea—with all the changes," Felicia said in high anticipation. "I hear it's really wild now."

"Kathy Rhodes was over last month. She gave me a list of shops we *have* to see. And a couple of jazz clubs and espresso bars not to be missed. She said Chelsea's a mixture of our North Beach around Grant Avenue, Greenwich Village, and the Left Bank. And the clothes are mad!" She whistled eloquently. "London's taken over the fashion scene. Courrèges and St. Laurent are dressing women," she said emphatically. "Mary Quant and the bunch of Chelsea designers are dressing the young. And *we* are the young."

"Do you know who Eva's insane about these days?" Felicia laughed. "The Beatles! It's weird to think of my grandmother flipping for them. Or maybe it's because they make her feel young."

"She saw them on Ed Sullivan's show last month," Jackie guessed. "Sexy."

"I came over with nothing to wear," Felicia exaggerated. "I expect to go home with a whole new wardrobe. If prices in the boutiques are what you claim. I'm not going to think about Miller Timber once the whole time we're here!"

"First thing tomorrow we'll hit the shops. They open at nine."

"We shouldn't waste today," Felicia complained.

"We won't," Jackie soothed. "We'll have breakfast in our suite, then conk out till cocktail time. Drinks at the American Bar—it's called that because they serve their drinks with ice. Then dinner at the Main Restaurant. And to bed early. Breakfast at seven," she warned, "when the Grill Room opens."

"Jackie, I'm in my car every morning at eight," Felicia shot back. "And you know how many nights I'm not home until two or three." All at once the excitement of being in London ebbed away. "Damn it, why did Naomi do this to me?"

"You could always marry somebody superrich and walk out on the whole deal," Jackie said after a moment.

"Everybody I know who's superrich is a bore," Felicia sulked. "Oh hell, let's just get to the hotel and go to sleep. I always have insomnia on these overnight flights."

At last the car turned off the Strand. Felicia's eyebrows lifted in astonishment as traffic suddenly flowed to the right.

"This is Savoy Court," Jackie explained. "The only street in England where traffic doesn't go to the left. I hear the Savoy had to get a special act of Parliament to make it happen."

"Why did it have to happen?"

"The traffic flows to the right to keep the Strand Theater entrance clear," Jackie said.

Felicia and Jackie were escorted into the hotel lobby, welcomed at the reception desk, and conducted to their suite.

"Yellow roses," Jackie commented as they walked into the sitting room, the decor an attractive blend of traditional and modern. The flowers graced a Louis XVI escritoire.

"Would you like the roses changed?" a maid asked solici-

119

tously from a bedroom doorway, for a moment pausing in her unpacking.

"Yellow is fine," Jackie assured. "The reservation was in Mother's name," she pointed out to Felicia. "They always bring yellow roses to her suite." In the second bedroom another maid was unpacking Felicia's luggage.

From their balcony they looked down upon the Thames. "Isn't this a marvelous view?" Jackie gazed at the array of bridges that span the river.

"Ask me later," Felicia flipped. "I want breakfast, a warm tub, and three or four hours sleep."

"The floor waiter will be here any moment. I'll show you the bathroom while we wait."

Felicia was admiring the elegant marble bathroom, whose fixtures included a telephone, when the floor waiter arrived with the morning newspapers and asked if they would like tea, coffee, or a drink.

"Breakfast," Felicia said crisply. "Scrambled eggs, smoked Scotch salmon, brioche, and lots of coffee."

"For two," Jackie instructed.

After breakfast Felicia and Jackie retired to their respective bedrooms, leaving a wakeup call for four o'clock. But exhausted as she was from their flights—first across the country and then across the Atlantic—Felicia had difficulty falling asleep. Damn! Wednesday night she'd be back in San Francisco. Thursday morning back in the salt mines. Maybe Jackie was right—maybe she should marry rich.

By nine o'clock Monday morning Felicia and Jackie were in the chauffeured Bentley Jackie had leased for their stay and were gazing avidly from the car windows. Chelsea belonged now to the young rebels. The shop windows, ablaze with color, demanded attention. Their audacious names evoked laughter. The mood here was defiant but happy; having fun, the unspoken rule.

Felicia inspected the hordes of young people already on the

streets. Girls in short, tight skirts, boots, and duffle coats—usually army surplus, their hair very long or cropped short, in the Mary Quant look. The young men with Beatle cuts, wearing skinny pants and leather jackets. The air seemed to ricochet with their enthusiasm for life. This was a different London from the one Felicia had seen in the past.

On Walton Street the chauffeur pulled up at the curb. Felicia and Jackie got out and crossed the sidewalk to their first destination.

"Kathy said Tony Armstrong is a terrific young designer—and everything is practically for nothing," Jackie whispered to Felicia as they charged into the small shop, its decor ultramodern silver, with no-nonsense lighting that showed off the clothes.

The two girls foraged zealously among the racks, squealing with delight as they read the price tags.

"Felicia, look at this!" Jackie marveled as she held a short chic dress against her slender body. "It's only ten guineas."

They tried on an endless array of dresses, suits, coats, debating about which to buy, dimly aware that girls who worked for a few pounds a week and lived in dismal little flats were buying the same clothes as the daughters of titled Englishmen and wealthy British professionals. The young were destroying social barriers.

Finally, laden with parcels, Felicia and Jackie emerged from the shop and headed for the car.

"We're going to Biba next," Jackie said. "Kathy says it's great."

Biba, on Kensington Church Street, was an amazing deep-red Art Nouveau boutique—barnlike in size—where they bought ostrich stoles dyed incredible colors, ultrashort skirts, skinny sweaters. Their routine for these three days was clearly indicated: shopping where swinging London shopped; lunching in Chelsea restaurants; resting up in coffee houses and espresso bars favored by the young.

They ignored Hardy Amies and Norman Hartnell but dallied at Mary Quant's Bazaar on Brompton Road, choosing the more expensive Bazaar specials that would not be seen anywhere else over the well-designed but cheap Ginger Group clothes. They went to Maxine Leighton on Conduit Street for knockout cocktail dresses from Chloe and Cacharel. To Cavanaugh's on Curzon Street for ravishing resort wear. They bypassed Cartier, Gucci, and Hermes on this trip, but bought avant-garde jewelry designed by Andrew Grima at Hooper Bolton on Sloane Street in posh Belgravia.

On their second evening in town—over supper in the Savoy Grill—Jackie brought up the subject of drugs, regarded far more casually in London than in the States. They'd smoked marijuana at parties back home, but neither had tried heroin or cocaine.

"Kathy gave me the name of this doctor in Mayfair who'll write us a prescription for pure cocaine. It's a phone call away," Jackie tempted.

"You know how I feel about drugs. I don't like anything that can take away my control. Not even too many martinis."

"Okay," Jackie said. "I just thought I'd mention it. I feel so damn pure. No marijuana, no cocaine, not even LSD. And LSD is so easy," she sighed. "I have trouble with joints—I don't even inhale cigarette smoke. With LSD you just nibble on a sugar cube drenched with the stuff."

"I've heard some wild stuff about what can happen when you're on LSD," Felicia objected.

"I know," Jackie said mockingly. "You always have to be in control."

Only three hours before the car was to drive them to Heathrow for their flight home Felicia and Jackie wandered through the maze of tiny streets and courts that run off Carnaby Street—where the men's shops glittered with splashes of color. Felicia bought a tie for Doug, suspecting its garishness would be an affront, and another for her father.

Felicia gazed out the window as their plane climbed above the clouds of London, her mind in high gear. Sure, she'd enjoyed dashing about Chelsea, shopping in those mad little boutiques. Playing at being part of the Chelsea girl revolution. She could understand their obsession for clothes. She shared it. But she didn't want to live the grubby little lives that they thought were so great because they were flaunting their independence.

The Chelsea girls left the excitement of King's Road to go to shoddy little flats. She had gone back to the Savoy. The clothes she and Jackie had bought were fun clothes. They'd wear them once or twice and throw them away.

Chelsea girls bought duffle coats at flea markets—she wore a pea jacket by Yves St. Laurent. Her clothes were young and exciting, too—but they were made of gorgeous fabrics and the lines were sensational.

The Chelsea girls were proud of talking uninhibitedly about their sex lives. Hell, in her small circle, girls said whatever they liked, did whatever they wanted—but they did it in Dual-Ghias or Alfa Romeos, in elegant mansions, or smart apartments. She and Jackie were as independent as any Chelsea girl—but money was part of their style.

These past few days made her face up to the importance of money in her life. But she'd come face to face with something else, too, in London: They were moving into a time when the young set the rules. Young people were earning huge chunks of money. The Beatles, Mary Quant, Jean Shrimpton, Twiggy. All under thirty.

All at once she envisioned herself as the driving force at Miller Timber. The beautiful and powerful head of the company. Making fantastic deals, important executives at her beck and call. She had a lot of years to wait to pick up her sixty million in stock—by that time it might be worth a hundred million—but she could handle this deal. Keep Anne in line. Control Doug. She'd find ways to supplement that fifty-thousand-a-year salary. Expense accounts, side deals, she thought—intoxicated by the possibilities that lay ahead. With Leon out of the way, she ought to be able to work up some terrific angles. Set up an inner circle within the company that

123

would be on *her* side, keep her informed of what was happening.

What was the name of that junior accountant Anne was having a fling with? Glenn something or other. He was as ambitious as hell—it kind of glowed from him. She'd lay odds he was sharp. The first thing to do when she was back at the office, was to check out Glenn Rogers.

Nine

IN the cool late March evening Anne leaned back against the front seat of Glenn's muchmaligned 1954 Chevrolet and listened while he reviled Berkeley student demonstrators who had abandoned their passive picketing of the Lucky Market on Telegraph for a "shop-in." The demonstrators recruited by CORE to protest the Lucky Market store's failure to hire Negroes for good jobs.

"Anne, they've made a mess of the store. Eggs, vegetables, canned goods, you name it, all over the floors. They're behaving like animals."

"Another group of students has gone in to clean it up," Anne reported. She'd been unnerved by Glenn's harshness toward the Berkeley students. He called them a bunch of spoiled brats. She admired their commitment. "But this has been a great evening, Glenn." She maneuvered the conversation into a less controversial area. Every evening with Glenn was great. "I'd heard so much about The Top of the Mark, but I'd never been there. The sunset was unbelievable."

In deference to Glenn's limited funds they'd had a drink at The Top of the Mark and then dinner in Chinatown before going to see *La Dolce Vita*. They'd sat in a lightly populated section of the movie house, holding hands and at intervals forsaking the screen to embrace, to kiss with a passion that was unnerving to Anne. She was relieved that Glenn had abandoned his pleas to go up to his apartment. He understood she wasn't ready for that. *"My beautiful little puritan,"* he jibed at intervals but with tenderness.

"Like some music?" Glenn asked, already reaching for the radio. The voices of the Beatles, singing "Love Me Do," filtered into the car.

"I heard a new Peter, Paul, and Mary last night," Anne said with a lilt in her voice. "Terrific!"

Glenn wasn't listening. "Somebody in the elevator of my building told me this morning that a larger apartment will be coming up for rent in ninety days." Stopping for a red light, he took one hand from the wheel to caress hers. "That would be one problem solved if we get married."

"Glenn, we've only known each other for a few weeks," she said uncertainly, but her heart was pounding. He hadn't come right out and talked about marriage until now.

"The apartment won't be available for ninety days. By then we'll have known each other almost six months." His eyes met hers in the spill of the street lights. "That's a respectable length of time," he said with mock seriousness. "Shall I check out the vacancy?"

"Yes," she said in a surge of exultation. If she married Glenn, nothing would change about the will. She'd still work and send money home to bail out Lazarus Timber. Glenn would understand she had to do that. Whatever problems came up, they'd handle them together. Like how would he feel when she told him they'd have to live in Naomi's house until she'd fulfilled the two-year residency requirement? "Glenn, let's keep it our secret for now."

"Our secret," Glenn promised and reached to kiss her, both ignoring the honking of cars behind them when the light changed from red to green.

Glenn would understand that they'd have to live in Naomi's house, she reasoned. He enjoyed luxury living. She sensed his pleasure when he took her, on rare occasions like tonight, to places that were the stamping grounds of the very rich.

She hadn't mentioned the dinner and chamber music concert at the museum tomorrow night. Doug and Consuelo were cochairmen of the benefit for Consuelo's favorite children's charity. Consuelo had cut short her month in Rio to work with the benefit committee. Tickets were five hundred a couple—far out of Glenn's range. She was going as Doug's guest. Glenn wouldn't mind that.

Tonight she lay awake far beyond the normal time. She wished Dad were here. That she could sit down and talk with him. Dad would like Glenn. At first he'd be upset that she was marrying out of her faith. He'd worry about problems arising over that. He said Grandma and Grandpa had been lucky. But Glenn always said he was nonreligious. They'd raise the children in her faith.

Tossing restlessly far into the night she heard sounds in the hallway. Felicia had come home. Doug hadn't said a word, but she knew he worried that Felicia wouldn't return on schedule. Felicia would push just so far and then backtrack, she comforted herself. Felicia had no respect for her family— but she respected the money at the end of the line.

Fighting yawns Felicia reached for the telephone on her desk, dialed Glenn's extension. Casual inquiries earlier this morning had confirmed her assumptions. Glenn was bright, ambitious, and on his way up at the company.

"Glenn Rogers," his voice came briskly to her.

"Hi," she drawled. "This is Felicia." No last name. She waited for recognition to sink in.

"Hi, Felicia." She sensed his surprise at her call. "Back from London already?"

"My uncle is a tyrant. I had to be back at the office today. I flew in last night."

"Is London as swinging as they say?"

"Fun for a few days," she acknowledged. "After that I think it'd be a drag. Do you have a tux?"

"Hidden away in the back of my closet." He was casual but she knew he was churning with curiosity. "For those rare occasions when I need it."

"I have a pair of tickets to a benefit dinner at the Naomi Miller Museum tonight." In San Francisco most servants were off on Thursday evenings. Thursday was a big social evening. "You can take me if you like. You'll meet some important people."

"I'd like that very much," he said after a faint hesitation. "Sounds like a great evening." Still casual. He was too sharp to come on strong. Felicia approved.

"I'll pick you up with my car at six sharp. There'll be cocktails first, then the concert, then dinner. What's your address?"

Anne would have liked to linger beneath the stinging hot shower, but she knew Doug would be waiting shortly to leave for the museum affair. Their determination to leave the office early had been aborted by a long-distance call from their Oregon mill. Doug had ordered her to listen in on an extension.

Mildred had laid the turquoise chiffon she had bought for an earlier museum affair across the foot of her bed, brought out the dyed-to-match silk pumps and the velvet coat inherited from her mother. Anne left the shower, wrapped her glistening wetness in a lush bath sheet, and tried to gear herself for the evening. These social affairs were still unreal to her.

Ever conscious of the time, she hurried with her makeup, and chastised herself for being inept as she struggled to subdue her mass of dark hair in a simple, sophisticated French twist. No jewelry except for the pearl earrings her grandmother had given her on her eighteenth birthday. *"With pearls you always look like a lady."*

Hearing Doug in conversation in the foyer with Mrs. Morrison she reached for her coat and evening purse and left the room. "You look beautiful," Mrs. Morrison said as she came down the staircase. She rarely offered compliments. "So much like Mrs. Miller in her younger years."

"Sometimes it startles me," Doug said. "The strong resemblance."

They might resemble each other physically, Anne told herself, but that was all.

At the brilliantly illuminated museum, radiating an aura of conviviality, the Miller limousine joined the parade of Rolls-Royces, Bentleys, and Mercedeses that paused briefly at the curb to discharge their passengers. Anne and Doug left the car, walked to the entrance and into the center hall of the museum. Already clusters of women in dazzling evening gowns and men in tuxes talked effervescently over cocktail glasses.

"Everything's under control," Doug reported with relief when he had checked their coats. "Connie's marvelous with these affairs. I'm cochairman, but she's done all the work. She's never been one just to sign checks."

"Doug, isn't Felicia with you?" In one of the ornate brocade gowns that were her trademark, Edwina strode toward them, sending a fleeting obligatory smile in Anne's direction. "She returned from London, didn't she?" Anne sensed Edwina's anxiety. They all lived on the edge of the volcano that Naomi Miller had created.

"She was at the office today," Doug confirmed and turned toward the entrance. "There she is now."

Felicia stood immobile at the head of the three wide steps that led into the central hall, a faint smile of amusement on her face, knowing the effect she created in her black crepe Givenchy. Now she turned slightly and reached out a crimson-nailed hand—with a calculated air of possessiveness—to a man approaching her from the checkroom area.

Anne stared, frozen in shock. *Glenn? Felicia had come to the benefit with Glenn?* This was some kind of nightmare. Last night, when he took her home, she'd told him she would be tied up late tonight with Doug and he'd said, *"I'll be working late."*

How long had this been going on with Felicia? What kind of crazy game was Glenn playing?

She saw his mouth drop open in astonishment when he spied her across the room. He'd thought she was working with

Doug—not attending the benefit. How long had he known Felicia? Where had they met? Felicia seldom came up to their floor. She never ate in the company cafeteria.

Glenn turned to Felicia at a remark from her. Anne understood; he was going to pretend there had been nothing between them. They'd played the scene very cool at the office—only Shirley knew she was seeing Glenn. And Doug, of course. He'd been around some of the times when Glenn had picked her up at the house or brought her home.

"Who's that with Felicia?" Edwina asked. "I don't know him. But then I don't know most of Felicia's young men."

"He's Glenn Rogers," Doug said grimly. He shot an anxious glance at Anne. He knew she'd been seeing Glenn. He didn't know they were engaged. "Our newest junior accountant."

"Handsome young devil," Edwina commented. "Leave it to Felicia to discover an interesting man."

"Anne, would you mind trying to find Connie for me?" Doug fabricated an errand. "I'm worried that we might be oversubscribed. We may need extra tables."

"I'll look for her." Anne contrived a smile.

She moved away with compulsive swiftness, turning her back on Glenn and Felicia, in conversation with other guests across the room. She would not allow Glenn to suspect the chaos he had created in her. It was all over between them, of course. She knew he realized that.

He'd caught bigger game. Felicia was top-drawer San Francisco society. She knew all the important people in the city. For a man in Glenn's position, to be Felicia Harris's escort was a coup.

But why that craziness last night? Why had he asked her to marry him when he was chasing after Felicia? No, she corrected herself in sudden comprehension, Felicia had done the chasing. But Glenn had been happy to be caught.

Later—when the agony of the evening was over and she lay sleepless in the dark solitude of her bedroom—Anne tried to deal with reality. Eerie the way family history was repeating itself, she thought painfully. Over seventy years ago Naomi had taken away the man Grandma expected to marry—and then had stolen her inheritance. Now Felicia was taking away the man *she* had expected to marry.

But there the repetition would end, Anne vowed. She had lost Glenn to Felicia but she would *not* lose her inheritance.

Ten

ANNE made a strong effort to avoid Glenn at the office. When she encountered him for a moment at a turn in the hallway, she was frigidly polite. He knew not to try to resume their relationship. He didn't wish to do that, she taunted herself. He was relieved to be off the hook. Not that Felicia would ever marry him. She would have a fling with him until she was bored, then toss him back into the pond. He wasn't bright enough to realize that. Or perhaps greed overrode common sense.

On Saturday afternoon Anne went with Shirley and Gerry, an appealing tiny replica of her mother, to the zoo at Golden Gate Park and then to dinner with them at one of the city's many inexpensive ethnic restaurants. While Gerry dawdled ecstatically over deep-dish apple pie and ice cream, Anne told Shirley about Glenn's arrival at the museum last night with Felicia.

"I knew you were uptight about something. Baby, he's not worth it."

"Shirley, I couldn't believe it. The night before the benefit he'd asked me to marry him." She hesitated. "I didn't let on to you about how serious we were because I knew you didn't like Glenn."

"I knew what was going on," Shirley said gently. "But I didn't expect this. Of course, I wouldn't trust either of them farther than I could throw an elephant." Shirley's eyes searched hers. "I hope you don't change your mind when he comes around with a hang-dog look."

"He's come and gone," Anne told her. "He knows I want no part of him. Anyhow, he's after bigger game."

"He's getting off the hook easy." Shirley's face radiated contempt. "Somebody else would give him a hard time."

"I suppose in a way it's my fault," Anne said after a moment. "You know how things are these days. I kept refusing to go up to his apartment. I told him I just wasn't that liberated. I'm sure Felicia is—"

"I don't call it liberation," Shirley shot back. "All of a sudden women are liberated, and men think that all they have to do is buy you dinner and you'll jump into bed with them. If not on the first date, then on the second." All at once she was giggling. "Can you imagine how hookers hate the 'new woman'? It's enough to make them unionize."

"I thought Glenn and I had something more going for us than a sexual attraction. But I know now," she said with sudden intensity, "that his primal urge is ambition."

"You going to the Acapulco house next weekend?" Shirley rechanneled the conversation. "It'll be the Easter weekend." She was familiar with the family schedule.

"I'd forgotten." Anne tensed. "Easter's early this year. The twenty-ninth of March. I don't know how long it'll last; but we're still following Naomi Miller's schedule. We'll leave for Acapulco Friday morning."

"For a woman who was a natural-born feminist," Shirley said caustically, "Naomi Miller never carried it beyond herself. Any man coming into the lowest office job starts off at ten bucks a week more than a woman. When you get powerful enough, Annie, you change that."

"That's a long way off," Anne laughed. But yes, there were a lot of changes she'd make at Miller Timber when—if—she had the clout to do it.

Sunday evening, in the midst of a long phone conversation with Shirley, Anne heard angry voices in the hall. Doug was just coming home with Eva after meeting her flight from Nassau. They had encountered Felicia, who was on her way out.

"What do you mean, you're not coming with us to Acapulco?" Eva screeched. "I flew back from Nassau so we could all be together at Acapulco as usual."

"Eva, let's stop playing this silly game," Felicia said. "Naomi's gone. I don't want to go to Acapulco next weekend. I'll be at the house at Squaw Valley. I'm going skiing with a friend." *Glenn,* Anne knew it must be.

"You can ski at Squaw Valley straight into July," Doug reminded. "The whole family will be at Acapulco."

"I won't," Felicia told him. "Now if you'll excuse me I have a date."

Did Glenn ski, Anne asked herself while Shirley reported on Gerry's mad love affair with a neighborhood golden retriever. No doubt in her mind that Felicia was going to the Squaw Valley house with Glenn. But not to ski.

On Friday morning at eleven Anne and Doug left for Acapulco on the smaller of the two company planes. The others had left earlier on the larger plane, planning to arrive at the house in time for lunch. Next month, Anne remembered as the plane lifted off from the tarmac, she'd be flying home for five days. Thank God, she'd said nothing to Dad and Mother about Glenn.

"We touch down in Mexico City for Customs clearance," Doug told her. "From there it's only another hour to Acapulco. But the trip won't seem long. I had a picnic lunch brought over from Bardelli's. After that we'll probably nap." With a complacent smile he pointed to a wicker basket that sat on the floor beside his leather-upholstered armchair. "Minestrone, cold beef salad, petit fours, and a thermos of coffee." He sighed. "You know my weakness for sweets."

"On you it doesn't show," she consoled.

Normally Anne enjoyed flying. It was a lovely parcel of time in limbo. Isolation from earthly problems. Views that elicited an inner serenity. But today the experience was marred by the knowledge that Glenn was holed up in Squaw Valley with Felicia.

"Have you ever been to Acapulco?" Doug asked.

"Never. I'm looking forward to it." She forced a festive smile. Oh God, she couldn't wait for those five days at home. She felt sick every time she overheard the gossip circulating around the office about Glenn and Felicia. She and Glenn had been discreet. Felicia was flaunting her affair with him.

"When we first went down there, Acapulco was still a small town with mostly dirt streets, though once the road from Mexico City was completed back in 1927 it was headed for a real-estate boom," Doug recalled. "Now it's a city with a permanent population of fifty thousand, and three hundred hotels capable of housing eighty thousand visitors at any one time."

Now Doug told her about the marble *palacio* Naomi had built in Acapulco.

"Somebody at a charity affair talked about the magnificent harbor—the best on the West Coast except, perhaps, for San Francisco. Mama insisted we fly right down to see it. She was eager for a hideaway house where the weather was always fine. The temperature in Acapulco never changes more than a few degrees from winter to summer, and from November to May it never rains. In those days," he reminisced, "we flew in a Sikorsky 538 seaplane."

"I know Acapulco is supposed to be an international resort." Anne struggled to appear interested in this discussion. Should she have fought for Glenn? *No.* Shirley was right— he was just an opportunist with an overabundance of charm. She'd been so lonely and homesick she'd been taken in by him. Yet her heart pounded as she remembered evenings of lovemaking in Glenn's car, parked in dark privacy near Telegraph Hill.

"My mother bought five acres high on a cliff and another two acres down below so we'd have a private beach," Doug continued. "Foreigners aren't allowed to own land within fifty kilometers of the coast, but we discovered that it could be bought through a Mexican bank trust. She didn't care about the style of the house, so long as it was palatial in size and the windows of her personal suite faced the ocean."

Anne remembered that her grandmother had been intricately involved in every small detail of the colonnaded white colonial built sixty-two years ago, in which she and her mother had lived all their lives. Hardly a palatial house but one rich with love.

"I was thrilled to be put in charge of the Acapulco house project." Doug glowed with recall. "I'd just seen Taliesin West—Frank Lloyd Wright's new masterpiece—and I was determined to have a house with the same sense of being one with the landscape. But I knew that Mama would not be impressed by volcanic rock or the like, which Wright had used for the walls and chimneys and terraces. I told the architect to focus on marble and stone. I think if I were ever to live away from San Francisco, it would be at the Acapulco house. Sometimes, when I feel I'm being overwhelmed by the business, I disappear for forty-eight hours." Anne knew the beach house was staffed year-round. "Only Leon knows where I can be reached," he said softly. "There's something wonderfully therapeutic about ocean waves rolling onto the beach. Walking along the sand, gazing out at the Pacific, I can pull my life together again."

Tears stung Anne's eyes. "My father has a cabin in the woods, where he hides away every now and then. He says it's his oasis of sanity in a crazy world."

When they were approaching the modern Acapulco airport at close to sunset, Doug told her—with a hint of regret in his voice—that within a year a jet strip would be completed, so that jets from all over the world could fly directly to Acapulco.

"Nobody ever wants to leave Acapulco," he said. "It has a magic all its own."

On the drive to the house Anne gazed avidly at the passing scenery. She was enthralled by the splashes of color on every side. Flowers she had never seen before, tropical trees. Acapulco Bay a sapphire ringed by hills.

The Miller house, high on a cliff overlooking the Bay, was laid out in such a fashion that each person in residence had absolute privacy. Endless terraces at different levels flanked the ten bedrooms. Purple bougainvillea spilled over the terrace railings. A small house to the rear provided quarters for the servants. The spectacular dining room, living room, and the pool were the central meeting places.

Their luggage in the hands of smiling native servants, Anne and Doug were welcomed by Consuelo and Leon, lounging on chaises beside the pool.

"Where's everybody?" Doug asked, gazing appreciatively at the orange-red sky.

"Edwina and Bruce drove into town to Peggy Pena's," Consuelo said, referring to a high-fashion boutique. "Edwina decided she didn't have a thing to wear. Eva was meeting some friends for cocktails at Villa Vera. Todd's down below surfing."

"You know Adrian's in Europe with a school group," Leon reminded, faintly apologetic, and Doug nodded.

"I was hoping we'd make it in time for the sunset," Doug said with satisfaction. "Let's go out to the terrace to watch."

"The Acapulco sunset has to be seen to be believed," Consuelo told Anne while she rose from her chaise.

The four left the pool area for the sweeping terrace that faced the Pacific. The entire Bay—bathed in splashes of orange, pink, and red—was on view before them. Caught up in the magic of the moment they stood at the railing in tacit silence.

"In a moment—with any luck at all—you'll see a mysterious phenomenon," Doug gently intruded into the quiet. "Once in a great while it happens in other places. Often in Acapulco."

As though mesmerized Anne watched the ball of fire that was the sun touch the horizon and begin to sink from view. And then a strange cry of wonder broke from her as the last sliver of red–orange burst into a brilliant green for the final moment before the sun sank beneath the horizon.

"That is the perfect Acapulco sunset," Doug said, his voice reverent.

They lingered at the railing while dusk settled over the water with amazing swiftness. All at once lights went on all around the Bay, in the residential areas that rose up into the hills. The rigging of each of the ships of the Coast Guard Squadron, at anchor in the Bay, was dazzlingly illuminated.

"God, I'd love to be able to paint that," Leon said quietly. "To do it justice."

How much alike Leon and Doug were in their love of beauty, Anne thought. And yet, she remembered with unease, part of a conversation aboard the plane coming down here. Doug had spoken with such contempt for the conservationists who were fighting the timber industry's demands that the Forest Service raise the cut of the coast redwoods in federal forests. Doug must understand that those trees would be forever lost to the world unless the government stopped that proposed slaughter.

Doug was two people, Anne analyzed. The Doug whose thinking had been rigidly set by his mother—and the Doug she saw at unwary intervals, who was warm and compassionate. He might have been born to Naomi Miller, but he was in truth more Rae Lazarus's child. How sad that Grandma had not been allowed to know him.

Todd arrived, full of high spirits after an afternoon of surfing.

"I'd better go change for dinner," he said reluctantly after he'd greeted Anne and Doug. "Hope it's soon," he grinned. "I'm starving."

"I'm going down to the beach for a walk," Consuelo decided spontaneously. "This is the most magnificent time of day here."

"I'll go with you." Leon exchanged a warm smile with his wife. Theirs was a fine marriage, Anne thought. The kind of marriage Dad deserved.

138

Though the trip entailed a rather long flight, Anne remembered that Consuelo and Leon sometimes came down to Acapulco for a three-day weekend. Consuelo had said it was their "escape hatch." When they were frustrated by another of Adrian's outrageous escapades, she surmised. Thank God, he wouldn't be here this weekend.

"Let's go into the living room for a glass of wine," Doug said. "The view from there is marvelous, also."

They settled themselves in chairs strategically placed by the living room window wall and sipped white wine from fragile glasses. Anne's mind was unwittingly invaded by images of Glenn and Felicia in the exquisite solitude of the Squaw Valley house. She could hear Rae's voice on that special evening when her grandmother talked about the man her sister had stolen from her. *"It took a long time for me to stop hurting, but then Marshall came into my life, and I knew this was real."* Anne knew that she, too, would hurt for a long time.

Edwina and Bruce arrived along with Eva, who was miffed at having been summoned from her cocktail party for the drive home.

"We really should have more cars here," Eva complained to Doug. "The limousine and a jeep just aren't enough." Now she turned to Edwina. "Darling, let's do go to La Perla this evening." In her customary fashion Eva behaved as though Anne weren't present. "I adore the divers."

"Yes," Doug said. "I think Anne would find that exciting." Anne saw Eva's mouth drop open in shock. Her eyes blazed. Doug ignored this, turned to Anne. "Three or four times a night divers jump by torchlight from a cliff a hundred and eighteen feet high into twelve feet of water, at sixty miles an hour. They've been trained to hit the water just as the waves come in."

Anne hesitated.

"It sounds fascinating, but I think I'll be falling asleep soon after dinner tonight."

"Perhaps tomorrow night," Doug nodded in understanding. "It has been a full day."

Over dinner—despite Doug's efforts to derail it—a battle erupted between Todd and his mother. Anne lowered her eyes to her plate, pretending interest in the superb fresh-caught fish broiled over a wood-and-charcoal fire.

"It's absolutely absurd to talk about taking off a year before going on to college," she shrieked at Todd, while his father displayed interest only in the Scotch and soda that accompanied most of his dinners. "You'll go on to Yale in the fall. You'll graduate from Yale, like my father and my grandfather!" His own father, Anne had heard, had graduated from Harvard and Berkeley Law School—pushed into law by his grandmother, she suspected. What would have been Bruce's inclinations if he had been left on his own?

"I don't know if I'll even be accepted," Todd said doggedly, reiterating his conversation at Squaw Valley. "The letters won't come in for another couple weeks." He seemed to cling to that delay.

"You'll be accepted," Edwina insisted. "Your grades are high, and it's a family tradition. Yale respects that."

After dinner Anne corralled Todd for a game of chess.

"What schools did you apply to?" she asked Todd while he set up the chess board.

"Harvard, Yale, Princeton," he rattled off. "And Columbia."

"I think you'd like Columbia," she said quietly. She didn't want to see Todd taking a year off on his own. He had few roots as it was. At boarding school since he was ten. Camp so many summers. With the family only on traditional holidays. "You'd be living on a college campus, but in reality the whole city would be your campus." She hesitated. "It's a very liberal setting." From stray remarks Todd had made about the Berkeley scene, she sensed he was emotionally involved in civil rights and the American presence in Vietnam.

"I don't know," Todd hedged. "A couple of friends at school are taking off a year. It sounds good to me."

"Think about it," she encouraged. "I loved Barnard. It's Columbia's sister school, you know."

140

Anne spent most of the weekend in the company of Consuelo and Leon or with Todd. Along with Edwina and Bruce, Eva was involved in the hectic social life of the resort. Doug gave himself over to solitary walks on the beach or long siestas on his private terrace.

With Consuelo and Leon, Anne explored the Zocalo, the main square of downtown Acapulco, where anything from a live chicken to a high-fashion gown could be bought. The narrow passages teemed with life, the lively conversation, multilingual. She shopped for a book for her father, a hand-painted scarf for her mother—remembering that her father had written that her mother's check from Naomi Miller's estate had arrived and was earmarked for a mink coat and a Paris shopping spree with Avis Moore in July.

Mother would never consider using her inheritance to help reduce the bank loan against Lazarus Timber or to invest in more timberland. And Dad wouldn't ask her—he was forever guilty that he hadn't supplied the riches she considered her due. Naomi Miller's wealth had always been a dark shadow over her life.

Anne sensed that Edwina was annoyed that she spent so much time on the beach with Todd. His mother couldn't understand his obsession to commit himself to something useful to humanity. Todd had a way of highlighting her own sense of guilt that she was making no real commitment. And increasingly she was concerned about Miller Timber's cutting practices. Doug insisted they were not acquiring the clear-cutting habits of other major timber companies: *"This is a major reason I'm anxious to acquire public timber at the Forest Service auctions. So that much of our old-growth forests can remain untouched."*

After an early al fresco lunch on Sunday, they all boarded the larger company plane for the return trip. Doug sequestered Anne in the small rear cabin that he now designated as his airborne office.

"It'll be a working flight away from the others," he said with satisfaction.

They lived such effortless lives, Anne thought in a corner of her mind. Private planes, limousines, fine houses—all the physical comforts money could provide. Yet who of Naomi Miller's family wasn't fighting private demons?

Anne dreaded going into the office on Monday morning. She could avoid encountering Glenn if she was careful, she comforted herself. Instinct told her that he would be just as anxious to avoid her. Soon Felicia would move on to somebody else, and she'd contrive for Glenn to be fired. Felicia had done her a favor, Anne reasoned. How awful it would have been to have married Glenn and then discovered what he was truly like.

How wrong for her to think about marrying, she rebuked herself. She couldn't tie herself down to the old-fashioned notion of home, husband, and children. She had charted a different course for herself. Women today were waking up—they expected more than second-class citizenship.

Not until late in the week did Anne come face-to-face with Glenn. He was impersonally polite, as though nothing had ever happened between them. Fighting for poise she hurried back to her office, trembling and cold. Only contempt was in her mind for Glenn Rogers. *Why did she feel this awful sense of loss?*

It was routine for Anne to go into the office for half a day on Saturdays, though the clerical staff worked a five-day week. At one sharp Anne left, knowing Shirley and Gerry would be waiting for her downstairs.

"Hi," Shirley greeted her exuberantly as she emerged from an elevator into the lobby. "It's a gorgeous day." Shirley was determined to divert her from her anguish over Glenn.

"We're having a picnic," Gerry said, her pretty little face luminous with anticipation. "And then we're going to the Japanese Tea Garden. But I'm not having tea," she added conscientiously.

"The cherry trees are in bloom at the Japanese Tea Garden,"

Shirley told her while they walked out into the brilliant sunlight. "It's a gorgeous sight." She giggled contagiously. "Even for two women in the timber industry."

"I remember Doug saying that his mother looked at the trees and never saw their beauty. To Naomi Miller a tree was just so many feet of lumber."

"And to Felicia it's probably a phallic symbol," Shirley drawled, then winced as she saw Anne tense. "To hell with Felicia—let's talk about more interesting people."

En route to Golden Gate Park they talked avidly about President Johnson's recent appointment of ten women to important government positions, about Margaret Chase Smith's campaign for the Republican presidential nomination, about civil rights demonstrations.

Shirley knew Anne was one of those Southerners who recognized that the time for integration was now. It seemed fairly certain that Johnson would put through his Civil Rights Act before the year was out. Anne's dad was optimistic about Belleville's accepting this gracefully. Others in town—including her mother—were not.

Anne waited impatiently for the first Saturday in May, when she'd fly home to Belleville for a brief vacation. Shirley had made her flight reservation, arranged for a car to drive her from Hartsfield Airport in Atlanta to Belleville, and to pick her up for the return trip to Hartsfield.

Immediately after dinner on Friday Anne went upstairs to her room to pack. Doug had gone off to the Pacific Union Club to meet with a pair of California legislators sympathetic to the needs of the timber industry. Neither Felicia nor Eva was home. Anne enjoyed being alone in the house except for the servants.

She paused in her packing, fiddled with the radio until she found music that pleased her. Bob Dylan was singing "The Times They Are A-Changin'." She sang along with Dylan, stopped short at the sound of an imperious knock on her door.

"Come in." She reached to turn off the radio.

The door swung open. Edwina strode into the room, her face telegraphing her rage.

"Where's Doug?" she demanded. "It seems to be a point of honor with Mrs. Morrison not to give out any information in this house."

"He had a meeting at the Pacific Union Club," Anne said warily.

"I want to talk to him! You've come into our lives, and everything's gone wrong!"

"What specifically is wrong now?" Anne asked with strained politeness.

"I had a call from Todd. I assumed he'd written to Yale to say he'd be registering for his freshman year. Instead he tells me he's going to Columbia. Because of all your meddling! That whole weekend at Acapulco you were stirring him up to go to Columbia!"

"That whole weekend," Anne told Edwina, "I was trying to persuade Todd not to take a year or two off before going on to school. I'm sure he'll feel comfortable at Columbia."

"It's not for you to say!" Edwina shrieked. "I know we're supposed to put up with you for Felicia's sake, but your meddling is too damn much. I want to talk to Doug. I think Eva's right—we should go into court to upset her mother's ridiculous will. We have important connections in this town. In the right quarters." She smiled in vindictive triumph. "Let's see if Naomi Miller's will can stand up in a court of law!"

Eleven

AT Hartsfield Airport Anne walked with an aura of anticipation toward the waiting limousine. The chauffeur, carrying her luggage, talked with remembered Southern charm about how nice it was that some of the dogwoods still remained for her to enjoy. She carried her coat over one arm—the day was summer hot, though without the torpid humidity that would arrive in another three or four weeks. The house, she thought, would be surrounded by masses of flowers.

Sitting in the car, she watched the passing scenery with a wistful realization that she would be here only for a few days. She remembered her conversation with Doug the night before about Edwina's threats to go to court—and his reassurances.

"It won't happen. Edwina and Bruce would lose their trust fund. They would be left with nothing but their house. I'll talk to Bruce and Felicia. They'll put Edwina straight."

For an instant last night she'd thought, let them go to court. Let them upset the will. She'd escape from this hostile three-ring circus her life had become. But she'd plummeted to earth quickly. How could she forget what was at stake? With her salary alone she was keeping Lazarus Timber from going under—as so many family firms were doing these days. She was working toward lifetime security for her father and mother and herself. How many people in this world could count on that? And—sweetest of all—she was taking back from Naomi Miller what had belonged to Rae Lazarus.

145

She had never expected to become so emotionally involved in Miller Timber. Like Grandma with Lazarus Timber. For Rae Lazarus her timberland had been a trust, to be handled with respect and affection. The way Annie Sachs had handled her timberland. But at Miller the forests were a commodity. The God there was profits. How much timber could be sold within a fiscal year? Never mind that the timber harvest in California was already almost double the growth.

She had tried to talk with Doug about her misgivings that the industry was pressuring the Forest Service to "up the cut" in the national forests.

"Anne, stop reading all that damn conservation literature!" He had exploded in a rare show of anger when she tried to express her fears. She read everything she could find that dealt with the timber industry. She read Thoreau, who wrote a century earlier about men "making the earth bald before its time." She read the reports issued by anxious groups trying to save the American forests. And she read the Forest Service reports—which had so often angered her grandmother. "They don't understand that this country is facing a serious timber shortage. It's time for the national forests to make a contribution. They can't get it through their heads that trees are a crop. *A renewable crop,*" he stressed—for the hundredth time. "All over northern California timber people have set up tree farms. Including us."

For the next few days she wouldn't think about Miller Timber—or about Glenn, Anne resolved as the limousine sped over a highway flanked by aromatic, towering pines. She'd just revel in being home. Being fussed over by Dad and Mary Lou. She'd make a point of listening to Mother's flow of imagined grievances as though she really believed them. And Mother promised there'd be no parties.

Her face lighted as they turned off the highway at the outskirts of Belleville. She leaned forward to talk to the chauffeur. "Follow the road to the right till we come to Magnolia Lane," she instructed. "Then take a left."

At moments, Anne thought this first evening home, it was

almost as though she had never gone to San Francisco. On the second morning she insisted on going in to the office with her father. He was in better spirits than she remembered for a long time. The financial pressure was off.

Their small office staff was, as always, warm and friendly. Reflecting Grandma's mood-setting through the years, Anne thought with nostalgia. As Miller Timber reflected Naomi's driving spirit. Sometimes the competitive atmosphere there was almost overwhelming.

Her father took her out to lunch at one of the charming restaurants in the outlying area.

"I'm celebrating your being home," he said tenderly when they had been seated at a cozy corner table and their orders taken.

"You're still having lunch at your desk," she scolded, but she understood. Loving Grandma, Dad was determined to build Lazarus the way she would have done. He utilized every waking moment. As Doug was doing with Miller Timber, Anne realized suddenly.

"Anne, are you happy out there?" Her father's face was serious.

"I haven't thought about that." She tried to laugh off the question. "My main concern is to keep this whole deal afloat." For almost twenty years she'd have to do this.

"Honey, I've told you before and I'm telling you again. Any time it gets too rough, you just get out of there and come home. We'll survive."

"I can handle it, Dad." She managed a smile. "As long as I can come home at regular intervals and keep talking to you over the phone every week. That's one of the bonuses," she laughed. "I never have to consider the phone bill."

Daughter and father spent hours each day probing into ways of improving the business, Anne ever conscious of the differences between the Pacific Northwest and the South. Aware of the increasing financial demands on a company in either area who wished not only to survive but to expand.

Anne was ambitious to see Lazarus Timber grow into a force in the South. A memorial to Rae Lazarus.

With disappointing swiftness her days at home were over and she was en route to Atlanta for the first lap of her flight back to San Francisco. Sitting in the limousine—oblivious to the splendor of the summer flowers—she grew tense in the knowledge that tomorrow morning she would be back at the office and trying to avoid encounters with Glenn. She'd be relieved when Felicia called off the affair and Glenn would vanish from the scene.

How could she have been so stupid? *It wouldn't happen again.*

In her latest Courrèges Felicia arrived late for "Monday lunch" with Eva at the St. Francis Mural Room—a longtime tradition among San Francisco's female socialites that legend claims began when a group of local ladies with growing bank accounts set out to show the city they didn't have to stay home on Mondays to do their own wash. The headwaiter, Barney— successor to the long-installed Ernest, who conferred social status in San Francisco by his seating—led Felicia to Eva's table. Off the center aisle and close to the door. The most desired locale.

"Darling, if dresses get any shorter," Eva complained while she held up a cheek to be kissed, "you might as well come to lunch in a bikini."

"Are you going to Paris next month for the collection?" While her grandmother had been in residence at the San Francisco house since her return from Palm Beach, Felicia rarely encountered her. Eva slept till noon.

"I'm going to see the collections," Eva sighed, "but I won't be buying. How can I, after what Mother did to me?"

"It's useless to fight the will," Felicia reminded her. A grim but indisputable fact.

"I have to talk to Doug about an advance. Felicia, you're so clever. Tell him that it's impossible for me to survive on the income from the trust. He's doing better than either of us. He's got his salary plus his trust. Mother was always partial to Doug," she said aggrievedly.

"I'll talk to him," Felicia promised. "He'll work something out."

"I've met this marvelous man," Eva confided. *Oh God, another one?* thought Felicia. "He's going to be a famous artist one day. But how can I be his patroness on my income?"

"Eva, don't mention your 'marvelous man' to Doug," Felicia warned. "Just tell him you're being dunned by your couturiers." Doug hated Eva's parade of ridiculously young lovers. "Offer to let him hold your diamond necklace as collateral."

"I won't give up my diamond necklace!" Eva gaped in reproach.

"Doug won't take it. But make the offer—"

Felicia ate, watched the fashion show that was part of Monday luncheon at the St. Francis, listened while Eva rattled off her latest supply of gossip; but her mind was mainly involved in the coming weekend at Lake Tahoe. While Doug remained alive, all the houses were at the family's disposal. Naomi took care of them in that respect, she conceded complacently.

In customary fashion the house at Squaw Valley had been closed up the week before and the staff moved to the Lake Tahoe house to get it into readiness for the summer. On Wednesday afternoon the staff left on their vacation. She would drive up to Lake Tahoe Thursday afternoon with Glenn. They'd have the house to themselves. The others would not be going up until the Fourth of July weekend.

Already Glenn had proved himself useful to her. No questions asked when she brought in her expense account for the business trips that were her current activity. One of the old boys—with the company over thirty years—would question every dollar. And Glenn was smart about the business. Doug was impressed at their Friday evening meeting when she'd talked—repeating Glenn's pronouncement—about how Boise Cascade had moved so successfully into the forest products industry and how that should be Miller Timber's next expansion. *Naomi always said, "You don't stand still in business—you go up or you go down."*

Of course, Glenn was a greedy bastard—but *she* fascinated him. He'd never known anybody like her. They looked great together. When they walked into a restaurant, everybody stared. And she could control him. Let Anne eat her heart out.

Tonight she had to be at the house for a business dinner with Doug and Anne. Doug wanted to discuss Anne's idea about their setting up a special warehouse in San Francisco to sell directly to home developers within their area. That sounded like a small-change operation, she thought arrogantly. A Lazarus Timber operation. For all she'd seen, Anne still didn't understand the scope of their business.

After the meeting—over by ten with any luck at all—she'd meet Glenn at The Top of the Mark for a drink, then they'd go down a few floors to the suite the company kept at the Mark Hopkins. She hated that ghastly little apartment Glenn lived in on Russian Hill. They only thing good about it was the address.

Sometimes sex with Glenn was sensational. He worked to make it great. Maybe tonight they'd smoke a little pot first. Everything seemed better after a few drags. Food tasted fabulous. Jokes were funnier. Even the Beatles sounded more sensational. Pot she could handle. She'd never do hard drugs.

"Darling, you will talk to Doug?" Eva punctured her introspection as they waited for dessert to be served.

"I'll talk to him," Felicia promised. "But make your new protégé understand you don't own a chunk of Fort Knox."

By quarter of six on Thursday afternoon Felicia was at the wheel of her Dual-Ghia, her weekender stashed in the trunk. She pulled on her fire-engine-red St. Laurent pea jacket because the salt-scented fog that swept in from the sea had brought the early June temperature down to 55 degrees—a common occurrence in the summer. In the valleys across the bay the thermometers registered close to 90 degrees.

She headed for Russian Hill to pick up Glenn for the drive to Lake Tahoe, a hundred-fifty miles northeast of San Francisco. There'd been no problem about her taking a "vacation day" on Friday and cutting the Friday evening sessions with Doug that had lately become routine. He had a gallery opening to attend that night. He could take Anne, she thought with caustic humor. Eva was off to Palm Springs with her current protégé.

She'd told Doug she was going up to the Tahoe house with Jackie for a long weekend. He was probably the only one in the company offices who didn't suspect she was going up with Glenn. It had been simple for Glenn to ask for a day off—he kept strenuous hours, like most Miller executives. Naomi had been in favor of three-day weekends at intervals. *"It recharges the batteries."*

When Felicia pulled up before the rather smart apartment house where Glenn lived, she spied him waiting at the entrance.

"Traffic is ghastly," she complained as he hurried to climb in beside her.

"Would you like me to drive?"

"When we're out of the city," she stipulated.

She knew he enjoyed being behind the wheel of the Dual-Ghia. She understood the sense of power this gave him. He was thrilled at the prospect of spending a weekend at Naomi Miller's Lake Tahoe estate. And he was avid to claw his way up at Miller Timber. He knew she could help him rise in the business. More important, he could be useful to her.

He was sharp about the business. If Doug's top-level executives knew how smart he was, they'd boot him out right now. He could be her right-hand man. Far more important than okaying her expense-account sheets.

Glenn soaked up everything like a sponge. He knew operating figures, sales volume, their margin of profit. He projected a sales growth—with a strong five-year plan—that doubled what Doug figured. In twenty years, when the stock was to be handed over, it could be worth ten times what it was today.

At the next conference with Doug she'd bring up Glenn's five-year plan.

How many years before Doug began to take a less active role in the business? Right now he was gung-ho to train her to fill Naomi's shoes. It was a commitment he was determined to carry out. But once he saw that she could run the show, she thought with exhilaration, he'd begin to back away. He'd never liked the business. The museum and that arty crowd he played with at free moments were all that really mattered to him.

In five years, she promised herself, she'd be ready to take over. It meant a lot of maneuvering, a lot of work, but she could do it. Anytime she ran into an impasse with Anne, she'd have Doug to vote on her side. She could see it already, she reminded herself in triumph. Doug was getting fed up with Anne's cry-baby routine about "saving the forests." Doug held the deciding vote when it came to a crunch.

Where normally she would have been swearing under her breath at the stop-and-go traffic, today she focused on the campaign ahead. She'd have Doug to vote with her—and she'd have Glenn, with his smart ideas about building the business, to help her fight for control. She'd have Glenn on a full-time basis, she told herself softly. She knew exactly how to bring that about.

"Have you ever been to Tahoe?" she asked Glenn.

"No," he said, one lean muscular thigh pressing against her own.

"You'll love it," she predicted.

He'd be shocked out of his skull tonight when she suggested—after the first time they made love—that they drive up to Reno in the morning and get married at the Washoe County Courthouse. In Reno all they had to do was walk into the Courthouse and take out a license, then walk upstairs to the judge and pay for the ceremony. Not a doubt in her mind that Glenn would be elated to marry her.

"Shall we stop for dinner somewhere along the way?" Glenn asked.

152

"We'll eat at Harvey's Wagon Wheel at Tahoe," she told him. "In the Polynesian-style restaurant upstairs." She chuckled reminiscently. "Doug calls the Wagon Wheel an eleven-story chunk of hardware. Actually, it's a great resort hotel. Doug liked Lake Tahoe better the way it was a dozen years ago, when it was a dull little town of about three thousand."

"I read somewhere that it has six million visitors a year," Glenn said. "Most of them heading for the gambling casinos."

"The lake's impressive, too. Tahoe in Indian language means 'Big Water.' The lake is twenty-two miles long, twelve miles wide, and a third mile deep. There it sits, six thousand feet above sea level, with the Sierra Nevada mountain peaks rising another three thousand feet higher."

"I'll bet you're lucky at the casinos," Glenn said.

"Why?" Her eyes left the road for an instant to clash with his.

"Because you've got good luck written all over you."

"I'm counting on that." Her smile was dazzling. She'd pick up where Naomi left off. Before she was thirty, they'd be writing about her in *Barron's* and *Forbes* and *The Wall Street Journal*. The brilliant and beautiful young successor to Naomi Miller.

Felicia and Glenn wasted little time over dinner at the Wagon Wheel. Both were impatient to be at the lakeside house.

"The casino across the street is run by Bill Harrah," she told Glenn as they headed back to the car. "He runs two others here in town. Sinatra and his pack own a hotel here, too."

"Big bucks." Glenn nodded in approval.

Naomi Miller's Lake Tahoe house was low and rambling, hanging right at the edge of the lake, with its own slip—though the boat was still in drydock. They garaged the car and crossed the oversized breezeway into the house.

"We've been coming here during the summers since I was about two," Felicia told him, flipping on the lights in the side hallway that ran the length of the house. She was getting that fluttery feeling down *there*, she thought with elation. Tonight

153

would be one of the good times. "Though I've been here less and less each year."

"How big a place is this?" Glenn asked, pausing in the hallway. She sensed he was impressed.

"Ten bedrooms plus the servants' quarters." She moved toward him, thrust her slim, firm body against his. "But one bedroom is all we'll need."

"Nobody else is coming up?" His mouth was already reaching for hers.

"Nobody," she confirmed, but the word was muffled by the intrusion of his tongue.

"Do we have to stay here in the hall?" he asked after a few moments.

"My room is at the end of the hall." She reached for his hand. "You'll wake up to a spectacular view of the Sierra Nevada peaks. And me—"

"You're driving me up the wall," he chided, an arm about her waist as they headed toward her bedroom.

"That's not the destination I have in mind," she laughed. "Should we detour to the bar for a bottle of champagne?"

"Who needs champagne tonight?" he challenged. "I'm high as a kite just thinking about us in bed."

Felicia reached for the wall switch, and her large, white, wicker-and-chintz bedroom was softly illuminated. The window-wall was discreetly draped.

"Go run a tub for us," she ordered, gesturing toward the bathroom. She ignored his grunt of protest. Let him wait. "I'll be with you in a few minutes."

Already she was hot with anticipation. She heard the sound of water running into the sunken, square, black marble tub that dominated the bathroom. She stripped to skin in moments, reached for the atomizer of Chanel No. 5, sprayed between her breasts. She didn't have much on top, but she had these huge nipples. That turned men on. And Glenn was really ballsy—half the time she didn't have to pretend with him.

With the sensuous stride she had cultivated her last year at boarding school and had been polishing ever since, she

154

walked naked into the black-and-gold bathroom. The mirrored wall steamed over. The moist air pungent with the scent of honeysuckle. Glenn had chosen her favorite bath salts.

"Hi." She posed provocatively while he rose beside the tub. Her eyes fastened to the indication of his instant arousal.

"See what you do to me?" he mocked and reached out to draw her close.

"No rush," she warned. For her the most satisfying part of sex was knowing that she was driving a man to frenzy. Except for that she could have the same feelings with a vibrator. "Glenn!" she reproached sharply because he was pinning her against the wall and impatient for entry.

"Honey, I'm not a one-shot man," he cajoled.

"Let's soak in the tub first," she insisted, nuzzling against him while he groaned. Tonight was going to be great. "Then you can kiss me from the top of my head to my Elizabeth Arden toenails."

Felicia awoke first. Glenn was still asleep, sprawled on his back, warm and naked beneath the sheet. Early morning sunlight spilled into the bedroom through the window wall that faced the mountain peaks. The drapes were left open in anticipation of the spectacular morning view.

They'd fallen asleep last night before she could bring up her plans for today. Laughter in her blue-green eyes, she leaned over Glenn and dropped a hand between his thighs, knowing he'd awaken quickly at her prodding.

"You're missing the most gorgeous view out there," she scolded as his eyes flickered open.

"It can't match the view right here," he said, his gaze fastened to the huge-nippled, delicate mounds that were her breasts. For a while she'd considered plastic surgery until she realized their effect on men.

"I've been thinking about us," she told him while she allowed him to lift her above him and to prod with sudden urgency.

155

"What were you thinking?" he demanded as they moved in an accelerating rhythm, one of his hands at her pelvis, the other at her rump.

"I was thinking that it might be fun if we drove over to Reno this morning and got married. We just have to go into the courthouse and take out the license and then go upstairs to the judge." All at once he was motionless. "Darling, don't stop now," she clucked. "First we fuck, then we get married."

Anne and Doug left the dining table to go into the library. Over dinner Doug had talked with much anger about the commercializing of Lake Tahoe.

"Casinos and bars all over the place," he said with distaste as they walked into the library. "I suspect that the south end will be a slum in thirty years if something isn't done to stop it." Anne remembered that the Miller house was at the northern end. "But worst of all is what they're doing to that magnificent lake. Mark Twain's 'noble sheet of blue water.' Not only is the scenery being desecrated but the lake itself is becoming polluted. But thank God, we have concerned residents who're forming associations to try to cope with the situation."

How strange, Anne thought in recurrent frustration, that Doug could understand and deplore what was happening to the water of Lake Tahoe yet be blind to what the timber barons—including Miller Timber—were doing to the forests of the Pacific Northwest.

"That must be Felicia," Doug commented at the sound of the doorbell. They heard Walter's stolid footsteps in the marble-floored foyer. "Eva's at the ice follies with Edwina and Bruce tonight."

"Is my uncle home, Walter?" Felicia's high-pitched voice drifted down the hall to them.

"He's in the library, Miss Felicia," Walter said.

"Come along, Glenn. Let's go say hello to Doug."

Anne sat tensely in her chair, fighting an inclination to flee. Doug frowned.

"Doug, I'm glad you're here." Felicia smiled effervescently and slid an arm through Glenn's. "Oh, hi, Anne."

"Hi." Anne forced an impersonal smile. Felicia was such a bitch. Taking Glenn's arm that way to remind *her* that he was her personal property. *How could she still feel the way she did about Glenn, knowing what he was?*

"How's Jackie?" Doug asked pointedly.

"Oh, that was a little white lie," Felicia drawled. "You two are the first to know. Glenn and I were married in Reno on Friday morning." Anne froze in shock. She'd never thought Felicia would marry Glenn. Everybody at the office thought it was just another affair. "We've been honeymooning at the Tahoe house."

Doug was silent for a moment. His face cold and remote. Glenn appeared uneasy. He was fearful of a storm. And her presence made him uncomfortable, Anne knew. He hadn't expected her to be here.

"Yes, I suppose a big wedding would be in bad taste with Mama dead just a little over six months," Doug said casually.

"It'll be all right if Glenn and I spend a few days at the Mark Hopkins suite, won't it?" Felicia said with deceptive sweetness. "I'll be back home—with Glenn—" her eyes lingered fleetingly on Anne, "by the weekend. And I'll be at the office in the morning as usual. This doesn't affect Naomi's will, does it?"

"No," Doug replied. "Not as long as you continue to be in permanent residence here at the house. I hope you two will be very happy." But it was clear that only Doug's good manners elicited this wish.

"I have to pick up a few things, then we'll shoot over to the hotel." Felicia hesitated. "I'll call Mother and Dad later and tell them. Will you tell Eva for me?"

"I'll tell her," Doug said politely.

"I'll still be Felicia Harris," she said and linked an arm through Glenn's. "Glenn understands that women keep their own names these days."

"I'll remember." Doug's smile told Felicia he was unimpressed.

"See you in the morning." Felicia and Glenn left the library.

"Do you want to go over Mr. Evans's report on the Eureka mill?" Anne asked Doug—pretending Felicia had not delivered a wrenching blow.

"I think we should," Doug said briskly. "I won't have time tomorrow morning. There's the meeting with the group from Canada."

How far would history repeat itself, Anne demanded of herself. Felicia had walked off with Glenn. She had married him. And now the three of them would live under the same roof. She could hear her grandmother's voice: *"Anne, you can't imagine the torment. Living there in the same house with Naomi and Joseph. Lying in my bed in a room just across the hall from theirs. It was the most awful time of my life."*

How could she let herself feel this way about Glenn, knowing what he was? She was lucky that Felicia took him away. But like her grandmother, she knew she would hurt for a long time.

Twelve

TIRED after a sleepless night, Anne sat hunched over her desk and stared at, without seeing, the report on the Oregon mill that Doug had given her to study. At just past nine the office was coming to life for the day.

"Hi." Shirley walked into the tiny office with a mug of steaming coffee in each hand.

"Close the door behind you," Anne told her, unfamiliarly terse.

Eyebrows uplifted, Shirley thrust the door shut with one foot and put the mugs on Anne's desk.

"What's up?"

"It'll be all over the offices in the next ten minutes," Anne predicted, bracing herself for what must be said. "Felicia and Glenn were married over the weekend. In Reno."

"I don't believe it!" Shirley gaped in astonishment.

"They're both here at work," Anne said with quiet distaste. "Honeymooning by night at the company's suite at the Mark Hopkins."

"They deserve each other. But I never thought Glenn would pull it off."

"He didn't," Anne guessed. "I'm sure it was Felicia's decision. She figures Glenn will be useful to her. He's well liked in the company. He knows everything that's going on. He's an ally against me." Anne laughed self-consciously. "I know, that sounds melodramatic—"

"At least, Felicia isn't walking out," Shirley said with an effort at optimism. "Glenn wouldn't let her—not with all that loot in the offing. How does the family feel about this?"

"Doug is livid, though he's being cool about it. I heard Eva screaming last night when Doug told her. And I doubt that Felicia's parents are enthralled."

Shirley reached for her coffee mug. "Let's go out to lunch today. Somewhere fabulous. My treat."

In the middle of the week Doug called Anne into his office for a conference. She was about to begin a new phase in her training. For the next few weeks she would be spending much of her time shuttling between their mills and the warehouses. She suspected Doug had arranged this to isolate her from Felicia and Glenn.

She was relieved to be away from San Francisco for three or four days each week. It was exciting to travel on a company plane—as though she was already an important executive, to become involved in activities that she had known heretofore only through reports. But often, lying sleepless in a hotel bedroom that was home for the night, she was haunted by memories of Glenn. How could she think of him with such longing, she taunted herself. The Glenn she'd loved had existed only in her mind.

Dutifully she joined Doug, Consuelo, and Leon at the Lake Tahoe house at the beginning of the long Fourth of July weekend, relieved that Felicia and Glenn were defying family tradition by spending the holiday at the Acapulco house. Eva was flying up to Tahoe with Edwina and Bruce on Saturday afternoon, and the three would remain for most of the month.

Anne enjoyed being with Consuelo and Leon. Of the San Francisco branch of the family they were the only ones who showed interest in their Georgia relatives. Doug always seemed uncomfortable in conversation revolving around his Aunt Rae. He considered it disloyal to his mother, Anne decided.

Anne was pleased when Todd arrived with his parents and grandmother, though she sensed immediately that there had been friction on the flight out. Todd had come to Tahoe out of respect for Doug's wishes. He was heading south for the summer with a group of school friends. He was elated, as Anne was, that President Johnson had signed the Civil Rights Act of 1964 just three days earlier. When a battle erupted between Todd and his father over dinner, Anne was upset by Todd's threats to enlist in the marines in the hope of being sent to Vietnam.

"I don't think we have any right to be in Vietnam," Anne said softly while Todd and his father stared belligerently at each other. "It could become another Korea. Nobody really won there—but an awful lot of lives were lost."

Todd turned to Anne.

"That's what Rick, my roommate, says," he admitted somberly.

"There's so much that needs to be done here in this country," Anne said, aware that Todd's parents were not enthusiastic about this approach either. "You'll see for yourself this summer." His parents pretended not to realize his summer down south with a student group would revolve around the civil rights movement.

"Why don't we run over to Harrah's tonight?" Eva intervened. "I feel lucky today. But Todd, darling, you're too young to be allowed in the casinos," she sympathized. "Settle down and listen to records while we're gone."

Anne had become adept at avoiding Glenn both at the house and the office, but immediately after the Tahoe weekend she turned a corner at the office—walking with her customary compulsive swiftness—and collided with him.

"Annie," he said softly, his hands at her shoulders.

"Excuse me." Instinctively she backed away. Her heart was pounding.

"Don't run away," he pleaded. "You keep avoiding me. I've wanted to—"

161

"We have nothing to say to each other." Her eyes blazed with a blend of pain and rage.

"Annie, I have to tell you. I'll never stop caring for you, but love isn't enough." All at once his eyes were bitter. "My parents loved each other early in their marriage, but poverty killed that. I saw my mother die because we had no money for decent medical attention—"

"You went out with me because of what you thought I could do for you," she challenged with contempt.

"No," he denied. "Maybe at first I figured it wouldn't hurt my chances for advancement, but that was only in the beginning. We had something great."

"I notice!" she jeered. Tears stinging her eyes.

"That isn't enough to make it in this world," he reiterated. "When Felicia phoned and asked me to take her to that benefit, I realized what she could do for me." *It had been Felicia who instituted the chase.* "Okay, I'm looking out for my own interests above all else. Felicia won't be hampered by your brand of ethics. She'll do whatever is to her advantage and to hell with everybody else. When it comes to a showdown, she'll win over you. I couldn't throw away the opportunity fate threw in my path."

"We'll see who wins!" Defiance lent sharpness to Anne's voice. Eventually either *she* would control the company, or Felicia would. They could never rule jointly. "Now will you please excuse me?" Her voice was low but urgent now that they were no longer alone in the corridor. "I have no time for socializing."

On July 15 Senator Barry Goldwater was nominated for president at the Republican National Convention, held in San Francisco. The Democratic convention would take place in late August in Atlantic City. Just a few days after the Republican convention riots broke out in Harlem—only blocks north of the Barnard campus but a painfully different world.

Early in August Doug corralled Anne to attend another

benefit dinner at the Naomi Miller Museum. She knew he considered it important for her to be accepted by San Francisco society, and at intervals he escorted her to various functions. In an odd fashion she felt she owed it to her grandmother to be accepted in the circles where Naomi Miller had been accepted.

"I know you're not mad about these affairs," Doug apologized, "but the family has an image to uphold. That was always important to my mother. And this benefit is particularly close to me. The funds raised go to support aspiring young artists."

"It's fun to dress up now and then," Anne conceded. "I don't want to be part of the jet-set circuit, but I can handle these occasional deals."

"San Francisco is a great dress-up town," Doug chuckled. "Perhaps because just a few generations ago San Franciscans were out there with picks and shovels in search of gold. Now they're out to show the world they've acquired sophistication and breeding along with money."

Accompanied by Shirley, prodding her to buy a spectacular gown to wear to the dinner, Anne spent a Saturday afternoon at Magnin's trying on a parade of dresses.

"Annie, that's it. It's gorgeous!" Shirley proclaimed when Anne stood before the dressing room mirror in an audaciously red chiffon that bared one shoulder and swept with classic simplicity over her slender body. "It just needs to be shortened."

"Shirley, it's so—so loud." Still, she was intrigued by the dramatic contrast of red against her near-black hair and alabaster skin.

"*You* can wear it," Shirley insisted. "You have that air of gentility that carries it off."

"I'm afraid to look at the price tag," Anne said and flinched when she did.

"Buy it," Shirley ordered ebulliently. "Every woman at that dinner will hate you, and every man will wish he was twenty years younger."

"I don't honestly want to go," Anne reminded. Yet,

strangely, part of her looked forward to the dinner. Each time she attended a San Francisco society affair she gained confidence. Rae Lazarus's granddaughter could play this role.

The August evening was shrouded in fog when Anne and Doug left the house for the Naomi Miller Museum. It seemed to Anne—and Doug insisted this happened occasionally—that the evening air held the scent of pines, as though brought down pure and undiluted from the Sierras. In the distance the fog horns blared in their deep baritone.

"Bless Connie for coming in from Tahoe to take care of all the last-minute details," Doug said gratefully while they settled themselves in the limousine. "I always feel secure when she's on the job."

Eva would not be at the dinner, Anne remembered. She was still at Palm Springs with her current young lover, supposedly an up-and-coming tennis star. In a drunken moment Bruce had declared the athlete was more eager to star in a rich old woman's bed than on the tennis courts. Felicia and Glenn had taken off to Acapulco for a week. Edwina was down at The Golden Door to lose ten pounds, at the same time Bruce was on one of his periodic "drying out" bouts.

The predinner cocktail hour had begun by the time Anne and Doug arrived. The usual festive scene, the usual faces. The women in designer gowns, the men in meticulously tailored evening attire. Waiters circulating with trays of champagne-laden glasses. Newspaper photographers on duty.

Most of the faces were familiar to Anne now. She disliked the required small talk but was learning to handle it. She was conscious of stares as she walked into the central hall. Almost everybody here knew she was Naomi Miller's grandniece, being groomed to share her empire with Felicia. No doubt they took bets among themselves about how long it would be before Felicia and she erupted into battle and broke the will. Everybody knew that if this happened the museum would inherit everything.

"Tess, it's been such a long time!" Doug was striding toward a tall, attractive woman with beautifully coiffed, prematurely white hair and a warm smile. "How've you been?"

After the two exchanged kisses, Doug introduced Anne to Tess Blumberg. Anne's face brightened in recognition. This was Arthur Blumberg's wife.

"Where's Artie?" Doug's gaze moved about the room.

"Out of town on a case," Tess explained. "Josh was shanghaied to come with me tonight. There he is." She lifted a hand to signal her son.

"Josh still at Berkeley?" Doug asked while a dark-haired young man with the trim but muscular body of a ballet dancer strode across the room toward them. He wasn't tall but with his figure and bearing he appeared so. And slightly self-conscious in his tux, Anne thought with immediate sympathy. The two of them were the only people in the room under thirty —there was a kind of kinship in that.

Anne remembered Arthur Blumberg talking about his son on her first flight from Belleville to San Francisco. *"He went to Washington in August for Martin Luther King's 'Freedom March.' All through high school he wanted to be a lawyer, then halfway through college he decided law was a dirty word."*

While Josh Blumberg carried on casual conversation with Doug, Anne was conscious of his covert but intense scrutiny. Instinctively she knew this had nothing to do with her role at Miller Timber. She doubted that Josh Blumberg even connected her with Naomi's will, though he must be aware that his father was the family's longtime attorney. Doug had introduced her as "my young cousin from Georgia."

She was disconcerted by his interest and by her own reaction toward him. He would have fitted right in with her close friends at Barnard/Columbia. All of them were scattered about now, making her feel guilty that she was uncommitted in an era when commitment was so important.

"Do you go to school out here?" Josh asked Anne while the other two were drawn into an exchange with a pair of new arrivals.

"I graduated from Barnard last year," Anne told him and saw his eyes light up.

"Then you were part of the Columbia scene," he guessed. "I hear there was a lot happening there last year."

"Sort of like at Berkeley." She nodded, warmed by this common bond between them. "Actually most students were just involved in the usual campus stuff—but there were those who were concerned about civil rights and why are we sending American soldiers to Vietnam?"

Anne listened avidly while Josh talked about the demonstration at the Sheraton Palace last March that had brought out two thousand kids. He told her about seeing films smuggled out of North Vietnam, about the weeks earlier in the summer when he'd been involved in voter registration in Mississippi. Both were oblivious to the convivial conversations around them.

"Going to school in New York was a real awakening for me," Anne said. "The campus was just a few blocks from the edge of Harlem. A bunch of us used to sit around on weekend nights at the West End bar and argue about how the world had to be changed. My father was one of the Southerners who understood early that we have to listen to the needs of minorities. Including women," she said with a spurt of defiance and Josh laughed. But it was a sympathetic laugh.

At dinner Anne was seated next to Josh at Doug's table. She suspected Doug had connived with Consuelo to change the seating to arrange for this. She was conscious of a heady exhilaration. She felt young again, released from the role she played at the office and even at the house. Emotionally and intellectually she and Josh shared the same world—the questioning, sometimes angry, sometimes euphoric student world. She doubted that Glenn had ever been part of that.

It seemed so natural, toward the end of the evening, when Josh said, "Why don't we go to a flick tomorrow night? There's a Bogie film over at the Guild in Berkeley."

"It'll have to be late," Anne apologized. "I have a business meeting that'll probably run close to ten."

"I'll pick you up at ten," he agreed.

There was nothing romantic about this, Anne told herself. She and Josh had formed an instant friendship based on shared convictions. They enjoyed exchanging ideas, arguing here and there. That was all.

Josh and Shirley helped Anne build a wall around her feelings for Glenn. At the office she could emotionally insulate herself from him. And she told herself she *could* live under the same roof with Glenn and not fall apart. She was relieved that they so seldom encountered each other at the house. Felicia carried Glenn into her jet-set crowd—shunned by Doug and alien to Anne.

Her life away from the business revolved around the time she spent with Josh or with Shirley and Gerry. Over dinners in Chinatown—at Songhay's on Jackson when they were budget-minded, at the Far East Cafe on Grant, with its lacquered screen and ivory-inset tables, when they felt lavish—she and Josh earnestly discussed the politics that disturbed many of the young. After dinner they'd walk to a North Beach coffeehouse—usually Coffee and Confusion or the Graffeo Coffee House—for coffee or beer. With the approach of the fall term Josh was anxious about the mood on campus at Berkeley and predicted student-administration confrontations.

On Saturday afternoons Anne went with Shirley and ingratiating little Gerry to Fisherman's Wharf or Golden Gate Park or the Planetarium. The three would have an early dinner in some inexpensive restaurant, and later Anne would meet Josh and go with him to a movie at the Guild or the Studio in Berkeley and then to the Mediterraneum for coffee and pastries.

On the Friday of Labor Day weekend Anne and Doug left the office at noon and headed for the airport to fly to Tahoe. Josh was leaving later in the afternoon with his family for their country house. Doug was unfamiliarly grim and taciturn on the drive to the airport. Not until they were airborne and having lunch did Anne realize what caused his ill-humor.

"By now," he said brusquely, "considering the difference in time between Washington, D.C., and California, Johnson has signed that damned bill. In the Rose Garden of the White House."

"What bill?" Anne glanced up from her cracked-crab, iced to perfection and sent to the plane by special messenger from Amelio's.

"The Wilderness Act of 1964 bill," Doug shot back. "The government is trying to set aside almost eleven million acres of national forest lands and talking about another fifty million in the future. Damn it, Anne, the timber business shouldn't be cut off like that! The country has a real need for more timber!"

"But it's important to preserve our wilderness," Anne said urgently, though she knew this was a delicate topic. "It's an obligation to future generations. We . . ."

"The lawyers will find loopholes," Doug surmised with a surge of hope. "We're not without friends in high places." He pushed aside his half-filled plate and reached for his coffee. "What we need in the timber industry is better management. We waste in a hundred ways. But . . ." he took a deep breath, "we still should not be stopped from cutting in the national forests. This country is in desperate need of housing."

Anne allowed Doug to redirect their conversation away from business. It was impossible to change his thinking, she told herself. Last night he had been outraged about the pollution of Lake Tahoe but he refused to see that the country's forests were being devastated.

Anne tensed as they approached the airport. Felicia and Glenn would arrive tomorrow morning. This would be the first time since they were married that she would be thrown into such intimate contact with them. Eva, her sons, and their wives had come out yesterday. Todd was in New York, at Columbia, Adrian at boarding school in Southern California. But probably everybody, except for herself and Doug, would spend most of the weekend at the casinos and nightclubs, she consoled herself.

On their first evening at the house only Consuelo and Leon joined Anne and Doug at the dinner table, and this was a pattern that continued. Felicia and Glenn slept till noon, swam in the pool, and sunbathed on the terrace or went sailing in the family boat, then in the late afternoon—like Eva, Bruce, and Edwina—took off for the casinos. But at odd intervals Anne encountered Glenn's eyes, somberly regarding her. Was he already regretting his marriage?

Felicia could handle their late-night social lives, Anne observed. She was at the office every morning well before most of the staff arrived, casual and unruffled by lack of sleep. Glenn appeared tired and slightly grim. He was angry, she suspected, because he had not been promoted when an executive two notches above him had retired in August. Doug had decided to eliminate the position. It had been part of his effort to streamline Miller Timber, as his mother had planned before her death. But then, Glenn was not one of Doug's favorite people since he had become his grandnephew-in-law.

Early Monday afternoon—to avoid holiday airport traffic—the entire party headed back to San Francisco on the larger company plane. Anne was conscious of the elation that radiated from Felicia and Glenn. But not until she and Doug were alone in the limousine the following morning did she understand.

"Just before we left Tahoe yesterday afternoon, I told Glenn he would become the departmental chief of Accounting." He frowned as she stared in astonishment. "I know, it'll have a hell of a reaction in Accounting. I hate the arrogant young twirp," he admitted unhappily, "but Felicia's right. *He's family.*"

Thirteen

ALTHOUGH Anne was spending sixty to seventy hours each week in the business—including after-hours conferences with Doug and Felicia—she was emotionally involved in the accelerating frenzy on the Berkeley campus. She spent as much time as she could manage with Josh. This was real. The rest of her world was not.

The moment Anne walked into the near-campus coffeehouse on this balmy evening a week before the opening of classes at Berkeley, she knew something calamitous had happened. The atmosphere reeked of tension. Pushing her way through the closely clustered tables, she caught fragments of indignant conversation.

"Traffic bad?" Josh asked as she squeezed into the tiny booth he had commandeered earlier. On occasion now Anne would borrow a company car for the fifteen-mile drive from the city to Berkeley.

"I missed the worst," she said. "What's happening?"

"Dean Towle just declared war." He leaned forward, his face grim. "All the student organizations just got notice that, effective immediately, the Bancroft Strip can't be used to recruit members, solicit funds, or make speeches for any off-campus action." The Bancroft Strip was a twenty-six-by-sixty-foot bricked-over area, just outside the main pedestrian entrance, where student activists had been free to operate. "The only area on campus that was open to us!"

"What's going to happen?" Anne asked.

"The students—undergraduate and graduate—won't allow the University to turn the campus into a concentration camp. This is the one action that could bring the students together into a united front. Everybody from the far right to the far left is outraged!"

Though not a Berkeley student, Anne stood with Josh outside the dean's office as several hundred students protested the suspension of eight students who had defied the order against manning the tables on the Bancroft Strip. The protesters vowed to remain throughout the night. Close to midnight Anne reluctantly admitted she had to leave.

"I'll walk you back to your car," Josh said, turning to forge a path for them.

"Josh, I can go alone."

"No," he said.

"Shall we stop for coffee before you take off?" he asked, as they walked to where she had parked. He was anxious about the situation on campus.

"Sure," Anne agreed. She knew Josh needed to talk.

"It's going to get worse before it gets better," he said when they sat at a table with steaming mugs of black coffee before them, and Anne nodded. "I don't understand why the administration can't see what this is all about." He slammed a fist on the tabletop in frustration. "They'll never get away with trying to keep the student body away from what's happening in the world. We can't live in a vacuum. The educational system should give students a bridge between ideas and social action. When it doesn't, then we have to fight for our principles."

"About every few weeks I hear from my exroommate at Barnard," Anne said somberly. "She's at Columbia, working toward her M.S.W. She said that Mario Savio and Tom Hayden have both been on campus this year. She says there's S.D.S. on the Columbia campus—but so far it has no teeth. But neither does a baby when it's born."

"What's happening at Berkeley will happen at Columbia,"

Josh prophesied. "Maybe it'll come from different quarters—but it'll come. Students today don't like what's happening to our country."

With reluctance they left the coffeehouse, and Josh walked Anne to her car. He had a class to teach in the morning. She had a job. She had never felt so close to Josh as tonight. Nothing romantic, she told herself self-consciously: a deep, caring friendship.

"There'll be a noon rally tomorrow. It could get rough," Josh said.

"Josh, be careful. I have a dinner meeting with Doug, but I'll call you afterward."

It was past midnight the following evening when, after several attempts, Anne was able to reach him by phone.

"The police arrested Jack Weinberg for manning a CORE table on Sproul steps," he reported. "Students surrounded the police car. God, there must have been two thousand! A bunch of them finally went into Sproul for a sit-in. I suspect the administration will have a mob of cops there tomorrow."

On October 2 the administration summoned police to quell the continuing student protest. Almost a thousand police arrived on campus and surrounded the demonstrators. President Kerr and other university officials agreed to meet with faculty members and student leaders. Finally they reached a tentative agreement. But the following day the Free Speech Movement was formed, swiftly labeled the FSM.

Soon professors were moving over to the students' side. The chancellor set up a Campus Committee on Political Activity, and faculty-student-administration conferences were held, calling a halt to the campus upheaval. When an impasse was reached in early November, the FSM began to demonstrate again. The campus was enveloped in civil war.

Anne was emotionally involved in FSM. Josh's Berkeley friends, including Stuart Lerman, with whom he shared a tiny off-campus house—were hers now. They knew she'd gone to Barnard, was sympathetic to the movement.

At intervals Stu, working for a Ph.D. in English lit, carelessly made sarcastic remarks about the Pacific Coast timber barons. He soft-pedaled this most of the time, Josh confided to Anne, because he knew she was with Miller Timber. Stu's older brother was a forest ranger in the state of Washington—but his opinion of the Forest Service and the timber industry bordered on the obscene.

With the approach of Thanksgiving Anne was conscious of a fresh wave of homesickness. Two days before Thanksgiving of the year before she had arrived in San Francisco aboard Naomi Miller's private plane, her whole personal world in tumult. Thanksgiving of 1963 had been a holiday lost in the trauma of the Kennedy assassination. All at once it was important for her to be home for this Thanksgiving, rather than to wait for a mid-December visit as she had planned.

Doug was encountering opposition to the usual family Thanksgiving at Squaw Valley. Felicia announced that she and Glenn were going to the new ski resort at Vail. Edwina and Bruce preferred to remain in town. In the face of all this indecision Anne asked Doug if she might fly home for Thanksgiving week.

Despite the on-campus trauma at Berkeley—a mass rally was scheduled momentarily—Josh insisted on driving Anne to the airport.

"What do you think will happen today?" she asked uneasily.

"There'll be another sit-in in Sproul," Josh anticipated. "Thank God, Thanksgiving recess is coming up. Everything will be on hold for four days."

"You'll be going to your family's country house for the holidays?" she asked and Josh nodded. His was a close family, she thought with respect, though Josh and his father often held different viewpoints.

"I'll go home and let Mom spoil me to death," he said humorously, "and argue with Dad because he's so much the establishment figure."

"It'll be good to be home for a few days," Anne mused. She could even look forward to spending time with her mother. Maybe now they wouldn't be on a constant collision course.

Arriving in Belleville Anne was startled to discover—after an affectionate welcome by her father and Mary Lou—that her mother had taken off.

"She'd been planning for weeks to join Avis and some friends for a cruise down in the Caribbean," her father apologized as they settled themselves on the living room sofa while Mary Lou bustled off to prepare dinner. Before she'd called and told Dad she'd be coming home for this week, was Mother set for that cruise? *Leaving Dad alone on Thanksgiving.*

"Mother must have been so excited." She forced herself to smile.

"She flew down to Miami with Avis this morning," her father continued. "But we'll have ourselves a fine Thanksgiving together," he said with an air of pleasure. "Mary Lou's planning everything you like."

"It's worth coming home just for Mary Lou's sweet-potato pie." She echoed his air of conviviality. Dad would have canceled any trip if he knew she was coming home. She was furious that her mother would dash off and leave Dad alone on Thanksgiving. It was a glaring revelation of the state of their marriage. Was Mother still playing the flirtatious Southern belle? Not that she'd wander off into an affair—she was just forever playing games.

"You look wonderful, honey." Her father scrutinized her face with remembered tenderness. "Maybe a little thinner. Are they working you too hard out there?"

"I can handle it," she said lightly.

"I don't have to tell you the money you send home is keeping the business afloat. I've had papers drawn up, Annie. I'm transferring my shares of Lazarus Timber to you."

"Dad, no!" She knew her grandmother had left 55 percent of the company to her father, 45 percent to her mother. "Grandma left that to you."

"I have to be sure that if anything happens to me, you'll control the business. It's the money you're pouring into it that

174

keeps us from going under. I want this transfer of stock for my peace of mind. The papers are all signed."

"Does Mother know?"

"All that interests your mother is knowing she still looks beautiful." He sighed. "She's talking about a facelift now."

Late Sunday evening, back in the San Francisco house, Anne talked on the phone with Josh about what had been happening at Berkeley over the holiday weekend. He was convinced there would be trouble when classes began again in the morning. Two FSM leaders, Mario Savio and Art Goldberg, were facing new disciplinary action. Tomorrow FSM would demand the charges be dropped.

"We're heading for a violent confrontation," Josh predicted and sighed. "Teaching assistants will strike if the administration doesn't drop the charges. We can't back down."

"I'll be tied up in an evening meeting with Doug, but call me late," Anne urged.

For the next two days she was involved in a series of Miller Timber staff meetings. In addition, Doug demanded her presence, along with that of Felicia, at private evening meetings. She listened respectfully but privately disagreed with much of what Doug said. Congress had passed an act that was meant to preserve the wilderness—but Doug, along with other timber leaders, was contriving to save the trees for logging.

In framing the Wilderness Act of 1964 Congress had declared that "no federal lands shall be designated as 'wilderness areas' except as provided for in this Act or by a subsequent Act." The timber industry meant to utilize this to its own advantage. Congress set aside certain areas as "wilderness" but provided for a ten-year review of other areas—a delaying action Doug appreciated.

Tuesday night, apologizing for calling so late, Josh told Anne that there was to be a major sit-in at noon the next day. The FSM meant to bring university activities to a halt.

"Everything peaceful. No violence," he stressed. "The sit-in will probably last through the rest of the day into the night. Let's meet for dinner on Thursday. The usual place, around seven. Okay?"

"Sure." It seemed so long since she'd seen Josh. She was astonished by how much she missed him. "I'll be watching the TV news."

She was relieved that she was alone at dinner on Wednesday evening. She asked for a tray in the library, where she could watch the early evening news. She heard about Mario Savio's passionate speech to a crowd of over fifteen hundred students and how the students—led by Joan Baez in singing "We Shall Overcome"—marched into Sproul and sat down.

Anne went to sleep relieved that the sit-in was peaceful. Shortly before six in the morning her private phone rang. Instantly awake, she picked up the receiver, expecting to hear Josh's voice at the other end.

"Hello—"

"Anne?" A husky voice—vaguely familiar.

"Yes." She was sharp in her anxiety.

"This is Stu. Stu Lerman."

"Oh. Hi, Stu." Often she and Josh had dinner or sat around a coffeehouse with him and dissected campus problems. "I didn't recognize your voice at first."

"I came down with laryngitis and left the sit-in at Sproul late last night when a bunch of others went home. Josh told me to call you if I heard about arrests being made. He said you were expecting to meet him for dinner tonight."

"Has Josh been arrested?" She was cold with alarm.

"The word just came through to me. They're all being arrested. About three hours ago at least six hundred cops showed up on campus. By orders of Governor Edmund Brown." His voice deepened with scorn. "The six hundred cops are taking away about eight hundred demonstrators, one by one. The kids aren't showing any fight—they're just going limp. The cops are dragging them down the steps and into the paddy wagons. It'll go on for the next ten hours."

"Thanks for letting me know, Stu."

Anne forced herself to wait until just past seven before calling Arthur Blumberg.

"What the hell is the matter with those kids!" he exploded when Anne had explained the situation.

"I thought you'd want to know," Anne stammered. She'd expected him to rush down to wherever the students were being held to bail out Josh.

"I do. I didn't mean to blow up that way," he apologized. "I'll see what I can do. I'll call you at the office as soon as I have some word."

Anne listened to the morning radio news before she joined Doug for breakfast. At exactly eight o'clock she and Doug headed for the office. She knew that when they left, Felicia and Glenn would come downstairs for breakfast, then drive to the office in Felicia's Dual-Ghia.

According to the news, activities at Berkeley were at a halt. Students were joining together to strike. Hundreds of professors were canceling classes in outrage at the calling in of the police. Nobody would predict how long the strike would last.

In mid-morning—calm but unhappy—Arthur Blumberg called Anne to say that the faculty members had gotten together to raise bail for all of the arrested students. They'd be released within twenty-four hours.

When Anne left the office on Friday afternoon, she found Josh waiting in the lobby for her.

"You all right?" she asked anxiously.

He grinned. "You might say that. Let's go somewhere and eat."

Over shish kebab at the Cairo Restaurant on Fourth Street, Josh told her the strike was continuing. "Students are wandering around the campus. Picket lines are up at all the buildings. No classes are being held. Some of the faculty are trying to formulate a solution, but so far all they've come up with are motions for a meeting of the Academic Senate on Tuesday. They're working on the wording now." He shook his head tiredly. "At this point I just wish to hell I could get away from the whole scene for a day or two. All kinds of rumors

177

are circulating. One is that the administration will bring in the National Guard."

Anne stared at him in disbelief.

"Josh, they wouldn't dare!"

"They're desperate. Another rumor is that the regents plan to expel at least a thousand students and a few hundred professors. And what have we done except ask for what the Constitution of the United States guarantees us?"

"Let's drive up to Marin County tomorrow," Anne urged, feeling his exhaustion, his despair. "Forget about the insanity on campus for a day."

He squinted in thought.

"You know what I'd really like to do?" he said quietly. "I'd like us to pack a picnic lunch and drive up to the family's country house. Nobody's going up this weekend—we'll have the place to ourselves. It's real country. Quiet and peaceful."

"How long does it take to drive up?" Anne asked.

"Usually around an hour and a half," Josh said. "And the weather's supposed to be great tomorrow."

"Then we'll go," Anne said exuberantly.

Before nine the next morning, picnic makings on the rear seat, Anne and Josh were in the 1958 Chevie he'd inherited when his mother bought a new car. They vowed not to say one word about the Berkeley crisis or about Miller Timber for the rest of the day. They talked about the fog that lay heavily over the city—rare in winter. About the His and Her planes in the Neiman-Marcus catalogue, for $176,000 a pair, postpaid. About the cleanliness of San Francisco because it burns little coal and most of its public transportation is electrified.

"Cold?" Josh asked solicitously when they had left the city behind them. "Shall I turn up the heat?"

"It would be nice."

Within moments a cozy warmth suffused the interior of the car. Outside, the fog was eerily beautiful. Josh drove slowly, concentrating on what lay ahead. Anne felt an odd sense of being cut off from the world. But it was a warm, comfortable feeling.

"We'll take the long way this morning, all right?" Josh asked, squinting ahead at an exit sign.

"Whatever you say."

"Careful," he laughed. "That's a broad statement."

Suddenly the atmosphere was electric. They'd never progressed beyond a casual good-night kiss, though at unguarded moments Anne thought that Josh was about to make stronger overtures. But each time he had retreated. That was the way they both wanted it, Anne had told herself.

"Why are we taking the long way?" she veered into less complicated ground.

"All this fog. Some of the turns on the shorter route can be dangerous."

"Do you have a fireplace up there?" Instantly she regretted the question. She was disconcerted by a mental image of herself and Josh sprawled on the floor before a blazing fire.

"How can you have a country house without a fireplace?" he chuckled. "I'd disown my parents for buying a place without one."

"Tell me about the house." They were just going up to picnic there, she told herself. To escape the city pressures. Josh was as intent as she on keeping their relationship casual. "Is it in the mountains?"

By tacit agreement they continued to keep the conversation light. The fog became a drizzle and then a winter rain as they traveled north. Josh reminisced about childhood weekends and vacations spent at the country place.

Anne knew he was fighting the same unexpected emotions that welled in her. It was just that they were both so relieved to be away from the problems they'd left behind, Anne told herself. It would be comfortable to be alone up here this way. *How could she be feeling like this about Josh when just a few months ago she'd been in love with Glenn?*

The Blumberg house sat on a wooded acre adjoining a game

179

preserve. A California ranch encircled by Douglas firs. A friendly house, Anne thought—inviting as the rain pelted the winter earth.

"I'll turn up the heat as soon as we get inside. It'll be warm in twenty minutes," Josh said, opening the car door on his side. "Let's make a dash for the house."

In twenty minutes, as Josh had promised, the pleasant living room was warm. Chunks of wood crackled on the grate. While Josh trailed out to the kitchen to put up coffee, Anne laid out her paper tablecloth and matching napkins on the floor before the fireplace, set two places, brought out the delicatessen bought at David's—open twenty-four hours a day.

"The coffee'll be ready in five minutes," Josh announced, returning to the living room. "Wow, everything smells great!"

"And why not?" Anne said perkily. "When I've been slaving over a hot stove all day."

"Every housewife should look like you," he said, all at once serious. "It'd make a man eager to come home at night."

For a heated instant their eyes clung.

"Does the fire need another chunk of wood?" Anne asked, her voice uneven.

"Let's be generous," Josh laughed. "I'll throw on another. We'll live dangerously."

Anne knew even before Josh went out to bring in the percolator that this was unlike any other occasion since they had met. She knew that tonight they would make love—and there would be no stopping.

They made a pretense of drinking their coffee. It was as though she were on the sidelines watching, Anne thought. When would they stop this inane conversation? She wanted him to take her in his arms and hold her.

"Anne—" He reached tentatively for her hand.

"I've never slept with a man before," she said shakily. "I'll probably do everything wrong."

"Whatever you do," he said, reaching for her, "will be right."

It was so natural to lie this way in his arms. His mouth clinging to hers. His hands seeking, arousing.

"Warm enough here?" he asked after a few minutes.

"Yes," she whispered.

In silent swiftness they undressed before the firelight and Josh drew her close again, moving with her while the wood on the grate popped as though in approval.

"Let's try the sofa," he said and prodded her along its comfortable length.

Her arms closed in about his shoulders as he found his way to her. It was going to be wonderful, she exulted, clinging to him, moving with him. *No need to worry that she wouldn't know what to do.*

They headed back to San Francisco at dusk, Anne's head on Josh's shoulder as he drove.

"I'm glad we came up here," she murmured.

"I'm glad, too." One hand left the wheel to fondle hers for a moment. "I'd been scared it could never happen this way for me." He paused. "I had a bad scene with a girl a few months before I met you. I thought I was mad about her. But she was all caught up in this 'new woman' thing. She thought she had to sleep with every male grad student on campus to prove she was free." *That was why he hadn't pushed their relationship into something heavier. He'd been scared of being burned again.* "But almost from the beginning, I think, I knew you were different. That was animal lust," he derided good-humoredly. "This is real."

Later she'd tell him about Glenn, Anne promised herself. Not tonight.

181

Fourteen

AT Glenn's insistence, and knowing it was the smart thing to do, Felicia agreed to participate in the traditional Christmas at the Squaw Valley house. But she was annoyed at the way he was catering to Doug.

"Felicia, we have to play the game," he countered when she reproached him. "The old boy made me head of Accounting. We owe him."

"You're not being paid what Leon was paid," she shot back. "Not even a quarter of what Leon had been drawing in salary."

"It's a start." Glenn was smug. "A hell of lot more than I was earning as a junior accountant."

"We'll trade in the Dual-Ghia for a red Ferrari," she decided.

"Let's keep the Dual-Ghia and buy a second car," he said. He'd junked his 1954 Chevie as being out of line with his new position.

"One car," she said sweetly. Better not let Glenn get overgreedy.

Felicia and Glenn flew to Mexico City to celebrate the arrival of 1965 at a houseparty given in a friend's villa. Back at the office Felicia was irritated when Doug refused to allow her to take off a week at the end of the month to accompany Jackie to Washington, D.C. Jackie was in pursuit of the son of a Midwest congressman. Felicia stalked out of Doug's office in rage and returned to her own to phone her friend.

"Let's meet for lunch." Jackie offered her usual panacea. "Doug can't stop you from that."

"Let's go to the Fleur de Lys," Felicia said. "I have a mad yen for cucumber soup. Theirs is great."

"Pick you up at one?"

"I'll be downstairs waiting." Felicia put down the phone. God, she was sleepy. They'd done a lot of partying down in Mexico City, but lack of sleep had never bothered her before. Glenn was the one who said he wasn't worth a damn at the office if he didn't have at least seven hours' sleep.

She mentally reviewed her encounter with Doug earlier that morning. He had been downright furious that she'd asked to take a week off. Glenn had warned her against asking. But damn it, she wasn't one of the support staff, with vacation days doled out according to years of employment. Executive status came with privileges. But she was wary of being on bad terms with Doug.

Go talk to him, instinct ordered. Mend fences. She pushed back her chair and rose to her feet. She needed Doug on her side. She suspected he had a sneaking affection for Anne, though he made a point of being impartial in their training sessions. If anything, she recalled with a flicker of complacency, he favors *my* way of thinking.

She'd talk to him about the industry's plans for setting up lobbyists in Washington. He was gung-ho to see the Wilderness Act manipulated to help the timbermen. Timber *people*, she silently corrected herself.

Shortly past one she was sitting with Jackie at a candle-topped table at the Fleur de Lys. They ordered cold cucumber soup and chicken champagne. She sipped at a glass of white wine, served in fragile crystal, and fought against sleepiness.

"I'm dying for that cucumber soup," she said restlessly, drumming on the table with one extravagantly long, scarlet fingernail. "You'd think it'd be ready to be served immediately."

"Felicia, the waiter just left the table," Jackie scolded. "Sweetie," she asked with an air of sudden suspicion, "you're not pregnant, are you? You're acting just like Eleanor." Her brother Paul had married Eleanor Lansing at a splashy wedding last April.

Felicia sat motionless, in shock.

"Oh God, Jackie!"

"You're late," Jackie guessed.

"A week or two. But that happens now and then. We're always so careful." She hesitated—remembering a night when they'd both been drinking, and she'd been too lazy to get out of bed after they'd made love.

"You ought to go on the Pill," Jackie said. "I feel so free now."

"I'll call my gynecologist." *God, how could we have been so stupid!* "I'll take the test. Let me phone her right now—"

"After lunch," Jackie stipulated. "Tell her she has to see you today. All you do for the pregnancy test is pee in a paper cup and she sends it to a lab."

Felicia said nothing to Glenn about her suspicions. She was relieved when he reported that he was staying late at the office, along with others in the accounting staff, to track down some error in figures sent down from the Eureka mill.

"When we're through, I'll call the house to see if Walter's free to pick me up with the limo." A faint reproach was in his voice because she had not agreed to their buying a second car. "If he's busy, I'll phone for a cab."

When Glenn had not come home by eleven, Felicia went to bed. She pretended to be asleep when Glenn finally slid under the blankets. She was in no mood for play tonight. Anyhow, he was so damn fast most of the time he left her at the starting gate. But still he managed to get her pregnant, she thought bitterly.

At ten the following morning her gynecologist phoned.

"The test was positive," she told Felicia. "Congratulations. I'll transfer you to my secretary. She'll set up an appointment for you."

184

Again Felicia met Jackie for lunch. Again at the Fleur de Lys because of her continuing yen for cold cucumber soup.

"Jackie, I can't believe it!" she reiterated for the dozenth time since they sat down. "One lousy time I don't get out of bed afterward, and I'm caught."

"It's an acceptable reason to take a year off from the office," Jackie consoled. "It's an act of God—you're not breaking the will."

"I'm not taking off a year." Felicia glared at her. "I'd come back and find that little bitch Anne in the driver's seat."

"So you'll go to some private little sanitarium for a D and C," Jackie said. "Voilà, no more baby."

"I won't have another abortion," Felicia whispered heatedly.

Jackie stared at her in astonishment.

"You never told me you'd had an abortion. We're so close and you never told me?"

"I never even wanted to talk about it. Something went wrong—I nearly died."

"When?" Jackie probed.

"My second year at Radcliffe. When you stayed home and played the postdebutante scene."

"That time when you were raped by that African prince? You never told me you were pregnant by him!"

"I wasn't," Felicia brushed this aside. "I was making it with three other students at Harvard. I set him up for cover."

"How?" Jackie was enthralled.

"I had that apartment in Cambridge, remember?" One of Naomi's little presents. "I invited him up for a drink one Friday night. Then in the middle of making love I started to yell that I was being raped. All of a sudden people were breaking down the door. He didn't know what hit him."

"Felicia, did he go to jail?" Her eyes reflected a blend of admiration and censure.

"Of course not," Felicia shrugged. "He had diplomatic immunity. But he did have to leave school."

"Then you had the abortion."

"And I was able to cut out of school." Her eyes glittered in remembered triumph. She had loathed the college scene, but Naomi kept insisting she earn a degree. Naomi had resented her sister's going off to Cornell while she'd stayed home. Naomi meant for Felicia to be the first woman on their side of the family to go to college. "Naomi sent me to Europe for six months after the abortion. To help me forget," she drawled. "She agreed that Europe would be better for me than therapy." Naomi considered therapy a sign of weakness.

"That was the summer I met you in Greece," Jackie remembered. "You said you'd been having a ball."

"Sensational!" Felicia recalled. "But I won't take a chance on another abortion." Her mind was charging ahead. Maybe her pregnancy wasn't such a bad deal after all. It would impress Doug with her maturity. She wasn't a kid anymore. "I'll have a fantastic maternity wardrobe," she went on. "Maybe by Oleg Cassini. Even if we have to borrow at the bank. Being pregnant isn't going to change my style, Jackie. And it might prove a terrific asset. Doug has such an obsession for 'family.' "

Felicia waited until they were home from Paul and Eleanor's dinner party and up in their bedroom before she told Glenn that she was pregnant. Her earlier acceptance of the situation had been infiltrated by doubts.

"You're sure?" he asked after an incredulous gasp.

"I'm sure," she said, her laughter brittle. "And I know just when it happened." Her voice crackled with reproach. "That night after the costume ball at the Burlingame Country Club. You drank too much."

"Not too much to get it up," he flared.

"Did you have to get me pregnant?" she lashed back. "That's all I need right now!"

"I figured you'd take care of yourself."

"So once I was careless. Why is it always the woman who has to 'take precautions'?"

"Because you always have." He was wary now, weighing

his new situation, Felicia surmised. Feeling their marriage on stronger ground now that she was pregnant. "Look, baby—" He paused as she flinched. "Felicia, honey," he substituted, "this means you have a legitimate excuse to take a year or so off from the office. Doug can't say you're breaking the will. He . . ."

"No!" she lashed at him. "Nothing's changing about the office. I'll work up to the last minute, be back at my desk two weeks after." She squinted in thought for a moment. "I need some sharp angle for the lobbying in Washington. Work on it. I want to take it with me to the evening meeting with Doug next week."

Anne was surprised when Felicia and Glenn appeared at the dinner table on a Sunday evening along with Eva, back from visiting friends in Palm Springs. She was surprised again when Edwina arrived as they were settling in the library for after-dinner coffee.

"Your father's off at his club for some business conference," Edwina told Felicia. Her voice was pitched high. "But since you said it was important, I came right over."

Edwina's eyes moved from Felicia to Anne and on to Doug. Edwina was scared to death either Felicia or she was walking out of Miller Timber, Anne surmised. *Why* had Felicia brought her mother here?

"Glenn and I have marvelous news." Felicia reached for Glenn's hand. "I just wish Naomi were here to hear it." Her uncharacteristic sweetness set off warning signals in Anne's mind. "I'm pregnant."

"Oh God, Felicia!" Eva chided. "You'll make me a great-grandmother!"

"You're sure about this?" Edwina asked after a moment.

"Quite sure," Felicia laughed. "The rabbit died."

"Congratulations," Anne said because nobody else seemed prepared to make the routine conversation. "I don't suppose the rabbit told you whether it's a boy or a girl? Before it died, of course."

"We'll take pot luck," Felicia murmured. A glint of satisfaction was in her eyes, as though this were some kind of victory over her, Anne thought. "Glenn says it's what I need to make me a totally mature human being."

Why did she suddenly feel so shaken, Anne reproached herself. *She was over Glenn.* At least, she'd thought she was. But he looked at her now with that strangely unhappy smile, and something happened inside her. She wasn't in love with Glenn, she told herself. He was a kind of obsession.

These months ahead were going to be awful. To live under the same roof with Felicia when she was carrying Glenn's baby. She was conscious of an overpowering sense of loss. That might have been their baby.

"Darling, you don't mean you're going to remain in the business?" Edwina asked after Felicia explained that her pregnancy would make only a ripple in her work schedule. Yet Anne sensed Edwina's relief that Naomi's will would remain in force. "At least, take off a year—" Edwina turned to Douglas. "Felicia can do that, can't she?"

"If she wishes," Doug said, but it was clear he didn't anticipate this.

"I'll probably go into labor in the middle of a business conference," Felicia predicted. "Women today manage to have children without sacrificing their careers."

This was the first time Felicia had verbally acknowledged she was pursuing a career. Normally she joked about "the prison sentence Naomi dumped on me."

Anne waited until she and Shirley went out to lunch the next day to tell her about Felicia's pregnancy.

"Women like Felicia have children the way they might pick up a kitten at a pet shop." Shirley never made a secret of her hostility toward Felicia and her ilk. "Her major participation will be trotting around with a big belly. The minute she drops the kid, there'll be nursemaids to do all the dirty work. To do all the loving," she added. "From what Joe Col-

188

ton tells me, the only real loving Felicia received was from Naomi Miller—and that was in bursts, when it was convenient. Every time Felicia came home from boarding school, Naomi would bring her into the office to show her off."

"But not Todd?" Anne asked curiously.

"You must know by now—Felicia and Todd are as different as two siblings can be."

"Like Naomi and my grandmother," Anne said softly.

"Todd's a good kid. I don't know how he ever landed in that family." Shirley's face softened. "When I think of the way Todd and Felicia were raised and I remember the love I share with Gerry, I know we're far richer in the ways that count than those two have ever been. When Gerry puts her little arms around my neck and hugs me, I feel richer than Naomi Miller."

"I can't wait for the two-year residency clause in the will to be over and I can move out of the house."

"Felicia won't ever move out," Shirley said with a wise little smile. "Not until Doug dies and the Museum inherits the property. And I'll bet you she'll try to buy the house from the museum. She wants to be Naomi Miller in every way."

Anne cherished her relationship with Josh. It was something they both needed, she rationalized, and neither wished for any permanent commitment. In truth, she told herself in a contemplative interlude, she had far more in common with Josh than she had ever had with Glenn.

Sex with Josh was terrific. Because she'd never been with another man? No, she rejected that. She wasn't some naive little kid. Sex had been a favorite dorm topic. Slivers of earnest, late-night, dorm talk replayed in her mind: *"Look, I don't want to sleep with just one man in my lifetime. How dull!" "I love being with Ed—but why do we have to fuck every night?" "Men are all alike. They ball you and go to sleep. I like to talk afterward."*

Josh was special. She'd known that right away. They seemed to recognize each other's moods. There was nothing awkward or embarrassing with him. Josh was important in her life. *Then why couldn't she push Glenn out of her mind?*

She had dinner most nights now with Josh rather than at the house. Felicia and Glenn were making a habit of being home for dinner frequently these days. It was as though they were trying to convince Doug that Felicia had put her jet-set life-style behind her.

Table talk always revolved around business. Felicia and Glenn lined up with Doug against Anne in what he referred to as the "new wilderness hysteria." To the timber barons the new Wilderness Act was a knife at their throats.

"But Congress *has* kept an eye on our interests," Felicia intervened in a heated dinner conversation between Doug and Anne. "And the Forest Service is making damn sure the best timber areas are not included in what's being set aside as 'wilderness areas'," Glenn pointed out.

"I don't like it." Doug echoed most timber leaders. "The Wilderness Act puts us in chains. If something isn't done, we'll be seeing a timber famine. While millions of board feet will be rotting."

The conservationists were proclaiming victory, Anne thought tiredly, but the Forest Service was out there fighting the timber industry battles—blatantly ignoring Congress.

Some nights Anne met Josh and they had dinner at a cafeteria, then—with the lights flickering across the bay—walked to the redwood shingled house he shared with Stu. Other nights—when Josh knew they'd have the house to themselves—they'd cook dinner there and go to his room to make love. Often she wished she didn't have to return to the mansion on Washington Street, where Glenn and Felicia shared a room only thirty feet away. Josh was a hundred times the man Glenn was. Why did she still hurt at unexpected intervals?

By the end of her third month Felicia was already into her glamorous and concealing Oleg Cassini wardrobe. She asked for no concessions because of her condition, Anne conceded—and for this Doug accorded her new respect. After all, Felicia was his grandniece. His sister's grandchild. He might have approved of her in the past, but Doug was so strong for family. And he must understand by now that Felicia was as bulldog-determined as she not to upset Naomi's will.

Anne was less tense about the problems at Berkeley. A lot of changes had taken place on the campus. At least on the surface, Anne amended her thought. Josh was not sure that peace would remain, though the atmosphere was incredibly relaxed now. Students were allowed to take part in political activity on campus. They could recruit, raise funds, debate about almost any political subject. Right now the hot topic was the presence of Americans in Vietnam.

On this brisk March afternoon Anne stood at a window of her office and gazed out at the city, emerging from the fog that had imprisoned it for much of the day.

"You staying late?" Shirley asked from the doorway.

"Not tonight," Anne said firmly. "I'm leaving in twenty minutes. I'm meeting Josh for dinner." For the past three nights Doug had asked her to be his hostess while he entertained visiting executives from the Washington and Oregon mills at the house. Except for the jet set, upper-crust San Franciscans preferred to entertain in their homes rather than at restaurants.

"Have fun," Shirley said. Her smile was sympathetic. She knew the business dinners had been exhausting. "A night off from school."

As she left to meet Josh at Kan's, she reminded herself that she was to tell him she'd just decided to move up her scheduled one-week vacation. She'd leave in ten days instead of waiting for mid-April. She needed to talk to Dad about what was happening out here with the timber people. She'd been disturbed by all the dinner talk with the Washington and Oregon executives about how the company could circumvent the Wilderness Act.

Wending her way through the evening crowds, she spied the headline of the evening *Examiner*. Thirty-five hundred

191

marines had landed in South Vietnam. Josh would be upset about that.

Over lemon chicken Anne and Josh discussed the Vietnam situation.

"It was bad enough that twenty-three thousand Americans are serving as advisors in South Vietnam. Now we have thirty-five hundred marines there. Not advisors," he railed. "They're combat troops."

"Thank God, you've passed your twenty-sixth birthday," she said softly. "You're not subject to the draft anymore."

"That's what Mom said," he chuckled, then grew somber. "But Bert can be called up. Not while he's in school. But this thing won't go away in a few months."

"I decided this morning to push my vacation ahead," Anne told him. "I'll leave in ten days."

"The rat race is getting to you." His smile was compassionate. He knew every small detail about her life now. "All this business about working around the Wilderness Act."

"My father respects the Wilderness Act. Why can't the big corporations do the same?" But she knew the answer. Their insatiable greed for money.

"They've clear-cut up and down the Pacific Coast," Josh said contemptuously, quoting Stu, she was sure. "Now they want to massacre the national forests."

"Miller Timber doesn't clear-cut," Anne said defensively. "Only to a small extent in the Douglas fir forests because they don't grow well in the shade of taller trees. We don't clear-cut our redwoods." Lazarus Timber did some minor clear-cutting—loblolly pine needed sunshine, too, for growth.

"Oh, come on, Annie," Josh jeered. "Miller is no different from the other biggies. You've flown up in that area often enough—you must have seen for yourself."

"I haven't seen anything," she insisted.

"What do you do when you climb aboard a Miller plane?" he demanded. "Put on blinders?"

"Most times I have a thick report to read before we reach the airport," she told him. "I read my way from one airport

192

to the next. But Doug's told me that Miller doesn't clear-cut. We've established tree farms in three states," she pointed out with pride. But Doug was fighting to have the cut in the national forests upped as high as possible. She remembered the stream of correspondence that went out to their congressmen.

"You believe Miller doesn't clear-cut?" Josh challenged, clearly skeptical.

"Yes! And I know—I've seen the diagrams—that we have tracts that won't be touched for another fifty years and some for a hundred years. Does that sound like the kind of planning that would allow clear-cutting?" she demanded.

Josh squinted in thought for a moment.

"Maybe I should just keep my mouth shut—"

"No, say what you want to say," Anne prodded.

"Stu's father has an air taxi service. Stu has a pilot's license—he can take us up. Anne, I think you ought to go up and see what's happening to Miller forests. Maybe I'm overly suspicious; but from what Stu says, Miller is no different from the others. His brother with the Forest Service says as much."

"All right," Anne said after a moment. "Let's go up and see."

On Saturday afternoon Stu took Anne and Josh up in one of his father's air taxis. Before taking off Anne had given him the specific location of Miller forestland within an hour's flying time of San Francisco. Flying north they avoided discussing forestland and talked about the situation on the Berkeley campus until Stu tersely interrupted Josh.

"Right below us, Anne. According to your map that's Miller property. I'm going down closer."

Sick with shock Anne gazed down at the bald patches that stretched for endless acres. Not her grandmother's biologically approved quarter of an acre to ten. Total devastation.

"It looks like the back of a mangy dog," Josh said in distaste.

"An ugly patchwork quilt," Anne described it and closed her eyes for a moment as though to wipe away its painful impact.

"That's not logging," Stu told them. "It's timber mining. First cousin to strip mining. To hell with the environment. Get the money and run."

"I've seen enough. Let's go back." Anne's throat tightened with rage. She had believed Doug when he said they were not clear-cutting.

"My father would kill me if he knew I'd taken you up today to see how Miller Timber handles its forestland," Josh said while he ladled tomato and mushroom sauce over mounds of spaghetti. "You know how loyal he is to Naomi Miller."

"Let's don't tell him," Anne said, bringing warmed-up sourdough bread to the table. They were alone in the house; Stu had gone off for the weekend. "And I know without seeing," she conceded grimly, "that what you showed me must be repeated on the hundreds of thousands of acres Miller owns in three states." How naive of her to have believed Doug!

"Naomi Miller long ago convinced Dad that she knew everything there was to know about the timber business. Her word was gospel. If she said they were managing their forests properly, then it had to be that way." Josh carried the saucepan to the range, then returned to sit at the table.

"My grandmother used to talk with such pain about the way the timber people slaughtered our forests through the years. She saw this from the time she was a little girl living in Michigan. She said that President Roosevelt—through the CCC—blessed the South with its second forests."

"Why just the South?" Josh asked curiously.

"The South has fast-growing species." Anne glowed with a messianic zeal. "The loblolly and slash pines—and the shortleaf—can mature in only thirty years. My grandmother predicted just before she died that within the next fifteen years the South would emerge as the largest producer of softwood sawtimber in the country."

"And here you are in California, where it takes a Douglas

fir a century to mature and redwoods a lot of centuries," he joshed, but his eyes were sympathetic.

"My instinct—after what I saw today—is to say that I want no part of Miller Timber. Yet what would I accomplish by walking out? I'm saving Lazarus Timber by working for Naomi Miller. In a little less than six years the banks will be paid off. Dad can begin to expand, the way my grandmother had hoped. And that's why I have to stay," she summed up with frustration and sighed. "Naomi may be dead, but she lives in Doug. How am I to turn him around?"

"I don't know," Josh acknowledged. "She's molded him in her image."

"But there's another Doug, too," Anne continued. "A man who's genuinely upset about the polluting of our lakes and rivers. A man who's warm and sensitive—"

"The only way to turn Doug around is by looking at the bottom line. What is Miller Timber losing in the long haul by clear-cutting?"

"Josh, the timber barons don't care about the long haul. Miller Timber isn't giving any serious consideration to reseeding or replanting. Much of the land may never heal sufficiently for that. I'd guess," Anne said bitterly, "that Doug will quote Naomi Miller saying that clear-cutting is economically advisable—and nothing else counts."

"You don't have to stay with the company," Josh told her. "You can survive without Naomi Miller's money."

"I have to stay, Josh," she reiterated. "I've felt guilty ever since graduation because I wasn't committed the way my friends at school are committed. But Josh, I *am* committed in another direction. I'm committed to do whatever I can to help save our forests."

"God knows, that's important enough on its own," Josh said somberly. "But Stu rails about how clear-cutting is causing serious soil erosion. How it's contaminating the forest watersheds that supply water to hundreds of towns. It changes courses of streams, chokes their water with silt."

"What happens when the forests are gone?" Anne demanded. "We know the cut far exceeds the growth. With sustained-yield logging the timber industry had a future. What happens when the forests are gone?" she repeated.

Anne talked with quiet intensity through much of the evening about the devastation inflicted on the forests for the past hundred-fifty years. She took pride in the knowledge that clear-cutting was not common in the South. Josh listened with a genuine interest and respect that was a pain-easing balm to her.

"Do you have to go home tonight?" he asked when they headed upstairs to his bedroom. "Stu won't be back until tomorrow night—"

"I can stay," she said after a moment of inner debate, relishing Josh's closeness. "Provided you can loan me pajamas." She strived for lightness.

"Annie, you won't need pajamas," he chuckled. "And I've got a spare toothbrush up there on the bathroom shelf."

"Then I'm staying." It was Josh who made life bearable for her in San Francisco, she suddenly realized.

Anne lay in the curve of Josh's arm while they watched a late movie on the tiny TV set atop his bedroom dresser. She felt cherished and protected, isolated from the rat race of daily life at Miller Timber.

"Feel like a mug of hot apple cider?" Josh asked at the commercial break.

"I'll fix it," Anne offered.

"No, you stay here. I relish the image of you in my bed."

"No snapshots," she warned laughingly.

He paused beside the bed. "I wish you could be here on a permanent basis." His eyes were wistful. "I wish we could spend the rest of our lives together starting right now. But God knows when I'll be able to support a wife."

All at once Anne's heart was pounding. With Josh she could survive anything. She could put Glenn forever behind her.

"Josh, you talk like a fifties man," she scolded. "Today's

196

young wives are partners. They carry their own share of the load."

Their eyes clung in mutual exhilaration.

"Annie, are you proposing to me?" he asked.

"You might say that." Her smile was dazzling.

"Then I accept!" He dropped to the edge of the bed to pull her into his arms.

"We'll have to live at the Washington Street house until I finish my term there," she warned and he groaned.

"Rough, but I can handle that."

"Come home with me to Belleville." Her face glowed with anticipation. "The school will let you take a week off. We'll have a civil ceremony here before we go, and then a religious ceremony at home. Your parents and Bert can go with us to City Hall. My parents will be there when the rabbi marries us in our living room."

"Oh God, you're making me respectable in the eyes of my mother and father," Josh chuckled. "Dad thinks you're a great little chick. He and Mother will figure 'once Josh is married, he'll forget all his crazy ideas.' "

"Don't," she admonished. "I like your crazy ideas."

Fifteen

FIGHTING guilt that she had said nothing to her parents about Josh until now, Anne phoned home to tell them about her change in vacation schedule and that she and Josh would be married while they were in Belleville. She was relieved that, as usual, her mother was not home when she called.

"Dad, you'll like Josh," she concluded earnestly, knowing she'd bowled him over with this sudden marriage announcement. "He's somebody special." She knew he was pleased that Josh was Jewish.

"Darling, if you love him, then we'll love him," her father said, his voice deep with emotion. "But let's don't tell your mother you've already had a civil ceremony. You know how she is."

"How will I explain our not getting a license and all?" Anne asked in sudden anxiety.

"Annie, she'll never think to ask. Just say you've come home to get married." Her father chuckled. "Or I'll be hearing for the next year about your being married without her being present."

"Make Mother understand," she pleaded, "that we want just a simple ceremony at home. Nobody there except you and Mother. And Mary Lou, of course," she added shakily. "It wouldn't be legal without her there. Afterward Mother can send an item in to the newspapers."

"I'll call Rabbi Kahn right away." Twenty-six years ago

Rabbi Kahn had married Anne's parents. "And Mary Lou's first question—after she cries a little about her baby getting married," he chuckled, "will be, 'what kind of wedding cake shall I make?'"

"Chocolate-pecan-bourbon—the kind she always makes for your wedding anniversary." But their marriage, Anne promised herself, would be different from her parents'. "Daddy, I'm sorry I didn't tell you earlier about Josh—" She slipped unconsciously into the childhood "Daddy." *Thank God, she'd never told him about Glenn.* "It's just that life's so hectic out here."

"I know, baby," he consoled. "And I can't wait to meet Josh. To use an old cliché, I'm not losing a daughter—I'm gaining a son."

Josh's parents rejected the prospect of an impersonal City Hall wedding.

"Oh no," Tess Blumberg tenderly reproached. "Your wedding day should be a beautiful memory. How can that happen in a two-minute ceremony in a municipal office?"

"We'll have a religious ceremony down in Belleville," Anne explained and hesitated, self-conscious at subterfuge. "My mother would be terribly upset if she knew I'd been married away from home. We'll tell my father, but not my mother, about the ceremony up here."

"Nobody will know if you're married in our house by a judge. We'll say nothing to the aunts and uncles and cousins until you've had a religious ceremony," she promised ebulliently. "There'll just be Artie and me and Bert. But you'll have pleasant memories."

On the Saturday evening before their departure for Georgia, Anne and Josh arrived at his parents' Tudor house in Burlingame for the civil ceremony to be performed in the charming, flower-banked living room. The elegance of the house and furnishings were a testament to Arthur Blumberg's success, though here was not the luxury enjoyed by Bruce and Leon and their wives in adjacent Hillsborough.

Moments later Shirley and Gerry arrived, simultaneously

with Stu Lerman, the three of them the sole guests outside of immediate family.

"I feel so guilty," Anne whispered to Shirley. "Being married here first."

"It's practical," Shirley reminded her. "You have all that business about getting a license taken care of here. Your father will understand—and your mother won't know." She reached to squeeze Anne's hand. "You look beautiful, Annie. If I didn't know you'd laugh at me, I'd probably be crying."

"Don't you dare." Anne reached to hug her. Shirley was the sister she'd never had.

The brief ceremony was performed by a distinguished judge who had known Josh since he was born. After they'd been pronounced husband and wife, Anne lifted her face to Josh with an air of happy incredulity. A few words, just like that, and she was Josh's wife.

Tess prodded everyone into the formal dining room, the area dominated by a magnificent crystal chandelier that hung over a damask-covered table. Anne relished the warmth that ricocheted about the room. There was a beautiful love in this family. Already she felt enveloped in that love.

Anne was grateful that neither Tess nor Artie Blumberg showed any awareness that their older son was marrying into prospective great wealth. At introspective moments she considered that her relationship to Artie might in the future be reflected in his attitudes toward Miller Timber. She was convinced that this would cause considerable annoyance in Felicia. But she knew, too, that for over thirty years he had been loyal to Naomi Miller—and she doubted that his being her father-in-law would make any concrete difference in that loyalty.

"Gerry looks adorable in that plaid taffeta dress and white lace tights," Anne said affectionately of Shirley's pixie daughter who was carrying on ebullient conversation with Josh.

"And her mother looks obese," Shirley sighed.

"Not obese," Anne contradicted. "But you'd be smart to forget the late-night ice cream binges."

"My substitute for sex," Shirley chuckled. "Unfortunately it shows."

"You ought to circulate more," Anne reproached. She worried about Shirley's contempt for men. "You're young and attractive—you could find yourself an interesting man."

"Oh God," Shirley clucked. "There's nothing like a new bride to push her friends into marriage. For me once was enough."

Anne and Josh spent their wedding night in the bridal suite at the elegant, history-drenched Palace Hotel—now the Sheraton Palace, which socialite San Franciscans preferred to ignore.

"The last time I was in the Palace," Josh reminisced, "was at a demonstration with a thousand other Berkeley students. I carried a sign that said 'Jim Crow Must Go.'"

"It's all right," Anne laughed. "The hotel signed a no-bias hiring pact."

"I suppose I'll have to sleep in a guest room at your parents' house," he teased. "Since your mother doesn't know we're married."

"I'll leave my door open," she laughed. "And drop sleeping pills in Dad and Mother's coffee."

They left on an early morning flight for Belleville. On this trip home Anne had waived the usual limousine waiting at Hartsfield in Atlanta. Instead, her father was there to pick them up. She sensed an instant rapport between Josh and her father. She sat between them on the front seat of the family car and listened with pleasure while they discussed President Johnson's televised address to the joint session of Congress. He'd asked for quick passage of legislation to bar discrimination against citizens trying to register to vote.

"Will you have problems with that in Belleville?" Josh asked seriously.

"Oh, we have some hotheads in town," Kevin told him, "but most people will respect the law. Anne told you, didn't she," he asked with pride, "that we're already integrating our schools here?"

Her mother was waiting for them at the house, along with a beaming Mary Lou. Anne dutifully kissed her mother, was swept up in a warm embrace by Mary Lou, then introduced Josh to the two women. After introductions Mary Lou—clearly approving of Josh—hurried out to the kitchen to prepare to serve dinner.

Her mother was polite and charming to Josh, yet Anne read the reproach in her eyes. She'd never given up hope that "darling Ted" would become her son-in-law.

"I don't know why we have to be so secretive about this wedding," Denise scolded. "It seems to me we should have had at least a small reception for close friends."

"I just want family," Anne insisted. "We'll spend our wedding night at the Biltmore in Atlanta and then fly right back to San Francisco."

"It just doesn't seem natural," Denise began but Kevin cut her off.

"Rabbi Kahn scheduled the ceremony for just after sundown on Saturday," he told Anne and Josh.

"I had Mary Lou press my wedding dress just in case you wanted to wear it, Anne," Denise said sweetly. "But I declare, I don't think it'll fit. I've always had such a tiny waist."

"I thought I'd wear Grandma's wedding dress." Anne fought off a sense of suffocation. Why did her mother always make her feel this way? She turned to Josh. "It's been hanging in my closet since I was sixteen. Grandma gave it to me then, hoping one day I'd wear it."

"You can't wear that old thing." Denise grimaced in distaste. "It's probably yellow with age. There's no way Mary Lou could bleach it after all these years."

"I'll wear it," Anne insisted. "Grandma would have liked that."

Each day Anne invented side trips to take Josh and herself away from the house for hours. They drove down to FDR's Little White House near Warm Springs and to Fort Benning on the outskirts of Columbus. They explored the Lazarus timberland and had a picnic beneath the pines.

On Saturday afternoon the house was permeated by tantalizing aromas that emanated from the kitchen. Mary Lou dashed ecstatically between the kitchen and Anne's bedroom, where Anne was dressing for her wedding. The dress that Rae Sachs wore the day she became Rae Lazarus lay across the canopied bed.

Earlier Denise had fluttered about the living room with an air of martyrdom, placing vases of fragrant, showy white star magnolias and arrangements of vari-colored crocuses. Anne knew her mother resented being deprived of the opportunity to play "the beautiful mother of the bride" before a vast assemblage. She had insisted that Rabbi Kahn's wife—who thirty years ago had abandoned a career as a pianist for marriage—be asked to play during the ceremony. The baby grand that sat at one side of the living room had been added to the furnishings years ago when Denise had nurtured visions of herself as a concert pianist, though these visions had been short-lived.

With dusk settling over the town—a balmy breeze bringing the fragrant scent of early spring flowers into her bedroom—Anne stood before the mirrored door of her closet and inspected her reflection. She felt poignantly close to her grandmother. Rae Lazarus's wedding gown—instep-length white silk with lace overskirt and a heart-shaped neckline—fit as though it had been custom-designed for Anne. About her throat she wore her grandmother's cameo on a narrow, white velvet ribbon.

The sounds downstairs told her that Rabbi Kahn and his wife had arrived. She reached for the ivory prayer book that her grandmother had carried at her own wedding but which her mother had considered "not chic." Theirs would be a fine marriage, Anne promised. The kind of marriage her grandparents had shared.

As prearranged, Mary Lou stood in the hallway to alert the rabbi's wife to begin the music. Her face was luminous as Anne appeared at the head of the stairs ready to descend.

"That's my beautiful baby," Mary Lou crooned, hugging

Anne in her capacious embrace but managing at the same time to wave a hand to signal for the music to begin.

Anne hesitated for a moment as the first strains of "Oh Promise Me" filled the living room. How serious Josh was, standing there at the red velvet *chupah*—the wedding canopy that is part of Jewish tradition. Her parents formed a tiny aisle. Unexpectedly she felt the sting of tears.

She walked slowly to the *chupah,* carrying her grandmother's ivory prayer book and a single white rose. They were married by warm and frankly sentimental Rabbi Kahn in a service from which the word "obey" had been eliminated—in compliance with the new feminist thinking.

When Anne turned to receive her father's embrace, she saw the tears of pleasure in his eyes. But he was wishing—as was she—that Rae Lazarus had been here to see her only grandchild married.

The Miller limousine, with Walter at the wheel, was waiting for Anne and Josh when they emerged from the San Francisco airport terminal. Anne had phoned Doug after the ceremony and told him about her marriage. He had not seemed truly surprised. She suspected Josh's father, who was sworn to secrecy, had given him the news. But he was pleased. He'd known she was seeing Josh and he was fond of all the Blumbergs.

"You and Josh stay at the company's suite at the Mark Hopkins for a week. And I promise, no evening meetings until you're back home."

After a very early continental breakfast in their suite at the Mark Hopkins on Monday morning, Josh drove Anne to the Miller house so that she could pack a valise to see her through the week.

"You go on," she encouraged Josh after a glance at her watch. "I'll ride to the office with Doug."

She crossed the sidewalk to the house with an air of defiant pleasure. The next time she came here, Josh would be with her. It wouldn't be Anne Forrest against the family any longer. Anne and Josh. Her face softened as she waited for one of the servants to open the door. How understanding of Josh's father to explain that they could spend weekends away from the house without upsetting the will. Thank God, in December they could move out—her two-year residency would be over.

In the hallway Mrs. Morrison greeted her with unexpected warmth. Anne was relieved that Doug had obviously told the others. "It'll be nice to have a pleasant young man in the house," Mrs. Morrison said. Her eyes glinted with dry humor. "A young man other than Mr. Rogers and Adrian." At intervals, Anne knew, Adrian had taken up residence here when his parents were off in Europe or the Far East.

While Anne packed a valise, she heard Doug in conversation with Walter in the hall. Doug was going downstairs for breakfast. That meant Felicia and Glenn would not be down for at least forty minutes. She was in no rush to encounter either of them.

She brought her valise downstairs, left it in the foyer, and went to join Doug for coffee in the breakfast room. After brief conversation about the Belleville wedding, Doug turned to business.

"You and I and Felicia will have a long lunch in my office," he told Anne.

"At noon?" she asked, disappointed that she wouldn't be able to have lunch with Shirley her first day back at the office.

"Noon sharp," he confirmed.

Anne was sitting at her desk, absorbed in a report from the Oregon mill when Shirley charged into the office with the usual mugs of coffee in tow.

"Good morning, Mrs. Blumberg," Shirley effervesced.

"It's still Forrest," Anne shot back with an impish smile. "During business hours, anyway." Like Felicia she subscribed to the new rule that said a young woman could retain her single name.

"You look rested," Shirley said, dropping into a chair before Anne's desk and setting down the two mugs. "Gerry's still euphoric at being allowed to attend the wedding and the dinner afterward. I think she's secretly in love with Josh."

"Only because he sneaked her a second piece of wedding cake. How's my foster niece behaving herself?"

"I love her madly, but Gerry's like every other kid over the age of five. They're all hard of hearing—except when they want to hear."

"I doubt that Felicia will ever even notice." Anne's exuberance ebbed away. "How is the coheiress?"

"As bitchy as ever. God, what she spent on her maternity wardrobe could support a family of four for a year. But I never thought she'd hang on to the job this way." A reluctant respect crept into Shirley's voice.

"Naomi Miller knew the power of money." Anne stirred restlessly. "The old lady is still ruling from the grave."

Normally Doug allowed himself only a Spartan lunch. On those occasions when he summoned Anne and Felicia together to an office luncheon, he ordered with consummate taste from Bardelli's. He was arranging the dishes on a small table kept in his office suite for such purposes when Anne arrived. Moments later Felicia sauntered into the inner office.

"Hi." No congratulations to Anne on her recent marriage, though Doug had told the family. "I've spent the morning going over those studies about Secretary of Interior Udall's trying to bulldoze that bill through Congress."

"What bill?" Anne asked.

"A bill to establish a Redwood National Park." Doug shuffled papers on his desk, avoiding Anne's eyes.

"But that's a safeguard for the future." Anne tensed. "Some of our redwoods must be protected."

"The bill will cut off redwood auctions," Felicia shot back. "Everybody in the timber industry will suffer!" She turned to Doug. "I think you're absolutely right. We must have our own lobbyist in Washington."

"What about The American Forest Institute?" She had

talked privately with Josh and Stu on endless occasions about the efforts to put through a Redwood National Park. Stu's impassioned voice echoed in her mind: *"We can't afford to wait fifteen or twenty years to get that bill through. It has to be fast—while we still have stands of redwoods left!"* "Don't they handle the industry lobbying?"

"We need more personal input," Doug said while they seated themselves at the white linen-covered table. "Weyerhaeuser, Diamond International, St. Regis, Georgia-Pacific—they have their own people in D.C. We all need to be in there pushing our point of view to Congress."

"What are we doing about it?" Felicia demanded while she dug into Bardelli's famous cold beef salad.

"I've talked with Arthur Blumberg. It's not enough to hire lobbyists at regular intervals. We need a permanent man—" He paused, smiled in humorous apology at Felicia, then Anne. "We need a permanent *person* in D.C. to express our views. I'm flying out next week to set up an office. Arthur will go with me. He has excellent contacts in the capital. It's a bad time for me to be away from the city, but it's essential."

"Doug, let me go in your stead," Felicia said with studied casualness.

"Now?" Doug was startled.

"The baby won't be born for months. And I have special qualifications for this deal. Jackie's staying at her fiancé's house in Georgetown right now. She's marrying Congressman Tyler's younger son late next month." Anne saw Doug's instant interest. "I'll meet a lot of members of Congress at parties. Members of the right committees," Felicia emphasized. "I'll be very useful."

"Glenn won't object?" Doug probed.

"It's my decision," Felicia said sweetly. "And it's not as though I'll be alone. Arthur Blumberg will be with me."

Anne sat back and listened while Doug and Felicia plotted the imminent trip to Washington. Felicia, Arthur Blumberg, and a member of his staff would go out on the company jet, remain for five days. Miller Timber was moving in a direction she loathed. Felicia glowed with satisfaction.

"Artie will make the deal with a lobbyist," Doug explained. "You circulate where it'll do us the most good. The lobbyist can make arrangements for official headquarters for us . . ."

"Why not utilize part of the apartment at the Mayflower as headquarters?" Anne felt driven to make a contribution to the plans. If she was ever to switch Doug to her way of thinking, first she had to prove her worth to the company. "You're there no more than a dozen days out of a year. It'll be a substantial savings."

"That makes keeping the apartment a realistic move." Doug nodded in approval.

"It could even be used for entertaining purposes," Anne charged ahead. "Another savings." Doug was ever cost-conscious, something engrained by his mother.

"I'll call Jackie tonight," Felicia picked up. "I'll tell her to line up some parties while we're there." Now she turned to Anne with what Shirley privately called her "drop dead" look. "I hear you were married while you were away. Anyone I know?"

"Josh Blumberg," Anne said with inbred Southern politeness. Doug must have told her! "Arthur Blumberg's older son."

On the point of leaving Doug's outer office with Anne, Felicia stopped short.

"Damn, I left an envelope behind," she lied. "I'll just duck back inside and pick it up." She crossed to the door to Doug's inner office and knocked.

"Come in." He glanced up from his desk in inquiry as she walked back into the room.

"Doug, I couldn't bring this up in Anne's presence, of course . . ." With an apologetic smile she sauntered across the lush carpeting to sit across from him. "But don't you think that Anne's marriage to Arthur Blumberg's son brings up problems?"

"No." His voice was acerbic. "I see no problems."

"It's a conflict of interests." She made an effort to conceal her irritation. Anne must be gloating like hell at having Blumberg on her side of the battle lines. "Naturally Arthur's going to be concerned about Anne's status in the company. Considering the kind of money that's at stake."

"Arthur has been our attorney for over thirty years." Doug was testy. "There's no conflict of interest. You and Anne are a team. *Together* you'll run this company one day."

"If anything happens to you, Doug, he controls your voting stock," Felicia pointed out bluntly. "He'll be on Anne's side, not mine."

Doug was silent for a moment.

"I expect to be around a lot of years yet. I control that stock. And if I should die or become incapacitated, I'm sure that Arthur will vote in the best interests of the company. He's proven his loyalty through the years."

"Anne's not happy about our fighting the Wilderness Act," Felicia pointed out. "Nor the bill for a Redwood National Park." A triumphant glint was in her eyes because she suspected this situation troubled Doug. "If she could, she'd stop our participating in the Forest Service auctions."

"Anne is bright." Doug was searching for words. "She'll come to see in time that these moves are necessary. And she was right on target when she said at our last meeting that we leave valuable timber on the ground to rot. I have a study in the works on that right now."

"She's bullheaded," Felicia warned, her cheekbones stained with color. "She'll use her sweet little ways to twist Arthur around to her way of thinking, and then he'll start on you."

"Anne may be bullheaded, but so are you," he shot back. "That is a trait you've both inherited from my mother. And nobody can change my thinking about the way this company is to be run. Naomi Miller laid down the blueprints a long time ago."

Anne returned to her office with a nagging uneasiness. She knew that Felicia considered the Washington trip a triumph for herself. Miller Timber would pull as many strings as possible to allow itself to circumvent the Wilderness Act; to help defeat the bill to establish a Redwood National Park. Stu said the bill was causing such overheated emotions that families were breaking up over it.

Her father, Anne remembered, had enormous contempt for lobbying. He had once declared it ought to be outlawed. And there were so many loopholes that allowed lobbyists to ignore the law calling for their registration. Doug had no intention of having their own representative registered.

Anne glanced up with a welcoming smile when Shirley arrived with letters to be signed, plus two mugs of coffee.

"I figured you'd need this by now." Shirley delivered one mug with a flourish.

"Felicia persuaded Doug to let her go to Washington in his place," Anne told her and Shirley whistled.

"She's not letting her date with the delivery room change her style. Did you ever see such gorgeous maternity clothes? With her belly popping out to there she's showing off her great legs in miniskirts. She'll probably go into the delivery room in a shift from the House of Dior."

"And the baby'll be born in a diaper by Oleg Cassini." Anne paused. "Are we being catty?"

"Yes." Shirley giggled. "And isn't it fun?"

On Friday afternoon Anne made a point of leaving the office on schedule. She and Josh were going to his parent's house for dinner. She wanted to change from her tailored business suit into something more festive. Felicia, too, was leaving at the traditional hour. They met in the down-going elevator.

"Glenn and I are going to Edwina's dinner party," Felicia

said. Glenn must be working up to the last minute, Anne surmised. "Will you be there?"

"No," Anne told her. She was never invited to Edwina's parties. Her marriage wouldn't change that. Josh wasn't rich and important. "Josh and I are having dinner at his parents' house." She was invited to other dinner parties—probably because of prodding by Doug, always her escort in the past. She felt obligated to accept these invitations. It meant she was becoming part of Naomi Miller's social world—a kind of retribution for her grandmother.

The elevator drew to a stop at the lobby floor. The operator opened the door and passengers hurried into the lobby with an air of relief that the business day was over and a few hours of freedom lay ahead. Almost immediately Anne spied Josh, in the green corduroy jacket and jeans that were his uniform. His eyes fastened on an open book.

"Is that Josh?" Felicia asked, her gaze following Anne's, an aura of surprise in her voice.

"Yes." Had Felicia expected him to have three eyes and a pointed head?

As coolly as she could manage, Anne introduced Felicia and Josh. Felicia's voice, her eyes, said that Josh turned her on. Was this Felicia's reaction to every man she met who was young and good-looking? *Hands off, Felicia. This one is mine.*

"When are you moving into the house?" Felicia asked Josh.

"Sunday," he told her with an amused smile. Josh was not taken in by Felicia. "We're playing by the rules." He reached for Anne's hand. "Can we drop you off some place?"

"I have my car here. See you around."

While she and Glenn dressed for Edwina's dinner party, Felicia brought up her misgivings about Arthur Blumberg.

"Knock it off, Felicia," he said. "Blumberg's Naomi Miller's man. He's paid well. He won't go off onto any of Anne's idealistic tangents. He's only interested in the bottom line." Glenn turned from adjusting his shirt studs to zip the back of Felicia's dinner dress. "But you should have tried harder to bring me in as part of the Washington team."

"I can push just so far, Glenn. Doug wasn't buying that. Now concentrate on giving me a crash course on lobbying." During the vacation at the end of his junior year at college, Glenn had considered becoming a lobbyist after graduation. He'd spent the summer in intensive independent study on the subject in Washington. "I want to know all the rules. Protocol. And how hard—and how—to push." In Washington, Glenn had said, the important lobbyists were labeled "the third house of Congress." And they exerted tremendous pressure on the other two houses.

"I don't like the idea of your flying off to Washington in your condition," Glenn protested and Felicia grunted in annoyance. How many times had he said that already?

"Pregnancy is a normal condition, darling. Women don't put themselves in cold storage until the delivery date." In truth, she looked forward to the trip. She was moving too damn slowly in the company. She churned for action. "We'll hole up at the house for the weekend," she cajoled. "You'll coach me on this lobbying shit." Thank God, Glenn was too nervous about her being pregnant to want to fuck every night.

At the Blumberg house Anne and Josh were greeted with the warmth she cherished.

"Bert couldn't make it tonight," Tess said, an arm about Anne's waist as they walked into the charming English Regency dining room. "He says Friday night is his night to howl."

True to his promise to Anne, Josh avoided talk of the troubles at Berkeley. The table conversation ranged from discussions of the San Francisco Ballet Company and the Sunday afternoon polo matches to the escalation of American participation in the Vietnam War.

"No more talk about Vietnam," Tess ordered when the maid appeared with dessert. "Bert is still subject to the draft.

I was so relieved when Josh reached twenty-six," she told Anne.

"You still have that group at Berkeley carrying on about our involvement in Vietnam?" Arthur asked Josh.

"Artie, enough," Tess warned.

"I just wish you'd settle down and get your doctorate," Blumberg told Josh. "All this delaying. And don't tell me the trouble on campus hasn't slowed you down. Anne, talk to him," her father-in-law urged. "At the major universities today a professor can just about write his own ticket. It's a better field than industry."

"Josh, how do you react to living in the Miller mansion?" Tess intervened. "You feel as though you're slumming when you come to dinner here?"

"We're moving out in December," Josh said with an anticipatory grin. "I'll manage till then."

"How did Doug persuade Felicia to go out to Washington?" Blumberg asked.

"He didn't have to. Felicia insisted on going," Anne said. "Her best friend is marrying Congressman Tyler's younger son. That should be a useful connection," she admitted.

She'd be glad when she and Josh could move into their own little house. Not that Felicia would make any inroads into Josh's affections. Josh wasn't Glenn. Still, she wouldn't feel truly married until they were under their own roof. In a way it would be like escaping a bit from Naomi Miller's tentacles.

Sixteen

IN a tweed "trapeze" above-the-knee dress designed to conceal her advancing pregnancy and with a cinnamon wool cape over one arm, Felicia strode across the tarmac to the waiting plane. Early this morning Walter had brought her collection of Vuitton luggage to the plane. She knew that with his obsession for punctuality Arthur Blumberg would already be aboard and waiting. They were scheduled to take off in six minutes.

She was amused by the glint of relief she saw in his eyes when she climbed into the forward section. Her delay in arrival had been deliberate. Let him understand that she was in charge here. Doug's alternate. Why in hell couldn't Doug agree to changing attorneys?

"Marvelous day for flying, Artie," Felicia said as she and Blumberg settled themselves in a pair of leather lounge chairs. The middle-aged, business-suited secretary had gone to the galley to put up coffee, Felicia assumed. "We'll be in Washington in time for dinner, their time, won't we?"

"If we encounter no problems," Arthur confirmed.

"I have a tentative appointment," she stressed. Making it sound a command to a subordinate. "With Congressman Tyler's son and Jackie Emerson." Doug had briefed Arthur on her connections. "You and your secretary will be staying at the Mayflower, too?" Not in the company apartment. She'd made it clear she expected to have the apartment to herself.

"We'll be at the Mayflower," Arthur nodded. "Always accessible to you."

He wasn't happy that she was here in Doug's place, Felicia thought. He resented taking orders from somebody half his age and female. But he'd been at Naomi's beck and call, and one day he'd be at hers—until she was in a position to dump him.

For the first two hours of the flight Arthur outlined what he was to accomplish while in Washington and how he meant to do it. This was a tacit agreement that his path and Felicia's would not overlap except on occasions where she felt his appearance would be useful. Along with his highly experienced secretary he would handle all the mechanics of setting up a lobbying organization. Felicia was to socialize in an effort to meet Congressmen and, particularly, members of the committee dealing with the timber industry.

"Let's liaise twice a day. You'll have my schedule at all times. Call me at your convenience. If I'm out on an appointment, leave word for me to get back," Blumberg wound up briskly. "We have a great deal to accomplish in the next four days."

After a light lunch served by the secretary, Felicia excused herself to retire to what had been Naomi's airborne bedroom. She meant to look beautiful and rested tonight. Being pregnant was only a minor inconvenience. Thank God, Doug had refused to approve Glenn's coming with her. She wanted him there in the office—a sharp pair of eyes and ears.

Blumberg's secretary rapped on the door when the plane was preparing to land at National. Felicia immediately joined Blumberg in the forward cabin, her mind detailing what lay ahead. A limousine would be waiting to take them to the Mayflower. She would go directly upstairs to the Miller suite. Arthur and the secretary would check into the hotel. Jackie was standing by for her call. She'd shower, dress, and wait for the Tyler car to pick her up.

Riding from the airport, Felicia paid little attention to the passing scenery as the chauffeur wove through the rush hour

215

traffic into downtown Washington. She'd been in D.C. a dozen times—always for some social event but never for longer than two days. As a child she'd "done Washington" with a group from boarding school. Her interest was not in the city but the people who could be useful to Miller Timber.

"We'll be at the hotel in a few minutes," Arthur assured her, believing that she was as irritated as he by the heavy traffic.

Felicia was barely conscious of the traffic. She was debating about what to wear for dinner. Jackie had made reservations at the Jockey Club. Where another Jackie—Jackie Kennedy— had her turtle soup and beef Stroganoff with Marlon Brando ten weeks after the assassination and found herself on the front pages of the tabloids.

Finally the chauffeur, who would be on call during her stay, deposited their small party before the historic yellow brick-and-limestone-trimmed Mayflower Hotel.

"Mrs. Miller adored this hotel," Arthur reminisced, gazing up at the heraldic medallions, the carved swags, the parapet urns. "She told me she'd been here for Calvin Coolidge's inaugural ball in 1925—which marked the Mayflower's opening."

When a maid arrived to press her dinner dress, Felicia phoned Jackie.

"Darling, I can't wait to see you!" Jackie trilled. "The last time we were together you'd barely popped out at all."

"I'm out now," Felicia assured her. "No discos, Jackie, I'd look absurd trying to dance." Jackie had told her that discos were "in" and the folk scene all but dead except for some college students.

"Bill and I will pick you up at quarter of eight. He's insisted on a dark corner table where you won't feel self-conscious about being so 'preggy.' "

"Tell him to call back and ask for a table in front, where everybody has to pass us," she ordered firmly. "I expect Bill to introduce me to at least two Congressmen tonight."

Felicia's billowing midsection was adroitly masked by a gray crepe Christian Dior trapeze dinner dress she had usurped

216

from Eva. Tonight she deserted her flamboyant jewelry for a "twenties" string of pearls and earrings in a gray several shades darker than her dress. She appeared unfamiliarly elegant.

During dinner at the dark-wooded, subduedly illuminated Jockey Club Bill introduced her to several men—including an Oregon Congressman whose campaign funds had been enriched by the Miller family, Felicia shrewdly recalled. All of them would prove helpful to Miller Timber. She'd arrange to have an early breakfast with Arthur at the Rib Room at the hotel. No, she changed her mind. In the company suite— where *she* was in residence. She relished the maneuvering that was required of her. She was exhilarated by the prospect of power these moves would instigate.

After dinner Felicia went with Jackie and Bill to the Marquee Lounge at the Shoreham Hotel to see Mark Russell. Even when Washington's favorite political satirist poked fun at Congressman Tyler, Bill couldn't control a furtive smile.

Leon had been right when he said at Edwina's dinner party that everybody went to Washington with an axe to grind. This was an atmosphere she enjoyed. She came here with a job to do—and she would do it.

For the next four mornings Felicia met with Arthur for an early breakfast in the company apartment. He was impressed—grudgingly, she guessed—by the contacts she was making. At Jackie's prodding Bill plotted her course. They lunched at the exclusive Four Georges and at Billy Martin's Carriage House in Georgetown, and at Paul Young's.

She was amused by the constant name-dropping. *"Oh, Vice-President Humphrey loves Conrad's for dinner." "The Kennedy clan makes Paul Young's their favorite hangout."* The women forever talked about Dorothy and Carol and Scooter—whose husbands were Arthur Goldberg and Abe Fortas and Dale Miller—all high in the D.C. hierarchy.

Arthur reported that he had lunched at The Monacle—favored by the lobbyists about town—and at the Ascot and the Rotunda, where Miller Timber's new D.C. representative introduced him to important diners. His afternoons were devoted to paperwork, then more socializing in the evenings.

Felicia spent the afternoons napping, to prepare herself for the strenuous evenings. Bill piloted her with Jackie to hastily scheduled dinner parties, which invariably ended by eleven-thirty in the Washington tradition. From the private dinners they traveled the Embassy party circuit, concluding their evenings with a visit to one of the coffeehouses that dot gas-lit, cobblestoned Georgetown.

"Felicia, how do you manage to make an eight o'clock breakfast every morning?" Jackie demanded on her final evening in town. "I have to sleep till noon or I'm dragged out."

"Felicia's one of those people who can survive on four hours a night and still look radiant," Bill said.

"Even when she's pregnant," Jackie sighed.

"I'm like Naomi—she could survive on four hours a night up until her final illness. Not Glenn," she said with an air of impatience. "He wastes too damn much time sleeping."

"Are you happy with what you've accomplished here?" Jackie asked curiously.

"Ecstatic. Thanks for all the introductions, Bill. And believe me, Miller Timber will be a heavy contributor to your father's next campaign. Even though he's from another state," she laughed.

Miller Timber contributed to both Republicans and Democrats. It was urgent to have friends on applicable committees whatever their party affiliations. Oh yes, she congratulated herself. She had pushed herself up the ladder in Doug's estimation by what she'd engineered in this town.

Next month she'd be Jackie's matron of honor. The wedding reception, to be one of the splashiest of the year, would be held in the Garden Court of the Sheraton-Palace.

The groom's guest list would include at least three or four congressmen, a senator, and a federal judge. Jackie said that one internationally known Japanese business executive was delaying his return to Tokyo to stop off at San Francisco for the wedding. She would make some marvelous contacts there. *Let Anne try to top that.*

Seventeen

INSTINCT warned Anne to mask her distaste for the company's lobbying efforts. Felicia had returned from Washington with the air of a general who has masterminded a major military victory. Doug scheduled a lunch meeting the following day with Felicia and herself and her father-in-law. There was no way she could redirect Doug's thinking at this time. What would be gained by antagonizing him? Especially now when she hoped for his approval for a project to reseed the bald tract she had seen from Stu Lerman's plane.

But business concerns were being displaced by Anne's suspicion that she, too, was pregnant. She was suffused with tenderness at the prospect of having a baby, yet simultaneously concerned that Josh would be upset. They had not planned to have children for at least five or six years. These days young couples waited to start a family.

A baby wouldn't cause friction in their lives—it would be an enrichment, she reasoned. She could handle motherhood and the business. Conflicts might arise, but they could be worked out. Don't wait any longer to tell Josh, she prodded herself. Tell him tonight. He loves kids. Look how sweet he was with Gerry.

They were spending the weekend, as usual, at the house Josh had shared with Stu for the past three years. Stu was great about clearing out on Friday nights and not surfacing until Sunday afternoons. He had a girlfriend who had an apartment in Haight-Ashbury, where rents were cheap and the young were settling in.

Usually she enjoyed having Stu hang around with them for Friday evening dinners. Tonight she was impatient for dinner to be over so she could be alone with Josh.

"This is great chili, Stu," Josh said, approving the dinner Stu had prepared. "Maybe you should open a restaurant."

"Who's got time?" All at once Stu was somber. "We've got to move our asses on setting up an anti-Vietnam committee on campus."

"We're already up to thirty-eight thousand Americans over there—and more are sure to go if something isn't done to stop this insanity," Josh said.

"What's with your lobbying deal in Washington?" Stu suddenly changed tracks.

"It's not my lobbying deal," Anne said defensively. "But the company's set up a representative there," she admitted. She hadn't realized that Josh talked about this with Stu—but of course, Stu would ask questions.

"The timber industry has to be stopped." Stu dug viciously at his chili. "I saw a Sierra Club survey that shows that in the past fifteen years eight hundred thousand acres inside the protected areas of the national forests have been taken out of protection and put into timber-cutting by the Forest Service. The Forest Service isn't protecting our forests—it's servicing the timber industry!"

"A lot of people are in the battle to save the redwoods," Josh reminded. "Congress will hear from them. Loud and clear."

Anne toyed with her dinner while the two men discussed the fight to save the redwoods. She'd seen correspondence at the office that told her that Miller Timber was fighting—along with other timber companies—for a share of the redwoods and Douglas firs in national forests. They'd slash as much as they could before Congress would pass a bill to establish a Redwood National Park. Would she ever gain enough power at Miller Timber to put a stop to their share of the slaughter? Was she harboring a ridiculous dream?

Anne had meant to wait until a romantic moment to tell Josh that she was pregnant. Instead, the moment she heard Stu's car backing out of the driveway—while Josh was reaching to put away the dinner plates—she told him.

He deposited the plates on the shelf and turned to her.

"Did you say what I think you said?"

"I'm probably pregnant," she repeated. *Josh was in shock.* "I know we didn't plan to have a baby for another five years," she stammered. "Please don't be upset. This won't . . ."

"Upset?" he reproached. "Annie, I'm thrilled." He reached to pull her into his arms with such tenderness that tears welled in her eyes. "I can't believe it." He laughed, rocking with her. "Our kid. You're carrying our kid. God, can't you hear Mom and Dad? They'll be out of their minds!"

"We'll have them over for dinner tomorrow night," Anne decided. "If they're not involved in something else. Then we'll tell them." She'd call Dad and Mother and tell them. And of course, Shirley, and Doug. "By the time the baby is born, Josh, we'll be able to move into our own house."

"You'll take six months off from the office," Josh plotted. "Unless you're ready to throw in the sponge on the whole deal? . . ." He drew away to search her eyes.

"Josh, no." She was shocked that he would consider this. "I'll take off the last month and then another six weeks after the baby is born."

"Annie, you don't need to push yourself this way," he protested. "In another six months I'll have my doctorate. I'll be able to . . ."

"Josh, I can't walk out on the will. It involves too much. In another five years Lazarus Timber will be free of loans— then Dad will start its expansion. I made a commitment to my grandmother when I came out here. I promised myself I would take back from Naomi Miller what belonged to her sister. And now, Josh, with the baby—this is our chance to guarantee a lifetime of financial security."

"You sound so damn practical," he derided but with tenderness. "Like Dad."

"And I won't stay away from the office a moment longer than absolutely necessary," she said softly. "I don't trust Felicia."

While Josh concentrated on coaxing a blaze from slightly damp wood on the fireplace grate, because the night was unusually chilly for this time of year, Anne went into their bedroom to phone her father. It was close to midnight in Belleville, but Dad wouldn't mind, she told herself. Mother stayed up till all hours, then slept till noon the next day.

"Annie, how are you?" His affectionate voice warmed her.

"I have terrific news, Daddy." The childhood term crept in again. "You're going to be a grandfather sometime in January."

"Oh honey, how wonderful!" She heard the rich, warm emotion in his voice—his love, his tenderness, his pleasure. "This is the most important news of my life—next to the night your mother told me *you* were on the way."

"You and Mother will come out to San Francisco when the baby's born," Anne told him firmly. "By then we'll be in our own house."

"You couldn't keep me away," he chortled.

"Is Mother there?" Anne geared herself to tell her mother the news. She'd react the way Eva had reacted when Felicia told them all about her pregnancy.

"Your mother's out somewhere," Kevin told her. How long since her father and mother went out together socially? Anne asked herself. Not for a dozen years.

They talked for a little while, then Anne returned to the living room.

"Shall we call your mother and father?" Anne asked on impulse.

"Why not?" Josh grinned. "This puts me back in favor with the family."

After a long phone conversation with Tess and Artie Blumberg, their pleasure in the news bringing tears to her eyes, Anne phoned Shirley.

"Hey, I'm going to be an aunt!" Shirley's voice crackled with approval. "Gerry will be counting the years till she's old enough to baby-sit for you!"

While they talked, Josh walked into the bedroom and deposited a mug of hot apple cider on the night table, his face alight with happiness.

"Tell Shirley I expect Gerry and her to keep me company in the waiting room when you go into labor."

"I heard." Shirley's voice came jubilantly over the phone line. "We'll be there."

Anne was enveloped in the love and concern of Josh's family, and touched by their sincerity. Her own dad was excited about the baby—he spilled over with a loving anticipation. But her mother had not once bothered to phone to talk about the baby.

Tess chose a topnotch obstetrician for her. All the Blumbergs concentrated on helping them find a house to rent. Later they would buy, Josh decreed. At moments he was self-conscious about his limited finances. And most of Anne's income went to pay off Lazarus Timber's huge loans. When her father tentatively suggested asking for an extension from the bank, Anne rejected this.

Felicia made condescending jokes about the two of them being pregnant at the same time. It was as though, Anne thought in distaste, that even in this they were in competition. On Saturday afternoons Anne went with Shirley and Gerry to shop for the baby, to choose the furniture for the nursery—which Tess and Artie insisted would be their gift.

Doug suggested, as though fearing rejection, that Anne and Josh might like to choose some pieces of furniture stored in the attic for their new home. Naomi had been an inveterate collector, particularly of the fine Far East cabinets and tables which Anne loved. He was delighted when they accepted with candid pleasure.

Josh was working on his doctoral dissertation with a new determination to earn his degree and improve his financial situation, yet he managed to be involved in the continuing hassles on the Berkeley campus.

As the summer arrived, Anne and Josh spent some weekends at the Blumberg country house, an occasional weekend with Doug at the Lake Tahoe house. Anne enjoyed the tenderness toward her unborn child—and Felicia's—that emanated from Doug.

"Actually, I've had very little experience with babies," Doug confided in the course of a Lake Tahoe weekend. "Eva kept her two boys pretty much out of sight—and of course they went off to boarding school at a very early age—like Felicia and Todd."

Somehow, in the years ahead, Anne told herself, she must reach through to the man Doug kept hidden away, imprisoned by the shadow of Naomi Miller—to the man whom she suspected more resembled his Aunt Rae than his mother.

Anne and Josh returned from the Blumbergs' country house on an August Sunday afternoon—upset by the reports they'd been hearing since Friday about the riots in Watts, down in Los Angeles—to find Mrs. Morrison on the library phone, grimly trying to contact Felicia's obstetrician.

"She's in labor and carrying on like this was the first child ever born," Mrs. Morrison reported.

"Mrs. Morrison!" They heard Felicia shrieking from the head of the stairs. "You tell that son of a bitch I want him here immediately."

"His office says he's off on his boat," Mrs. Morrison said. "And I'm trying to track down the associate who's covering for him."

"I'll go talk to her," Anne said quickly.

"Anne, be careful on the stairs," Josh cautioned. "You have to stop rushing the way you always do."

"Felicia, are you packed?" Anne tried to be calm as she mounted the stairs.

"I've been packed for weeks. Glenn's putting my valises in the car."

"You've remembered everything?" Anne questioned, as though she were talking to a small child.

"Everything. Glenn wanted to know why I insisted on packing a dozen silk sheets—" Suddenly she stopped dead and clutched her stomach. "Oh, God! If a man had to go through this, we wouldn't have to worry about overpopulation!"

"Are you timing the contractions?" Anne asked.

"Fifteen or sixteen minutes apart." Felicia gripped the banister post and grimaced in pain.

"Then you won't be leaving for the hospital for a while. Why don't you lie down now?" Anne coaxed.

"I told Dr. Ornstein I wanted to enter the hospital with the first contractions!" Felicia spat at her. "Where the hell is he?" She had changed obstetricians in her fourth month.

They both turned to gaze down below as the front door opened and Eva, followed by Walter with several valises, sauntered into the foyer.

"Eva, my stupid O.B. is out on a boat somewhere!" Felicia told her grandmother.

"Darling, has the time come?" Eva demanded, hurrying up the stairs.

"I'm in labor, damn it," Felicia shrieked. "I'm paying his absurd fees so he can gallivant on his boat."

"Dr. Ornstein's associate will meet you at the hospital," Mrs. Morrison called from the foot of the stairs. "And Dr. Ornstein is being contacted."

The door swung open and Glenn charged into the foyer, pale and grim.

"The car's out front and ready," he reported. "Have you phoned your mother?"

"When was Mother ever where she was needed?" Felicia

225

scoffed. "She's in Acapulco. I'll take the elevator down." The seldom-used elevator had been installed years ago for Naomi Miller.

"Darling, I'll go with you," Eva said dramatically. "I'll be there when you need me."

Anne and Josh were watching the late evening TV news with Doug when Eva phoned.

"Felicia had a son." Her shrill voice carried into the room. "Seven pounds two ounces. He's the image of her."

"How is she?" Doug asked.

"Fine but giving everybody a bad time," Eva replied. "Glenn looks ready to collapse."

"Give her our love," Doug said perfunctorily. "And remind her she doesn't have to run back to the office right away."

"Shall we call and have flowers sent?" Josh asked, seeming harried at what amounted to a dress rehearsal for Anne and himself.

"I'll have my secretary send flowers first thing in the morning," Doug said, a glint of amusement in his eyes. "I'll bet the hospital staff will be glad to see the end of Felicia."

Anne made a duty call to the hospital to see Felicia. She lingered briefly in the heady sweetness of Felicia's flower-laden suite, where Felicia held court in a peach satin Christian Dior negligée, then went to stand before the nursery. She gazed with a surge of tenderness at the tiny, red-faced bundle that was Felicia's son, to be named Timothy Dalton Rogers. Unconsciously she rested a hand on her stomach. Her face lighting as a tiny foot kicked within her. For all the worries that nagged at her, this was the most beautiful period of her life.

"Everybody says he looks like Felicia." Glenn's voice startled her.

"It's too early to say," Anne contradicted, turning to him. How strange to remember that she had once thought she was in love with Glenn! How could she have felt such anguish when Felicia walked off with him? "Wait till he's a year old. Then you'll know."

"Nothing in life ever works out the way you expect, does it?" His bitterness was unmistakable.

"I never expected to be living in San Francisco and part of Miller Timber." Anne strived for lightness. "But I can't say that I'm sorry about it."

"I made one hell of a mistake," he said quietly. "And I'll spend the rest of my life paying for it."

"You have a beautiful son, Glenn." Her eyes met his in faint reproof, refusing to recognize what his eyes said. It would have been the mistake of *her* life to have married Glenn.

"In your own way," Glenn said with what seemed to be sudden awareness, "you're just as ambitious as Felicia. But never forget for one moment, Anne. She's a dirty fighter."

Eighteen

FELICIA returned to business when Timothy Dalton Rogers—almost immediately called Timmy—was fifteen days old. She was pleased that Doug had offered no objections to transforming Naomi's suite—closed since her death—into a nursery for the baby and a bedroom for his nurse. The suite was far down the hall from the bedroom she shared with Glenn.

Doug had made some fatuous remark about Naomi being pleased that her first great-great-grandson would spend his early years in her rooms. *When the hell would he decide it was time to step down in the company and let her take on more responsibilities?*

In mid-morning on Felicia's first day back Doug sent word that she and Anne were to lunch with him in his office. He'd be reporting to them on the results of that Forest Service auction he'd attended up in Eugene, Oregon, she surmised. This afternoon there'd be another long, dull board meeting. Of course, the Board had no real say—they could only make suggestions. That was the way Naomi set up the business.

She left her own office at one sharp. Promptness had become part of her campaign to win over Doug. A small point, Glenn had pointed out, but one the old boy would appreciate. She smiled in satisfaction as she caught a glimpse of her silhouette in a glass door. How great to be flat again. Almost flat, she conceded inwardly—the lines of her dress contributed to the look. But she exercised every morning.

She knocked lightly and entered. Doug glanced up from his usual chore of setting up their luncheon table from the hamper sent over by Bardelli's.

"How does it feel to be back at work?"

"I like it," she said—a reversal in her thinking that still astonished her. Glenn was wishing she'd take some time off, allow him to represent her at the company. Couldn't he understand that wasn't the way this game was to be played?

Anne arrived, faintly breathless, before Doug could reply. "I hope I haven't kept you waiting. A last-minute phone call—"

"Why don't you two look over those figures on what I've bought at the auction," he said, pointing to a pair of reports lying on a corner of his desk. "We'll discuss them while we eat."

For a few moments Felicia and Anne were absorbed in digesting the figures. Then Doug summoned them to the table.

"You paid high," Felicia noted. *Doug didn't want them to be "yes" women.* "The bidding must have been heavy."

"I walked every one of those two hundred and sixty acres," Doug said crisply. "I know exactly how much it'll cost us to put in the roads to get the logs hauled out. I have a strong conviction that market prices will surge upward in the next five years." He gazed from Felicia to Anne. "I want to hear comments."

"We have a substantial tract of national forest land that we haven't cut yet," Anne said seriously. "In addition to our private lands. And lumber prices are soft right now—"

"And stumpage rising," Doug nodded.

"It's a bad situation for smaller companies," Anne interpreted. "They'll go out of business if prices keep soaring."

"We're not pushing sales." All at once Felicia followed Doug's thinking. "You're saying that now is the time to buy—even at somewhat inflated prices—and we should hold

229

on to our timber. Because with the large companies like Miller keeping logs off the market, the prices will rise."

"On the nose." Doug gestured in approval.

"I talked with Ted Houston up at Eureka this morning." Anne leaned forward with the intensity that always alerted Felicia to resented competition. "He's sending in his report on my guideline for a more cost effective clean-up system. He has documented proof of what I've been saying all along. We're leaving forty to fifty percent of the volume uncut on the ground. And these are logs that can be hauled out at a reasonable cost—without our having to buy any new equipment."

"I look forward to seeing it." Felicia tensed at the respect in Doug's voice. Damn, Anne had been on that kick for months. Up till now Doug had been unimpressed. "We'll take it up at the board meeting this afternoon. That's the kind of action we . . ."

"Doug, I have a project to present to the board this afternoon," she interrupted with calculated enthusiasm. She must make a point of cultivating Ted Houston. Maybe he could be persuaded to reverse those statistics. "I'm convinced this is something that would show a huge profit—and on a long-term basis." She had planned to spend more time breaking down the fine points with Glenn, but this was too hot an opportunity to let pass. "It's time we moved into the export scene. Other majors are out there selling. Japan, for example."

"We're selling to Japan," Anne said and Felicia grimaced. *That operation was small change.* "Since the end of World War Two." The Japanese forests had been overcut and burned during the war years. Japan was hungry for timber. "Whatever we cut and don't market domestically goes to Japan."

"That amounts to peanuts," Felicia shrugged. "I have a whole new angle."

"Our man in Washington tells me there's talk in Congress about slapping on export bans," Doug told her.

"That won't happen for years," Felicia asserted. "The lobbyists will see to that." Her mind was operating in high gear.

She'd met Takaji Tsuda at Jackie's wedding. He was head of one of the world's largest manufacturers of photographic film. He'd built retirement communities and resort hotels. He had his own sawmills. He was a prime market for Miller Timber.

"I'm not sure the profits would be enough to warrant expansion," Doug hedged.

"It can be." Felicia radiated a confidence that was only skin-deep. This whole deal could backfire, her reasoning told her. But she had to grandstand. She had to make Doug understand *she* was the one to fill Naomi's shoes. "Look at the facts. There are a lot of small timberland owners in northern California with trees arriving at the forty-year point. At that age in this state they have to start paying taxes—unless they cut them. That tax on forty-year-old timber goes on year after year."

"And it hurts," Doug picked up.

"I say, let's buy their logs—letting them keep the land—and export to Japan. Japan is willing to buy even small logs. They need whatever they can latch on to."

"Before we export," Anne urged, "let's consider moving into home building. That's a natural expansion for us. There's a market waiting to . . ."

"It would be foolish at this point," Felicia jumped in. "Look at the capital investment. We can do this for far less."

"Provided we can develop a strong long-term export market," Doug concluded.

"Let me go to Tokyo." Felicia was super-charged. "I met Takaji Tsuda at Jackie's wedding." She paused to allow Doug to digest this. He knew Tsuda by name. Everybody did. "He's very close with Jackie's father-in-law. I can write and say I'll be in Tokyo and would like to talk with him about our working together."

"That's an expensive selling trip if nothing comes of it." Doug squinted in thought. "We'll talk about it at the board meeting."

"It could be a real coup," Felicia pushed. "Naomi always said that nothing works better in business than the right connections."

"It seems to me that when this country is in such urgent need of housing it's slightly obscene to plot to ship huge amounts of timber to Japan," Anne said to Doug.

"Darling, it's never obscene to make scads of money honestly," Felicia shot back. Wasn't Doug sick of what he called Anne's passion for candor? *She* was. "That was Naomi's firm belief."

Felicia awoke slowly in her seat aboard the Pan Am overnight flight to Tokyo. She checked her watch. They'd be landing in Tokyo in another hour. She was pleased that the fourteen-hour nonstop flight from San Francisco to Tokyo brought her into the city in the morning. No time wasted.

Everything was working out as she'd plotted. A hell of a lot more money was involved in this sale than in Anne's campaign to salvage timber left on the ground after cuts. She was confident the team Doug had set up would buy sufficient nontaxable timber to fulfill a huge contract. Glenn had surveyed the field. He said many of these small owners were hurting at the prospect of laying out tax money. And it was a commonly held belief that the taxes would keep rising.

Glenn was a nervous wreck—he thought she'd jumped too fast. But that wasn't the real reason as she analyzed it. He was upset because she was chasing off on business when Timmy was only three weeks old. God, at that age he didn't even know her! And both nurses—the sleep-in woman and the one who relieved her—were efficient. Glenn could look in on Timmy every evening when he came home from the office.

She knew when she'd talked to Tsuda on the phone that he was intrigued at the prospect of doing business with a woman. Particularly a young attractive American. Tsuda was thoroughly Westernized, a self-made multimillionaire who traveled between his various companies on a private jet. But the Japanese had not yet elevated women to the top echelon in business.

She would have to sweeten the deal with Tsuda to encourage him to sign a long-term contract with them. He'd said nothing about previous commitments—he was open to negotiations. It was she—not Glenn, she thought with satisfaction—who had realized Tsuda was eager to cater to Congressman Tyler. Bill said there was something about a foreign investment bill his father was sponsoring.

In twenty minutes the jet was approaching Tokyo International Airport. She gazed down at green velvet countryside surrounding a huge dark stain that was the city and remembered Tokyo's infamous smog. Leon and Consuelo had talked about that when they returned from the summer Olympics here last summer.

Emerging from the plane she saw throngs of Japanese on the observation deck. They held up bright red-and-yellow name flags to signal arrivals. And then all at once she was aware of being approached by an expensively tailored young Japanese man, who clearly held special status to be allowed here.

"Miss Harris?" he asked in slightly British English, with no trace of Japanese as a first language.

"Yes."

"I'm Bob Tsuda," he introduced himself. A nickname, she understood. "My father sent me to welcome you to Tokyo. I have a car waiting."

"Where did you learn English?" she asked curiously.

"I went to boarding school near London," he explained. "Then to Harvard. This year I took off because my father wanted me to spend a year at home before going back to Harvard Business School."

"I spent two years at Radcliffe." Felicia and the young student exchanged a loaded glance of mutual approval. "I probably left at about the time you arrived."

They spent a few moments reminiscing about life at Cambridge, Massachusetts. The Radcliffe Yard was located just across the Cambridge Common from Harvard. They were delighted to discover they had studied with the same professor

233

in two subjects, though at the time Felicia had felt only arrogance toward all her professors.

"Will you be my official escort while I'm in the city?" she asked. It would be fun to spend four days seeing Tokyo with Bob Tsuda.

"I suppose you could say that." Bob's smile was ingratiating. "This evening my father has arranged a small dinner party at your hotel. Tomorrow morning he will meet with you at his office to discuss business."

Bob moved her through customs with commendable speed. Then they were seated in the chauffeured Rolls Royce for the drive into the city, which he warned would take an interminable time. "The first time you won't be bored," he told her. "But traffic in Tokyo is like Manhattan at its worst."

The new Olympic Highway carried them from the outer suburbs, past rows of small houses and shops, and on to the glass towers of downtown Tokyo. In the city, the most populated in the world with ten and a half million people, they encountered endless construction sites and torn-up streets.

"In Tokyo eight hundred major new buildings are started up every year. And my father is always involved in at least one of those," he added with a grin. "This is 'new Japan.' "

Bob deposited Felicia at the luxurious new Okura Hotel, opposite the American Embassy and built into a hillside. He arranged to pick her up for a predinner drink in the hotel bar. Later in the evening he would take her sightseeing on the Ginza.

The five-hundred-fifty-room Okura provided a beautiful interior that subtly blended Japanese and Western decors. At Consuelo's urging Felicia had asked for a Japanese suite. *"Felicia, you'll have all the Western amenities—TV, telephone, Western style bathroom, plus your own small rock garden with a pool and exquisite miniature trees. It's a delightful experience."*

Felicia was amazed by the aura of tranquility that permeated her charmingly uncluttered suite, in such contrast to the frenzy of Tokyo streets. She had meant to waste not a moment in sleeping this afternoon, when an exotic new city lay just beyond the hotel walls. But what was anticipated as a brief nap extended to four hours.

At the prearranged time Bob presented himself to escort her to the elegant hotel bar for a drink.

"Not sake," he teased, his eyes admiring her pleated, sapphire chiffon dinner dress. "Sake should be drunk warm and with food. We can have very civilized martinis here."

The guests at the small dinner party were all considerably older than she and Bob. The women smartly gowned in couture designs. The men in formal attire. The conversation roved from the recent highly successful Japanese productions of plays by Ionesco, Tennessee Williams, and Edward Albee, to a recent fashion show presented at one of the luxury hotels by Paris designer Guy Larouche and a bevy of imported models, to the merits of one golf club versus another. This might have been a dinner party in Paris or London or San Francisco.

No mention of the business that had brought Felicia halfway across the world was introduced into the conversation. This was a sophisticated, Westernized gathering. Still, at intervals Felicia was conscious of Takaji Tsuda's quizzical inspection. She would have to convince him she could offer a better deal than he was able to achieve elsewhere—but her path would be smoothed, she promised herself again, because he had something going with Congressman Tyler.

The dinner party ended at an early hour, since Takaji Tsuda made a point of being at his desk by seven in the morning. Felicia remembered a joke made at dinner—"to keep from wasting time at lunch, Tsuda workers eat instant noodles at their desks." But for Felicia and Bob the evening was just beginning.

Felicia went to her suite to change from the sapphire chiffon to an ice-blue shift, striped with spinach green, by Courrèges, and to wait for Bob to return, also casually attired.

Arm-in-arm Felicia and Bob strolled along the bizarrely illuminated Ginza. The air was filled with the blare of loudspeakers sending cabaret jazz onto the street, the constant honking of car horns, the drone of pitchmen, the howl of the Japanese streetcars.

"What does Ginza mean?" Felicia asked.

"Silver foundry," he explained. "This was the site of an old mint."

"It's dazzling," Felicia said, gazing at the endless staggered array of neon signs. The wall of a department store, an acre in size, glowed with a splash of eerie colors. "Oh, wow!" She stared upward at a full-sized Japanese car, headlights blazing, that revolved on a pedestal. Perhaps a hundred feet beyond a twenty-foot-high owl—plugging a brand of gasoline—rolled its eyes heavenward.

For hours they made their way through the festive hordes that crowd the Ginza every night gazing into shop windows that were witness to Japan's industrial magic. They paused before the tubular San-ai Department Store, blazing like an enormous Roman candle, and glanced at intervals off the Ginza to the lanterned side streets. Finally they acquired a taxi to drive them to the Okura Hotel.

"Nobody in the States would believe a strawberry-pink taxi," Felicia giggled. Most of the taxis were tiny Renaults. She was astonished when Bob told her the drivers never expected tips. "Not like back home," she laughed.

"My father insists I stay here in Tokyo for a whole year. He's eager to make me understand that the next century will be the 'Century of the Japanese.'" All at once Bob was somber. "But everything is not as fine as it appears on the surface. The average Japanese doesn't live like my family." She was surprised by his sudden bitterness. "Most of our people have the lowest living standard among the developed countries. Almost eighty-five percent of Japanese homes are not connected to sewers. Only about one day out of seven can we see Fuji-yama from Tokyo—because of the pollution."

"It's beginning to sound like Los Angeles." Felicia was bored by the sudden switch in conversation.

"Pollution diseases are given the names of the Japanese cities where they've caused such devastation. TV antennas have to be replaced every year in some areas because of the pollution."

"Grim," she said with an effort at politeness.

"Would you like to see the other side of Tokyo?" he asked with intensity. "The side we don't show tourists?"

"Not really." Did she have to come all the way to Tokyo to tangle with another campus rebel? He was as stupid as Todd. "I like to see the exciting sides of places I visit."

How could she have thought Bob Tsuda was sexually attractive? His father, perhaps. Power was an aphrodisiac. But instinct warned not to invite Takaji into her bed. Then she would be just another woman.

At ten the next morning, attired in an exquisitely tailored but deceptively simple white linen suit, Felicia sat at a conference table with Tsuda and three of his top executives. Earlier she had made it clear that Congressman Tyler—*"he's like family to us"*—would be pleased to see Tsuda doing business with Miller.

"Tell us, in simple words, what you can do for us, Miss Harris," Takaji Tsuda said.

For almost forty minutes Felicia explained what Miller Timber could offer the Japanese firm, answering a barrage of astute questions from the four men.

"How do we know that we can receive these shipments?" Takaji challenged. He was intrigued by the prices Doug and the accountants had worked out, based on what they expected to pay.

"Because Miller Timber has never not delivered in the over seventy years it has been in business," Felicia told him. "We can do this because we know every phase of the industry. We have the right connections. Our own people are in important places. Like Congressman Tyler," she emphasized. "Sign a five year–contract with Miller and your timber problems are solved for that period. What you require you'll receive."

Tsuda glanced from one to the other of his three associates. Felicia's heart pounded. *She had to put across this deal.*

"We have certain penalties we will demand should your company fail us," he warned. "These will have to be incorporated in the contract."

"Such as?" she parried, for a moment alarmed. Doug had mentioned no such commitments. Glenn hadn't brought up that aspect.

She listened while Tsuda listed his demands. The penalties were absurd, her mind cautioned, but she knew she would go along with what he said. This was the kind of deal—if there were no hitches—that Naomi would have applauded.

"If you have the contracts drawn up and signed before I leave on Thursday, I'll take them home with me. My uncle, of course, will sign for Miller Timber. That's just a formality. We have a deal." Why in hell couldn't *she* sign?

Inwardly Felicia exulted in what she had all but consummated with Tsuda Industries. She owed herself a treat, she decided, intoxicated by her success, her mind churning. Jackie was in London with her mother. Bill—now part of the Congressman's staff—had gone on to Washington with his father, but Jackie and her mother refused to settle into their Georgetown houses until the ghastly summer heat was over. They'd be in London for another ten days.

All right! She'd change her flight schedule, go home in the opposite direction. Two days in Paris to buy two or three of those marvelous new "Mondrian" dresses St. Laurent was showing in his fall/winter collection. Drop in at the Courrèges salon for something way out. Glenn would scream at the expense—he wanted them to put money into stocks—but she deserved something after what she'd pulled off.

From Paris she'd fly to London. Stay for a few days with Jackie and her mother. Then fly to New York with them if she could get a seat. God, after all those months of tearing around pregnant, she deserved a holiday!

She'd cable Doug that she was bringing home a contract—but returning by a slightly longer route. He'd be furious. So would Glenn. But fuck the two of them. What could they do to her?

Nineteen

A mid-morning rain beat a mesmerizing rhythm on the windowsills of Anne and Josh's bedroom. Josh sprawled on the bed and carried on an impassioned phone conversation with Stu about the results of last month's round-the-clock antiwar teach-in at Berkeley, while Anne lounged in a chintz-covered armchair before a blazing fire that provided a spurious comfort.

In about four hours she would endure her first Thanksgiving dinner with what Josh wryly called "the extended family." Last Thanksgiving she had gone home. The Thanksgiving before that had been lost in the horror of the JFK assassination—and Naomi's final hours. She dreaded these gatherings of the clan, the atmosphere civilized on the surface but hostility seething underneath.

She knew Josh was not comfortable here, though he was determined to conceal this. After two years she herself still felt a stranger in Naomi Miller's mansion. But as soon as the baby was born, they would move into their newly rented house. For convenience's sake—because next week would be her last at the office until she gave birth—they remained here at Doug's urging. She would be able to have nightly business conferences with Doug except for the evening or two each week when social engagements usurped his time.

At recurrent moments this morning she remembered this was the third anniversary of her grandmother's death and the second of Naomi Miller's. She knew that Doug would be thinking of his mother with fresh grief. She'd thought he would be upset when Felicia asked to take over Naomi's suite for Timmy and his nurse, but he hadn't been. He gloried in Timmy's arrival—an extension of Naomi Miller's dynasty by yet another generation. She smiled tenderly as she remembered walking into the nursery the evening before—lately a compulsive habit—to find Doug standing beside Timmy's crib with a glow of rich affection.

Doug was furious with Felicia for not returning immediately after completing her business in Tokyo the month before last, though he had been delighted with the contract she had negotiated. Still, the company had paid for Felicia's exorbitant expenses in Paris and London. Two days at Le Crillon in Paris, five days at the Dorchester in London, plus tabs at the best restaurants. She had learned this not from Doug but from lower echelon personnel in Accounting. Doug was afraid that Felicia was sufficiently temperamental to walk out on the terms of the will if he pushed her too far.

"How're you feeling?" Josh's solicitous inquiry punctured Anne's introspection.

"Fine," she reassured him. The week before a hint of false labor had frightened them. The baby wasn't due until mid-January. That was when Josh—and Tess backed him up—insisted she take time off now from the office. "The doctor says there's nothing to worry about, so stop stewing," she scolded. "What's with Stu?"

"He's going to his folks' for Thanksgiving dinner, but tonight he has a meeting with his Redwood Park group." Stu was active with one of the local groups fighting for the establishment of a Redwood National Park. "Georgia-Pacific and Arcata Redwood are logging like crazy within the boundaries being proposed for the park." He hesitated. "What about Miller?"

"We're not cutting what we've bought in that area from the Forest Service," she reported. "I understand from the last

241

board meeting that we're selling some of our own acres to the government for inclusion in the park."

"What do you want to bet that what Doug has agreed to sell has been partially clear-cut already?" Josh challenged, leaving the bed to sit on the hassock before the fireplace.

"I don't know." She was faintly sharp.

Josh continued. "The timber lobbyists—including Miller Timber lobbyists—are working overtime on Congress." She felt the rage charging through him. "They're having more impact, it appears, than the public outcry against clear-cutting the redwoods."

"Josh, I feel so useless. So guilty that I'm personally benefitting from what Miller Timber is doing."

"Annie, you can't expect to change things on your own," he said gently. "You're one person."

"Naomi Miller would have had an impact," she said in frustration, "if she had thought as we think and acted on it. I don't know how to change the situation. If it comes to a showdown about the course Miller takes, Doug has the deciding vote. Why can't he understand what the timber industry is doing to our forests?"

"He's been conditioned by Naomi." Josh reiterated their comprehension of the situation. "The welfare of the company comes before all else."

"If I thought I could never change Doug's thinking, I'd walk out of this silken jungle tomorrow." She paused and sighed. "No, I wouldn't," she said. "Not with my salary what it is. Josh, I have to make Doug understand what's happening in the industry. Miller Timber could lead the way to saving our forests. In a tiny way my grandmother was doing that in Belleville. Miller Timber could do it in a large way."

"Stop tormenting yourself." Josh reached for her hand. "Today let's just think of us."

"Josh, come hold me," she said urgently. "Tell me I'm doing the right thing to stay with the company."

As Anne and Josh descended in the tiny elevator, they heard the shrill, combative sounds of voices on the lower floor.

"The family in full force," Josh remarked. "I suppose we should be grateful Doug gave up on Thanksgiving weekend in Squaw Valley. At least we're escaping after dinner." Anne and Josh were going to the Blumbergs for Thanksgiving-eve supper. Tess and Bert had been laboring all week over gourmet dishes for Thanksgiving dinner—to be served, also, at the late supper.

"It's so good to see Todd," Anne said affectionately. Todd had arrived from Columbia the night before. He was staying here rather than with his parents in Hillsborough. Dinner last night—with Doug, Todd, Josh, and herself at the table—had been a warm, festive occasion. Felicia and Glenn had been off to one of their endless parties. Edwina and Bruce had returned this morning from Palm Springs, along with Eva. "I hope he isn't serious about taking next year off from school."

"I hope he doesn't mention it to his parents. At least not yet."

Except for Felicia and Glenn, they were the last to arrive in the family sitting room, where the family gathered on such occasions until dinner was to be served.

Doug was off in a corner in somber conversation with Leon and Consuelo. Anne gathered they were discussing Doug's campaign for the museum to support upcoming young artists. Clutching a cocktail Bruce slouched in a club chair facing the fireplace, a shaker of martinis on the table beside his chair. Todd and Adrian were in a wary discussion about colleges. Barring the unforeseen Adrian would graduate in June and enter college in the fall. Of course, with Adrian, Anne thought grimly, the unexpected often occurred.

"Why don't we cut out of here after dinner and head for one of the new ballrooms?" Anne heard Adrian suggest to Todd. "I hear they're real spacey. Everybody gets stoned, and they've got these wild lights projected through glass slides. You know," he said with an air of arrogant superiority as his eyes focused on his parents, "strobe lights, psychedelic posters,

LSD." Anne recalled uneasily that LSD—pioneered in the East by former Harvard professor Timothy Leary and in the West by Ken Kesey—was legal in California.

"My God, you're enormous," Eva greeted Anne with a specious smile, her eyes antagonistic. "I'll bet you're carrying a boy. Still playing 'follow the leader' with Felicia," she drawled.

"You have a fifty-fifty chance of being right." Anne forced herself to ignore the barb. "But Josh and I don't care whether it's a boy or a girl. We just want a healthy baby." For a moment she was uneasy, remembering the false labor. *Please God, let the baby be all right.*

"You look absolutely radiant," Edwina gushed and Anne managed a polite smile. "Both of you do," she told Josh.

"I feel radiant," Josh told her with a grin.

"Are you serious about moving into that absurd little house Felicia said you've rented?" Eva inquired.

"It's a charming house," Anne corrected. She sensed that Felicia felt a kind of triumph that she and Glenn were remaining in the Miller mansion. Doug was not enthralled. He wasn't upset about having the quietness disturbed by a baby's presence. He was annoyed that Felicia was beginning to entertain at lavish dinner parties—an expense that strained the proceeds of the trust fund set up to maintain Naomi's collection of houses. "And yes, we'll be moving as soon as the baby arrives."

"Yes, I suppose you would be more comfortable in those surroundings," Eva commented.

"Annie, how are you?" Consuelo walked swiftly toward them. As always she made a point of providing a barrier between Anne and Eva.

"Impatient," Anne laughed. "I gather the last two months are always the longest."

"And the most precious," Consuelo said softly.

Anne remembered Consuelo had suffered four miscarriages before finally giving birth to Adrian.

"Hi!" In one of her St. Laurent Mondrian dresses, Felicia, followed by Glenn, strode into the room to greet her mother and grandmother, waving insouciantly to her father across the room. "Another dreary holiday."

After exchanging a quick embrace with Eva and Edwina, Felicia sauntered across the room to Todd and Adrian. Glenn stood by, appearing bored with the family enclave.

"How's the son and heir?" Josh asked Glenn. He was surmising—as she was, Anne thought—that neither Timmy's grandmother nor great-grandmother had bothered to go up to the nursery.

"Oh, Timmy's fine." Glenn's face lighted with a fleeting pride. "Growing like crazy."

How much time did Glenn spend with his son, Anne wondered? Five minutes in the morning, another five at night?

Wong appeared in the doorway to announce that dinner was ready to be served, and everyone left the family sitting room for the formal dining room. As usual no one sat at the head of the table. To Doug that place belonged to Naomi Miller. Even in death.

Anne was glad that little was required of her at the table in the way of conversation. In her mind she was trying to deal with Eva's hostility. Her mother and father were scheduled to come to San Francisco when the baby was born. She would not tolerate Eva's being nasty to them. How was she to handle this?

Though their house would be ready then, Doug insisted that Anne's parents occupy the company suite at the Mark Hopkins during their stay in San Francisco. She accepted this because she knew it would please her mother. But they were sure to encounter Eva. Consuelo and Leon would give a small dinner party for them. Doug had announced his intention of entertaining them at the Miller house.

Then in a sudden spurt of inspiration Anne knew how to handle the situation. Felicia would deliver the message to Eva. Now she was impatient for dinner to be over so she could confront Felicia.

Three hours later—when Josh went to bring the car to the front of the house because they were preparing to leave for his parents' home—Anne sought out Felicia in her room. She knew Felicia was alone. Glenn and Bruce were in heated discussion about the stock market.

"Come in," Felicia called out in response to her knock, and Anne opened the door and walked inside. Felicia lifted her eyebrows in surprise.

"Felicia, there's a matter that we have to discuss." Anne kept her voice casual, yet it was clear this was important to her. "It's about your grandmother."

"What Eva does or says is her own business." Felicia's eyes glittered in irritation.

"This time it concerns you," Anne said quietly. "I don't have to tell you that Eva is unconscionably rude to me. I make a point of ignoring it. But my mother and father will be here in a few weeks. I won't tolerate Eva's being nasty to them."

"Tell Eva. Not me," Felicia flared.

"No. You tell Eva." The authority in Anne's voice elicited a new wariness from Felicia. "You explain to her that if she makes one snide remark to my parents, I'm walking out of this whole deal."

"That's absurd!" Felicia was pale but defiant. "You have too much at stake!"

"You make Eva understand," Anne ordered, "or I'm walking out. Our shares of Miller Timber will go to the Naomi Miller Museum."

"I don't believe you." Felicia radiated contempt. "You're as greedy as I am."

"But there's one difference between us. I won't allow anybody—or anything—to hurt my mother and father. Unless you're willing to gamble on losing everything, you'll make Eva understand my point. I can live without great wealth. Can you?"

Trembling but with an air of confidence Anne walked from the room and down the hall to her own. Felicia was scared. She'd talk to Eva. Felicia couldn't take the chance that she was bluffing.

He was tired, it was late, but Doug was reluctant to leave the library and go upstairs to his room. Here, with a cluster of photographs of his mother arranged atop the fireplace mantel, he felt almost touching-close to her. Tonight those final few weeks of her life ticker-taped across his mind. A proud smile lifted the corners of his mouth as he recalled the front-page headline of her death: TIMBER BARONESS DIES.

Would there be a family timber baroness to replace Naomi Miller? God, how Mama wished for that! He had always realized he could never fill her shoes. He lacked her instincts, her daring, her strength. He could only carry out her orders. Felicia and Anne were both so young. Both with an instinct for the business, yet so different. Each amazingly strong in her own fashion.

He frowned at the sound of voices in the hall. Eva was home, along with that absurd young man who was her current escort.

"Bruno darling, I know you mean to be on the tennis court early tomorrow morning, but this is Thanksgiving Eve." She managed to be simultaneously coquettish and petulant. "You have to stay for one little drink with me."

"Just one," Bruno stipulated.

Doug sighed in resignation and rose to his feet. He could be polite for a few minutes. Eva was leaving for Palm Springs on Saturday.

"Doug, are you still up?" Eva paused in surprise at the library door, Bruno towering behind her.

"I do on occasion stay up past ten," he told Eva and nodded to her sun-bronzed Adonis. What kind of ego permitted a young hulk like that to live off old women like Eva?

"Are we disturbing you, sir?" Bruno asked in the diffident fashion that made Doug feel ancient.

"Not at all," Doug said with a smile.

How could Eva demean herself by pursuing men a third her age? Just a few years older than Todd. Bruno was clearly

247

impatient to be off—probably with friends of his own age. How much was it costing Eva to keep him? She was forever being dunned—by the couturiers, jewelers, even the beauty spas. He must stop giving her money every time she was cornered.

"Would you like a drink, Doug?" Eva was sharp, snapping him out of introspection. "Bruno's asked you twice."

"A glass of white wine," he told Bruno, standing at the bar. Mama had loathed Eva's parade of young men—a part of the scene even before she was widowed. Mama had contempt for most of the family, he remembered in pain.

"This is the third Thanksgiving that we've sat down to dinner without Mama at the table," he told Eva while Bruno prepared their drinks. "I can't believe she's been gone two years."

"Felicia remembered," Eva acknowledged. *She* hadn't. "She mentioned it this morning. I think it's marvelous the way Felicia has taken hold. It's absurd that Mother brought in that little bitch to share the company with her."

"Eva, you will not refer to Anne as 'that little bitch,' " he ordered in restrained anger. "She's a bright, fine young woman—and Mama's only grandniece."

"Who is robbing me, my sons and grandchildren of our inheritances!" Eva's face flushed in fresh rage. "She didn't even leave me one of the houses!"

"Eva, your drink," Bruno interrupted.

Eva's mouth dropped in shock. For a heated moment they had both forgotten Bruno's presence. Eva was upset. Because Bruno had just learned, Doug interpreted, that Eva was not the superrich heiress she pretended to be. Seeing the mental anguish that darkened her eyes, that added a dozen unbeautiful years to her age, he felt an impulse to take his sister in his arms and comfort her. Being Naomi Miller's daughter had not been easy.

Twenty

AWKWARD in late pregnancy, Anne settled herself in the limousine with a disconcerting realization that this was the last time Walter would drive her to the office. When she returned to the business, they would be in residence in their new house and Josh would drop her off at the office each morning en route to the campus. God, it would be wonderful in a house of their own!

At intervals she thought about her blunt confrontation with Felicia after the Thanksgiving dinner eight days ago. *"Annie, you're learning!"* Shirley had applauded when she told her. Two years ago she wouldn't have had the nerve, Anne thought humorously. But these two years packed the wallop of ten.

She walked into the Naomi Miller building with the uneasy awareness that she would not be here again for at least ten weeks. It was absurd to worry that Felicia would be operating beyond her wary, watchful eyes. Neither she nor Felicia could bring about a meaningful change of direction in the company. The board of directors made recommendations. Doug made decisions. She and Felicia were in training.

In the elevator, Anne exchanged gentle kibitzing with the elderly male operator, who had been there for thirty-eight years. Emerging on her floor, she saw the glint in the receptionist's eyes that told her everybody knew this was her last day in the office before the baby was born.

"So you decided not to have the baby here," the receptionist bubbled. "Now we'll have to go to the hospital to see him."

"Are you running an office pool?" Anne laughed. "What are the odds that it's a boy?"

The clerical staffs here at the main office and in the field offices made it clear they preferred her to Felicia. Shirley said they called Felicia—behind her back, of course—"Her Imperious Highness" because of her habit of expecting the obeisance that had been accorded Naomi. Middle-management was divided. The top echelon was cagey about showing preferences, yet she knew that Felicia was favored. They never truly regarded her as "family," nor was she "Old San Francisco Society."

"Let's go somewhere insanely expensive for lunch," Shirley greeted her ebulliently. "My treat."

"How can I turn that down?"

She and Shirley ignored her huge salary. They were two young women working for a living. Shirley knew that most of her income went home to pay off Lazarus Timber's bank loans. Now, she reminded herself with momentary somberness, she would have to hold back money to pay for the housekeeper and nursemaid. But, as Shirley kept reiterating, this was part of her business expense—she couldn't work without domestic help. She wished Josh didn't feel so uncomfortable about this. Today, wives expected to share financial responsibilities.

Three weeks ago Josh had delivered his dissertation. At any time now he'd be called in to defend it. Once he had his Ph.D. he'd move into a professorship—his salary would rise substantially. He'd feel better, she consoled herself.

Every small incident of the day took on special significance because she knew she'd be away for weeks. When she left at three o'clock—as she had been doing for the past six weeks—Shirley went downstairs with her.

"When you come back, you'll be Mommie Forrest-Blumberg," Shirley teased as they emerged from the lobby and headed for the waiting limousine.

"Once the baby is born, I'm going to be Anne Blumberg. How can I explain to my child that his name is Blumberg and mine is Forrest?"

"He won't be asking for a while. And you did say 'he,'" Shirley pounced. "Your subconscious told you it's a boy."

"Do you suppose Felicia will allow Timmy to play with him?" Anne's smile was affectionate. She adored Felicia's tiny son, and worried that in the years ahead he might be ignored by his parents, as his mother and uncle had been by theirs. Yet for all that, she thought with a sense of wonder, Todd had grown up a fine, compassionate human being.

"Gerry's fretting about how old she'll have to be before you'll allow her to baby-sit for him."

"She'll have to flip with Tess," Anne laughed. Her mother-in-law was impatient to spoil her first grandchild. How different from her own mother! But Dad would love him—or her—enough to make up for Mother.

"I'll call you tomorrow," Shirley said fondly while Walter reached to open the limousine door. "Take care of yourself, Annie."

Anne grunted in protest, feeling herself wrenched reluctantly from sleep. The bedroom was night-dark, without a hint of morning seeping between the drapes. Then all at once she was fully awake. The dampness of the sheet beneath her telegraphing an eloquent message.

Her heart pounded in alarm. *The baby wasn't due for almost six weeks.* But he was beginning his journey into the outside world. For a few moments nothing existed for her except this silent communication between her child and herself. Her hands caressed the protuberance that was the moving life within her.

She froze in startled pain at the first contraction. No, not the first, her mind corrected. The first had jarred her out of a deep sleep.

She hesitated. Should she wake Josh? He slept so soundly beside her—on his stomach, face buried in his pillow. It would

251

probably be hours before she had to leave for the hospital. But this wasn't false labor, she told herself in towering anticipation. Josh would want to share the whole experience.

"Josh," she said tentatively and fondled his shoulder.

"Hunh?" he mumbled. Then—as she continued the gentle shoulder massage—he swung to his side with a start. "You okay?"

"I've sprung a leak."

"The baby's coming!" He sat upright, reached for the bedside lamp.

"Not for quite a while," she soothed and glanced at the clock. It was eight minutes before five. "We'll check with the doctors in a couple of hours."

"Not if the water broke." All at once Josh was in command. "He'll want you in the hospital right away." He reached for the phone. "You're open to infection now."

Anne lay motionless beneath the light blanket while Josh conferred with the obstetrician, alarm spiraling in her. The baby was five or six weeks early. *Was he all right?* Those last weeks could be crucial. Belatedly she remembered that she herself had been two months early. She'd weighed in at under four pounds, and her mother had retreated into what she had ever afterward called "my nervous collapse." But with the care of dedicated nurses she had survived.

Was the baby coming early because she had worked so far into her pregnancy? Her fault, she chastised herself. The baby should have been considered above all else. *Her fault.*

"We're going to the hospital now," Josh said with a cheerfulness she suspected was synthetic. "I'll pack for you. Can you dress while I do that? Should I help you?"

"I can dress myself." She hadn't meant to sound sharp. "Josh, do you think the baby's coming early because I kept working too long?"

"Annie, no guilt trip," he commanded and chuckled. "The character is impatient. Takes after his parents."

"I'll call Shirley from the hospital. They'll let me phone, won't they?"

"One of us will call," he promised while he pulled a valise from a closet. "This is a first baby—he'll take a while. That's what you're always telling me."

By the time they were in the car the contractions were six minutes apart. From Josh's pale facade of calm she knew he was shaken to see her in pain.

"Josh," she whispered, at a merciful lapse between contractions, "I'm glad you're the father of my child."

"Destiny." He grinned and squeezed her hand. "I knew it the first time I saw you—even though I fought against it for a while."

They left the car in the parking area and walked to the hospital entrance.

"You're going to be fine, honey," he said while they stopped short at the door and she grappled with a contraction. "They're coming fast, aren't they?" He was trying to mask his anxiety.

"One on top of another," she gasped, perspiration dampening tendrils of her hair. "We won't have to wait long for this child."

Josh sat on a Danish modern sofa beside Shirley and clutched at the paper container of coffee she had brought to him moments ago. He was grateful that they were alone in the waiting area on the delivery floor.

"Why is it taking so long?" he demanded. "The contractions were coming fast."

"Josh, these things take time." He knew she was being matter-of-fact to reassure him, but her casualness only exacerbated his anxiety.

"If anything happens to Anne, I'm going to throw my clothes and books into the back of the car and cut out," he said grimly.

"Nothing going to happen. She's in the delivery room pushing your kid out into the world. It's been that way for thousands of years, Josh."

"I never thought I could love anybody the way I love Annie. It kills me, the way she works fifty to sixty hours a week in that rotten job. Taking all the shit she does. I wish she could be just a normal wife and mother. Instead of a slave to Naomi Miller's will."

"Anne can walk out any time she chooses," Shirley reminded him. "Nobody's holding a gun to her head."

"She's holding the gun," he flared. "Damn it, we can live without Naomi Miller's money."

"Josh, there's much more involved than that," Shirley protested. But he wasn't listening to her. The obstetrician was walking down the hall with a broad smile. Josh leapt to his feet.

"Congratulations, Josh. You have a five-pound-thirteen-ounce son."

"How's Anne?" Josh asked.

"Fine. You can see her in a little while. And don't worry about that young fellow," he anticipated Josh's next question. "He can handle himself without an incubator. He'll catch up in weight in no time."

"Shirley, I have to call Mom and Dad." Josh's face was incandescent. "Do you have change for the phone?"

For the next twenty-four hours Anne and Josh were caught up in the miracle of having brought a child into the world. Josh commuted between Anne's hospital room and the nursery, enveloped in love and awe.

"He's so tiny, yet so perfect," Josh marveled repeatedly. "I can't wait till we get him home and I can hold him!"

Anne's room—she had rejected the luxury of a suite—was a colorful bower of potted plants and cut flowers. Josh's parents and brother had rushed to visit with her and to see their grandson and nephew. Doug came, hiding his obvious emotion behind business talk. Edwina and Eva appeared for a few moments, made polite remarks about the baby, and left. But their conversation made it clear that Eva would behave to

Anne's parents when they arrived. Felicia had delivered her warning.

Consuelo and Leon lingered in affection, extravagantly approving the newest Blumberg. Anne knew Consuelo was reliving the memory of Adrian's birth after her four miscarriages. Consuelo was pleased that Marshall Brian Blumberg had a pair of doting grandparents living right in San Francisco.

Anne's parents arrived a day later in an aura of high excitement, Kevin humble and delighted at becoming a grandfather, Denise enthralled at being installed in the company suite at the elegant Mark Hopkins.

"Doug met us with the limo at the airport," Denise reported, impressed by this reception. "Sugar, they're all being so sweet," she said with a hint of reproach in her voice. Anne had been less than flattering in describing most of the clan. "Doug says that Consuelo is giving a family dinner party for us Thursday evening, and he's taking us for dinner at the Blue Fox—and I understand from Avis that's as swank as you can get in San Francisco."

Anne didn't salvage a precious hour alone with her father until his fourth, and last, day in San Francisco. She sensed that he was not comfortable with the life-style of the Miller side of the family, though he confided to an instant rapport with Tess and Artie Blumberg. Over dinner in the Blumberg house Tess had told him she would take care of all the details for a "very proper *briss*" and regretted that Marsh's maternal grandparents—already the diminutive "Marsh" had been bestowed on the baby—could not remain to share this festive occasion.

On the eve before his departure for Belleville, Kevin sat with Anne on the chintz-covered sofa in a corner of her room and gazed searchingly into her eyes.

"Annie, are you happy here in San Francisco?"

"Dad, you know I am!" She was enveloped in the ecstasy of new motherhood. "Except that I wish Belleville were twenty minutes away. But it's not that far by plane." She was determined to dispel even a hint of gloom. "We'll see each other more often from now on. We'll fly to Belleville, and you and Mother will fly to San Francisco. Marsh has to know his Georgia grandparents."

"Anytime Naomi Miller's straitjacket gets too much for you, you walk out on the deal, you hear?" he exhorted earnestly.

"I can handle it, Dad." She smiled, tears filling her eyes. He was always so concerned for her. "After all," she lifted her head in pride, "we're building Lazarus Timber for a fourth generation. That's great backup if Miller Timber becomes a bust."

They talked with familiar anxiety about the Wilderness Act of 1964—proclaimed the "greatest conservation victory of this century." But the Forest Service and the other agencies involved were dragging their feet. The timber industry helped in these delaying tactics. Wherever there were desirable trees in a national forest, the Forest Service—prodded by timber magnates—fought the new Wilderness Act.

"You know, Annie, there were times when I was not fond of the timber business." Kevin's smile was wry. "I wasn't fond of any business." Anne remembered he'd wanted to be a journalist, but her mother had quickly aborted that dream. "But through the years—mainly because of your grandmother, may she rest in peace—I grew to respect it. I realized what a wonderful heritage our forests are. I've never respected a lot of people in the timber field—just those like Rae Lazarus, who understood our responsibility. But we're not doing too well—"

"The situation will change, Dad. It *must*. People who care about this earth are making themselves heard."

She felt a glorious rush of exhilaration. It was so good to be sitting here with Dad and talking this way. And those changes would come. She would help them come.

By the end of her first week at home Anne knew she would be returning to the office within another week. She loved their

256

house—extremely modest by Naomi Miller standards but charming, spacious, with a fine view of the bay. The furnishings were eclectic, ranging from the exotic Far East pieces she had chosen from the attic at the Miller house, at Doug's invitation, to the antique Boston rocker that had been what Rae Lazarus humorously called her "thinking chair" and which Anne's father had painstakingly crated and shipped out to her.

But she wasn't needed here on a full-time basis—and she was restless. Mrs. O'Malley, the middle-aged widow who was Marsh's nurse, was a treasure—loving, bright, and devoted to Marsh. The housekeeper—sister of Tess's housekeeper—was a friendly and efficient woman. Anne knew she was blessed.

In jarring contrast Timmy's nurse was a cold martinet whom Anne had disliked on sight, and the relief nurse was little better. Glenn had made weak protests during their first weeks on duty, but Felicia insisted that both women were qualified and reliable. Glenn was less an enthusiastic father after the first weeks of euphoric fatherhood. He and Felicia had little time for parenting. They spent long hours in the business, more in the socializing Felicia relished.

"Annie, you're sure you want to go back to the office so soon?" Josh was ambivalent when she discussed it with him.

"I won't be depriving Marsh of anything." She tried to sound logical. Josh was thinking of his mother, who had always been at home with her sons. But that was another era. Today, women could raise their children and still continue their careers. "I'll spend all my time away from the office with him." What was being called "quality time." "Josh, I have this burning compulsion to be there at the company. To know what's happening. To fight for what I think is the right direction for the company to take. I know," she continued before he could interrupt, "Naomi laid down the rules a long time ago, and at this point what I think is not terribly important. But I *am* making Doug understand what Grandma always said—that the wasteful habits in logging are sinful. I'm beginning to make a dent."

"Okay." He nodded in agreement, yet she felt an underlying frustration in him.

Part of her restlessness was due, she understood, to her distrust of Felicia. Often Glenn's warning about Felicia darted across her mind: *"But never forget for one moment, Anne. She's a dirty fighter."* Thank God, she had friends in most divisions of the business, both here in San Francisco and in the field offices. She couldn't prove it, but she was convinced Felicia was behind those amended reports that the Eureka office filed with Doug on the waste problem.

Doug fought to have the family—including the two newest additions and nursemaids—gather at the Squaw Valley house for Christmas. *"God, it's like the Kennedy compound!"* Anne heard Felicia grumble to Glenn. But Doug won. Eva didn't arrive until Christmas Eve and left after the traditional mid-afternoon Christmas dinner, but the rest of the family was there for most of the weekend.

Felicia had agreed to go to Squaw Valley because Jackie and Bill would be at nearby Sugar Bowl, and the two couples could spend most of their time together. Todd and Adrian were both on school vacation. Todd spent much of his time—when he wasn't on the slopes—in earnest conversation with Anne and Josh about the campus upheavals. Adrian—like Josh's brother—was totally removed from campus rebellion. Even now Anne felt wary of Adrian—she still remembered the time he tried to run her down with his bike her first Christmas at Squaw Valley.

Back from Squaw Valley Felicia argued with Doug about increasing their allocation for the Washington lobbying efforts. Anne, with support from two members of the board of directors, was campaigning for the establishment of a research department. Though she had taken no definite steps in this direction, Naomi had sent out endless memos about the advisability of this, Anne discovered from the files. In truth, Naomi had been more concerned about immediate profits.

Early in February 1966 Anne was astonished when Felicia phoned from her downstairs office.

"Are you free for lunch today?" Felicia asked with an air of mystery.

"Yes," Anne said, immediately wary.

"Great. One o'clock at the English Grill at the St. Francis?"

"One o'clock," Anne agreed.

"I'll meet you there. I'll be coming from an outside appointment," Felicia explained. "We can drive back together."

"Sure thing."

Another expense account luncheon, Anne thought automatically. Shirley's longtime friend in Accounting was incensed by the way Glenn approved Felicia's endless luxury luncheons—often with personal friends rather than business associates.

"Don't say anything to Doug about meeting me," Felicia cautioned. "I'll explain later."

At a choice table in the English Grill—where Felicia was obviously a pampered patron—Felicia explained.

"Friday a week is Doug's seventieth birthday. That's kind of a landmark age. I thought we ought to throw him a surprise party."

"That's a lovely idea." Anne was touched by Felicia's unexpected show of sentimentality. "At the Museum?" She was instantly caught up in this pleasant intrigue.

"No. At the house. Just family. Leon and Consuelo will be back from Palm Beach. We can work out all the details with Mrs. Morrison. You'll have to keep Doug late at the office. I'll go home early and see that everything's rolling. I'll buzz you when it's time to steer him home."

"I'll say something about Josh's being tied up on campus until late and may I drive home with him for dinner," Anne plotted. The Miller kitchen was geared to irregular dinner hours and varied table settings.

"He'll be totally surprised," Felicia said with satisfaction. "Naomi would never allow birthday parties for herself or Doug as long as I can remember. Every added year was another enemy."

Not until Anne was sitting down to dinner with Josh and

reporting on the surprise birthday party did the first inkling of Felicia's campaign seep through to her. Josh's derisive smile triggered her mind into action.

"You think Felicia's serving notice on Doug that he should consider taking a back seat?" Indignation soared in her. "Naomi was ninety and still in total charge of the business when she died!"

"Felicia's impatient. She hopes to push Doug into something like semiretirement. And she'll rush to assume a chunk of his responsibilities."

"Over my dead body!" Anne's voice crackled with determination. "You and I will make a point of stressing that he's seventy years *young.* I want Doug there running the company. Neither Felicia nor I is at the point where either of us can take over. We've each got a point of view and strong opinions—but we don't have the background to run a huge corporation. Doug has over forty years of being second in command to Naomi Miller. The company needs him. I defy anybody to deny that."

"The party could become a cat fight between Felicia and you." Josh grinned. "The others may not suspect it, but my sweet little kitten has a bit of wildcat in her."

"No cat fight," Anne predicted. "Glenn will be coaching Felicia on the sidelines. He knows it would be a mistake for Doug to step down. He wants to keep the company healthy for his own sake."

"I don't know how much clout Glenn has these days." Josh frowned. Anne lifted her eyebrow in question. "I know, you figure Felicia's campaigns have been formulated by him. But I suspect the situation is changing."

"Why do you say that?" Her mind charged into high gear.

"It's a feeling. Nothing concrete," he granted. "But when I see Felicia and Glenn together, there's something different between them."

"I think I know what you mean." Anne was considering the situation with freshly opened eyes. "There's a kind of arrogance in her now. I know," Anne laughed, "she was as arrogant as hell before. But now she believes in herself. She sees herself as Naomi Miller."

"That's about it."

"We're walking a dangerous tightrope," Anne said softly. "With no safety net down below."

Outwardly Doug's surprise party was a smashing success. The house vibrated with an unfamiliar conviviality. And when Felicia deviously talked about Doug's allowing himself more time for relaxation, Anne and Josh went into low-keyed but effective action. Both Naomi Miller and Rae Lazarus had remained at the head of their businesses far beyond his age, they reminded eloquently. Doug would follow suit.

Anne sensed that Doug was suspicious of Felicia's motives. Still, he enjoyed the surprise dinner party. To Doug nothing was quite as important as family—and except for the two away at school and the two babies, he was here surrounded by family.

As Anne waited in the hall for Josh to retrieve their coats, she heard Doug and Eva in a muffled verbal battle in the library.

"Damn, Eva, you've got to stop these insane extravagances. I can't bail you out every time you're being sued. And what is *this?* Twelve hundred dollars for a man's watch? For Bruno?" His voice reeked with contempt.

"Doug, it was his birthday. You're both Pisces," she tried to coax him into a less belligerent mood. "There are all those stupid girls after him," she sulked. "I have to encourage him to stay with me. It was just a little birthday gift, Doug—"

Anne hurried down the hall to the foyer, where Felicia was in whispered conversation with her mother. Both women were irritated because the birthday party had not elicited the response Felicia had anticipated.

"How's Marsh?" Edwina asked with cloying sweetness as Anne approached. "I do hope Josh's mother isn't spoiling him to death."

Next weekend, Anne remembered, weather permitting, she, Josh, and Marsh were going to Josh's parents' country house. It would be so good to spend time within a normal family circle.

Twenty-one

AT the curb before the Miller mansion on a balmy early April evening, Eva paid her taxi driver with a grunt of impatience. Walter should have been at the house when she phoned from the airport for a pickup, she thought irrationally. She stepped from the taxi in an above-the-knee black wool dress topped by a too-youthful crocodile-and-mink bomber jacket.

At this distance a stranger might have thought this was a pampered young woman of thirty. Eva kept herself bone-thin. Her hair was colored at first hint of gray roots. She moved with the dogged resilience of the young. At close range—even with her most recent facelift—she appeared her seventy-two.

"Is my brother home?" she demanded imperiously of the maid who admitted her, her face etched with a blend of rage and fear.

"No, Miss Eva," the maid told her. "He wasn't home for dinner tonight."

"Tell Mrs. Morrison I'll want a tray in my room immediately." She swept past the maid toward the stairs. "And try to find somebody who can fix me a decent martini." Normally that would be Walter, but he must be off chauffeuring Doug.

In her cloyingly feminine, all-white bedroom—the lighting devised to be flattering—Eva stripped to skin and inspected her reflection in the cheval mirror with myopic eyes. She didn't see the small sagging breasts, the flaccid thighs and stomach because she willed herself not to see these.

263

Why did Bruno stare like that at that stupid girl in the red bikini? She could see him getting an erection just looking at her. He was dying to throw himself all over her.

She walked to the closet wall and pulled a white satin, feather-trimmed Jean Harlowesque negligée from a satin hanger and slid into it. Maybe she shouldn't have screeched that way at Bruno. As soon as she was on the plane, she wanted to run back to the house and say, "Bruno darling, I'm sorry!"

She'd left him there on the beach—still drooling over that young slut—and returned to the house. She'd shoved a handful of bills into a pocket of a jacket he'd left hanging over a chair. That would pay his fare home.

She slouched at the edge of her bed and phoned Edwina, willing her to be home. Wasn't this the night she was giving a dinner for that artist she was sure would be the next Picasso?

"The Harris residence," a maid responded.

"Dora, please put my daughter on the phone," Eva ordered.

"She's entertaining at dinner, ma'am," the maid said hesitantly.

"This is important. Tell her I must speak with her immediately."

"Mother, I thought you were in Acapulco," Edwina's voice came to her moments later.

"I had an awful fight with Bruno. Darling, I'm devastated." Eva reported in vivid detail the heated battle with Bruno on the beach.

"I have to make up with him, Edwina. I can't bear to lose him." Her voice was a high, thin wail. "I know what I'll do!" she said in a split-second switch in mood. "I've told you how he loathes that North Beach hovel he shares with a bunch of hippies. I'll rent a smart little apartment for us," she concluded in triumph. "Our little hideaway."

"Can you afford it?" Edwina seemed dubious. "You know how you're always running short."

"I'll tell Doug my dentist is dunning me. He'll bitch, but he'll advance me money." How could Mother have done this to her? Leaving her almost destitute. Having to grovel for a few dollars. "I'll rent a little apartment and send him a sweet note of apology and enclose the key. That'll bring him back, Edwina." She felt giddy with triumph.

Within three days Eva had rented an apartment in a newly fashionable section of town—furnished it in the stark modern Bruno admired—on the seventh floor because he always said that seven was his lucky number. She contrived to have an unlisted phone installed immediately. She sent her note of apology—with an ecstatic description of the apartment—and the key by messenger.

She waited expectantly for a call. By the end of the second day—with no word from Bruno—she was distraught. She bombarded his North Beach home with hourly phone calls, frantic that the word was always the same: "Bruno's not here."

On the second afternoon of her telephone marathon Bruno came to the phone.

"Darling, how can you punish me this way?" she scolded. "Enough already!"

"I'll meet you at the apartment in an hour," Bruno told her. So brusque, she thought. Still punishing her.

She changed from her white wool pantsuit to a navy coat-dress from St. Laurent, inspected her reflection anxiously. She didn't care what the doctors said about the dangers of a facelift after seventy—because of the anaesthesia. If Dr. Bronson refused to do it, she'd go to that man in Paris.

She called for Walter to drive her to the apartment she'd rented for Bruno. She'd send Walter back home—he'd be able to pick up Doug as usual. Bruno and she would make love, then go out for cocktails and dinner. An early evening, she exhorted herself with a show of virtue, because Bruno would be on the tennis court by nine tomorrow morning.

Bruno arrived moments after Eva had let herself into the apartment.

"Sweetie—" She darted toward him as he unlocked the door and walked inside.

"Eva, I want you to stop this crazy calling," he said tersely and tossed the key on the foyer table.

"Bruno, I had to reach you," she pouted. "I know I behaved disgracefully, and I'm sorry." She moved toward him, arms extended.

He dodged her arms.

"Eva, you have to understand me. It's over." He cleared his throat uneasily as she stared at him with disbelieving eyes. "No more phone calls," he reiterated. "It's awkward for me." She continued to stare at him, trying to assimilate what he was telling her. What did he mean—it was awkward for him? "Eva, I've got something else going."

"Bruno, don't keep punishing me this way!" She threw herself at him, struggling to close her arms about his neck. "Darling, you know how marvelous it can be for us."

"Knock it off, Eva," he said impatiently and pulled her arms away from him. "You're an old woman. I'm twenty-six years old. *Look at yourself in the mirror.*"

For a moment she froze. "Get out!" she screamed. "Get out of my sight! Get out!" She repeated while he stalked from the foyer and slammed the door behind him. "Get out!"

She stood shaking, cold, her mind in turmoil. Incapable of movement. She heard the elevator arrive, The door slid open, then closed. Bruno was gone. Out of her life. He called her an old woman. He told her to look at herself in the mirror.

She stumbled from the foyer into the living room. To the huge mirror that hung over the white leather sofa. Her reflection devastatingly frank in the sunlight that poured through the picture window. *She was an old woman. Bruno didn't want her anymore.*

She stumbled into the bedroom, dialed Edwina's number, then hung up before a maid picked up. Edwina wasn't there— she had left this morning for a week at La Costa. Call Felicia. Trembling uncontrollably she dialed the number for Miller Timber, too upset to remember Felicia's private number.

"I'm sorry. Miss Harris is not at her desk at the moment," a secretary told her, and Eva slammed down the receiver.

It was over. Her life was over. Her own mother had sentenced her to death. With the money that should have been hers she could have held on to Bruno. They could have been so happy. But now it was all over.

Her mind focused on the one way out that she could see for herself. But first, call Doug. Let him know what his precious mother had done to her daughter. Damn, what was Doug's private number? Call the switchboard. They'd connect her to Doug's suite.

"I'm sorry, Mr. Miller is in a meeting," Doug's secretary told her. "May I have him . . ."

"I have to talk to him now!" Eva's voice was shrill in hysteria. "Get him out of that meeting. Tell him he has to talk to his sister before she dies!"

"One moment," the scared secretary gasped. "Please hold on. I'll get him."

Eva's eyes swung to the open window—where sheer tailored curtains fluttered in the breeze. A rear window looking down on the courtyard seven floors below. She didn't want to wait for Doug to come to the phone. *Go now! Let it be over! Over.*

Doug excused himself and hurried from the conference room to his office. He reached for the phone with a mixture of alarm and exasperation. Eva could be so melodramatic. She'd frightened his secretary out of her wits.

"Hello, Eva—" He waited for a reply. "Eva?" A sudden premonition drained his face of color. "Eva!" They were still connected but Eva wasn't answering. "Eva!" He saw his secretary's eyes widen with fear. "Did my sister say where she was?"

"No." It was a strangled whisper.

"Get Felicia up here. I'll call the house on another line."

He talked to several members of the domestic staff. Anguishedly aware that every moment was crucial. No one knew where Eva might be. Only that she had gone out earlier. He was dialing Edwina's number when Felicia strode into his office.

"Do you know where Eva might be this afternoon?" he asked tersely.

267

"I haven't the faintest idea," Felicia shrugged, but her guarded gaze told him she was lying.

"Felicia, she just dragged me out of a meeting with a weird message about having to talk to me before she dies. Where the hell could she be calling from? When I picked up the phone, I got dead air!"

"Oh my God—"

"Where, Felicia?" He ignored the voice that was responding at Edwina's house. "Where might she be?"

"She rented an apartment a few days ago." Doug waited impatiently while she came up with the address. "For Bruno," Felicia admitted.

"We'll go right over," Doug said, then turned to his secretary. "Call the police. Tell them to rush an ambulance over there. Possible suicide. Let's go, Felicia."

Doug and Felicia were at the elevator when his secretary summoned him back to the office. A police officer was on the phone. A woman had just jumped from a seventh-floor apartment, he reported. A bill found in a pocket of her dress was addressed to Eva Harris.

Even before Doug arrived at the morgue, he knew the body he had been asked to identify was Eva's.

The morning was overhung with a dank fog as family and friends gathered at the gravesite for Eva's burial. A montage of images darted through Doug's mind. Eva's terror when— as young children—they had to flee into the streets when the Great Earthquake hit San Francisco. Eva's outrage when she accused him, unjustly, of telling their mother that he'd seen her kissing their handsome new chauffeur when they were both home from boarding school for the Christmas holidays. Eva on her wedding day—eighteen and admitting she didn't really want to marry Roger Harris. *"Mother says I have to marry him. It's very important for us socially."*

Last night Edwina had accused his mother of being responsible for Eva's death. *"It was mean and vindictive to treat her daughter and her grandsons as though they were suddenly pariahs. To leave almost half her fortune to somebody she'd never seen until she was dying. Eva couldn't cope with living on limited means."*

It wasn't fair to blame Mama. Eva was difficult. She should have been able to live well on a million dollar trust fund. Maybe he should have helped her more, he thought in remorse. He knew she resented the salary he received from the company—in addition to his trust fund. But damn it, he worked for that. And the income from his trust fund went to the Museum—as Mama knew it would.

Would the situation have been different if he'd helped Eva more financially? Could he have saved her from going out that window?

Twenty-two

IN the midst of dressing for a dinner party they were giving this evening at the Miller house Felicia and Glenn stared at each other as though they were a pair of gladiators in an arena in ancient Rome. Glenn had abandoned struggling with his shirt studs. Felicia's exciting new Galanos—about whose cost Glenn had chastised her earlier—lay forgotten across the king-size bed.

"Felicia, I can't write off a trip to Cannes as a business expense!" Glenn exploded. "In November you flew to New York for United Cerebral Palsy's 'Evening in Vegas' at the Hilton—"

"It was for a good cause," she interrupted with a shrug.

"You spent a fortune on clothes at Martha's while you were there," he reminded grimly. "In December you went to New York for the International Debutante Ball at the Waldorf—"

"I stopped off in Washington to consult with our lobbyists," she pointed out with an air of triumph. "It was a business trip. I flew on a commercial plane—I didn't take the company jet," she added virtuously. "And we didn't go to Kentucky for the Derby as we'd planned."

"Because your grandmother had just died. Felicia, I can't keep approving these trips."

"You're the head of the department," she said imperiously. "Nobody dares to question you. And there's no way we can live on our salaries."

270

"Most of the world lives on a hell of a lot less, Felicia."

"I'm not other people," she said with an arrogant lift of her head. "I'm Felicia Harris. I'm accustomed to a certain life-style, and I won't give it up. God, I work my butt off. You know that. I deserve these little 'quickie' trips."

"One of these days somebody is going to leak your little 'quickie' trips to Doug—when he thinks you're off on another field conference. And my ass is going to be in a sling."

"I am going to Cannes for two weeks in June—with or without you," she drawled. "It won't be wildly expensive. We'll be staying with Jackie and her mother in the villa they rented for six weeks. And it'll be written off as a business trip," she said sweetly, "because I'll be conferring with Bill Tyler while we're there. His father is important to our lobbying efforts."

"I don't like it, Felicia." His eyes clashed with hers. "We've got a great deal going here if you don't fuck it up. Maybe you're on safe ground, but Doug can fire me any moment he likes. If you didn't blow money the way you do—and we can keep rolling the way we are—we could buy a house of our own."

"Don't start that again!" Damn him with his stupid, middle-class ideas. "I like living here. And we have absolutely no expenses. We'll lose the house, of course," she admitted bitterly, "when Doug dies. But meanwhile let's enjoy it. We could never afford anything like this. Not until I own the stock outright, and the freeze on dividends goes off."

"I don't enjoy living here. It's Doug's house. I feel as though we ought to ask permission every time we entertain."

"Don't be absurd. This has been my home most of my life. When I wasn't away at school, I was usually here with Naomi. My parents were rarely home—you know that. And if Doug resents our entertaining, too bad." She knew he was irritated by her parties—he didn't like her friends. "But Doug isn't looking for a fight with me." Her smile was smug. "He'd die if either Anne or I walked out on the business. His whole life revolves around training me to take Naomi's place."

"Don't discount Anne," Glenn cautioned. "Doug has a lot of respect for her ability."

"But more for me. Even the board was pleased at how I handled the Japanese deal." So Glenn had developed the project. *She* had sold it. "Anne's getting nowhere with all that crap about investing in research."

"She's not entirely wrong," he said and Felicia bristled. "With money put into research the company might come up with ways to cut the time it takes to bring in marketable Douglas fir from ninety to a hundred years to maybe forty or fifty years. That could close the gap between . . ."

"Glenn, I don't give a shit about what happens in forty or fifty years. What concerns me is now. I don't see us throwing a fortune into something that may or may not be an asset to Miller Timber in my old age. I want to see the company moving into other fields. That's your job, darling. Look around and bring me some ammunition to take to Doug. And meantime," she said, moving in to him with an amorous glint in her eyes, though she knew there was no time for a sexual romp, "in the meantime, plan on two weeks in Cannes in early June—before the summer madhouse begins. We'll stop off in London for three or four days first." She knew Glenn was dying to see London. Not "swinging London," she thought with amused superiority. Tourist London. Buckingham Palace, Westminster Abbey, the Tower of London.

"You're living dangerously," he warned, but she knew he wasn't going to fight her any longer.

"I love living dangerously." She reached to help him with his bowtie. "Any other way is boring."

"We won't stay with Jackie and her mother," Glenn stipulated. "We'll stay at a hotel."

"At the Carlton," Felicia promised. "It's palatial. You'll love it."

Glenn never felt genuinely comfortable with most of her friends, she remembered—despite his love of luxurious surroundings. But he liked Jackie's husband. Jackie said Bill would be there the first two weeks in June.

Moments before their first guests arrived, Felicia and Glenn headed downstairs. She relished the knowledge that they were a striking couple. Everybody remarked about that. Almost every woman she knew envied her. She was young, beautiful, potentially very rich—and she was embarked on a successful career.

When the hell was Doug going to realize that she could handle far more responsibility than he gave her? The Japanese deal should have made that clear. At least, she had most of the board of directors eating out of her hands. They saw her as the next chairman of the board.

It recurrently irritated her that Anne's office was in the penthouse, along with those of the top echelon, while she was sequestered with middle-management. Why didn't Doug stop this nonsense about keeping Naomi's suite unused? He could move into Naomi's suite, and she could take his. For now. In five years, she promised herself, she would be sitting behind Naomi's desk and running this company.

Anne thought small. *She* thought big. *She thought like Naomi.*

Felicia settled Timmy and the two nursemaids at the Lake Tahoe house for the summer. Then she and Glenn flew to London for three days. His normally sophisticated facade evaporated as he played the tourist scene alone while she shopped at Hardy Amies, Norman Hartnell, and Gucci. He was grim when he saw the elegant parcels that arrived at their suite on their last day at the Savoy.

"Darling, if we run short, we can always borrow at the bank," she dismissed his anxieties. At times he could be as stuffy as Doug. "Aren't you having fun?" she challenged.

"I'm not sure." His eyes were opaque. "I'm enjoying the sightseeing. God, London's full of Americans!" *Time* and *Life* had made London the American tourists' mecca. "It's wild to read in the *Evening Standard* about the 'hippie communities' in San Francisco, and in the *Times* about Timothy Leary and LSD."

"LSD is available right here in London," Felicia drawled. "For free at the World Psychedelic Center in Knightsbridge."

"To hell with that. What bugs me is that you're so damn extravagant, Felicia. You don't think beyond tomorrow." That wasn't what was bothering him today. He was pissed off because she'd pretended to be asleep last night when he got all hot and bothered.

"Of course I think of tomorrow," she contradicted. "I know exactly where I'm headed. But I need to live a little if I'm to have the drive to get there."

"I need a drink," he said tautly. "Let's dress and go down to the bar."

In the morning they left for Nice. Jackie met them at the airport in the chauffeured Rolls that came with the rented villa. Under a magnificent blue sky they drove along the turquoise Mediterranean, fringed with palms and cypresses, bougainvillea and mimosa. All colors were enhanced to an incredible brilliance by the light that such masters as Van Gogh, Matisse, and Cezanne had labored to reproduce. Jackie was full of gossip about the two-week extravaganza early last month that was the Cannes International Film Festival.

"This was the twentieth anniversary of the festival," Jackie reported, "and I hear it was très serious. Not the usual madness. Princess Margaret and Lord Snowdon were forty minutes late to see *Modesty Blaise*—you know, the female James Bond—and the audience *booed* them. And *Doctor Zhivago* had to be shown out of competition because the Soviets were bitching so. Afterwards MGM threw a Russian party—tons of caviar and vodka and smashed glasses."

"The Cannes Festival is big business," Glenn reminded her with respect. "I understand around thirty-five percent of any year's productions are hatched in Cannes. That's a lot of money."

"The summer season hasn't really begun," Jackie explained. Only in the past twenty years or so had Cannes enjoyed a brilliant summer season in addition to its winter season. "But of course that means it's not insanely mobbed like it'll be later. Still, you're lucky to have gotten rooms at the Carlton," she effervesced. "After the fifteenth there's absolutely nothing available until September."

"Is Bill here yet?" Glenn asked.

"He arrived three days ago." Jackie giggled. "He's spending his nights at the casino—he sleeps most of the day. Even all those long-legged girls in bikinis don't lure him to the beach."

Felicia saw the glint of approval in Glenn's eyes as the car drove along the wide, two-mile-long beachfront Boulevard Croisette, its promenade lined by tall palm trees and colorful beds of flowers. Luxury hotels, elegant mansions, and fashionable shops on one side, the Mediterranean and white-sand beach on the other. Now they drew up before the white, multi-balconied towered palace that was the Carlton Hotel, host to the crowned heads of Europe and Asia, lesser royalty, and the fabulously wealthy since 1912. The Carlton's view— a panorama of sea, shore, mountain ranges, and islands—was spectacular.

"Change into something casual and meet me at the terrace restaurant in an hour and we'll have lunch," Jackie said. "I have to pick up a necklace being repaired for my mother at the jewelers."

In the hotel Felicia and Glenn were swept up in a welcome that was reminiscent of pre-World War I opulence. Their suite looked out upon the sea. While Felicia showered, Glenn—changed into casual slacks and summer sweater acquired on London's Savile Row—lounged against the brass bedstead.

Glenn whistled in approval when Felicia emerged from the bathroom swathed in a lush white terrycloth bathrobe provided by the hotel and whirled about to show the legend emblazoned on the back in glorious red: CARLTON.

"I wouldn't mind taking one of those home as a souvenir," he told her.

"Do it," she encouraged. "No one will say a word to you—they'll simply add it to our bill."

"What are all these buttons?" he asked curiously while she began to dress. "I figure one is for room service—" He stared at the four buttons beside the bed.

"One each for the valet, the maid, the waiter. The fourth is for a private servant for guests who bring one," she explained. She debated between a white linen pantsuit and a Mondrian minidress, settled on the mini. "I came here once with Naomi when I was about twelve. We traveled with one of her secretaries—and she kept that fourth button busy." Even when she was presumably running away from the business to relax, Naomi carried the business with her. That was where she and Naomi differed. But even as she thought this, in a corner of her mind she remembered that Congressman Tyler was running for reelection in November. She must remind Bill that his father could count on a substantial contribution from Miller Timber.

"You miss the old lady." With an air of astonishment Glenn interrupted her mental notation.

"Now and then," Felicia dismissed the sentiment, "when I'm not swearing at her for trying to run my life." But Naomi had made her realize the excitement of power. The kind of power that would one day be hers.

Felicia and Glenn met Jackie for luncheon as planned.

"Bill will meet us for cocktails and dinner," Jackie told them. "He thought you might want to go with him to the casino tonight," she said to Glenn. "He's spending all his time there until he has to go back to work. Having a mad affair with baccarat."

Glenn glanced uncertainly at Felicia.

"Play a little baccarat," Felicia shrugged. Glenn was too cautious about money to lose more than a few hundred dollars. "Jackie and I will find a party somewhere."

"Felicia, did I tell you? Gary North and Alice are here." Their eyes tangled with electric recall. "She finally hooked him, you know."

"He adored being caught," Felicia drawled. "We weren't invited to the wedding. That was darling Alice being bitchy."

"She's had a plastic on her thighs," Jackie giggled. "So she could wear her white mink tennis dress with the striped crushed silk tights."

After lunch they changed into swimwear and settled on the bikini-littered astonishingly narrow strip of beach—umbrellas in readiness after the requisite amount of sun had been ingested. After a period of lolling on chaises Jackie insisted they all have siestas before meeting again for cocktails and dinner.

"Otherwise you'll feel like sacking out by eleven."

In the bedroom of their suite Felicia pretended to nap. Glenn was prowling about the sitting room. She'd been conscious of his growing restlessness these past few weeks. It was finally getting through to him that he wouldn't go any higher in the business than he was now. *He was doing damn well. He ought to be grateful.*

She enjoyed having him at her side at social events. He was smashingly handsome. He wore clothes well. He turned women on like mad. Why didn't he turn her on anymore?

No man lasted long with her. Every now and then she looked at Josh and wondered what it would be like to make it with him. Maybe because he belonged to Anne, she told herself in blunt candor. Instinct warned her to steer clear of Josh. She needed Anne in the business.

At dusk Felicia and Glenn joined Jackie and Bill on the breezy terrace that faced the Mediterranean harbor. Sipping their drinks they watched the multinational parade of strollers along the promenade, admired the sailing vessels and the closely clustered yachts at anchor. Jackie reported that her brother Paul and his wife would be driving down from Antibes to join them for dinner. Her mother was entertaining a few friends at the villa.

"She's psyching herself up to hit the campaign trail with Dad in August," Jackie explained sympathetically. "But first she'll stop off in Paris for the fall/winter collection."

They dined in the huge Carlton dining room, which Felicia

assured Glenn was one of the most impressive in Europe. The white-and-gold decor was distinctly rococo, with marble pillars, mirrored walls, lush red carpeting, and glittering chandeliers. After being seated by the maitre d'—who remembered that Felicia had always ordered fish on earlier visits and recommended the sole *meunière*—they were surrounded by a *sous-maître,* the wine steward, and two waiters while a deferential young man with a silver water pitcher filled their glasses.

In the course of dinner they spied Gary North and his bride of several months across the room. Felicia waved a convivial greeting. Did Alice ever guess that Gary and she had cavorted in bed at Gstaad while *she* waited for his return? And how would Glenn feel if he knew she'd had a couple of flings with Gary—heading now for their table. Not that she was interested in Gary anymore. He was history.

While they lingered over coffee and liqueurs, Felicia became aware of a man three tables away, who was gazing intently at their table. At her. Not young. Probably in his forties, Felicia surmised. Streaks of silver in his dark hair. But he was ruggedly good-looking, with an arresting air of self-confidence.

"Jackie, who's the character three tables down?" she whispered while the others talked about demonstrations against the Vietnamese war two weeks ago, at both the White House and the Washington Monument. "The one who keeps staring at our table."

"That's Craig Preston," Jackie told her. "The Texas oilman. He has drilling operations in Spain and Libya as well as Texas. Mucho money." She smiled eloquently. "Don't you remember his wife Hera? She threw that marvelous party at Palm Beach three years ago. We were there. You had something going with that Moslem prince—and then his father had him practically abducted and taken back to their yacht."

"I thought they were divorced." Felicia saw Preston rise from his table, where he had been dining with two debutantes she remembered vaguely and an older man. In great shape for a man his age, she decided. He probably worked out regularly.

"There was talk of a divorce, but they just go their separate ways. They have a couple of teenagers at boarding school back home," Jackie briefed her.

Preston paused to exchange a few words with diners at the next table while his companions moved on. Felicia liked the way he carried himself. As though he owned the world. He owned a sizeable chunk of it, she thought with inner laughter. Hera—wasn't her father a Greek industrialist?—was ultrarich in her own right.

"Jackie—" He paused at their table with a dazzling smile, his eyes an amazing blue against his Riviera tan. "I haven't seen you since Saratoga last August."

Jackie introduced them all, and for a few moments they exchanged small talk. Felicia suspected Glenn was deeply impressed by Craig Preston. After all, Preston was one of the richest men in the world.

"I'm having a few friends out to the yacht this evening." Preston assumed that everybody present would know his yacht. It was *The Star of Texas,* she recalled. "I have a print of *Doctor Zhivago.* We'll be showing it around eleven." His eyes lingered fleetingly on Felicia—but long enough to tell her he was eager to know her better. He would not consider her husband a hindrance. "I hope you'll join me. There'll be a dinghy at the Carlton pier to bring you out."

She and Jackie would go to Craig Preston's yacht tonight, Felicia plotted. Bill was already talking about taking off for the casino with Glenn. No sweat in getting Glenn off her hands. Paul and Eleanor would go with Jackie and her. Paul was bored out of his skull with his wife. And everybody talked about the parties on the Preston yacht.

As Felicia had anticipated, Craig Preston's yacht was a hundred-eighty-foot masterpiece.

"Larger than Stavros Niarchos's hundred-and-two-footer and smaller than Ari Onassis's three-hundred-twenty-five-foot *Christina,*" Craig described in his somehow sensuous Texas drawl, his eyes approving Felicia's above-the-knee turquoise-sequined evening dress. "Not bad for an American who's Greek only by marriage."

He was reminding her that he was married—and of course, so was she. So it would be a brief but outrageously stimulating relationship, she told herself. They were very much alike. Two equals on the battlefield of sex. Already she was aroused.

The few guests swelled to about fifty. Glittering personalities from a variety of countries. The lounge—converted tonight to a screening room—would accommodate seventy. A table beside the bar offered a variety of patés and a dramatic mound of caviar.

Craig made a point of sharing a mauve velvet love seat with Felicia. In the darkness he casually dropped an arm about her shoulder as the film grew more intense, as though to whisper a comment without disturbing the others. She knew he noted that she had come without Glenn.

"Would you join me for dinner here tomorrow evening?" he asked, moments before the lights came up again. "I have only another four days in Cannes—"

"A late dinner," she stipulated—with no pretense of game-playing. "Around eleven."

She and Glenn were having dinner with Jackie and Bill and Jackie's mother at the villa tomorrow. An early dinner. Mrs. Emerson liked to rise by seven when she was on the Riviera. *"It's not chic to sleep late here. Besides, the morning is the most marvelous time of day. I have breakfast on the terrace, then soak up the early sun for an hour."*

She'd peck at dinner. They'd break by ten-thirty. Bill would take Glenn off to the casino. She would be at the Carlton pier for her pickup by eleven. She had not felt so exhilarated in years.

By the time Felicia arrived on board *The Star of Texas,* a storm seemed imminent. It was weird, she thought as they settle themselves at the dining table set up in the sitting room

280

of Craig Preston's private suite, how fast the weather could change on the Riviera. In twenty minutes a star-lit sky could erupt into violence. A dazzling sun could give way to a gale.

"I thought we'd eat on deck," he apologized with a charismatic smile, "but the gods decided otherwise."

Dinner, served by a pair of white-jacketed stewards, was superb. But then, she considered, Craig Preston would tolerate nothing less. She inspected the beige silk moiré-covered walls of the sitting room, hung with paintings by such modern masters as Roy Lichtenstein and Frank Stella. With his obsession for modern artists Doug would be ecstatic if he could own these.

By the time they were sipping their espresso, the storm broke. They could hear the rumble of thunder, the crash of lightning outside.

"Would you like to go outside and watch the storm?" Craig asked with a sudden glow of excitement. "I'll have a pair of raincoats brought for us—" He was already buzzing for a steward.

"I'll kick off my shoes first," Felicia warned.

"Honey chile, you can take off anything you like," he drawled, his eyes heated when they met hers.

"I'll start with the shoes." She was caught up in his mood. For all his patina of high sophistication, he always radiated an earthiness that said he never totally forgot his early background as an oilfield worker.

In over-size raincoats, hoods drawn over their heads, they went out onto the deck. Rain pelted them. The sky was ablaze with lightning. Somewhere in the distance they heard the split of timber as lightning hit.

"Ever see anything like this?" Craig demanded while their eyes scanned the panorama of beach, lush hotels, the ancient weathered walls of the Old Town that rose high on the hills, plus the awesome light show that enveloped the sky.

"Fascinating," Felicia agreed.

Suddenly everything on shore went black. A bolt of lightning had temporarily suspended electricity throughout Cannes.

"Wow!" Felicia was conscious of a dizzying exultation. "Did you put in an order for this?"

"Just for you." In the darkness Craig reached to pull her close. "It'll be at least an hour—perhaps two or three—before they restore service."

"Isn't this rather public?" she said unsteadily while he reached inside her raincoat to run a hand across her breasts. It was so rare she felt this way.

"Not really," he soothed in the darkness, his hands expert. "This is my private deck. Nobody comes here unless summoned."

"I've never made love on the deck of a yacht in the midst of an electrical storm," she mocked. "Will it be good?"

"Sensational," he boasted and reached for her mouth.

Surprisingly she discovered she relished the rain pelting them as they clung together. He kissed with the thoroughness of a master, she thought approvingly while his hard, lean body thrust against hers. Their raincoats afforded a certain protection against the downpour, though already her hair was drenched, plastered about her small, well-shaped head as though a silken cap.

"You're overdressed," he clucked and with one sweep thrust her short evening dress above her hips and tugged at her pantyhose. He'd already discovered that she was not wearing a bra. "Hold on," he cautioned while he coaxed the pantyhose down the length of her.

"I hope you have a steam room," Felicia murmured huskily. *This was insane.* Not that she was making love with Craig Preston. That they were exposing themselves to such physical discomfort. Yet that in itself was an aphrodisiac for both.

She waited, holding her face up to the rain, while he stripped away his trousers and shorts. She assumed that was what he was doing, she told herself in a surge of humor. Everything was black. She wondered in a corner of her mind if her mascara was truly waterproof. But to hell with that. All she cared about now was to have his hands moving over her again. To have him pushing into her.

"There's a deck chair here somewhere—" Craig was maneuvering her in the darkness. His breathing heavy.

"Here." She felt the extension hitting against her legs.

"Oh God, you turn me on," he said thickly, helping her onto the deck chair and sitting on the edge. His hands everywhere, searching for the areas that elicited grunts of approval. Her dress rolled into a belt that rested above her breasts. "I was waiting for this evening ever since I saw you in the Carlton dining room."

"Then let's get this show on the road," she said in soaring impatience.

His mouth was at a nipple. His hand fondling between her thighs. Their raincoats swinging wide, permitting the rain to pelt their bodies, too hot with passion to be aware of the night chill.

She cradled his head while his mouth followed a southward trail. She cried out in abandon—feeling them alone in the world—when his tongue probed and a pulse went berserk within her.

"Now," she ordered, her hands tugging at his shoulders. "Now!"

She thrust with him in pleasurable anguish, straining to draw him within her, willing these moments to last forever. Why couldn't it happen this way for her more often? Never anymore with Glenn.

They left the deck while Cannes remained in darkness and hurried to the comfort of Craig's steam room. They lay together on one narrow cedar slab, smug in their mutual satisfaction, his hands fondling her to fresh arousal.

"We can't stay in here too long," she cautioned. "We'll pass out from the steam."

"But what a way to go," he chortled.

They rose in cedar-scented nudity and left the steam room for the king-size bed in the adjoining bedroom. Later she'd worry about her sodden pantyhose and dress.

Craig said he'd be here for another four days. She had plenty of time to talk to him about his reputed close contacts with Lyndon Johnson. They were both Texans. Maybe Craig could make the shrewd old bastard understand what he was doing to the timber industry with his damn Wilderness Act.

Twenty-three

"READY to go out for lunch?" Shirley sauntered into Anne's office with a smile that said "Today I love the world."

"A couple of secs." Anne acknowledged Shirley's presence but hovered uneasily over the report she had been studying for the last hour. Basically the report confirmed her fears. The company was extending its lobbying operations. It supported the American Forest Institute's insistence that stronger public relations must be built to keep the public from fighting against cutting in federal and state forests.

"Annie, that can wait," Shirley scolded. "It's not every day I receive not only a big raise but a new title. Gerry's awfully impressed."

"You deserve it." Anne pushed aside the report and reached into a drawer for her purse. Her smile was effervescent but her eyes serious. "How many times did I swear I'd walk out of this madhouse, and you calmed me down?"

"You shoot off steam," Shirley laughed. "You know I'll be around to pull your feet down to the ground again."

"We're lunching at the Garden Court at the Palace. Walter's waiting downstairs with the car to drive us over." Doug had put the family limousine at her disposal on those rare occasions when she needed it.

"Such style! Should I talk to the rest of the secretaries after this?" Shirley joked.

"You're not my secretary anymore," Anne reminded her.

"You're my Administrative Assistant." She knew that Felicia was furious that Doug had handed over a fresh segment of the business to her, but she'd worked hard for it.

"I hope this is an expense-account lunch?" Shirley asked as they hurried down the corridor toward the elevators.

"No way." Anne shook her head with eloquence. "This is between two friends."

"What do we want to bet Felicia's Cannes vacation comes in as expense account? I'll know next week."

"You have your spies everywhere," Anne clucked, but she knew Shirley always looked out for her interests. "I can't say anything to Doug, Shirl. First, because it would make me look like a 'snitch.' Secondly, I can't afford to chance a head-on collision with Felicia."

"She's not walking out," Shirley said confidently.

"I don't think so," Anne agreed, "but I can't take the chance that she might. And she feels the same way about me. Naomi Miller knew exactly how to keep the two of us in check."

"How do you like this dress?" Shirley dismissed shop talk. "Do you think my tummy sticks out a teeny bit?"

"It's a lovely dress. But you'd better watch those late-night trips to the refrigerator." Anne knew that Shirley fought a constant battle against weight gain.

"It's funny, you know? At thirty the tummy's flat and the rump is curved. Twenty years later the tummy's curved and the rump is flat."

"Stop being philosophical at my lunch party," Anne chided.

At the huge, glass-domed multi-chandeliered Garden Court they focused on the serious business of ordering. Both settled on the Palace Court shrimp salad—and agreed to ignore prudence when the pastry cart arrived. When the waiter departed, they leaned back in their chairs with a mutual air of pleasure.

"This is what I always think a Grand Hotel should look like," Shirley confided. "It makes me think of turn-of-the-century novels of intrigue."

"I can imagine the kind of hotel Josh is staying in tonight," Anne mused. "Their budget is tiny."

"How long will he and Stu be down there working with that civil rights group?"

"Another week in Alabama, then three days in Georgia. Josh will get over to Belleville for a few hours to see my parents." Todd's parents didn't know he was with Josh. They thought he was visiting a school buddy at an Alabama plantation. It would have been pointless to tell them. There would have been an ugly scene—and Todd would have gone along anyway. Edwina and Bruce never probed very deeply. That might prove uncomfortable for them.

"You miss him." Shirley's eyes were sympathetic.

"More than I thought," Anne confessed. "We're separated so much even here in the city—but when I climb into bed at night, he's there."

"Are things going to be less crazy on campus this fall?" Shirley asked.

"Josh doubts it. He's expecting trouble the day school opens. Actually, he's fighting three battles. Civil rights, the anti-Vietnam protests, and the establishment of the Redwood National Park."

"Aren't you glad he's too old for the draft now? Plus being married and a father."

"He's awfully uptight about the way the war's being escalated. The draft calls are up ten times over last year. A lot of college students are losing their deferments. Josh says kids on campus are threatening to burn their draft cards."

"I'll bet Josh's parents worry about Bert," Shirley sympathized.

"Right. Law school isn't a protection anymore."

"We're living in such a screwy world. I'm glad Gerry's so young. Her major worry is how soon she can buy another Simon and Garfunkel record."

"What's happening with you and Stu?" Anne probed. She'd made a point of throwing them together after Stu broke off with his girlfriend.

"We like each other," Shirley conceded. "We like each other a lot. And thank God for the Pill." She shot an impish grin at Anne. "That's what you're after, isn't it? I slept with him the night before they left for Alabama. And it was good. But I don't want any commitments. Once was enough."

"Stu's special," Anne said softly.

"That's why I made it clear I'm not marrying again. I don't want to see him hurt. I have my family—Gerry. And I want her to know she always comes first."

"She might appreciate a father," Anne tried. Shirley was a warm, vibrant woman. She could give so much to a man.

"I think women's lib was made for me. Now will you stop trying to get me married off again, like every married woman I know? I like my life the way it is. No strings. I do what I want when I want. And face it, darling—I can always find sex if I need it. The pill revolutionized life for us women."

Anne allowed herself to dawdle over lunch. Her meeting with Doug and Felicia was scheduled for three. This would be the first meeting since Felicia returned from Cannes three weeks ago. Doug had been out on the ranch for a week on a much-needed holiday, then up in Oregon and Washington for ten days on business. She and Felicia had kept clear of each other.

She'd encountered Felicia once in the elevator. Felicia had been absorbed in conversation with Joe Colton, the oldest member of the board and 100 percent behind her. Suddenly Anne wondered, had Felicia discovered yet that Timmy had taken his first shakey steps in her absence?

At three o'clock sharp Anne arrived at Doug's office. As always Felicia was a few minutes late.

"I'm having a rough old time getting back into the groove," Felicia greeted them. "Everything's so leisurely in Cannes."

"I gather you enjoyed it." Doug reached for papers on his desk. He was impatient for the meeting to begin.

"Oh, I could live in Cannes forever," Felicia drawled.

"I doubt it," Anne said softly. "In France it's against the law to cut down trees."

"You're joking." Doug was startled.

"No," Anne insisted. "I've heard of people on the Riviera who've built their houses around a tree."

"Thank God, the rest of the world is more practical." Felicia fished in her pocket for a cigarette, ignoring Doug's instant frown. He loathed cigarette smoke in his office.

"Unlike Glenn you came home with a tremendous tan," Doug commented. "Doesn't he like the sun?"

"Glenn spent most of his time in the casino with Jackie's husband." Anne was surprised by the coldness in Felicia's voice. Discord in her marriage? Normally Felicia pretended they were the Perfect Couple. "He might as well have gone to Vegas. Shall we get on to business, Doug?"

Felicia sat behind the wheel of her new red Mercedes and swore under her breath as the lineup of cars ahead remained motionless. She'd have to pull off at the next gas station and go to the Ladies Room. What a place to be caught this way! She fidgeted in discomfort for a moment, then froze. Her mind hurtling back to the months before Timmy was born. Those first few weeks she was always running to the john.

Her mind focused on the date. Shock zigzagged through her. Was she pregnant? She was three weeks late. She'd been too busy to notice until now. *She was never late since Timmy was born.*

It had to be by Craig. She hadn't had sex with Glenn for almost six weeks. How could she have been so stupid? It must have happened on the first shot—after that first night she'd taken care of herself, as usual. But she hadn't got back to the hotel on the night of the storm until dawn. Glenn was in bed already. She'd lied about having been at a party with Jackie. She figured nothing would happen on a first round with Craig.

She sat in a cold sweat, fighting off panic. She couldn't go through another abortion. *Work this out.* She wasn't the first wife caught this way.

She commanded herself to plot an out for herself. Tonight

Glenn would discover his wife was in an amorous mood. He'd be pleased. He'd been guilty because they'd had trouble the last couple of times. She felt color rise in her cheeks as his accusation raced across her mind. *"Damn it, Felicia! Most of the time you're as frigid as the Arctic Circle."*

Tonight they were going to that benefit concert. Afterward she'd insist they come straight home. She'd pretend the concert made her sentimental. In the car coming home she'd drop her head on his shoulder. A hand on his knee. Her hand would travel. Not too much, she exhorted herself with a flicker of humor. She didn't want Glenn to smash up the new Mercedes.

Oddly, the prospect of being pregnant again was all at once less obnoxious. She was carrying Craig Preston's child, but no one would ever guess. Not even Craig. Doug—with his obsession for family—would be delighted. Another child for Naomi's dynasty. A plus for *her*.

She could carry this off with no sweat, she told herself in fresh optimism. But this time, she promised herself, she would insist on a cesarean. The baby would be born on a date she chose—and there'd be no labor.

She felt a giddy satisfaction at the prospect of keeping a secret of this proportion from the whole world. What chaos its discovery could cause! Felicia Harris pregnant by Craig Preston.

As Josh had predicted, the situation on campus at Berkeley did not improve with the new academic year. Students were calling shrilly for free speech, an end to the war, legalized abortion, the abolition of ROTC, and an end to capital punishment. Josh pointed out, too, that there was a newly developing chasm between students. The black students were heavily into civil rights and black power, less involved in the antiwar movement. Most of the white students were focusing more on an end to the war in Vietnam and less on civil rights.

Sometimes Anne was disquieted by the realization that most of her own thinking focused on the business and on Josh and

Marsh. At times she felt isolated from the world. Josh was her connecting link.

"Do you suppose the Berkeley situation will improve if Ronald Reagan is elected governor?" Anne asked.

"I doubt it." Josh's face tightened. "He's being promoted by a very rich group of right-wing businessmen. He's after the antiblack, antistudent, antiobscenity voters with a song about 'it's time for a change' deal." He sighed. "And the odds are that he'll win."

"I wonder how Adrian's doing at Yale." Not that she cared about Adrian—she always felt uneasy in his presence, but she knew how important it was to Consuelo and Leon that he do well.

"I'll guarantee he's not a campus rebel." Josh grinned. "He'll never go to Alabama to work on voter registration during school vacations."

"Edwina's furious that he made Yale," Anne told Josh in amusement. "She's sure that Consuelo pushed him into applying to make *her* unhappy."

"Edwina's still pissed off at us because we encouraged Todd to go to Columbia."

"Something went wrong with those two kids. Consuelo and Leon should have Todd for a son, and Edwina and Bruce deserve Adrian." Her smile was rueful. "Misplaced genes?"

"Todd was great this summer. I'm glad he's decided to go on to law school after Columbia. Of course, Bruce and Edwina would be livid if they knew he wants to devote his law practice to the disadvantaged."

"This family is split right down the middle," Anne said with a recurrent sense of astonishment. Though Bruce and Edwina, like Felicia, hardly considered her family. "It's Grandma and Naomi all over again."

In December—only weeks after Ronald Reagan defeated two-term Governor Pat Brown with a million-vote victory—the Berkeley administration called for the police to evict an antiwar recruiting table from the student union. A mass meeting was called to plan a new strike. In the early years of the sixties students had rallied behind "Solidarity Forever." Now it was the Beatles's "Yellow Submarine."

To Anne it seemed that Berkeley students were forever on strike. She was looking forward to Christmas weekend at Squaw Valley because it was another world from the Berkeley campus. Returning from a Hanukkah dinner party at the senior Blumbergs' house, she reminded Josh about the Squaw Valley weekend.

"Oh God, I'd forgot about that. What a bitch." In the darkness of the car she sensed his grimace rather than saw it.

"Josh, it's gorgeous up there," she protested. "We'll enjoy it." *Despite the hostility that always permeated these family get-togethers.*

"I doubt that," Josh rejected. "It makes me livid the way Edwina and Bruce and Felicia all just wait for a chance to take potshots at you. Even that young kook Adrian."

"Todd will be there," she pointed out. "You know you're dying to talk with him about the troubles on campus at Columbia." Todd had not come home for Thanksgiving—they hadn't seen him since last summer.

She knew Josh was ambivalent in his feelings toward Doug, though he was always respectful and friendly. And he was compassionately aware of how deeply Doug had been hurt by Eva's suicide. But he railed against Doug's participation in fighting the Wilderness Act—along with other major figures in the timber industry.

As Anne had anticipated, she and Josh spent many hours at Squaw Valley in earnest conversation with Todd. Josh wanted to know every minute detail about the public debates at Columbia during the fall, about the efforts of the SDS, the student march into a campus building to protest the presence of a CIA recruiter on campus, and the march by five hundred students on Low Library the following week.

Anne sensed Josh's frustrations about the progress being made by students. He was afraid conditions on campuses across the country would grow worse before they improved. She worried that so much of his energy was being sapped in these efforts.

She relished the lighter moments, when they skiied with Todd, lounged comfortably before the living room fireplace with Leon and Consuelo. And both she and Josh reveled in taking Marsh and Timmy out for joyous encounters with the snow, though Felicia accused them of spoiling the nursemaids.

Discovering that Doug had made no plans for New Year's Eve—and she knew how empty the house would be this year—Anne invited him to join a small gathering she was setting up to welcome in the new year. An eclectic range of guests included her mother-in-law and father-in-law, whom Doug liked enormously, Shirley and Stu, and Todd. Edwina and Bruce would be in Palm Springs. Along with Adrian, Consuelo and Leon were flying to New York for a reunion with Consuelo's two sisters and their husbands, after which Adrian would join a school friend until school reopened. Consuelo and Leon were to fly down to Rio for their annual visit with her parents.

Felicia and Glenn—Felicia was calling her pregnancy a "piece of cake"—were hosting a party at the Acapulco house. Anne had been surprised when Felicia announced she was pregnant again. Felicia's succinct statement after her first delivery had been "once is enough to go through that."

Sometimes Anne worried that Josh, and perhaps his parents, thought she allowed the business to take precedence over Marsh. She loved Marsh with an intensity she had not thought possible. She cherished their time together. Weekends Mrs. O'Malley was off. She and Josh were with Marsh every minute.

Todd, refusing to adhere to his mother's demands that he "cut that ghastly long hair," remained in San Francisco for the winter break. He told Anne that Doug had clucked in mock dismay when he brought a trio of psychedelic posters to hang in his room.

"He'd rather I hung something by Picasso or Toulouse-

Lautrec," Todd guessed good-humoredly. "But Uncle Doug's an all-right guy."

On a mid-January evening—the night before the planned "Human-Be-In" in San Francisco—Todd persuaded Anne and Josh to go with him to a rock concert at the Fillmore Auditorium. He was proud of the San Francisco groups, just beginning to make an impact on the rest of the country.

"Usually when Anne and I go to a concert these days, it's some symphony giving a benefit performance," Josh told Todd as they joined the crowds pouring into the Fillmore. Everyone was obviously anticipating the three bands scheduled to appear, the fanciful light show of colored projections, the stroboscopic lights, slides of paintings and drawings already being cast on the auditorium walls and surrounding the patrons with a frenetically changing visual environment.

Anne listened with part of her mind while Josh and Todd discussed the excitement and meaning of rock, the individual merits of The Grateful Dead and the Jefferson Airplane.

"People don't come here just to dance anymore," Todd pointed out enthusiastically. "They sit and they listen. Rock is becoming a fine art."

Did Josh miss being part of the young night world? Anne asked herself guiltily. Most of his time was spent with students on campus, with young faculty members. She and Josh weren't kids anymore—they were family. They had responsibilities. But he seemed so animated, so happy in this atmosphere, she had to acknowledge. This *young* atmosphere. Did he regret giving up his independence for marriage? The possibility was unnerving.

Sure, Josh grumbled—like all men, Tess said—each time he had to dress for some formal affair. But they didn't go out constantly like Felicia and Glenn. Three or four formal affairs a month at the most. These were occasions their position in San Francisco demanded. They were part of "Naomi Miller's family."

"Annie, come to the 'Gathering of the Tribes' tomorrow," Todd urged. It was to be held in Golden Gate Park—not far from the Haight-Ashbury district, where young hippies—as they had been dubbed by the *Examiner*—had been taking up residence for over a year now, bringing with them marijuana, LSD, and casual sex. "It'll be real jazzy."

"I don't think so." Anne glanced involuntarily at Josh. He didn't want to go, did he?

"That's not quite our scene, old friend," Josh said, his face all at once cautious.

"Josh, it's not just the kids in their beards and bare feet and crazy-colored ponchos who float up and down Haight Street. I can see how you might not dig them. But the political radicals will be there. The young who want to make changes," Todd said earnestly. "And the Hell's Angels are going to be on duty."

"I can live happily without them." Anne rejected Allen Ginsberg's latest definition of them as "saintly motorcyclists." "They're a nightmare come alive. Remember the Vietnam Day peace march from Berkeley?" Anne turned to Josh. "The Hell's Angels charged into the marchers and bashed in heads, and the Oakland police just looked the other way."

"I'll give you a report on the happenings," Todd promised, refusing to abandon his enthusiasm.

The newspaper reports on the event in Golden Gate Park were colorful. On the platform were Timothy Leary—chanting his "Turn on, tune in, drop out" philosophy—Jerry Rubin, Gary Snyder, Allen Ginsberg. Bands played rock. Off the platform the crowd, reputed to number over twenty thousand, passed out flowers, burned incense, banged on tambourines, and dropped acid. A bunch calling themselves the Diggers handed out thousands of tablets of top-grade LSD—though LSD was now illegal—along with free turkey sandwiches.

Todd was ambivalent about this scene.

"Sure, it's exciting," he told Anne and Josh. "I've smoked pot—it's on every campus. Even on high-school campuses. But LSD scares the shit out of me."

"Remember that, Todd," Anne said softly.

"I have a gut feeling that whole situation is going to jump out of hand," Josh warned. "Eventually it'll get ugly."

"The word around town right now is that hordes of kids will pour into the Haight once school closes, Todd said. "I think maybe I'll hang around town this summer." His eyes glowed in anticipation. "It might get real wild."

Twenty-four

ON the day specifically chosen by Felicia as being the most comfortable for her schedule—supposedly three weeks before "due date"—she entered the hospital in preparation for a cesarean section the following morning. She was outraged to awaken shortly past midnight in hard labor. She ignored the pleas of her obstetrician and of Glenn to allow this new child to be delivered in the normal fashion.

"I won't go through this!" she shrieked between pains. "Dr. Bernstein, you get me into surgery and do it fast!"

Within three hours Felicia had given birth to a daughter, to be named Karen Naomi Rogers. As previously planned, a procedure was performed, also, to make sure this was Felicia's final pregnancy. By mid-morning her suite was a bower of flowers, and Felicia—violently sick from the anaesthesia—was reviling the grim private-duty nurse who was unable to relieve her nausea.

Felicia refused to see her daughter until three days after delivery, when she was reluctantly on her feet and indignant to discover that recuperating from a c-section was not the picnic she had anticipated. She inspected tiny Karen with something less than maternal ardor.

"She's gorgeous, Felicia," Glenn said with the same paternal pride he had exhibited toward his son. Briefly. "Already she looks just like you."

At intervals Felicia had nurtured disquieting fears that this new child would resemble its father. All babies had blue eyes, but even if Karen's should turn out to be brown, it would be all right. Both Glenn and Craig had brown eyes. Nobody would ever guess—she told herself with fresh confidence— that Karen was Craig Preston's child.

"Tell Doug that I want a business meeting with him and Anne here in my suite this evening. You can fend away visitors till we're finished."

"Do you think you should?" Glenn was ambivalent.

"I want to know what's happening with the Japanese shipments. Anne may try to delay them—she's making kooky noises about a housing crisis being predicted here in this country within the next eighteen months. We're making a fortune on that Japanese operation. It was *my* deal—it makes *me* look good."

Damn Anne for moving up her trip to Georgia by almost three weeks. As soon as she found out the date scheduled for the cesarean, she'd switched her own date. The little bitch, pretending to do that out of consideration for Doug. She was forever buttering him up. That wasn't going to help when the real crunch came.

When was Doug going to step down and let *her* get her teeth into running the company? He'd been lucky so far. He was still operating along the lines Naomi had prescheduled. But that was running out—and Doug was no Naomi Miller. Maybe she ought to start working on Fred Armstrong to pressure Doug. Armstrong knew he'd be her second-in-command. And it wouldn't hurt to start some campaigning with a couple of the other members of the board.

As often happens in August, San Francisco was fogbound this day, the air damp and salty. Josh walked swiftly, shoulders hunched in tension in his olive-green corduroy jacket that was welcome in weather more reminiscent of late October in northern England than summer in California. He was hurrying to meet Stu for a late lunch on Kearny Street in Chinatown.

This was his first summer of teaching. In truth, he thought, the teaching was a kind of escape. He honestly didn't want to spend another summer chasing around Alabama and Georgia among hostile whites and sometimes suspicious blacks. And he knew how Anne worried about him when he was down there.

The summer teaching seemed kind of required of him. He'd be bringing in extra money, such as it was. Piddling compared to what Anne earned. He always felt he wasn't kicking in enough—though God knows, Anne never uttered one word of complaint. But their monthly bills—between the mortgage on the house and salaries for Mallie and Hester—were mind-boggling.

Sometimes he felt like piling the back of the car with clothes and books and saying to Annie, "Let's get the hell out of this madhouse. Just you and me and Marsh. We'll manage without Miller Timber and Berkeley." But Annie was a pit-bull when it came to her inheritance.

What would she say if he laid it right on the line? *"Annie, I want you to throw in the towel. I want us to be just a normal couple with a kid. We can live on my salary."* He didn't have the guts to say that, he silently recognized.

He'd said nothing to her about his growing disenchantment with teaching. He didn't want to spend the next thirty years in a classroom or lecture hall. What had made him so sure this was what he wanted to do with his life? But if Annie would give up the rest of the crap, he'd hang in there at Berkeley.

Josh brushed past hordes of East Coast tourists, loudly comparing New York's Chinatown with the San Francisco version. Nothing was like San Francisco's Chinatown, he thought with pride.

He was conscious of the aromas that emerged from the restaurants, the smells of temple incense, fresh baking, fish on ice, exotic teas. And the cool, fresh scent of watercress. He turned into a narrow, dark doorway and climbed up a dank but clean stairway to the second-floor restaurant where he was to meet Stu.

Emerging into the small, comfortable room he spied Stu at a table for two by the window. While Stu, too, was teaching this summer, he had no class today.

"I break my hump teaching all morning, and you sit here reading that shit," Josh grumbled as he eyed Stu's collection of erotic poetry with good-humored contempt.

"Did you finish up that letter to the *Chronicle*?"

"Yeah—" Josh sat opposite Stu, unzipped his briefcase, and withdrew a sheet of paper. He grinned. "I managed to get it onto one sheet—I didn't want to overwhelm them with the length." He leaned back in his chair while Stu read with absorbed attention.

A waiter arrived with tea, and they focused for a few moments on ordering. God, he was bushed. He'd got up at a few minutes past five this morning to polish off the letter before he had to leave for the campus.

"Not bad," Stu approved.

"It's great," Josh insisted. It had been a joint effort originally, then submitted to a committee for suggestions. After that, he'd taken on the final polishing.

"You tell Anne yet?" Stu poured tea for the two of them.

"About the letter?"

"About the organization," Stu pinpointed. "That we've launched still another 'save the redwoods' group." He grinned sheepishly. "My old man could understand our breaking our butts for civil rights. He understood the importance of the Wilderness Act of 1964. But he looks at me and says, 'you're spending your bloody summer trying to raise support for a Redwood National Park at Redwood Creek? Don't you know, it takes fifteen to twenty-five years to establish a national park?'"

"The redwoods don't have fifteen to twenty-five years," Josh said bluntly. "We were a drop of water in the ocean as far as the civil rights movement goes. Fighting for the park we can see ourselves making progress. And it's urgent!"

"You still have to tell Anne," Stu prodded. He hesitated. "You're putting her in a weird position. She's a wheel at Miller Timber, and her husband's fighting against the timber industry."

"Annie won't be upset." Josh exuded conviction. "She feels exactly the way we do about the redwoods. She felt that way before I did," he said with candor. "Remember—way back—when you took us up in your father's plane to show her how Miller Timber was clear-cutting? Wow, was she shaken! Annie grew up in a family that considered saving a natural resource a personal obligation."

"One side of the family," Stu reminded. "But with you involved in this, she'll come in for heavy flak from the Miller board of directors. I can't figure out why you haven't already told her."

"We don't see that much of each other these days." Josh frowned in recall. "Annie's been flying around from one mill to the other. She's forever tied up in meetings. She's so tired after dinner—if she's not running off to another meeting—that she falls asleep on the sofa. Saturday afternoons—the ones when she doesn't get hung up at the office—and Sundays are dedicated to Marsh."

"Hey, how's the little character? He's been asleep the last two times you had me over for dinner."

"Annie's already planning his second birthday, even though it's almost four months away. We're talking about flying down to Belleville with him to celebrate it down there."

"Tell Annie how we're breaking our backs to get some action on the park," Stu exhorted. "Before your letter hits the *Chronicle.*"

"Yeah. I'll tell her tonight."

Josh waited until they'd had their special prebedtime session with Marsh and were at the dinner table to tell Anne about the group Stu and he had formed to help combat the foot-dragging of the Forest Service in regard to the Redwood National Park.

"What's happening to the forests in Humboldt County is

nothing less than carnage," he said heatedly. Much of Miller timberland was in Humboldt County, north of San Francisco. "In ten or fifteen years we won't have a redwood left on private lands."

"There won't be much left on federal lands if the Forest Service keeps on with the auctions," Anne added. "That's why the Redwood National Park is so important."

"Are you upset about what Stu and I are doing?" Josh asked.

"How could I be upset?" Anne replied. "You know I'm rooting for that park." Her smile was wry. "I know. I'm with a company that's fighting every way possible to prevent choice forests from being included in the Wilderness Act protected areas." Her face tightened in rejection. "A company that's fostering—though Doug closes his eyes to it—personal and economic harassment of people in favor of the park. God knows, the timber industry holds no love for the labor unions; but now they're buddies, fighting together against the park."

"The union leaders are scared shitless that some jobs might be lost in the area if the redwoods are saved."

"Josh, I hate what we're doing with the lobbying and with our public relations department. But what I say doesn't count."

"To the public it's going to look as though you and I are on opposite sides of the fence in this park situation."

"My body may be on the timber industry side," she tried for humor, "but my heart's on the other side." Her face softened. "Josh, I'm so glad you're home this summer."

"I'll be writing some blistering letters to the newspapers." How could Stu have thought even for a minute that Anne might be upset? He knew her better than that. "I may be *persona non grata* at the Miller house."

"I can live with that. Write your letters, Josh."

Several mornings later Anne looked up from her desk to see Felicia charging into her office.

"Have you seen this morning's *Chronicle*?" Felicia tossed a folded back copy of the morning paper before Anne.

"I never read the newspaper until lunchtime," Anne said, suspecting she would find Josh's "Letter to the Editor" in this morning edition. Josh said it was about time for his letter to run. "Oh." She glanced briefly at the letter and gazed up at Felicia. "You mean Josh's letter about the proposed Redwood National Park."

"That diatribe against the timber industry!" Felicia bristled, "How does he have the nerve to write something like that?"

"He sat at his typewriter—and after a few rough drafts—came up with this letter." Anne refused to abandon her cool.

"You let him send that letter to the *Chronicle*? You didn't tell him to knock it off?"

"I don't issue orders to Josh," Anne said quietly.

"What kind of control do you have over him?"

"I'm his wife, not his jailor." Anne's color was high. What kind of life did Glenn lead with *his* wife?

"You're letting him get away with this garbage?"

"Josh doesn't tell me how to run my life. I don't tell him how to run his. I'm sure he'd be much happier if I were not here at Miller Timber, but he doesn't try to tell me to cut out."

Anne saw the flicker of alarm in Felicia's eyes. She'd struck a nerve—as she'd meant to do. Felicia would die if she walked out on their deal.

"I think you're a stupid little ass," Felicia hissed and stalked out of the office.

Anne struggled to dismiss the encounter from her mind. Why did she let Felicia get under her skin this way? *They had to work together.* It would be easier for both of them if they could stop walking this damn tightrope.

She started at the jarring ring of her telephone, reached to pick it up. "Anne Blumberg."

"Annie, this is Todd." The tension in his voice alerted her to trouble. She worried that Todd was spending so much time on the Haight-Ashbury scene. It was becoming ugly. "I

303

wouldn't be calling you at the office, but I don't know who else to call. I couldn't reach Josh at the house, and Uncle Leon is . . ."

"What's up, Todd?" she broke in. Her voice sharp with anxiety.

"I'm on the corner of Masonic and Haight. I just ran into Adrian—"

"I thought he was in Europe." Anne remembered that Consuelo had mentioned receiving a stream of postcards from Adrian before she and Leon left for two weeks at Bar Harbor.

"That's what his parents think. He bribed a classmate who did go on the tour to mail the cards for him. Annie, I don't know how long I can trail him, but he's here and he's freaking out. I think he's on LSD. He doesn't even recognize me. He thinks he's a Hell's Angel, and he's yelling that somebody stole his bike, and he'll kill him."

"Stay with him, Todd." Anne's mind charged into action. "I'm coming over with a car." Doug was out of town, but she'd phone and ask Walter to pick her up with the limo. "I think I can get hold of Josh—"

"That would be best." Todd sounded relieved. "I'm not sure the two of us can handle him. And Annie, keep the windows of the car rolled up."

"Right. And keep your eyes on Adrian—try to keep him out of trouble."

Within a few moments Anne had arranged for Walter to pick her up at the office. She'd tracked down Josh at the print shop where he and Stu were stapling a bulletin to be distributed by their "save the redwoods" group. He was driving straight to Masonic and Haight. She knew Walter was upset at having to drive into Haight-Ashbury. It had acquired a nasty reputation these past weeks. But they had to take care of Adrian for his parents' sake.

With commendable speed Walter headed down Market Street into Haight. The "Hip Hop Tours" run by the Gray Line had just been discontinued, but this in no way stopped the tourists from piling into the district. The streets were clogged with a mixture of hippies, would-be hippies, and gawkers from out of town. Young people in bare feet and headbands, carrying a single flower and seemingly absorbed in inaudible music, moved along the street or sprawled in doorways or at curbside. Fast-food places—where cooks wore love beads—offered Love Burgers and Love Dogs. Button stores were everywhere. Love was offered to all, but the tarnish was beginning to set in.

"This is Masonic and Haight," Walter told her and slowed to a crawl.

"Do you see Todd or Adrian?" Anne asked him, her eyes searching the scene in soaring alarm.

"They're not here," he said after a moment. "Should I try driving farther on?"

"Please."

A block ahead she spied Josh's car, precariously double-parked. Todd and Josh were trying to subdue Adrian while disinterested passersby strolled near them.

"Walter, help them!"

While strangers watched now with morbid interest, the three men restrained Adrian and prodded him into the limo. Walter and Todd positioned themselves on either side of him and Josh went off in search of a public phone so he might appeal to his father for advice in handling the situation. They were reluctant to take Adrian to a public psychiatric hospital, and anxious about the legal aspects, since Adrian was a minor and his parents three thousand miles away.

Anne slid behind the wheel of the limo. Adrian was lapsing into incoherent jibberish now, abandoning the attempt to free himself.

"Here's Josh," Anne said in relief.

Josh hovered at the window beside the wheel and reported on his father's advice. They were to take Adrian to a private sanitarium. Josh's father was already making arrangements. He gave Anne specific directions to the sanitarium, adding that he would follow directly behind them.

"Dad's handling everything," he reiterated. "Everything's

under control." He smiled reassuringly but his eyes were somber. "Damn, at times like this I wish I had gone to law school!"

Within hours Adrian was being treated in the private sanitarium, and Consuelo and Leon were aboard a chartered flight from Bar Harbor to San Francisco. By the time his parents arrived, Adrian was in a semicoma, but the doctors were confident he would recover. They prescribed in-hospital psychiatric care for an indeterminate period.

Consuelo insisted on remaining at the sanitarium until Adrian emerged from the semicoma.

"I have to be here when he comes out of it," she said quietly, her eyes moving from Todd to Anne to Josh. "Leon and I will never be able to thank you enough for taking care of Adrian this way."

Anne, Josh, and Todd left the sanitarium a dozen hours after Todd's morning phone call. It seemed a year, Anne thought. Exhausted and famished, they stopped off at an all-night delicatessan for pastrami sandwiches and coffee. While Josh and Todd talked about the troubles on the Columbia campus—the first actual outbreak of violence had happened in April, and Todd predicted that the coming year would be tumultuous—Anne reran in her mind a conversation between Consuelo and herself earlier in the evening, when Consuelo had prodded Josh into taking Leon and Todd off for coffee:

"I don't know where we went wrong with Adrian. Maybe I should have put a stop to all Naomi's spoiling but there was no handling her. When Leon married me, he wasn't in love with me. That came later." Her smile had been warm and confident. "He married me because my family down in Brazil is very social." And very wealthy, Anne recalled. "Both boys—Leon and Bruce—were under Naomi's orders to marry into the best social circles. Edwina's family was high on social prestige and low on money. She figured Naomi was her one real chance at wealth and then Naomi cut them off."

"A million-dollar trust fund—and the use of all the houses—isn't exactly cut off," Anne had said with a wry smile.

"Not to normal people. But Naomi raised her grandsons—and make no mistake about it, Anne, Naomi controlled their upbringing—to regard themselves as Crown Princes, heirs apparent to her kingdom. Both, of course, were disappointments to her. I don't know how, but Leon and I have to turn Adrian around. He must learn to live in our world—Leon's and mine. Not Naomi's."

"Adrian's going to miss out on the school term." Todd's pronouncement invaded Anne's introspection. "Of course, Aunt Connie will come up with some doctor's note about an emergency appendectomy or something. You know, it's funny. When I was a little kid, I used to envy Felicia and Adrian because it was so clear that Great-grandma Naomi loved them more than she loved me. She used to say, 'Felicia and Adrian have *chutzpah.*' That's a Yiddish word she learned from your father, Josh." Todd turned to Anne. "It means . . ."

"I know what it means," Anne laughed. "Even before I went to school in New York I knew."

"Great-grandma might have been something of a Wasp, but she had great respect for Jewish brains."

"Ah-ha," Anne pounced, "so that's how I got into this kooky family."

"Sometimes I ask myself if being part of Naomi Miller's family is a curse." All at once Todd was somber. "I thought about that when Grandma died. Nobody in this family has ever seemed in touch with real happiness. But if it is a curse," Todd said, "then I intend to break it."

Twenty-five

ANNE invited Todd and Doug to dinner on the evening before Todd was to leave for his senior year at Columbia. Doug begged off on the grounds of a meeting at the museum. Anne understood; he was angry that Josh was involved in the fight for the Redwood National Park. He was polite but distant to Josh when they met socially, but it was clear he had no intention of being a guest in Josh's home.

Todd was invited into the nursery to visit with Marsh before Mallie put him to bed. Marsh was exuberant and affectionate. Anne relished the love she felt between her tiny son and Todd. She knew Todd had seen little love in his time. He always seemed so relaxed and happy when he was here.

As usual much of the table talk was about the campus unrest, which showed no signs of letting up. It was infecting campuses across the nation. Todd talked about the hippie community up in Cambridge—the third largest in the nation, after San Francisco and New York—where he occasionally visited a buddy studying at Harvard.

"What's doing with the redwoods?" Todd asked. "I know Doug didn't come to dinner because you're working to promote the park, Josh."

"We're fighting, Todd. A lot of people—not just in California—want to see those trees saved. It took millions of years to create those wonderful old-growth forests." Josh's voice deepened with rage. "And before the end of this century they could be gone forever."

"I don't actually understand—" Todd was apologetic. "I mean, Doug keeps pointing out that Miller Timber cut down redwoods through the past sixty-some-odd years, but he says they've replanted. That the company is rebuilding its forests."

"Naomi Miller replanted redwoods, yes." Josh leaned forward, his face revealing desperate frustration. "Like Weyerhaeuser did. But they replanted with plans to cut in fifty years—and that's what they're doing! Todd, it takes four hundred to a thousand years to bring a redwood to maturity. They're cutting down striplings, with no thought of restoring what nature spent millions of years in creating!"

"I'd like to work with you next summer," Todd said quietly.

"You'll run into trouble with the family," Josh warned.

"I'm always in trouble with the family." Tod grinned. "Let's say I'll be in trouble with part of the family. You and Anne are family, too. Great-grandma Naomi realized that. Otherwise, Annie, she wouldn't have dragged you into the business. I don't think it was just that she felt you would be a real asset to Miller Timber. I think she felt it was time to end the old family feud."

"Don't try to sell that to your parents and your sister," Josh chuckled.

"I just received my ten-thousand-dollar inheritance from the estate," Todd said. "Your father made the official presentation yesterday," he told Josh. "Dad figured I ought to put it toward my tuition and board and room at Harvard Law."

"I thought you're going to Berkeley." Anne stared in shock.

"I am," Todd reassured. "They're just assuming I'm going to Harvard. We don't see much of each other, you know."

"I'm glad you're going to Berkeley," Anne said with warmth. "That way we'll be able to see lots of you. Marsh will be pleased." Todd was one of his favorite people.

Todd hesitated. "I want to contribute five thousand dollars

to your 'save the redwoods' group," he told Josh. "I want to work with you."

Anne listened anxiously for the sound of car wheels on the gravel of the driveway. Had Josh forgotten that they were going to Amelia Devonshire's party tonight? With Josh so exhausted these days—between campus and the redwoods group—she would have manufactured an excuse not to go to Amelia's dinner, but Shirley had tipped her off that Congressman Evans would be there.

Doug had been invited—he was Amelia's favorite "extra man." And Felicia and Glenn would be there. She suspected that she and Josh had been included because Amelia knew of Josh's activities in the campaign for the park—and Congressman Evans was openly in favor of it.

Felicia would be intent on trying to sway the congressman's viewpoint. Let Josh be in there fighting. And she'd be right there beside him, making every effort to keep Felicia and Evans apart.

Anne froze at attention. She heard the crunch of gravel in the driveway, sighed in relief. Josh was home. He'd have to cut short his time with Marsh tonight, she thought guiltily. But with Congressman Evans there, this party was important. Meeting the congressman on a social level could be productive.

Josh grimaced when she reminded him of the party.

"Damn, I'd forgot about it. I suppose we dress?"

"We dress." She smiled cajolingly. "But you'll have a terrific opportunity to talk with Evans. With any luck at all we'll be sitting at his table."

"Annie, you're a conniver," he chuckled and dropped an arm about her waist as they headed for Marsh's room.

Normally society dinners in San Francisco were small, no more than fourteen or sixteen guests. But Amelia Devonshire was a New Yorker before her marriage a dozen years ago to the San Francisco industrialist, and her parties were unusual

310

and large. That would mean a collection of small tables, Anne expected.

Had Amelia been annoyed when she called to drop a hint that she and Josh would like to be seated with the congressman? She had made it clear to Amelia that, since she was on Consuelo's committee for the Christmas charity ball, she'd return the favor.

"You look particularly spectacular tonight, Mrs. Blumberg," Josh teased as they walked into the huge, marble-floored foyer of the Devonshire mansion.

"I wasn't sure about the dress." Anne wore a copy of an Yves St. Laurent evening dress, all sequins and paillettes from white, silver, gunmetal to black and with a brief skirt of black ostrich feathers. "It isn't really me, but Shirley insisted it would be a great conversation piece."

"Not that you ever run short of conversation," Josh ribbed her and then whistled softly. "Oh, wow," he whispered. "Look what just blew in."

Felicia had arrived with Glenn. She wore an evening suit of turquoise velvet knickers and jacket.

"Would you call me catty if I said that outfit is ugly?" Anne said under her breath.

"My sentiments exactly," Josh agreed.

Felicia's smile lost some of its conviviality when she spied Anne and Josh walking into the palatial drawing room. She reached to press Glenn's arm. He turned to Felicia, followed her gaze.

"Oh, hell," he muttered. "Why did Amelia invite them?"

"Ever since that trouble with Adrian they've been thick as thieves with Consuelo."

"Consuelo's not here," he pointed out. Consuelo and Leon had gone down to the Acapulco house for a week.

"Consuelo probably told Amelia to be sure to invite them," Felicia guessed. "She knew Josh would jump at the chance to talk socially with Evans." Now Felicia contrived a dazzling smile. "Amelia, darling, what a marvelous dress. Galanos?"

Felicia discovered forty minutes later that Anne and Josh

311

were seated at Evans's table. "You can be damn sure Anne engineered that," she whispered to Glenn. "And Amelia is bitchy enough to enjoy doing something to annoy me. Everybody knows Evans is infuriating the whole timber industry with his loud-mouthed support for the redwood park."

A festive air filled the elegantly appointed, darkly paneled dining room, set with small tables to accommodate the sixty guests invited for dinner and to hear a jazz concert afterward. As everyone anticipated, the dinner—served on Directoire plates flanked by gold flatware and Waterford goblets—was superb.

Felicia ate without tasting. Anne and Josh must be filling Ezra Evans's ears with dramatic reasons to push for the park. It meant nothing to Anne that Miller Timber owned substantial forests within the area being talked about for the park. The government could condemn and take over that property. It would cost the company at least a million dollars in lost profits.

With Glenn at her side, Felicia contrived to chat briefly—unsatisfactorily—with Evans. Stubborn old bastard, she told herself in irritation. He wasn't as easy to handle as some other California congressmen and senators. But he was up for reelection next year.

"Glenn," she said when they were in the Mercedes en route home, "dig up some seedy private eye and have him look into Ezra Evans's background. There's got to be something there we can use to fight his reelection. Put it on the books as some kind of research."

"Why?" Glenn was curious.

"Because, darling, Doug might be squeamish about our prying into Evans's private life. He doesn't have to know. You'll find a way to write it off. Just maybe Ezra Evans won't be going back to Washington after this term."

Josh sprawled pensively under a light blanket on the queen-size bed he shared with Anne. She walked out of the bathroom and joined him under the blanket.

"You enjoyed talking with Evans, didn't you?" she asked, too stimulated for sleep.

"He made me understand how ill-equipped I am for what I want to do." The frustration in his voice startled Anne.

"He was impressed by you," she reproached. "His eyes lighted up when you talked about how you and Stu are working for the park."

"He couldn't figure us out. Here you are, being groomed to become one of the two big wheels at Miller Timber, and here I am fighting to keep outfits like Miller from desecrating our redwoods."

"Josh, I think he knows where my sympathies lie." And she knew how little impact she had on Miller Timber. Thus far.

"The man thinks so clearly," Josh said in a rush of admiration. "He knows every ploy the timber barons are using to fight against the park. That they're prodding the unions to fight it—not that the unions need much prodding," he conceded humorously. "He knows there are whole towns in some states that are in economic bondage to the timber companies. Towns where as much as seventy percent of the jobs are tied in with the business."

"You know those things, too." She struggled to follow Josh's thinking. What was bugging him tonight?

"I know them, yes." A nerve quivered in one eyelid. "But Annie, Evans can talk with knowledge. He knows the law. He practiced law for a dozen years before he moved into Congress."

"Are you saying that you wish you'd gone on to law school instead of moving into teaching?"

"Yeah," Josh admitted after a moment. "Isn't that the pits? I was mesmerized by the educational process. Maybe I dug the image of myself as a pipe-smoking professor," he jibed. "I never learned to smoke a pipe."

"It's not too late for you to go to law school." She was

313

deliberately matter-of-fact. Her mind trying to cope with this unexpected admission.

"Annie, Bert graduates from law school in June. My kid brother. I'm almost twenty-nine years old. I'd be taking the bar exams when I'm thirty-two."

"That's not ancient," she shot back. Now she understood his restlessness this past year. "You won't have any trouble getting into Berkeley Law."

"I can't give up my job to go back to school," he protested. "I goofed. I admit it."

"You're going to law school," she said strongly. "I know no rule that says you can't change career directions because you're past twenty-five. Josh, you know now what you truly want to do. Go for it!"

He hesitated, then shook his head with conviction.

"Annie, we can't afford for me to quit work. Not with our expenses. We have firm commitments."

"We can afford it." She pulled herself up against the headboard and reached for Josh's hand. "The way we've reduced Lazarus Timber's loan, I can go in and refinance, spreading the payments over more time, reducing the monthly payments. It makes sense! It's an investment in our future." *She must make Josh understand this.*

"I don't know." His eyes were troubled. "Your father would be upset—"

"Dad won't be upset. If anybody in this world can understand what you're going through, it's Dad. He never wanted to be in the timber business—my mother pushed him into it. He belonged on a college campus teaching—or editing a literary magazine. Maybe it's too late for this term, but you get yourself enrolled for next term at Berkeley Law. You'll go to summer school. Before we know it, you'll be taking your bar exams."

Josh reached to pull her close. "Did I ever tell you that you're a very special lady?"

"A few times," she said tenderly. "But I won't let it go to my head."

Twenty-six

ANNE was upset by the continuing breach between Doug and Josh, fostered she knew by Felicia. Knowing the situation between the two men, Artie and Tess insisted that this Thanksgiving Anne and Josh, along with Marsh, attend a family dinner at their home.

"Doug promised to drop by for a late supper," Artie said diplomatically.

Anne knew that Doug dreaded the holiday, the second Thanksgiving since Eva's death. And she suspected he was upset that he was losing his battle to keep the family together on major holidays. They used Naomi Miller's houses as it pleased them—not for a gathering of the clan.

Edwina and Bruce explained that they would be in Palm Springs again for Thanksgiving. Todd would remain in New York because of his involvement in the turbulent student unrest at Columbia. Adrian was still in the sanitarium, and Consuelo and Leon would leave immediately after the mid-afternoon Thanksgiving dinner at the Miller house to visit with him.

Anne decided to wait until Thanksgiving morning to tell Josh that she was pregnant again. By then she knew it was a certainty. While they had not planned on having a second child just yet, she was joyous at the prospect. Her one concern was that Josh might refuse to go on to law school now. That

315

he might feel the responsibility of another child demanded he continue with his teaching.

"Annie!" His face glowed when she told him. "You're sure?"

"I'm sure."

"Thank God, they haven't hired a replacement for me yet at school. They're still interviewing."

"Josh, this doesn't change anything," she insisted. "You're going to law school."

"With two kids you expect me to go to law school?" he derided.

"You damn well better." She braced herself for a battle. "I want my kids to be proud of their father. You'd be miserable if you stayed with teaching. You'd never be able to accomplish what you want to do—and that's important for them, too."

"It's not right. You tied down to the Miller Timber straitjacket, and I go off to play being a law student."

"It's not playing," she said with a touch of impatience. "You're serious about law. I'm doing what I want to do. You have to do the same. Your heart and soul are in public service—and I love you for that. Three years of law school won't be so awful."

"We'll play it by ear," Josh hedged. But Anne knew she had won.

"I told the family we'd be over early," she said. "I'll help Tess in the kitchen, and you three guys can spoil Marsh and watch football." She paused. "Don't say anything just yet about the new baby. Let's tell them later in the day." She nurtured a shakey hope that the announcement of her pregnancy might bring Josh and Doug together again.

Anne still relished the warmth and love that enveloped her in the Blumberg household. Artie was proud and happy that Josh would shortly begin his studies at Berkeley Law, though he was uncomfortable that his older son was fighting a long-time major client of his law firm. Anne remembered how he had talked about Josh on that flight aboard the Miller jet when

316

he brought her from Belleville to San Francisco four years ago.

"Josh is bright and warm and compassionate. But I don't understand him. I worry about him."

The clash of values might bring on angry words, but love prevailed.

Not until late in the evening—while Doug sat with Artie before the blaze in the living room fireplace and argued good-humoredly about the memorable football game between Southern California and UCLA on the eighteenth—did Anne announce that Marsh would have a baby brother or sister sometime late in June.

The discussion of the football game was arrested as Anne's words reached Doug and Artie. The living room was suddenly electric with pleasurable excitement. Artie jumped from his chair to go to embrace his daughter-in-law. Tess flung her arms about Josh. Bert hoisted Marsh into the air with comic delight.

"Josh, that's marvelous news," Doug said, extending a hand. Anne exchanged a vibrant smile with her mother-in-law. "I'm very happy for you both." Doug grinned. "And for you, too, Marsh." He reached to take Marsh from his young uncle. "You have any preferences, young man?" he teased. "Sister or brother?"

Again, Anne's waking moments were dominated by the knowledge that she was carrying a second child. As with Marsh, she would continue to be at the office until close to delivery. At Christmas she and Josh, along with Marsh, joined the family at the Squaw Valley house. Anne suspected that Felicia had ordered her parents to be part of the family circle.

Felicia resented the familial closeness between Doug and Anne. To Felicia she was an outsider—no matter that Naomi had been her great-aunt. Todd was there, as well as Consuelo and Leon—three on her side, she tallied humorously. Adrian would remain at the sanitarium until the first of the year.

The first months of 1968 were hectic. On January 5 Dr. Benjamin Spock and Rev. William Sloane Coffin of Yale were indicted for conspiracy to aid and abet draft evasion. On February 1 former Vice-President Richard Nixon announced he would be a candidate for the Republican presidential nomination. Eight days later former Governor of Alabama George Wallace announced he would run as a third-party candidate.

Edwina and Bruce were indignant when Todd did not come home for the spring break. Instead, he was working as a volunteer for Eugene McCarthy in the New Hampshire Democratic presidential primary. Again, Edwina railed at Anne for encouraging his activities.

"Be glad Todd isn't taking off the next term," Anne said coolly. "Some students are doing that so they can work for McCarthy full time until the convention in August."

"He couldn't do that!" Edwina shrieked. "He graduates this year!"

None of the political upheaval in the country touched Denise Forrest in Georgia. Her major grievance was that Avis and her husband had gone to the south of France for the month of March, abandoning their usual plans for a month in Palm Beach early in the year. She had been invited to join them at their rented villa at Nice for two weeks, but Kevin insisted they couldn't afford to buy all the clothes she would demand plus the money for the airfare.

Why couldn't Kevin ask Anne to get the money together for her, she asked herself at reproachful intervals. In her situation Anne could walk into any bank and take out a loan. She harbored unceasing resentment toward Naomi Miller for leaving her out of the will. That ten-thousand-dollar bequest— long gone—was just ridiculous.

On this mid-March morning—in a red velvet housecoat because the weather was cool—Denise lingered before her dressing table mirror and focused on her eye makeup with the dedication of a Hollywood makeup artist. Attractive eyes drew attention away from the fine lines. Not that anybody who didn't already know would ever dream she was almost fifty-three. Ross thought she was forty-one. A year older than he.

Her whole life had changed since Ross Leonard moved into town and opened up his antique shop. Ross understood her. He was so sweet and attentive.

Ross knew about Anne and her inheritance. He didn't know Anne had a child who was past two and that she was pregnant again. Thank God, he was away on a business trip when Anne and her ménage came to celebrate Marsh's birthday down in Belleville. He'd gone up to Charleston to arrange for the shipment of the rest of the antiques from his shop up there—his share of the divorce settlement.

Now Denise listened for sounds from the kitchen that would indicate Mary Lou was about to leave. On Wednesdays she made the beds, dusted, fixed a casserole for their dinner, and took off for the rest of the day. It was ridiculous of Kevin to insist that Mary Lou have Wednesday afternoons off in addition to Sundays. He spoiled her rotten. Still, it was most convenient now that she was seeing Ross.

Ross said he'd drop by around one-thirty or two. That was when he could take off from the shop and pretend he was off to inspect an antique up for sale. She preened with satisfaction. He insisted she be his consultant—on a voluntary basis, of course—when he opened up the interior decorating department at the shop. He was bringing in a professional decorator, but he said he'd feel more secure knowing she was keeping an eye on things.

"Miss Denise, I put the casserole in the fridge." Mary Lou appeared at the bedroom doorway. "You jes' sit it in the oven and turn the temperature up to three hundred degrees for about twenty minutes. The salad's made, and I baked a bread pudding for dessert. And there's a plate of those little finger sandwiches you like for lunch and a perc of fresh coffee."

"That's lovely, Mary Lou," Denise said sweetly. "Now you run along and enjoy your afternoon."

When she heard the front door close downstairs, Denise left her bedroom to go down to the kitchen for the plate of sandwiches and a cup of coffee. A faint whisper of heat rose in the radiators that had been installed in the house just before she married Kevin. She'd fix herself a tray and have it in bed. Then she'd look refreshed when Ross arrived. Nobody suspected anything—even though he popped in this way every Wednesday afternoon. Folks knew she was artistic and interested in Ross's new interior decorating department.

She finished her lunch, leaned back against the pillows with her eyes closed for fifteen minutes in the conviction that these brief rests erased the lines in her face. She carried the tray downstairs, dumped the dishes in the dishwasher, went to the front door to make sure it was unlocked so that Ross could come right upstairs to the bedroom as usual.

At the second-floor landing she paused to shift the thermostat upward five degrees. She wanted her bedroom warm so she could wear one of her lovely nightie-and-peignoir ensembles. She changed into a black chiffon ballerina length, lace-trimmed nightie with matching peignoir. She inspected her reflection in the mirror with approval. The ballerina length was so much more romantic than those silly "baby dolls."

She glanced at her watch. Ross wouldn't be here for another fifteen minutes, at least. Slide under the covers until the heat came up stronger. Then she could smooth out the spread again.

Ross adored her in black. He said it made him just want to climb the walls when he saw her like this. All white skin under black chiffon. She never allowed herself to tan, no matter how chic it was supposed to be. Men worshipped white, white skin.

At the sound of a car turning into the driveway she left the bed, rearranged the ivory chenille bedspread, and crossed to her dressing table for the bottle of Chanel No. 5. Just a bit more between her breasts and behind each ear. Now she walked out into the hall.

"Ross?" She stood at the landing with a welcoming smile, feeling herself a thirty-year-old Marilyn Monroe.

"Hi, baby." Ross was bounding up the stairs now.

"I thought you'd never get here." She pretended to pout. Lord, he was good-looking. When he walked into a room, every woman turned to stare at him. A lot of men in this town were envious of him. They called him a womanizer. Just because he had been married and divorced twice.

"I had to wait for Joe to return from lunch," he explained and set down his briefcase—which was supposed to explain his absence from the shop—to pull her close. "You looked absolutely gorgeous last night at the day-nursery benefit dinner. I wanted to pull you out of there and throw you into the bushes."

"Ross, you do carry on." He thought she was gorgeous and sexy and great in bed.

Arm-in-arm they walked into her bedroom. The heavily lined floral drapes were pulled closed to bathe the room in shadows. Flattering shadows. Denise abandoned herself to Ross, pretending an impatience that matched his own. Knowing he wouldn't rush. She still had a marvelous body, she thought complacently while Ross whispered heated endearments.

Now she steeled herself to respond to his ardent invasion. The one advantage of menopause, she congratulated herself, was that she didn't have to worry about getting pregnant.

"Wouldn't it be sensational if we could do this every night?" Ross lay back against the pillows with an air of satisfaction.

"Darling, don't be greedy," she scolded. Once a week was quite enough. And he knew she'd never divorce Kevin. Despite all that talk about the "new woman," folks in Belleville would be shocked if a wife divorced her husband after so many years of marriage. "Now tell me about the interior decorators you interviewed up in Atlanta yesterday."

She made a pretense of listening while he elaborated on the

problems in choosing just the right decorator, then began to outline his latest plan for expansion.

"I can't do this on the small scale I originally planned," he said seriously. "I'd be doomed to failure. This shop has to be a huge success."

Ross was forty, Denise remembered while he continued, and obsessive about becoming successful. But the shop should do well. Women were just drawn to Ross. Then all at once she stiffened beneath the flower-sprigged sheet, *What was Ross getting at?*

"I can manage on twenty-five thousand, Denise. You'll be my silent partner. Nobody has to know."

"Ross, I don't have twenty-five thousand to give you."

"You can get it from Anne," he insisted.

"I can't get ten cents from Anne," she said, fury blending with humiliation in her. *All Ross wanted from her was money. Everything else was lies.*

"You talk a blue streak about how rich your daughter is!" A vein pounded at his temple. "You can't buy clothes like you wear on what Kevin brings home!"

"My aunt left me ten thousand dollars. I spent it on wardrobe." She felt suddenly sick. "Ross, I think you'd better go."

"You led me on!" He sat upright in bed. "All that shit about your daughter being worth sixty million . . . damn you!" He slapped her a dizzying blow across one cheek, and she screamed in sudden terror. "Shut up you little bitch! Shut up!"

She screamed again. Ross grabbed at her throat.

"Shut up before the whole town comes running!" His large muscular hands closed in to silence her screams. And then she wasn't screaming anymore. She was silent. Hanging limp and lifeless from his hands.

Anne was just about to leave for lunch when her private line rang. She reached for the phone.

"Anne Blumberg."

"Annie—" Her father's voice, harsh with anguish.

"Dad, what is it?" Terror ricocheted in her. "Daddy?"

"I don't know how to tell you this. I can't make it easy for you, baby. A little while ago I received a phone call from the police." He was struggling to talk. "The McFeeters next door heard a scream in the house and called them. Annie, your mother's dead. She was raped and murdered."

"Oh my God." Anne was ashen. "Dad, I'll be on the next plane home."

"You shouldn't travel when you're this far into your pregnancy. And there's nothing you can do. You stay there, Annie. But I had to tell you."

"I'm coming home." She couldn't let him go through this alone. "I'll call you later and let you know when I'll arrive."

She sat motionless at her desk, trying to absorb what her father had told her.

"Anne?" Expecting to go to lunch with her, Shirley appeared in the doorway. "Annie, what's happened?"

Haltingly, enveloped in shock, Anne told Shirley about her father's phone call. They talked in hushed tones for a few moments.

"I have to go home and pack." Anne pushed back her chair and rose to her feet. "And I have to call Josh. Marsh will be all right with Josh and Mallie while I'm gone."

When Anne told Doug about her mother's death, he insisted that she fly home on the company plane. The crew would stand by to bring her back after the funeral.

"Josh will go with you, of course," Doug said. "Don't worry about Marsh. He loves Mallie. And I'll drop by to see him every day. Shirley will, too—and Tess and Artie. Just tell me what time you want to leave. I'll have the flight crew waiting at the airport."

Late in the evening eastern time the Miller plane landed at the Belleville airport. Kevin was waiting for them. While she clung to her father in grief, Anne automatically read the

323

headline of the evening newspaper left on a bench in the waiting room: BEAUTIFUL SOCIETY MATRON MURDERED.

Anne fought to make her father understand he was not responsible for her mother's death, but he clung to this conviction.

"If I had agreed to her going to France with Avis, this would not have happened. I'm always so damned conservative."

"It's not your fault, Dad."

Standing between her father and Josh while the rabbi delivered the graveside service, Anne remembered Todd's words: *Sometimes I ask myself if being part of Naomi Miller's family is a curse.*

Only hours after the funeral Anne and Josh boarded the plane for the return trip to San Francisco. She clung to her father with a desperate wish that he could come with them to California. As a child she had taken it for granted that she would live and die in Belleville. But this was a world where families were divided. Physically as well as emotionally. One child in one part of the country, another thousands of miles away.

"Dad, you'll come out when the baby is born," she ordered. "And tell Mary Lou I want to bring her out, too."

"You'll never get Mary Lou on a plane." Her father's laugh was shakey.

"Then she'll come out on the train. In a drawing room," Anne promised lavishly. Mother had been Mary Lou's "baby"—though Mary Lou was only fifteen years older than she. And in turn she had been Mary Lou's "baby." Mary Lou was family. She could retire now because—unlike so many others with domestic help—Dad had insisted on paying social security for Mary Lou, including Mary Lou's share. But Mary Lou had told her—her big brown eyes red from weeping— that she would be there to look after "my Mister Kevin."

"You tell her she has to come out to San Francisco to see my babies."

Like most Americans Anne reeled from the events of the next few weeks. Days after her mother's funeral Senator Robert Kennedy announced he would be a candidate for the Democratic presidential nomination. On March 31—in a dramatic TV appearance—President Johnson announced he would not seek another term. At Berkeley activists told themselves that at last hope was ahead. Parties erupted spontaneously. Cars drove through the streets, drivers honking in jubilation.

On April 4 civil rights leader and Nobel Prize winner Dr. Martin Luther King, Jr. was assassinated. Few were surprised by the week of rioting that occurred in the urban ghettos. Nineteen days after the King assassination Columbia students—rebelling mainly against the slum-owning university's tie-in with war-related research and its disregard for the needs of the neighboring black community—occupied campus buildings.

After eight days of efforts at negotiations, Columbia's President Kirk called in the police. A thousand policemen came onto campus in the middle of the night and arrested 692. Todd managed to phone home. His parents were at the Homestead, but he reached Anne and Josh.

"I'm okay," he insisted. "Just a bunch of bruises. The fuzz think Columbia students are a bunch of spoiled rich kids," he added bitterly. "But this isn't over. We're calling for a student strike. We'll close the university."

At Columbia, Todd wrote later, students sat in on classes on the lawns, picketed the classroom buildings. The police remained everywhere. It seemed an agonizingly long time, Todd reported on his return to San Francisco, before the school year was over. He was glad, he said, that he'd dropped some courses so he could focus on what was happening at school—even though this meant delaying graduation for another year. "Anyhow, there are some prelaw courses I should take."

Then shortly past midnight on June 4, Robert Kennedy was shot. Twenty-five hours later he was dead. For the second time in a little over two months the nation was in mourning.

Late in June Anne gave birth to a daughter, to be named Robin Denise Blumberg, after her great-grandmother and grandmother. Though Mary Lou, fearful of flying, made up excuses not to come, Kevin flew out to see his second grandchild. He looked old beyond his years, Anne thought. He closed his mind to the commonly held belief that his wife had died at the hands of her lover. Ross Leonard had committed suicide when the police began to close in on him as the murderer. There had been no question of rape in the minds of the police.

"Robin is the image of you when you were born," Kevin told Anne with pride and pleasure. "That same mane of heavy dark hair. The same high cheekbones. Thank you for giving me a beautiful granddaughter."

"I wish you'd stay for a while," Anne tried again, but she knew he would insist on returning home quickly.

"I have a company to run," he reminded, his face suddenly serious. "I worry about the way lumber prices are soaring. It's the timber industry manipulating again. Carrying on about a timber shortage."

"And that allows them to demand that the Forest Service up the cut in the national forests." Anne nodded in agreement. "I know Miller has an enormous amount of uncut timber we've bought in the national forests—enough to keep us going for at least two years even if we didn't cut one tree on our private lands."

"The lumber shortage is the result of several factors, Annie," Kevin said. "First, we're exporting too damn much to Japan—"

"I've been fighting with Doug and the board about that," Anne told him. "I'm getting nowhere."

"Then the country's been plagued by a dock strike," Kevin continued. "We're all having problems with the shortage of railroad boxcars for domestic shipments. And too many retailers—figuring wholesale prices have to drop again—are keeping their inventories down to the very minimum. It adds up to a possible lumber crisis, particularly with all the talk about soaring demands for new housing."

"In some way," Anne said determinedly, "I must make Doug and the board understand how many small or dead trees are being left to rot on logging sites. That's a lot of potential lumber—and it's there. And we have to learn at our sawmills not to waste wood residues the way we're doing. You don't at Lazarus," she added with pride. "I had Doug on my side about the wastage until reports I'd received were recast. I can't prove it, but I know Felicia was somehow responsible."

"I had a long talk with Josh last night," Kevin said. "He's so aware of the responsibilities of the timber industry to the environment." His affection for Josh was obvious. "He didn't say much about his law studies. Is he happy about the switch?"

Anne's face lighted. "Very much so." She knew, though, that Josh was upset that he wasn't contributing to the family budget. That wasn't important right now. "Dad, I've been thinking." She knew how her father still grieved for her mother, still blaming himself for her death. The memory of the long, painful years of his marriage had been replaced with the recall of the sweet months of their courtship. He remembered only the lovely, bewitching young Denise. He needed a strong distraction. "Dad, I think it would be very smart of Lazarus Timber to expand its holdings."

He lifted an eyebrow in doubt. "When we're just moving into a comfortable financial situation?"

"Lazarus can't stay small—we have to enlarge to compete today. For Grandma, let's make Lazarus one of the most important companies in the South."

"Annie, you're talking big money." He was ambivalent, yet she knew he was intrigued by the challenge. And he knew she was right. There was no middle road anymore.

"I'll have no trouble enlarging our bank loan. Dad, I can handle it," she persisted. "Look how Weyerhaeuser is moving into the South. Grandma always said the South would dominate the industry before the 1980s."

"What would you like to see us do?"

"Most of the timber in the South is in small plots," she reminded. "Let's buy up wooded plots from farmers who're willing to sell. With proper management—and Dad, you know how rare that is today—we can double the yield. Even at current prices we'll be ahead of the game. We'll be extending the company," she said with a surge of exhilaration, "and at the same time we'll be utilizing the forests the way they should be utilized. We'll cut selectively—and promptly reseed and nurture." *When would she be able to make Doug understand the urgency of setting up a research department?*

"Spoken like your grandmother," Kevin said tenderly, and in her mind Anne heard Doug making this same comment to Felicia. "We'll have to work out the figures," he cautioned, but she sensed his excitement. "We don't want to go overboard."

Dad would be so absorbed in this expansion he'd have little time to blame himself for her mother's death, Anne congratulated herself. This was the kind of challenge he'd grown to respect through the years. He was helping to continue Rae Lazarus's dynasty.

All at once Anne was wistful that she would be here in San Francisco instead of sharing this new campaign. She was conscious of a towering sense of homesickness, of a yearning to walk out on this whole insane way of life. But here she must remain—despite the constant hostility, the covert efforts of Felicia and her clique to sabotage her own efforts to bring about dramatic changes at Miller.

How could she walk out when so much depended upon her remaining here? Josh and law school. Her father and Lazarus Timber. And precious financial security for Marsh and Robin. She wasn't Anne Forrest of Belleville, Georgia, anymore. She was part of the tapestry woven by Naomi Miller.

She had chosen this path.

Twenty-seven

UP until the final moment, the timber industry fought to control the boundaries of the proposed Redwood National Park. Their influence was clear in the final bill presented to Congress.

"The terms are pretty much to our liking," Doug announced at a board meeting a few days after passage. Anne flinched as she remembered how Josh had raged that the proposed park was being used for political bargaining and power plays.

On October 2, 1968 President Johnson—who had made a public commitment to save the redwoods—signed the Redwood National Park bill. The Pacific Coast timber companies were smug; the compromises that had brought about the bill allowed them to log their lucrative remaining old-growth timber in the Redwood Creek watershed.

Anne and Josh listened to the reports on the late TV news, then he switched off the set with a grunt of frustration.

"Soon there won't be anything left in Redwood Creek except bare slopes. They'll put in more tractor-made roads and create gullies that send topsoil into the rivers, plugging it with dirt and rocks. Where once there had been such great beauty," he said bitterly, "there'll be only ugliness."

"It's a beginning, Josh." Anne strove for a positive note.

"We've got a long, tough road ahead if we're to save this country's forests. I'm not talking just about the redwoods. The

Forest Service is fighting the Wilderness Act in nearly every state with a national forest."

"Oh, I picked up something that you might want to discuss at your next meeting." She wasn't being traitorous to Miller Timber to feed these tidbits to Josh's conservation group, she thought defensively. Miller Timber—like many other companies—was being traitorous to the American people in the way they handled the nation's heritage. "There's serious talk at the American Forest Institute about cleaning up the industry's image. In the next few months that'll be coming under intense study."

"You mean they'll be dreaming up ways to convince the public that it's important for the timber companies to log more trees. And they'll be working again with the labor unions about how many jobs will be lost if the cuts aren't upped in the federal forests."

"They're considering huge advertising campaigns, from what I understand. In consumer magazines and newspapers. Probably radio and TV coverage."

"We'll be on the lookout," Josh promised. The timber companies and related businesses would rush to contribute financially. "They have so much money behind them," he sighed, "and we have so little."

The atmosphere in the comfortably large kitchen of the younger Blumbergs' house was mellow on this early morning of the first day of 1969.

"It was a great party," Shirley told Anne while the two of them piled the dishes that could not fit into the dishwasher into the sink to soak. "Gerry was so excited to be allowed to come. I never thought she'd make it through to midnight, but she was determined."

"Gerry considers herself practically grown up," Anne laughed. "She's a baby-sitter in training now." Gerry had finally been coaxed to go to sleep in the den.

330

"Will you two stop fussing and come sit down with us?" Stu ordered with mock sternness.

"I'm bringing fresh coffee," Shirley said. "That's why you're rushing us to the table."

"What do I have to do to make this woman marry me?" Stu demanded of Josh while he patted her rump.

"Stu, this is a new year," Shirley noted. "You made a resolution to stay off that track. Besides, I'm too old for you."

"Every year it seems less," he shot back and sighed. "I look at Josh and Anne, and I'm jealous." But Anne suspected he knew it was futile to push his relationship with Shirley into a formal one. In another era, she thought—where feminism was not becoming such a strong issue—Shirley would have married him by now.

"Thank God, 1968 is over," Josh said with a rueful smile. "What a bastard it's been!"

For a charged moment there was silence in the kitchen, the four remembering a year that included two assassinations, campus violence across the country, no sign of peace in Vietnam, the horrors of the riots in the Negro district of Miami beginning the day before the Republican convention in Miami, and the brutality of the Democratic convention in Chicago.

"I'm scared to think what Nixon is going to do about forest conservation," Josh said tautly. "Johnson was our friend. Nixon will play ball with the timber big wheels."

"My crystal ball says we're in for some rough times." Stu shook his head in pessimism.

"Finish your coffee and take me home," Shirley jibed, "or you'll be in for a rough time." She turned to Anne. "Thanks for keeping Gerry here overnight."

"Yeah." Stu grinned. "It's almost like a honeymoon for us."

In his bedroom in the luxurious Hillsborough house that his great-grandmother had given to his parents as a wedding present, Adrian sprawled across his bed and listened to the sounds down the hall. Within the next hour his parents would be heading for the airport on their usual safari to Rio, he thought smugly. He'd have the whole house to himself. The servants would be on vacation for all of January.

Of course, his parents expected him to stay with Doug and Felicia at the Miller house until it was time to return to school. But he wasn't going back to school. He'd say good-bye, pretend to head for the airport, and come back here. He'd had all he could take of the school shit. He'd face his parents when they came back. He'd talk about all the drugs on campus and how he was scared he'd get hooked again.

In nine weeks—on his twenty-first birthday—he would collect his ten-thousand-dollar inheritance from Naomi's estate. She'd always told him and Felicia that they were the only ones in the family worth a damn. She let them believe they'd inherit almost everything. She was putting Felicia through hell to get her share, and he ended up with nothing.

He didn't have to wait until his birthday to collect, he thought with sudden exuberance. He'd talk to Felicia about loaning him the ten thousand now—she knew he'd pay her back in a few weeks.

"Adrian—" His mother's voice called from down the hall. "Darling, we're ready to leave for the airport. We'll drop you off at the house en route."

"I'm not ready to leave." He leapt to his feet and crossed to the door as his parents approached, switching on the potent Adrian Harris charm. "I'll throw my gear together later and call Walter to come over for me."

"Be sure you lock up the house before you leave," his father instructed. "And for God's sake, Adrian, stay out of trouble."

"Be cool, Dad," he chuckled. "I won't get into any trouble. Have fun down in Rio."

Late in the afternoon he called the house to have Walter drive over for him. Settled in his room at the Miller house he debated about going out to North Beach to see what action he could dig up, dismissed this. Tonight he'd have dinner at the house. If Felicia was home, maybe he could find the right moment to ask her about advancing him the ten thousand.

He was listening to Janis Joplin on the library stereo when Doug arrived home and walked down the hall to the library doorway.

"Good Lord, Adrian, are all you kids of this generation hard-of-hearing?"

"Be cool, Doug," he drawled. "Cool" was his favorite adjective these days. "I'll turn it down." Doug was pissed off that he was going to be here until school opened.

"I gather your parents took off on schedule?"

"Right. They're already headed for Rio."

"We'll have dinner in about half an hour. Felicia and Glenn have to leave early for the theater."

Adrian realized when he joined the other three in the dining room that he wouldn't be able to talk to Felicia tonight. Okay, so it could wait a day or two. He wasn't going anywhere.

Over dinner, as usual, most of the talk was about business. He listened without absorbing what was said until the conversation became heated.

"Doug, we have to fill our export orders to Tsuda! We make a fortune on that deal," Felicia said.

"You know about the 1968 export ban," Doug replied, his face taut. "We can't use our national forest cuts for export. And we've already logged everything we bought for Tsuda."

"Then we'll go out and look for more," she insisted. "The situation hasn't changed. Small timberland owners out here are still stuck with paying high taxes on forty-year-old stands."

"There are not that many stands out there now," Doug shot back.

"We'll find them," Felicia said coolly. "It may take a while, but we'll find them. We can't screw up with Tsuda."

"I have no time for that." Doug was testy. "Put it on your agenda."

"I'll start on the project in about two weeks." She wasn't

333

happy about having it dumped on her shoulders, Adrian noted. "We can't afford to mess up on the Japanese exports."

Adrian listened with covert attention as the other two, along with Glenn, dissected the possible availability of small stands in northern California and Oregon. Maybe there was a way here for him to make a real deal for himself. Using his ten-thousand-dollar inheritance as option money.

Two days later Adrian took Felicia out for lunch.

"We'll put it on my expense account," Felicia said indulgently when they were seated at a table at Trader Vic's. Adrian knew she was curious about his luncheon invitation, but there was always something special between them. Everybody had always known they were Naomi's favorites.

Felicia's eyes grew wary as he explained his mission.

"Sweetie, Glenn and I are always just one jump ahead of our pay checks," she apologized. "Some months we borrow."

"I have a deal going, Felicia," he said softly. "How the hell do I borrow against the inheritance?"

"What kind of a deal?"

"Business." He grinned. "Naomi always said that you and I had her business sense. I can't tell you till it's set, but I'll at least double that ten thousand. Possibly quadruple it," he boasted with a confidence he sensed she respected. "I can't wait till the middle of March. I need it fast—" He paused. "Within the next week."

"You won't get it from a bank," Felicia warned. "You're under twenty-one, for starters."

"Where can I get it?" he demanded. "You know any loan-sharks?"

"Glenn does. But that's risky business. And expensive."

"No risk," he dismissed this. "I pick up the check at the lawyers' offices on the morning of my twenty-first birthday. And I can afford the tariff."

"I'll have Glenn set it up for you. Adrian, I hope you know what the hell you're doing."

Adrian's smile was smug. "I know."

In twenty-four hours Adrian was depositing ten thousand

dollars in his personal checking account—regarded as his "school account." He was to repay twelve thousand within nine weeks. With the money deposited he rented a car and began his search. By early the following week he had spent most of the ten thousand on six-month options on small tracts of wooded land in northern California.

On Wednesday evening at the dinner table Adrian brought up the subject of his options.

"I have enough acreage optioned to handle your Japanese exports for a year," he assured Doug and Felicia. He'd listened closely to their conversation about their needs. He'd made mental notes. "Exactly what you talked about at dinner last week. The options are yours for fifty thousand."

"They cost you ten thousand," Felicia shot back.

"You'll pay fifty thousand," Adrian sparred. "The timber is all there with no sweat for you. I have six-month options. If you don't want the stands, I'll peddle them somewhere else." He ignored Doug's glazed stare of disbelief.

"Adrian," Felicia scolded, "you're a greedy bastard."

"A smart bastard," he said calmly. "I have what you want." Felicia exchanged a swift glance with Doug.

"We'll buy," she said. "Be at the office tomorrow morning at ten."

This was just the beginning, Adrian told himself in triumph. Felicia knew he was smart—and she respected that. Felicia stood to control the business when she finally got around to pushing out Doug. And he meant to be Felicia's second-in-command.

He had to take care of himself. The old lady left him out in the cold. He'd never see anything from his parents. They were always crying about being broke. They'd even cut back on his allowance. Felicia was the one to follow. Together they made a sensational team. Together they'd take care of Doug. And then they'd take care of that dumb bitch Anne.

335

Twenty-eight

"OH shit!" Felicia slammed on the brake with an intensity that the car resented, but she avoided smashing into the bumper ahead.

Most days she left the office late enough to avoid this bumper-to-bumper rush hour crawl, but she wanted plenty of time to dress for tonight's gala at the Naomi Miller Museum. Usually Glenn drove, which allowed her to use traveling time to study Adrian's latest proposal. Some of them were off-the-wall, she admitted, but some were shrewd.

The traffic was not the major reason for her irritable mood. Doug was mainly responsible. How could he have been so stupid as to say he'd seriously consider setting up a research department at the company, she asked herself yet again. That would cost a fortune and was unnecessary. Let the others spend money on research. It was easy enough to infiltrate and learn what they were coming up with.

Anne had been beating the drums for that damn research department for years. Let Weyerhaeuser and Georgia-Pacific waste profits—and valuable time—on that. Adrian had a talent for digging up employees who'd hand over info for a price.

The cars began to move. Again, she noted, the tieup was due to a disabled vehicle. But she'd have plenty of time. The days were long past when she needed two hours to dress for a party.

Normally she was bored by the galas at the Naomi Miller Museum—which were command performances for family members in town. Tonight she was eager to attend.

"Craig Preston's in town on business," Doug had mentioned this morning. He had no idea that she and Craig had a mad fling at Cannes summer before last. Craig didn't know—nobody knew—that Karen was his daughter. "You know how Angela Conway always takes two subscriptions to every museum event in town." Angela was an eighty-five-year-old patroness of the arts, who delighted in bringing important men to these affairs. "She's bringing Preston tonight in the hope that he'll make a big contribution to the museum."

It seemed incredible that she and Craig hadn't run into each other since Cannes—but they were both on a treadmill. And her traveling took second place these days, she remembered grimly. She'd never expected to change her life-style this way. She hadn't expected to be mesmerized by the potential of becoming a second Naomi Miller.

But now she was sick of fighting for control of the company. Doug would stay on until he was ninety—like Naomi. He'd never feel sure enough of her, or of Anne, to let go. She was kidding herself to think he would.

Didn't he understand that he *needed* her? Naomi had known he didn't have the shrewdness, the imagination, the conniving mind to keep Miller Timber moving ahead. But damn it, she'd wasted close to six years in this rotten rat race. Married to Craig she could have everything she wanted. Mistress of half a dozen gorgeous homes, a yacht, a private jet on call. Fuck Miller Timber.

In her bedroom—pleased that Glenn had flown up to their Portland office this morning and wouldn't be back until tomorrow evening—Felicia concentrated on dressing. Alert to the passing time she inspected her reflection in the full-length cheval mirror. Yes, she decided with satisfaction, Craig would approve. The beaded minidress from Yves St. Laurent's spring collection was marvelously flattering to her.

Nobody had ever excited her the way Craig had those few

days in Cannes. Had he turned her on that way because she knew he was one of the richest and most powerful men in the world? Or was it because she thought—then—that he was unattainable? There was no man who was unattainable if the right approach was used. Again rumors were flying that he and Hera were talking divorce. *Was she ready to trade in Miller Timber for Craig Preston?*

She started at a knock on her door.

"Yes?" She crossed to her dressing table for the atomizer of Miss Dior.

"We have to leave for the museum in five minutes," Doug called through the door. "I'll be waiting for you downstairs."

"I'll be right down," she said.

In exactly five minutes—because she made a point these days of not antagonizing Doug—Felicia took her sequined evening coat from the closet and hurried down to the foyer. Her parents, she remembered, would not be there tonight, they were at a houseparty in Pasadena. Consuelo and Leon would be there. Consuelo was on the gala committee. And Anne and Josh never missed an affair at the museum. Always playing politics with Doug.

Consuelo would be there early, Felicia imagined as Doug followed her into the limousine. She would casually mention that she had met Craig Preston at Cannes and suggest the seating arrangements be adjusted so that she could sit at his table. She'd hint to Consuelo that she might be able to persuade Craig to make a major donation to the Naomi Miller Museum.

At the festively illuminated museum she immediately sought out Consuelo—busy with a last-minute check of the dining areas—and contrived for the change in the seating arrangements.

"It's no problem," Consuelo assured her. "Angela Conway is his hostess while he's in town, but she's ill again, poor darling. I was having an awful time trying to find him a suitable dinner partner tonight. I'd put Joyce there because I always have to find a partner for her. Now she can sit with Doug."

338

Walking down the wide, circular staircase Felicia saw Craig arrive. Alone. Aware of a flicker of passion she strode toward him. It was so rare that she felt this kind of excitement. Sex with Glenn was dull and predictable. He always complained she was cold. Right now she wasn't cold. A pulse was going crazy down there. For Craig.

"Hi," she drawled and he swung toward her with an electric smile.

"I figured you'd be here tonight." He extended a hand as though in casual greeting, but the pressure of his fingers was eloquent. "That's why I agreed to come. Where have you been keeping yourself?" he scolded. "It's been too damn long."

"I'm a working woman, remember?" Her eyes were mocking. "I don't play the jet-set circuit these days."

"You do make occasional escapes," he challenged.

"I do," she conceded. "And by the way, I connived to be your dinner partner tonight."

"What about after dinner?" he asked, his smile a charismatic invitation.

"Where are you staying?"

"At the Mark Hopkins."

"I'll meet you at The Top of the Mark half an hour after I walk out of here," she told him. She'd have Doug drop her off en route to the house—*"I'm meeting some people for a few drinks."*

The evening dragged unbearably, though under the dinner table Craig's knee pressed hers in hot promise while he simultaneously carried on a somber conversation with the woman on his right about the war in Vietnam, where U.S. combat deaths had passed those killed in the Korean war. At the next table she heard Josh in volatile discussion with a member of the state legislature about the student protests at Harvard University and Cornell. Why did Anne let Josh get away with quitting teaching to go back to school? Couldn't she see he was just using her? Why should he work when she was willing to support him?

Three hours later, in the bedroom of Craig's lush suite, Felicia lay nude and satiated beneath the sheet with him. He was incredible, she marveled. As hot as some highly sexed eighteen-year-old.

"I have to leave very soon," she told him, a leg tossed across his.

"You can make some excuse." His eyes were amorous.

"Not tonight," she said firmly. If she didn't show up at the breakfast table, Doug would be upset. He was so square.

"I'm flying to New York tomorrow afternoon," Craig told her with an air of apology. "I'll be there, up to my eyebrows in conferences for the next two weeks. Then I'll fly down to Bermuda, where the yacht will be docked. Meet me there? May is great on the island."

"I might be able to arrange that," she said. "For a long weekend."

"Let's schedule it," Craig said. "These little 'quickie' meets just whet my appetite."

"We'll work out the details," she agreed.

But at the moment Craig had something more urgent in mind.

Felicia carried on a long telephone conversation with Jackie, recuperating from a miscarriage at their sumptuous new house in Georgetown. It was arranged that Felicia would fly to Georgetown to comfort Jackie. Strictly a "girls' weekend," she would explain to Glenn—though instinct told her he wouldn't object to a few days on his own.

When she arrived in Georgetown, Felicia plotted, Jackie would insist they fly down to Bermuda for the weekend because she needed a change in scenery. In truth, Jackie was not unhappy about the miscarriage. She was in no rush—though Bill was—to start a family. Jackie would not go down to Bermuda with her.

Felicia was in high spirits as the day of her departure for Georgetown approached. Glenn knew how close she was to Jackie. It was natural for her to want to fly out to console

340

her friend. And, of course, if Jackie felt a need to run down to Bermuda, then they would go. No problems.

Early Thursday morning Felicia was aboard an eastbound flight. God, she felt as though she were out on parole. She would have preferred to travel on the company plane, but Doug would never buy that. But Craig was sending his private jet up to Washington to bring her down to Bermuda, she remembered in pleasurable anticipation.

He hadn't said anything about the rumored divorce. Still, everybody had known for years that Hera and he had no real marriage anymore. It could be exciting to be married to Craig Preston. Not only one of the world's wealthiest and most powerful men but damned attractive. And sensational in bed. Would he be sensational if they were married? she asked herself in candor.

Craig was mad about her. Was he wondering how *she* felt about divorce? If she became the third Mrs. Craig Preston, there would have to be a premarital financial arrangement because she'd be giving up at least sixty million. *Should she tell Craig that Karen was his daughter?* It provided her with a delicious satisfaction to know what nobody else on this earth knew. It was a strange kind of power.

It would be worth walking out on Naomi's will, she thought with vindictive amusement, just to see Anne fall on her face. Anne would die. Not only would she lose her inheritance—she'd lose her job. The business would go to the museum. The new board of directors wouldn't keep Anne on at her fancy salary— plus a five-thousand-dollar escalation every bloody year. How would she support two kids and her husband—not to mention her father down in Georgia—without those big checks every month?

It would be a snap to push Glenn into a divorce. He was sleeping with Norma, that secretary in the accounting department. A divorce would be no problem. She must make that clear to Craig.

Jackie was waiting for her at National Airport with the white Jaguar that had been her parents' consolation prize for losing the baby. She talked ebulliently about life in George-town as she drove Felicia to the sprawling estate she shared with Bill.

"I think this whole feminist thing is getting out of hand," Jackie declared. "I adore Betty Friedan, and I thought it was just super when NOW members sat in at the Oak Room at the Plaza in New York to protest that 'no women at lunch time' deal. But those other women—Robin Morgan and Ti-Grace Atkinson and Valerie Solanas—they're too far out for me."

"But men *are* getting away with murder," Felicia said. "Two men behind me on the plane were talking about some woman one of them had just met, and one asked the other if she was terribly good-looking. And he said, 'Oh, she's a bitch.' And you know what the other bastard said?" Felicia was angry in recall. " 'I can handle that. Is she gorgeous?' They look at every woman as a sex symbol."

"Darling, if Craig wasn't looking at you as a sex symbol, you wouldn't be flying down to Bermuda in the morning," Jackie clucked.

"But I'm using Craig," Felicia shot back defensively. "I don't care about pleasing a man in bed. That's past history. I want him to please *me.*"

"Bill's always asking me, 'did you come?' But I don't think it's because he's worried about pleasing me," Jackie said with candor. "I think a man figures he's not great in bed unless the woman has an orgasm, too."

Felicia nodded in agreement. "To a man sex is just one way to prove how sensational he is."

"Bill can't understand that some women don't have or-gasms. He can't see that I have a ball just from his holding me and touching me."

"Sweetie, men are a breed apart. Don't try to understand them. Just enjoy them." She wanted more than the holding and touching, Felicia thought. She wanted Craig going crazy in her. *That* was a terrific kind of power—to know she could do that to a man.

In the morning Jackie drove her to Dulles International, where Craig's jet was waiting to take her on the eighty-minute flight to Bermuda. Earlier she had phoned Glenn to explain that she and Jackie were headed for Bermuda and gave him the phone number of the Hamilton Princess where she would supposedly be staying. Craig's yacht was at anchor in the harbor, five minutes from the hotel.

She sipped coffee and flipped through the past weekend's edition of the *Bermuda Sun* while the jet sped south. Thank God, no fog for three days. No office phones jangling every other minute. No hectic office conferences. No dealing with stupid, short-sighted company employees.

When she left the plane at the airport, she found Craig's rented Rolls waiting as planned. Only Bermudians, she remembered, could own or drive a car—though she remembered Naomi working out a deal once to buy a car and sell it back on the understanding she'd be spending a month on the island. Naomi had commuted to San Francisco once a week during that month-in-residence.

"Take the South Road, please," she instructed the chauffeur.

She would register at the Hamilton Princess, leave one of her two valises, and rejoin the chauffeur in the Rolls for the brief trip to the harbor. If the hotel maid wondered that her bed was never slept in, Felicia thought humorously, that was her problem.

She leaned back in the car, ignoring the spectacular view she had specifically requested. She had not been in Bermuda for years, she realized. She hadn't been anywhere since Naomi died. She blocked out recall of her frequent escapes from San Francisco and the business. The prospect of marrying Craig Preston was increasingly enticing.

Within thirty-five minutes they were in Hamilton. She gazed with admiration at the immaculate sun-washed streets of the capital city. Probably this was the most relaxing spot on earth—though she doubted that she would care to remain amid such serenity for more than a few days at a time.

343

Craig had a palatial house, she'd been told, in posh Tucker's Town. Still, he preferred living on the yacht when he was in Bermuda. He preferred the yacht in most situations, she imagined. It was his private kingdom.

At the Hamilton Princess she registered, instructed that one of her valises be sent up to her suite, then rejoined the chauffeur in Craig's rented Rolls, where a second valise was stashed. When she arrived at the yacht, Craig was on deck to welcome her.

"You look sensational." His eyes swept appreciatively over her sleek, slim figure in a white gaberdine pantsuit. "As always."

They made love in the bedroom of his private suite, and it was almost as good as she remembered. Afterward they were served lunch on the private deck off his suite. The blue of the sky matched the brilliant blue of the sea. Lunch out of the way, they lay on a pair of chaises and drank Bloody Marys. She felt emancipated, Felicia thought with relish.

"Felicia, I know you had a short flight, but still it was tiring." Craig reached for her hand, but she intercepted the furtive glance at his watch. "Why don't I have Albert drive you back to the hotel for a siesta before you dress for dinner?" His smile was ingratiatingly apologetic. "I have a couple of business associates coming onboard to discuss a deal, but I'll pick you up for dinner at eight sharp. What would you prefer? Veal Cordon Bleu at The Waterlot Inn or lobster at Tom Moore's?"

"Lobster," she said instantly. But she was piqued that he would bring her down here and then go off on a business conference.

In her suite at the Hamilton Princess she made a pretense, briefly, of napping. Then she reached for the phone and called Miller Timber. At dinner in Georgetown last night she'd made a point of picking Bill's brain and had acquired a pair of useful items. One for Doug, one for Adrian—that would benefit the private corporation the two of them were setting up.

She talked first to her secretary to check on mail and phone

344

calls, then with Doug, then Adrian. She felt immeasurably better. Craig might have dismissed her for business associates, but at Miller Timber her decisions carried weight. She'd come a long way since Naomi had thrown her into the jungle.

She was dressed and waiting when Craig arrived at the Hamilton Princess to escort her to dinner.

"You're in a smug mood," she observed when they were seated at Craig's favorite table at Tom Moore's in Bailey's Bay. "Business went well?"

"It usually does," he said, his eyes fastened to the cleavage of her turquoise-sequined sleeved jumpsuit. "It's a matter of timing, mostly."

"I know," Felicia said with a crispness that captured his attention. "I made a few calls to my office. I had dinner last night in Georgetown. The table talk was enlightening."

"How long do you plan on playing at being the woman executive?" he demanded indulgently.

"I'm not playing at it, Craig." He was such a male chauvinist! "My great-grandmother built Miller from nothing to a major company in the industry. I stand to take over totally in another five years." She'd promised herself that would happen before she was thirty—but that was less than two years away.

"You're so damn sexy when you talk like the ambitious woman executive," he murmured, his knee finding hers beneath the table. "If it were any other woman, I'd be turned off."

After dinner they moved on to the nightclub at the Princess but lingered only briefly despite the topflight comic appearing there. Craig was hot to take her to bed. In Craig's bed, she told herself with towering satisfaction, she was in control. Would it be that way if she were Felicia Preston?

Felicia slept till noon. She knew Craig had risen early. He worked out for an hour every morning in the ship's gym whenever he was onboard. She leisurely showered, inspected the brief selection of clothes she'd brought to the yacht, and chose a pair of daffodil yellow shorts—cut to display as much as was acceptable—and a skinny ribbed sweater because the day was still cool. She was debating about calling to the galley for breakfast when Craig appeared at the bedroom door.

"We'll have breakfast on the deck," he told her. "My second breakfast. We'll start with chilled papaya, picked at the house thirty minutes ago," he boasted. While the house was reported to be a showplace, Craig seldom stayed there. His wife, his mother, and business associates were in residence at intervals, Felicia recalled. "The eggs and butter were flown in from Charleston. The bacon and sausages," he chuckled, "are from Miles Super Service Market—and top quality." Miles was the local gourmet market.

"Less talk and more action," she reproached, walking with him on to the deck. "I'm famished."

"At around two o'clock some characters are coming aboard to discuss a business deal. Stay up here out of sight. I'll wrap up the conference by three. We'll go ashore to the Jermone Hollis boutique at your hotel and pick up a souvenir for you." He reached to pull her close but quickly abandoned this as a steward approached with their breakfast tray.

Felicia's smile was brittle. Again Craig was letting business intrude on their weekend. Why had he coaxed her to fly all the way down here when he had business conferences scheduled? Probably another tomorrow—Sunday would mean nothing to a man like him. *And what was that crack about her staying out of sight?*

Craig gave no inkling that he was aware of her irritation. The Craig Preston charm was switched on full wattage. Once he offhandedly mentioned Hera. Another time he talked about his two teenage daughters, at school in Switzerland. What would he say if he knew he had another daughter—just a month away from her second birthday?

The kids were sweet, she thought with a moment of pride. The new p.r. woman, hired to build the Felicia Harris image into celebrity status, said they were great to use in magazine stories. The beautiful young woman industry leader and her two beautiful children.

"You're quiet this morning." Craig was quizzical. "Tired from all that exercise last night," he grinned.

"Darling, sex never makes me tired." Her eyes were a challenge. "I can keep it up forever."

He hesitated, ran the tip of his tongue across his lower lip. The usual sign of arousal. For a man well into his forties he was sensational.

"After I dump the three guys," he stipulated, "I'll take you up on that."

When Craig left to welcome his guests, she changed into a bikini and settled on a chaise with the morning's *Royal Gazette*. For a moment she'd thought he'd cancel the meeting. She'd wanted to see him do that. Not for the sake of afternoon sex, she conceded, but to show that she could pull him away from business.

At ten minutes past three Felicia left the deck and changed into a pantsuit, her mind churning. Craig had said he'd wind up the conference by three. Clearly he wasn't doing that. At twenty minutes past three she began to throw her clothes into her valise. Damn him! He treated her as though she was some call girl he'd ordered sent out for the weekend.

By three-thirty—with no indication that Craig was concluding the business conference—she called for a steward to say she was leaving the yacht. *Let Craig fuck his three business associates.*

She was about to leave the hotel suite when the phone rang. That, no doubt, would be Craig. She ignored the phone, went to the lobby to check out, and requested a cab to take her to the airport. If she were lucky, she'd be on a flight out within an hour.

Craig would be burning up the wires when she got back to San Francisco, she anticipated. Tough. She wasn't accepting his calls. She felt humiliated. Degraded. She wouldn't take this from any man.

Twenty-nine

AT intervals Anne fought against a towering sense of helplessness. She was constantly in conflict at Miller Timber—passionate in her efforts to reshape logging practices that were harmful to the environment but, thus far, those efforts were ineffectual. It seemed to her that the campus troubles at Berkeley—almost ten years old—were insurmountable. And now the Black Panthers were becoming highly visible on the Berkeley scene, and this terrified her. The Black Panthers were armed revolutionaries, prepared to shoot it out with the police.

She was tired from the endless grind. Josh was tired. *And what were they accomplishing?*

She concealed her irritation when Doug announced that Adrian was coming into the company in a marketing capacity. *"He's family, Anne. Mama would be pleased to have him ask to come into the business."*

Adrian was a college dropout who'd connived his way into a sharp deal. How did that qualify him for what she knew would become a major role at Miller Timber? A new member for Felicia's team.

With the school term ending Anne was indignant when she discovered that neither Todd's parents nor his sister were arranging to attend his imminent graduation at Columbia. She went to Doug and urged that the two of them—representing family—fly to New York for the occasion.

"I think it would mean a lot to Todd to have us there."

"Right." Doug's eyes mirrored compassion and frustration that those closest to Todd could be so callous. "We'll fly out, Annie." It was the first time Doug had called her "Annie," she realized and was touched.

Anne and Doug flew to New York on the company plane, which would stand by to fly the three of them back to San Francisco. From their suite at the Pierre Anne phoned Todd.

"Hey, you came for graduation!" Todd was frankly jubilant.

"And to fly you home in style," Anne laughed. "Are you all tied up tonight or can we have dinner together?"

Wrapped in nostalgia—her Barnard days seeming suddenly close—Anne sat at dinner with Doug and Todd in a booth at the West End Bar, across from the Columbia campus.

"I'm a pariah, you know," Todd said humorously. "As far as my parents and Felicia are concerned. I refused to apply to Yale or Harvard Law. My mother said 'we can't afford an expensive school like Yale or Harvard, but we would have made the sacrifice.' They can't bear to have their friends know I'm going to Berkeley Law."

"They can afford it." Doug was uncharacteristically blunt.

"Anyhow," Todd forced a smile, "they've told me their responsibilities as parents are over. I'm out on my own."

"Todd, you can always live at the family house," Doug told him. "But I'm sure you know that."

"Thanks, Uncle Doug. But I'll be settling into a pad with two buddies who've also been accepted at Berkeley. I still have a chunk of money from my inheritance."

Not until the plane was about to come down at International Airport did Todd mention that he would be working during the summer with Josh's "save the redwoods" group. Anne saw Doug flinch. To him this reeked of disloyalty to Naomi Miller.

At the airport both Walter and Josh were waiting to provide transportation. Doug went home to the Miller house. He

349

politely rejected Josh's invitation to an impromptu small welcome-home dinner for Todd.

Over plates piled high with spaghetti—Josh's one culinary accomplishment—the young people lapsed into somber discussion about the coming school year.

"It's going to be a rough year again," Josh prophesied. "Not only at Berkeley. On most campuses."

"Tell us something new," Stu mocked.

"At least, Nixon committed himself to withdraw twenty-five thousand troops from Vietnam," Anne interjected. "That's a beginning."

"I'll believe we're out of Vietnam when I see it," Josh said bluntly.

"This is supposed to be a party," Shirley reproached. "Not a wake."

"It's going to be a great summer," Todd said with determined enthusiasm. "I need that before the law-school grind."

As Josh had prophesied, the school year had barely begun when the fires of campus unrest were ignited again. Anne was secretly relieved that between law school and his conservation group Josh had little time for campus revolution. She was frightened by the violence that had emerged.

This summer, Todd apologized to Josh and Anne, he was taking a month off before working with the "save the redwoods" group. He was going to backpack in Europe with two law school buddies. "To clear my head." Josh was doggedly taking summer classes because this would see him through to his law degree.

"Hey, when you come back," Josh gloated to Todd, "I'll almost be able to touch that diploma."

Only ten days before Todd was scheduled to fly home, Edwina received an urgent call from the American Consul's office in Athens. Todd had been arrested, along with two friends, on charges of smuggling forty pounds of hash into Greece from Turkey. Edwina called Felicia. "They woke me up out of a sound sleep. It's only a few minutes past nine," she finished indignantly.

"Don't get hysterical," Felicia ordered. It was just like Todd to get caught in some stupid deal like this. "Who did you talk with in Athens? Tell me exactly what happened."

She listened impatiently while her mother filled her in.

"Todd insists he's innocent," Edwina repeated. "He was just traveling with the other two—he didn't have anything to do with bringing in drugs. Felicia, you have to do something," she shrieked. "Todd's your brother."

"Where's Dad?" Felicia hedged. Did they expect her to drop everything and fly to Greece? "Does he know about this?"

"Where do you think he is, Felicia? Sleeping off a drunk. I tried to reach Doug—he's out of the office. Maybe he'd know how to handle this."

"Doug's in Seattle at an auction." Felicia's mind moved into high gear. All at once a quick trip to Greece sounded inviting. She could line up a lawyer for Todd in Athens. The people at the embassy would help her. Then she could play for three days on one of the Greek islands. She needed a break from the rat race. "I'll fly to Athens and make sure Todd has a good lawyer."

"The man at the consulate warned me Todd might sit there waiting trial for months, Felicia." Edwina's voice was strident again. "How could Todd put the family in a position like this?"

"I might be able to pull some strings." Felicia felt a flicker of excitement. "Craig Preston's father-in-law is powerful in Greece. I'll track Craig down and—"

"Craig's in Majorca," her mother broke in. She seemed calmer now. "I read an item in somebody's column."

The yacht would be in the harbor at Palma, Felicia surmised. "I'll fly over there. Don't sweat it—we've been through worse."

Felicia put down the phone and plotted her course. She wouldn't try to discuss this over the phone with Craig. She'd fly to Majorca. Doug couldn't complain she was taking time

351

off from the job—this was a family crisis. And Majorca was marvelous in early August.

So she walked out on Craig in Bermuda eighteen months ago, had refused a half-dozen calls here in San Francisco. She'd never really washed Craig out of her mind. He came under the heading of "Unfinished Business." She'd pick up a phone in Palma and coolly say, "Craig, you called?"

Accustomed to imperious demands, her travel agent scheduled a flight to New York within five hours. She would have only a two-hour layover in New York. A suite was reserved for her at the Victoria in Palma—a second home, Felicia recalled, for Prince Juan Carlos. And she had confirmed that Craig's yacht was, indeed, in the harbor at Palma.

Twenty-four hours later—aware of Craig's habit of arising early wherever he was—Felicia phoned him on the yacht from her elegant suite at the Victoria, conveniently located in the heart of Palma, the capital of the island.

"You called?" she said casually as planned and was amused by his startled intake of breath.

"I behaved like a bastard in Bermuda," he apologized. "When can I see you?"

"In about twenty minutes," she suggested and laughed at his grunt of astonishment. "I'm at the Victoria."

This morning Felicia was impatient with the in-season traffic that delayed her progress. Belatedly she felt some real anxiety about Todd's situation. The newspapers had been warning Americans—particularly student-age travelers—about the foreign crackdown on drug smugglers. Italy, Spain, West Germany, Greece, Lebanon all had a growing population of American prisoners. A best-selling author was serving four and a half years in a Corfu jail. *Playboy*'s December playmate was serving ten months in Averoff Prison in Athens. *How could Todd be so stupid?*

Craig welcomed her with ingratiating warmth. They settled on the deck off his private suite and nibbled at croissants flown in from Paris and sipped Craig's special brand of Columbian coffee. His eyes made passionate love to her while they exchanged casual conversation. She knew he was waiting for her to explain her sudden appearance.

"I have a problem," she said at last. "At least, my brother Todd has a problem."

As succinctly as possible she explained the situation. At one point Craig—his eyes serious now—interrupted to ask a question. So he knew she was here because she needed a favor. That was fine, Felicia told herself. Don't let him think she was on the prowl for him.

"I'll have to make phone calls," he said. "Stay right here."

Twenty minutes later Craig rejoined her on the deck.

"We'll have some word in a couple of hours." He smiled confidently. "Jet lag got you down?"

"No way," she drawled.

"Then let's not waste those two hours."

They were lying smug and satiated in Craig's bed when the phone rang.

She tried to interpret Craig's brief comments. *What the hell was happening?*

"Sure, we'll fly down to Chile together. I've already given the crew orders to stand by." Craig listened with a show of impatience. "I'll clear flight time with you tomorrow night."

Craig was flying down to Chile with his father-in-law. To meet Hera, she surmised. Hera was presumably mad about winters in Chile.

"Well?" Felicia demanded. Her tone faintly sharp. She knew Craig took this for anxiety.

"He'll be released within the next twelve hours and put aboard a flight for New York. But tell him to stay the hell out of Greece for a couple of years."

"Thanks, Craig. The family appreciates this." Put it on a "family" basis. "I'll be flying back tomorrow afternoon if I can book a flight." Don't let him guess she was disappointed he was cutting out for Chile. "Complications at the office." Let him understand her career was important to her.

"We'll make the most of today and tomorrow," he cajoled. "Sorry about having to rush down to Chile. The old boy doesn't know it, but Hera's planning an anniversary party for her parents."

So much for the new divorce rumors, Felicia told herself. What did she have to do to persuade Craig to divorce Hera? They hadn't slept together for years. The children were always off at boarding school or summer camps. *What tied Craig to Hera?*

For Thanksgiving, 1970 Anne and Josh and the children flew to Belleville. Anne cherished this four-day escape from Miller Timber. Mary Lou's grandniece came in to watch over the children so that she and Josh could spend some time at the Lazarus office with her father.

She knew her father was pleased with the progress of the business, though he worried about the continuing escalation of lumber prices.

"At the same time Nixon's carrying on about building two-point-six-million homes every year, lumber prices are beginning to put them out of reach of a lot of Americans. The public's going to demand a price freeze." Kevin shook his head in frustration. "I hate the way the big timber companies people are manipulating."

"I hate the way they're mismanaging the forests," Anne reiterated a long-standing complaint. "Including Miller Timber. I'm making some inroads on the board," she acknowledged and smiled faintly. "Of course, the board has no real say. Doug makes the decisions—and he still thinks the way Naomi Miller thought."

"Miller is in fine shape financially, but times are rough for the small lumber companies," Kevin said somberly. "They rely on private timber—and most of that's been cut out your way. And once their equipment needs replacing, they're in deep trouble. There was a time you could replace practically everything in a sawmill for anywhere from twenty-five to fifty-thousand dollars. Today you're talking about millions because to make a profit you need that expensive equipment. The old peckerwoods can't afford it."

"You're doing great here," Josh said with determined cheerfulness and Kevin's face brightened. "Anne and I are proud of you."

In mid-December Anne and Josh went to his parents' home for a dinner party to celebrate Bert's engagement to a young teacher. Bert was now a junior partner in his father's law firm. A conventional "young man on the way up." Josh had passed the bar exams and joined a group of young attorneys working in the public service sector. And of course, he was immersed in the fight to save the redwoods.

Anne was aware that Josh was unfamiliarly taciturn on the drive home.

"Tired?" she asked sympathetically. He drove himself so hard—between his law practice and the redwoods group.

"I was thinking about Bert," he said. "The sane pattern of his life. He and Janice will get married, buy a pretty little house—"

"Don't you like our house?" she asked defensively. He'd objected at first when their landlord offered to sell, but only because the mortgage payments had temporarily alarmed him.

"I love the house," he admitted. "But how much time do we spend in it? We're both on such mad schedules. Bert will come home from the office every day no later than six," he predicted. And bring home an attaché case packed with work, Anne mentally added. "Janice will probably get pregnant right away and settle down to being a housewife and mother."

"You resent my being with the company—" Though the car was toasty warm with the heater on, she was suddenly cold.

"I always feel I come second." He kept his eyes on the road ahead. "That the children and I come second," he amended. "Our lives revolve around the needs of Miller Timber."

"You're saying you want me to give up on the deal," she said after a moment, her heart pounding. They were back to *that* again.

"I know you won't," he said tiredly. "But yes, I'd like to

know that we have lives of our own. Naomi Miller rules us from her grave."

"Josh, I've put seven years into this. How can I walk out now?"

"I said before—I don't expect you to do that," he said testily. "Let's drop it, Annie."

"No." She hesitated. Shaken as she realized the depth of his bitterness. She'd been too wrapped up in the business to see what she should have seen. She'd dismissed his occasional gripes as temporary irritations. "You have to understand, Josh." She spoke slowly, searching for the right words. "It's not just all that money—though God knows, it's important, for what it can do for us. Maybe it's an obsession with me—the way you say sometimes. But I have to feel that I've taken back for Grandma what belongs to her. And I want to turn the company around to the way Grandma would have run it."

"Annie—" His voice deepened with compassion. "Do you honestly believe you can do that?"

"I have to believe that, Josh. Because if I can do that with Miller Timber, maybe we can help lead the way to saving our forests. Not just the redwoods, damn it!" she said in a surge of rage. "All the forests."

"We want the same thing, Annie," Josh said tenderly. "Like your grandmother. And whatever contributions we can make toward saving the forests we must make." One hand left the wheel to squeeze hers as they stopped for a red light. "But let's never forget we're a family. Let's find time to celebrate that."

Anne could not erase from her mind the bitterness that had surfaced in Josh. It had gone under wraps again—but she must never forget that it was there. To Josh the company was an enemy that usurped part of her.

Grandma had worked all her adult life, up to the day she died. But Grandma had managed to maintain a happy marriage and a stable family life. What was *she* doing wrong?

know that we have lives of our own. Naomi Miller rules us from her grave."

Anne sat across the table from Shirley in the company cafeteria, deserted except for themselves because they'd delayed till almost two to go to lunch.

"I thought I knew Josh so well," Anne said quietly. "And then that craziness last night after Bert's engagement party."

"Look, he's being typically male. The men haven't caught up with the female revolution. They want the little woman in the kitchen. A second-class citizen." Shirley was matter-of-fact. Anne knew how involved she was in the women's movement, but—thank God—she wasn't part of the lunatic fringe.

"Josh isn't the typical male! He's bright and clear-thinking and a liberal."

"And a man. It'll take a while, baby, before they come around to our way of thinking." She hesitated. "And you have to admit you're not the nine-to-five working wife. You're in the career-woman category—and that's a whole different ball game. Women on the way up don't get away with a thirty-five or forty-hour work week. It's a dozen hours a day plus some weekends—and the briefcase stuffed with work that goes home with you."

"I know the women's movement is claiming that marriage is unimportant, and the big deal for women is self-fulfillment and achievement." Anne hesitated. "But isn't it normal for a woman to want a husband and children?"

"When men are reeducated, it'll work. Right now it's a rough scene. Why do you think I won't marry Stu? Six months after we were married, he'd start with the little-wife-at-home bit. And he'll want kids. I remember those years when Gerry's father walked out and I was breaking my butt to survive. I did it," she said with a touch of defiance. "Now I'm in charge of my own life. I won't give that up again."

"I can't believe that Josh thinks the company comes first with me—before him and the children." Anne closed her eyes for an anguished instant. "Why can't he understand that what I'm doing is for us?"

"Let's face it." Shirley was frankly cynical. "Every man wants two wives. One to stay at home and cook his meals and clean his house and iron his shirts. And the other to go out in the business world and bring in the bucks. And one or the other—depending on his mood—takes care of him in bed."

Thirty

EARLY in the new year Felicia was miffed that Anne was planning an elaborate seventy-fifth birthday party for Doug without asking her to participate in the arrangements. "Buttering up the old boy again," was Glenn's comment, echoed by Adrian.

But this annoyance was forgotten when she received a pair of diamond-and-sapphire earrings from Craig, along with a formal invitation to a weekend house party at his just-acquired villa—near Acapulco—on the weekend prior to Doug's birthday party. According to instructions, his jet would be waiting at the San Francisco airport to transport his guests to Acapulco.

"The earrings are spectacular," she told Jackie in a call to Georgetown. "And I suspect the guest list to the houseparty will consist of one."

"He figures you're not coming out to the yacht again," Jackie guessed. "Didn't I see an item in somebody's column about the gorgeous place he's bought down there?"

"I know the house," Felicia acknowledged. "It's not far from Naomi's. Enormous," she added with respect. "A marble *palacio* hanging over the bay."

Off the phone with Jackie at last, Felicia considered her situation. After those days in Palma Craig couldn't get her out of his mind. All right, handle this right and she could marry Craig. Her first objective, she told herself with conviction, was to divorce Glenn. He'd back down fast enough when she

359

accused him of sleeping with Norma. A Mexican divorce, she resolved. No time wasted.

She waited until the following evening to confront him. "Glenn, don't try to lie to me," she warned while he stared at her, his eyes glazed, his face drained of color. "Everybody in the company, it appears, knows you're sleeping with Norma. I've got too much pride to stay with a cheating husband. I want you to go to Mexico immediately for one of those 'quickie' divorces. You and Norma can stay in your jobs—as long as you're useful to me," she stressed. He understood there'd be no financial settlement. "There'll be bonuses when you help me in important deals."

"Will you put that in writing?" he challenged with shaky bravado.

"Glenn, you're in no position to bargain. If you want to remain with the company, okay—but on my terms. You can see Timmy and Karen whenever you like."

Forty-eight hours later Glenn was in Mexico. Norma gave two weeks' notice. She'd find a job somewhere, Felicia guessed. She was one of those stupid, conscientious secretaries who'd break her back for any boss. Doug was grim about Glenn's remaining with the company, but Felicia insisted. In a limited fashion Glenn was sharp. He was useful to her.

"I want Glenn to stay on," she told Doug with a slight aura of martyrdom. "For the children's sake."

On a Friday afternoon in early February Walter drove Felicia to the airport, where Craig's plane would be waiting. To her astonishment she discovered other guests from San Francisco would be flying down, also. So Craig was pretending it was a real house party, she told herself nonchalantly. He wasn't taking chances on her walking out again. She'd spend her nights at Acapulco in Craig's bed. And at the right moment she'd tell him about her divorce.

Craig had invited a dozen guests for what he now announced as his housewarming. Felicia knew most of them: the men ultrarich and powerful, their wives attractive, bejeweled by Van Cleef and Arpels, Bulgari, Harry Winston. Though the women at this point were dressed casually in keeping with their setting, Felicia knew that at dinner they would be gowned by the likes of Galanos and Oscar de la Renta.

Felicia was conscious of an unexpected flicker of contempt for these coddled women. God, she'd spent too long at Miller Timber, she mocked herself. What was so fascinating about fighting to become CEO of a timber empire?

Arriving at the house with the other guests she listened along with them to Craig's gloating report on how he had outbid an Arab prince and deposed royalty for the Acapulco house.

"When I set my mind on something, I usually acquire it," he said complacently, his eyes grazing hers for a heated moment.

The multilevel house—with a dozen guest suites—was set in the midst of exquisite gardens and looked down upon the harbor. A marvelous house, Felicia agreed. But no more so than Naomi's place less than a quarter mile to the north— which would go to the museum at Doug's death, she remembered with revived anger. She mentally noted that she would prefer to see some of the priceless antiques here replaced with less ornate pieces. Still, the house was a showplace.

After a Lucullan feast, Craig—known as a movie buff— corralled his guests into the projection room to see a film that had been flown in from Hollywood.

"Acapulco is for relaxation," he announced as they settled themselves about the sofas and lounge chairs to view the evening movie. "Early breakfasts, a walk on the beach, swim and sun—and *muchas* siestas."

As Felicia anticipated, Craig contrived for her to join him in his suite when the other guests retired to their own. Within five minutes after she arrived there, they were making love on the white-satin-sheeted king-size bed. Afterward they retired to his private sauna.

"I leave the sauna absolutely euphoric," he boasted, walking naked with her into the large, cedar-lined room—with a window that provided a magnificent view of Acapulco Bay. "And passionate as hell."

"Isn't that contradictory?" she challenged. So, he'd want to make love again.

"I'll prove to you that it isn't."

They lounged side-by-side on the heated cedar planks, wider than she recalled ever encountering. But, of course, Craig would insist on the ultimate in comfort. His hands moved with insidious slowness over her nakedness, and she sensed that in a very few minutes he'd be more demanding. But now it was oddly pleasurable to lie in this cedar-fragrant heat while he devoted himself to their fresh arousal.

"Let's go back to the bedroom," he said in a few moments. "I wouldn't want us to fall asleep in here."

He rose from the plank with a pride in the lean, taut body that spent an hour a day—wherever he might be—in serious workout. Still, there was that tiny hint of sagging jawline that belied the body of a thirty-year-old, Felicia thought detachedly while she strolled with him into the bedroom again.

"Did I remember to tell you that the earrings are gorgeous?" she murmured while he prodded her across the width of the bed and lifted himself above her.

"Meet me in Paris in April," he coaxed while his hands fondled her thighs and he teased her with his mounting passion. "We'll pick up the necklace I ordered to go with it." She murmured appreciation now as he sought entry in her. "Can you clear a week in April?"

"Darling, I'm a free agent now," she told him, seizing the moment. "I have a Mexican divorce that's two weeks old."

"Oh?" She felt his hands grow tense on her. She was aware of his diminishing passion.

For a moment he was immobile. Then he drew away.

"Why don't I call down for a bottle of champagne? That bastard Raoul was supposed to have left it in an ice bucket by the bed."

The damn prick, she thought in inner fury. She'd scared the hell out of him with that news about the divorce. He had no intention of divorcing Hera. He just wanted to sleep with her when it was convenient for him. When it amused him.

"Champagne sounds great." Her smile was dazzling. She'd be damned if she'd let him guess what had been on her mind. *Damn all men.* "We'll drink to my freedom. I'm an emancipated woman. Marvelous feeling, darling."

After this weekend she'd never let that son-of-a-bitch within ten feet of her. He'd go to his grave without ever knowing that Karen was his daughter.

Felicia pretended to doze on much of the flight back to San Francisco. She had been out of her mind to think of marrying Craig, she chastised herself for the hundredth time. Craig would have tried to run her life—and she'd allow no man to rule her.

She had been bored much of the weekend. She'd moved so far beyond those women. She could never settle again for that kind of life, she told herself with towering pride.

Craig was *amused* that she worked. He couldn't conceive of her ever being as powerful in the business world as he. But Naomi had been his equal in that rarified world of business. And in time she would be. No more playing games. Miller Timber was the kingdom she would conquer.

So she had divorced Glenn. That was fine. She didn't need a permanent man in her life. What she needed, she told herself with a rush of exhilaration, was the power to control the company, to plot the moves that would enlarge it beyond even Naomi's dreams.

Doug was a week away from his seventy-fifth birthday. She had to chip at him until he threw his votes with hers to appoint her CEO—to replace himself. A moment would show itself when she would make him understand that *she* was the logical replacement for Naomi. She must watch for that moment.

On Monday her mother called and ordered Felicia to meet her for lunch at the St. Francis Mural Room.

"I thought you were staying in Palm Beach until the end of the month," Felicia hedged.

"Your father insisted we come back for Doug's birthday party," Edwina said with annoyance. "I don't know why— since none of us will ever see a cent out of Doug. Meet me at one. I have gossip for you."

At shortly past one Felicia was escorted to the table in the Mural Room where her mother waited.

"Your tan is marvelous," Felicia said diplomatically when they had exchanged carefully manipulated kisses that caused no havoc on expensive coiffures. "But the sun is awfully drying to the skin."

"Are you saying I need a face-lift?" Edwina bristled, reached into her Gucci bag for a mirror.

"I'm saying the dermatologists are warning women that sun adds lines long before they should be there."

"Actually I've been thinking about a face-lift, but your father is so frantic about every dollar I spend. And as long as I'm going in for the face-lift, I might as well have a fanny-tuck at the same time."

"What's the gossip?" Felicia demanded when their waiter had arrived and departed.

"It's about Craig," Edwina told her. Lowering her voice though it was unlikely she could be heard at the next table. "If you've been nurturing ideas about marrying Craig, forget them."

"I don't want to marry again," Felicia said defensively. She had talked to her mother in Palm Beach and told her about the divorce. "I divorced Glenn because I like being free. But what's this about Craig?" She pretended to be amused.

"Bruce played golf with Hera's brother-in-law a few days ago. Hera's father and Craig are involved in some huge takeover—but the old man insists that Hera and Craig reconcile before he puts up his share of the money."

"Hera's going along with this?" Felicia was dubious.

"For the equivalent of one million dollars in Greek drachmas from her father. Plus I hear Craig has bought her a marvelous showplace of a house in Acapulco."

In the months ahead Felicia focused on the problems confronting the timber industry. On the plus side the export business—especially to Japan—was booming. Housing starts were soaring. The demand for second homes was approaching astonishing levels. A recent survey showed that close to three million households owned a second home—most of them wood-built. But the specter of price controls hovered over the industry.

Felicia flew to Washington in May for conferences with the Miller lobbyists. In July she traveled to Washington again. The word came through: A price freeze on lumber would go into effect on August 15 of this year. Back in San Francisco she relayed the news to Doug. He called an emergency board meeting for the following morning.

Felicia lay sleepless far into the night, too wound up to sleep, instinct telling her that how she handled herself in this situation could be crucial to earning Doug's support. Ever-present in her mind was the knowledge that her 45 percent of voting stock tied to Doug's 10 percent could make her CEO. Anne would continue to own—in escrow, like herself—45 percent of Miller Timber. But Anne would have no clout in running the company. Nor would she walk out and void the deal, Felicia reminded herself. Anne was in this for the full course.

In the morning—with a steamy hot shower pounding on the tense muscles of her shoulders—Felicia pulled from her mind a solution to the price-freeze crisis. It was so obvious, she exulted while she enjoyed the sting of the spray on her body. Of course, she'd have to convince Doug that it was the way to go. With Naomi gone he could become so exasperatingly ethical.

Call Adrian and tell him to be there in the conference room by eight-thirty. Doug and she would go directly there and have coffee while they waited for the board to arrive. Adrian could be an effective backup. Doug didn't like him—but ever since Adrian pulled that option bit, he had respect for Adrian's business thinking.

Call Glenn and tell him to be there about a quarter of nine. Glenn would be more backup—and he was familiar with all the rulings on the industry that Congress kept spewing out.

As Felicia anticipated, Doug suggested they go directly to the conference room on their arrival at the office. A few moments later Adrian joined them.

"I know Adrian can't be present at the board meeting, but he does come up with some constructive ideas," she told Doug while his secretary appeared with a carafe of coffee for them. "This is a bitch of a situation."

"We've pulled through worse," Doug said with an air of confidence, but his eyes were troubled.

"Thank God, you didn't listen to Anne with her crazy ideas about our moving into home-building," Felicia said, gearing herself to introduce her proposal.

"I'm not sure that wasn't a smart idea," Doug shot back, his smile quizzical.

"But with lumber prices frozen where's the profit?" Adrian countered.

"We can talk about moving into housing later," Felicia said briskly. Wrong subject to bring up now, she rebuked herself. Damn, Anne had been right about that. One of Adrian's spies had told him Weyerhaeuser was projecting construction of as much as five thousand houses in 1972. "Right now our major problem is to figure out how to get around the price freeze."

"Good morning." Glenn smiled cautiously as he walked into the conference room. Felicia saw the slight elevation of Doug's eyebrows that so clearly said, *"What the hell is Glenn doing here?"* Doug would understand in a few moments.

While Glenn made a pretense of interest in Felicia's efforts in Washington, Anne arrived. Why did Anne always have to be ten minutes early, Felicia fumed in silence. But she knew the answer to that. Anne was aware of her efforts at pre-board-meeting conferences—with her own team there to back her up.

"I don't expect the board to come up with any real solutions," Doug said with wry candor. "But we listen to what they have to offer on the chance that something they say may point us in the right direction."

"I think I know how to handle this crisis." Felicia was deliberately low-keyed.

"How?" Doug, too, was low-keyed.

"As I understand it, the price freeze won't affect imports." She turned to Glenn. He'd confirmed this when she'd called him earlier. "Am I right on this?"

"On target." Glenn nodded.

"Then let us set up a Canadian corporation. Sell logs to the corporation. The corporation contracts to have the logs reduced to lumber. We import—with no price controls. The demand is there—builders will pay whatever we ask."

"That doesn't sound legal." Anne was politely ambivalent. Later, Felicia suspected, she'd offer her customary impassioned protests.

"It's legal until the government says it isn't." Felicia feigned amusement at such naïveté.

"We'll need something cleaner than that," Glenn intervened. "In the past the IRS has stepped in and called these separate corporations a tax dodge. They could levy claims for back taxes, interest, and substantial penalties."

"Forget setting up our own corporation. Make a deal with a Canadian sawmill," Adrian proposed. "First, sell them logs. Then buy them back as lumber. At preset prices. We're clear of price freezes."

"That should work for a while," Glenn judged. "But run it past the lawyers."

"It'll be at least a year before the Price Commission makes noises," Felicia said. "Doug, let's go with that."

"That's twisting the law," Anne objected. "It's sure to backfire."

"This is not a church bazaar." Felicia was terse. "We're run-

367

ning a business. Until the Price Commission says we can't do it, we can operate through a Canadian intermediary. Take it to the board, Doug. They'll agree." Doug would make the ultimate decision—as always, but he was happy when the board agreed.

"We'll see a lot of finagling," Doug admitted. "Right down the line."

"It's unethical operating," Anne repeated, and Felicia saw the rage in her eyes. "It could backfire."

"It's sharp business." Felicia's voice rose in triumph. "It's exactly what Naomi would do if she were here."

"Glenn, fly up to Vancouver and look for a deal with one of the bigger sawmills." All at once Doug was decisive. "Take Adrian with you—he's got a sharp eye for these things. Damn if we're going to be crippled by some ridiculous ruling!"

Thirty-one

ANNE grappled with towering frustration while Glenn and Adrian commuted between San Francisco and Vancouver over a period of several weeks. At last they made the contact Felicia sought. Felicia flew to Vancouver, argued details of a deal, and returned to San Francisco with a contract that could earn Miller Timber a million in profits within the coming eighteen months.

"It'll take at least a year before the government moves in to cut off this kind of operation," Adrian pointed out at a business luncheon called by Doug with Anne, Felicia, and Glenn also present. "The red tape may give us two years of operation." All of them were convinced the government would step in eventually.

By the end of the year the company was stocking the warehouse with "imported lumber" that could be sold at escalating prices. The public was screaming, but it was hungry for lumber. As Felicia had predicted, the public bought as much as could be delivered.

Exhilarated by her successful maneuvering Felicia talked at an early February evening meeting with Doug and Anne about the importance of their becoming a multinational corporation, producing lumber and lumber products for the world. There was no limit to Felicia's greed, Anne thought in momentary shock. Naomi Miller had built a company that was among the top five in North America. Felicia wanted to dominate the industry worldwide.

"If we plan properly we'll catch up to Weyerhaeuser in three years." Felicia's face was luminous in anticipation. "In five years we can be right up there with Georgia-Pacific. Look at the figures. This last year our profits climbed by twenty percent—and you know damn well the 1972 figures will be higher."

"Weyerhaeuser is closing its mill in Eureka." All at once Doug was somber. "And more closings are rumored."

Anne realized Doug was concerned about all the people who would be thrown out of work. Naomi Miller had been proud, he often said, that she had kept Miller Timber running even in the worst conditions. Because she knew, Anne comprehended, that this guaranteed a loyalty from their loggers and sawmill operators that was invaluable. A policy motivated by sharp business judgement—not compassion.

"Doug, they don't need those mills. They're moving into underdeveloped countries," Felicia pointed out. "They can operate much more economically, for example, in Indonesia."

"Mama disapproved of long-range operations," Doug objected. "We'd spread ourselves too thin."

"Doug, think of the potential!" Felicia bristled.

"Think of the danger," Doug countered and gestured for dismissal of the subject. "Let's talk about the new equipment we may have to buy. Anne, you've been working up a report on that. What's the story?"

At a board meeting early in April Anne protested that they should cut back rather than increase their exports, as Felicia was demanding, with three board members supporting her. Export prices—like those of imports—were not controlled.

"The domestic market needs lumber," Anne reminded them, and Felicia muttered in irritation. "Our first loyalties belong to our domestic customers. Most of them have been with us for many years."

"Our Japanese customers deserve our loyalty, too," Felicia shot back, and two board members nodded in agreement.

"The Japanese government curtailed the cutting in its own national forests," Anne said, "because they figure this country is stupid enough to allow exports to go through. Why devastate their own forests when we'll sacrifice ours for them?"

"Sometimes it's so clear, Anne. You expect Miller Timber to become a philanthropic institution." Felicia smiled mockingly. "This is a business, and we must operate as such. The Japanese are building houses like mad—they'll send the prices for lumber skyrocketing. With the windfall-profits tax what it is under capital gains, we've never been so healthy."

Through all the travail of Miller Timber Anne was gradually aware that all was not right with her marriage. After the confrontation with Josh the night of Bert and Janice's engagement party he avoided any discussion of his feelings about being second to the business. Much of their dinner table talk revolved around the coming Democratic convention, to be held in Miami Beach in July—with George McGovern appearing the likely Democratic candidate. Still, she knew Josh resented her long hours at the office, the trips to their various mills.

But wasn't Josh away from the house three or four evenings every week? He and Stu were always encountering some crisis that threatened the existence of their "save the redwoods" group. Along with Todd—who'd graduate from law school this summer—they were constantly embroiled in fund-raising efforts.

When Josh was home, he usually retreated to the den after dinner to work. And she was *not* neglecting the kids, she told herself defensively. She spent quality time with Marsh and Robin. When Marsh was in a school play last month, she was there—even though it meant rescheduling an important meeting. His father didn't take time off from business—his mother did. She'd be at Robin's nursery school for their "commencement exercises" next week. She spent every waking moment on Sundays with Marsh and Robin.

She wasn't an absentee parent, like Todd and Felicia's mother and father had been. Couldn't Josh understand that he and the children meant more to her than anything else in the world? If she ever thought she was depriving her family by being with the company, she'd walk out.

But her concern about her personal life moved into the background through the summer and into the fall because the government was accusing some timber companies, including Miller Timber, of cutting off domestic customers in favor of Japanese. Homebuilders—backed up by the construction trades—were demanding the practice be stopped. The administration talked about building twenty-six million homes in ten years—but exporting timber could deny a lot of Americans those potential homes, they argued. And cost American jobs as well.

On November 7 Americans went to the polls and gave Richard Nixon a landslide victory. But thinking Americans were shocked by the intensifying drop in voter participation. Only 55.7 percent of eligible voters bothered to go to the polls.

"Did you read what Shirley Chisholm said?" Josh asked Anne over dinner a few nights after the election, and quoted from the *Examiner:* 'The lower voter turnout was a disturbing barometer of the air of apathy and resignation which permeates the nation's political atmosphere.' "

"More than apathy," Anne said somberly. "Disenchantment."

Then a few days after the election the deputy executive director of the Price Commission announced at a news conference that the government was investigating three hundred fifty lumber and wood-products companies on suspicion that they were finagling to defeat price controls. Doug immediately called an emergency meeting with Anne and Felicia.

"I find this very distasteful," he said frankly. "They know and we know our Canadian deal was set up to avoid price controls."

"We've had a year and a half of high profits." Felicia was undisturbed by the prospect of an investigation. "So we'll get a slap on the wrist and be told to stop it. And we don't even

372

know that our Canadian deal will come out. It's more likely the Price Commission is out after obvious violations."

Doug sighed.

"I'm not sure what we're doing is any better. I dislike the inference that we're guilty of shady operations." Normally Doug appeared fifteen to twenty years younger than his age. At this moment he looked his seventy-six years, Anne thought compassionately. To him this investigation might prove to be a reflection on Naomi Miller.

"It's not shady," Felicia protested. "It's a solid business maneuver. Look at all the other companies who're playing the same game. And we don't know that the Commission will uncover it at all," she repeated. Felicia had promoted this whole scene, Anne remembered—and up till now it had won points for her.

"I want us to stop the Canadian operation immediately," Doug said after a moment. "Maybe we can come out of this clean."

On January 22, 1973 former President Lyndon Johnson— architect of the "Great Society" programs for blacks and the poor—died at his Texas ranch. Thirteen hours later President Nixon announced that an agreement to end the war in Vietnam had been reached. The longest war in American history— twelve years of fighting—was over.

The IRS was actively investigating the burgeoning practice of shipping logs to Canada and bringing them back in as lumber. A blatant attempt, the IRS declared, to work around price controls. Doug was plagued by constant fears that their own involvement would be uncovered.

But Doug was cheered by a new ruling on price controls. Again, Nixon was proving a friend to the timber industry. Mandatory price controls on food and health products came into effect early in the month, but now logs were categorized as agricultural products and exempt from controls. Also, lumber mills were permitted to pass along the increase in log prices to their customers. As a timber company with its own lumber mills, Miller Timber would benefit greatly. The following month the cut in the national forests went up by 10 percent.

"Damn it!" Josh railed to Anne. "Nixon believes everything the timber lobbyists throw at him. The last thing this country needs is to increase the cut in the national forests!"

By early spring Doug conceded that Miller Timber was in the clear, though the Price Commission had levied penalties against two small companies for price-gouging.

Now Anne worried that Felicia might manipulate Doug into agreeing to cut stands of old-growth redwoods Naomi had decreed were not to be cut until the year 2000. Felicia's words ricocheted in her mind: *"Doug, we've got stands that are scheduled for cutting way into the twenty-first century—that's unrealistic!"* They were encountering difficulty in satisfying the ever-hungry Japanese market. Felicia talked grandly about pulling out of the northwest and moving into the south when they ran out of timber.

At an after-dinner meeting at the Miller house—a week before Doug's proposed family Easter weekend at Acapulco—Anne forced herself to conceal her annoyance as Felicia pressed this project once more: the old "cut-and-run" technique that would rob the world of its trees.

"Doug, face facts," Felicia urged and Anne sneaked a glance at her watch. The meeting was running long. Mallie left at seven on Fridays for her weekend off—Josh had to be home with the kids. It was absurd to feel guilty, she rebuked herself—but each time Doug called a Friday evening meeting she felt guilty at dumping the kids on Josh. Especially now. Josh was so uptight about the just-released Forest Service study, which claimed the ceiling set on the cut in some national forests could be up to 30 percent too high. Again, the timber lobby had paid off.

"We're working on a schedule my mother considered inviolate," Doug brought Anne back to the meeting. Yet she sensed a disturbing ambivalence in him tonight.

"Naomi would understand the need for revisions," Felicia

said. She, too, felt doubts infiltrating Doug, Anne realized. Felicia wouldn't let up now. "We're having trouble competing with lumber companies in the south and in eastern Canada. You know that, Doug. We can make more money exporting logs than in operating our five sawmills. Glenn's done an extensive survey. We . . ."

"We *shouldn't* have trouble competing," Anne interrupted heatedly. This was territory close to her. "I've spent a lot of time these past three months exploring the problem with the superintendent in each of our mills. They all agree. Our equipment is outdated. We've got to modernize." She'd tried to focus on this at the last board meeting, but the prospect of spending huge sums on new equipment seemed to unnerve most of the members. "How can we compete when we're not keeping pace with the new technology? Weyerhaeuser is. So is Georgia-Pacific. And don't tell me we can't afford the investment," Anne forestalled Felicia's retaliation.

The atmosphere in the Miller library suddenly exuded overt hostility. Then Felicia pulled her gaze away from Anne and focused on Doug with a devious smile.

"On the subject of new investments I have a proposal before we close up shop." Felicia had a knack for shifting debate when she was cornered, Anne thought in frustration. She'd have to manage to talk alone with Doug about their need for new equipment. "I asked Glenn to search for some loopholes to cut down our excess-profit tax."

"It's horrendous," Doug agreed.

"Glenn says this is the perfect time for the company to build a mountain retreat, where we can entertain important clients. A house at Big Sur could be useful."

"That's hardly a new tax dodge," Anne said derisively. She suspected that all of Naomi's out-of-town houses had been written off as business expenses. "Doug," she tried again, "We should consider installing new . . ."

"We can build a house at Big Sur for practically nothing." Felicia forged ahead as though Anne had not interrupted. "Our only cash layout will be land and labor. It's a marvelous investment for the company. Real estate there is sure to soar in the next ten years. And it would represent a substantial tax savings."

"We'll discuss it another time," Doug hedged. He was upset that Felicia was promoting a change in Naomi's schedule, Anne understood. He knew most members of the board would back up Felicia. All they would see was the immediate profit.

"I'll tell Glenn to work up some figures," Felicia said with a hint of triumph in her voice. "This year we need all the tax relief we can get."

"Tell him to have his report ready before we leave for Acapulco," Doug said. "I'll study it while we're down there."

Anne tensed. Was he going to use a house at Big Sur to bury her equipment program?

Anne glanced at her watch as she slid behind the wheel of her Valiant. It was almost ten. Marsh and Robin would both be asleep by the time she reached the house. She'd hoped the meeting would be over by eight-thirty. On Friday nights the kids were allowed to stay up until nine. Tenderness welled in her as she visualized them in their pajamas, waiting up for Mommie.

It was rare that Robin stayed awake past seven-thirty. She was so intense, so vital about everything—she'd be awake one moment and fast asleep the next. To Marsh it was special, she suspected, to have dinner with Daddy and then watch TV with him. Robin wore her intensity like a badge. With Marsh it was under wraps, but she knew it was there.

Letting herself into the house Anne was conscious of the night stillness. Josh would be in the den, she told herself, and headed down the hall in that direction. A moment later his voice shattered the quiet.

"Stu, I don't give a shit what the Forest Service says. More logging roads in that area mean major erosion and landslides." He turned from the phone and saw her standing at the doorway. "Stu, Anne just came home. We'll talk more tomorrow, okay?"

"Fresh problems?" Anne took off her coat, tossed it across a chair, and dropped onto the deep, comfortable sofa.

"Same problems," he said tiredly. "Thank God for the Sierra Club. They go into the courts to sue to stop the roads." He rose from the desk to walk to the coffee pot that was always close at hand when he was home. "I just made fresh coffee. Want a cup?"

"No. I had my quota for the night." Anne kicked off her pumps and drew her legs onto the sofa.

"Marsh was upset that you didn't get home before his bedtime." He poured himself a fresh cup of coffee.

"I didn't expect the meeting to run this long," she said defensively. "I told Marsh I'd *try* to be home before he went to sleep."

"You know kids," Josh reproached. " 'Try' means 'I will.' He kept watching for you. Mallie put Robin to bed before she left, and Marsh and I watched TV. But he kept listening for you."

"All right," she said, striving for patience when she was tired and tense from the drawn–out meeting. "The next time I won't say 'I'll try'. Then he won't be upset."

"What mammoth decisions did the Mighty Three at Miller Timber arrive at tonight?"

Anne ignored the edge of sarcasm in Josh's voice. "The Mighty Three" was normally said in tender jest.

"Felicia's hammering at Doug to reschedule our old-growth redwoods. Right now he's ambivalent, but she scares me."

"You won't let her get away with it?" He froze at attention, cup halfway to his mouth.

"Josh, I try. I can't give Doug orders." She hadn't meant to sound so sharp, but couldn't he understand she didn't make policy? "Felicia is trying now to sell Doug on the company's building a house at Big Sur. For the entertainment of clients. Another tax dodge," she conceded, hoping to derail him from the more painful subject. *She shouldn't have mentioned the old-growth redwoods.*

"The rich save on taxes, and the little people pay more," he said scathingly. "But what about this rescheduling of the old-growth redwoods?" Josh demanded. "I thought Doug considered Naomi's wishes sacred."

"He always has—but Felicia keeps insisting that Naomi would revise the schedule if she were alive and saw the situation—"

"That there's a market for the oldest and finest trees on this earth!" His voice thickened with impotent fury. "It's like the old lumberjacks sing—'Over the rivers and through the hills, we rape the land to pay our bills.' Annie, get out of Miller Timber while we still have our sanity. They're against everything we believe in. Go in there tomorrow morning and tell Doug you're through."

"I can't do that!" How could Josh ask that of her? "We can't afford to—"

"You're saying I'm not providing for my family," he broke in. "That I ought to find myself a job with a real law firm—with clients who can afford to pay through the nose."

"I didn't say that. I just said it would be impractical for me to walk out on Naomi's will. I've put in close to ten years of my life on this. I'm drawing a terrific salary—"

"That pays the mortgage on this house, pays for your domestic staff, pays for that fancy nursery school Robin attends—"

"Will you stop this?" Anne's voice soared into shrillness. "You've got to understand what—" She paused, stricken by the sound of Robin crying in her upstairs bedroom.

"Now look what you've done!" Josh lashed at her.

"What do you mean—what *I've* done?" She was trembling. She and Josh had fought before—but he'd never stared at her the way he was staring now. As though she was a stranger. A stranger he loathed.

"Go to Robin," Josh ordered, and she stumbled to her feet and hurried toward the door. "If you want to stay with Miller

Timber, you stay. I'm getting out of this straitjacket. I've had all I can take of Naomi Miller's family, her business, her will." His voice followed Anne down the hall. "You don't need money from me. You don't need anything from me. You're the successful, self-sufficient seventies woman. There's no room in your life for a husband!"

Thirty-two

ANNE sat across from Shirley in the company cafeteria and toyed disinterestedly with her shrimp salad. The cafeteria was near-deserted because she preferred a late lunch hour, when most employees were back at their desks.

"How long since you've seen Josh?" Shirley asked sympathetically.

"A week tonight." It seemed a month.

"What will you tell Doug when you and the kids show up alone for the flight to Acapulco?" Shirley's eyes were troubled. Only she knew that Josh had walked out on his marriage.

"I'll say that Josh has to work over the weekend." Anne tried to sound matter-of-fact. "Doug will understand that."

"What about Marsh and Robin?" Shirley prodded. "What are you telling them?"

"The same thing."

"Not about the weekend, Annie," Shirley chided. *This was unreal. How had she let it happen?* "About why Daddy isn't home. I didn't have that problem—Gerry was a baby when her father walked out." But even now, when Gerry was sixteen, that was a bitter memory.

"They see Josh every day," she said defensively. "Mallie says he hasn't missed a day yet. He tells them he's busy with work." Mallie was upset about the break-up but protective of her. "I suppose he'll skip weekends. I'll be home then."

"Annie, call him," Shirley urged. "This is crazy."

380

"I don't know where he is," she hedged. "He wouldn't go to his parents. He knows how upset they'd be." But they'd have to know soon.

"Ten to one he's with Stu," Shirley said after a moment.

"Is he?" She clutched at this indirect contact.

"Stu says he isn't taking sides, but that doesn't mean Josh isn't at his pad."

"I won't call him," Anne said firmly.

"He's probably saying the same thing to Stu right this minute. You're acting like a pair of stubborn kids."

"And that's the way it'll stay." Anne jabbed at her shrimp salad with unnecessary vigor.

"You know what's the matter with you and Josh? You've both lost your sense of humor."

"Should I offer a reward for its return?" Anne's eyes belied the flippancy in her voice.

"You two have got to sit down and talk this out. You and Josh have one of the few truly good marriages I've ever encountered."

"Had," Anne corrected. "Wrong tense."

"Talk to Josh," Shirley repeated.

"We can't talk anymore," Anne confessed in anguish. "We take potshots at each other. Maybe Josh is right. Maybe there is no room in my life for a husband."

"Bullshit. You both said things you didn't mean. Because you're running yourselves ragged. Call up Josh. Don't go to Acapulco tomorrow. Leave the kids with me, and you and Josh go off alone somewhere."

"That won't change the situation." Anne felt drained of strength. "I have no intention of leaving Miller Timber, and Josh is unable to accept that fact." She reached for her purse. "Let's get back to the office."

By the end of the following week Anne conceded she couldn't conceal the rift in her marriage. She suspected Todd knew already and was distressed. Doug was shocked when—

trying desperately to sound matter-of-fact—she told him Josh and she had separated. Not the truth, she tormented herself. Josh had walked out on her. She was grateful that Consuelo and Leon were spending a few weeks in Europe and she didn't have to tell them just yet. Maybe this would be a remembered nightmare by the time they returned.

Tess and Artie were stunned when she forced herself to tell them. She realized Josh had said nothing.

"What the hell is the matter with Josh?" Artie railed. "He's always been so damned unrealistic. Annie, I'm going to talk to him."

"No," Tess intervened even before Anne could object. "Annie and Josh have to work this out by themselves." But Anne saw tears in her eyes.

"I can't walk out on Naomi's will. The money I'm putting into Lazarus Timber is building it into a substantial business. It's a safety valve for us. Even if Felicia should walk out some time during the next ten years," she said with an effort at humor, "we won't fall on our faces financially. Each year I stay on Lazarus grows stronger."

"Annie, you don't have to explain to us," Tess said gently. "Josh loves you, and he loves the children. I can't believe he won't come back soon and say, 'Annie, I made a terrible mistake.' "

"I want that," Anne said shakily. "I want that so much." Deep inside she felt a wrenching guilt. She had failed Josh. She'd made him feel unnecessary in her life.

Marriage was a partnership. They should have been able to discuss their problems, work them out. The only partnership she seemed able to manage, she reproached herself, was that with Felicia. Based on greed and obsession.

Anne knew the children were anxious about Josh's absence from the house. They'd both heard that ugly battle. How had she let that happen? Children were so impressionable. They might not have understood the words, but the hostility—between the two people closest in the world to them—had been blatantly clear.

She strained to keep up the pretense that nothing had changed in their lives. *"Daddy's busy with work. You'll see him tomorrow,"* was her routine response when Marsh and Robin asked, "Where's Daddy?" She contrived to hide her anguish from them, but the nights alone in the room she and Josh had shared since Robin's birth filled her with despair. Empty hangers in the closet, where his clothes should be hanging. Empty drawers in the chest that had been his. How had this happened?

At the end of three weeks Marsh confronted her. Waiting, Anne observed in a corner of her mind, until Mallie had taken Robin off to bed.

"When's Daddy coming home? I mean, to stay," he said forcefully. Anticipating her usual response.

"I don't know, darling." Her smile was casual. Her heart pounded. "But you see him every day. You know he loves you very much."

"We don't see him on weekends." Reproof was in his voice. Up till now she and Josh had spent every waking moment of the weekends with Marsh and Robin. Every moment from the time she came home from the office on Saturday afternoon, she corrected herself conscientiously. *"You* don't see Daddy ever," Marsh accused.

"Daddy's so busy right now." She was startled by his perception. But he was seven years old and bright. "You know how hard he's working for the redwood park—and he has a lot of people to help in his law practice."

Marsh had friends whose parents were divorced—he knew these things happened. *The next time she heard from Josh, would it be to discuss a divorce?* The possibility was shattering.

With the school year coming to a close Anne called a real estate broker about a summer rental. A change of scenery would be good for Marsh and Robin, she decided—it would divert their minds from their father's absence in the house. In past summers they'd divided their weekends between Naomi's Lake Tahoe and Acapulco houses—where Marsh and Robin played happily with Timmy and Karen—and remained in town midweek. But this summer Felicia insisted on sending her two children—Karen six and Timmy eight—off to camp.

"I'll need a place close enough to the city to commute," Anne explained to the broker. And close enough so that Josh could drive out daily. "In a wooded area," she stressed. It was important to her that Marsh and Robin grow up with a love of trees and nature.

She kept waiting for Josh to make an overture to return to them. Mallie told her he was at the house daily. From Shirley, via Stu, she was aware of his activities. While most of his efforts thus far had focused on saving the California redwoods, Josh was fighting now, along with Stu, to expand their work. It was important to alert the American public to the threatened destruction of wilderness areas throughout the country.

She knew, too, that Josh was waiting for her to concede that he was right—that she should walk out on what he'd always called her "thralldom to Naomi Miller." Each day that passed—the lonely nights when she battled insomnia—intensified her fears for her marriage.

In June, shortly before the children and she were to take up residence in the mountain house, Anne planned two birthday parties for Robin: an afternoon party with half a dozen of her small friends from her nursery school as guests, and a dinner party with Tess and Artie, Shirley and Gerry, Todd, and Doug in attendance. Robin was ecstatic.

"With two birthday cakes?"

"Two," Anne promised.

Waking this Saturday morning—Robin's fifth birthday— Anne was especially conscious of Josh's absence from their lives. That night five years ago seemed so close. They'd been so pleased that this second child was a daughter. She had insisted it would be. Josh couldn't have forgotten this was Robin's birthday, could he? No, Mallie said Robin had told him about both parties.

She'd been hoping that Josh would take advantage of the occasion to bridge this awful rift between them. She prayed he would show up for the children's party—or for the dinner party. *Would he come?*

Gerry arrived at the house shortly past ten to take Robin and Marsh off to the zoo—away from the frenzied activities of the household. The afternoon party had mushroomed from a guest list of six to fourteen children plus mothers or nursemaids. Fearful that there might be a lapse in entertainment, Anne had hired a clown and a magician. Todd was coming over to take photographs.

To Anne's relief the children's party was a success from the moment the first little girl—Robin's "best friend"—arrived until the last exhausted but ebullient small guest was persuaded by her mother to leave. But all through the afternoon Anne was poignantly conscious of Josh's absence, overreacting to the ring of the telephone, the doorbell.

An hour before the dinner guests arrived, a messenger appeared with an enormous parcel for Robin. Marsh helped her unwrap it. Inside was a stuffed panda taller than she.

"Mommie, Mommie, he's beautiful!" Robin hugged the panda ecstatically.

"There's a card tied around his neck," Anne pointed out, fighting to hide her pain. Josh wasn't coming. "Shall I read it to you?"

"I can read," Robin reminded her with pride. "Some." She stared hard at the card. "To the—" She hesitated. "I don't know this word—"

"To the birthday girl," Anne read. "From Daddy, with all my love."

All at once Robin was silent. She lifted her blue-green eyes to her mother. They were stormy and accusing.

"It's my birthday. Why isn't Daddy here?"

"He's in Washington," Anne fabricated, her color high. "He and Uncle Stu had to go there to talk to some people about saving the trees. Now let's go phone your grandmother and remind her to bring over that birthday cake—chocolate on the inside and white on the outside, like you asked for, darling."

Why couldn't Josh have come for Robin's birthday? Did he hate her so much that he couldn't bear to be here tonight?

On schedule Anne settled the children, Mallie, and Olivia, the new housekeeper, in the rented cottage set on a heavily wooded acre an eighty-minute drive from the city—provided she avoided the freeways at high-peak hours. Mallie had provided Josh with detailed instructions about the location of the cottage and how to reach it. He'd told the children he'd drive up three or four mornings a week.

"Daddy's coming up for breakfast," Marsh reported happily. And she saw a poignant glint of hope in his eyes that they would sit down to breakfast as a family again. "He wants us at the table by seven in the morning."

Josh knew she was always at the office shortly past eight, Anne interpreted. That meant she'd be leaving the cottage no later than six-thirty. He could drive up for breakfast three or four times a week and know he wouldn't run into her. Was he annoyed that she'd brought the kids up here for the summer? No, she rebuked herself. Josh would be pleased.

In conjunction with the long, tension-riddled days at the office Anne admitted the commuting was exhausting. After the first week she stayed over in town on Wednesday nights and had dinner with Shirley and Gerry. Much of the talk— once Gerry took off for socializing—revolved around Josh and Stu. They were promoting a heavy letter-writing campaign by voters to members of Congress to complain about the shortage of funds for reforestation in the national parks.

In July Miller Timber began to close its offices on Saturdays. On the second Friday in the month Anne joined Doug and Felicia for a dinner meeting at the Miller house, then headed for the cottage. En route she listened to news on the car radio. Since the break-in of the Democratic National headquarters at Washington's Watergate complex a year earlier, each week seemed to bring more shocking disclosures.

"Today," a newscaster's voice reported, "Representative

Robert F. Drinan of Massachusetts introduced a resolution listing four actions as grounds for impeaching President Nixon: the bombing of Cambodia, the taping of conversations, the refusal to spend impounded funds, and the establishment of a 'supersecret' security force within the White House. The public's confidence in President Nixon has sunk to a new low."

And this, Anne thought ironically, was the man who was elected president by the greatest landslide in American history.

Now the commentator was discussing the weather. Again, another weekend without the badly needed rain, he warned. The earth was dry, lawns parched, and there was talk of water rationing in some California towns.

Marsh and Robin were both asleep by the time Anne arrived at the sprawling, redwood cottage, set in the midst of woods that afforded perfect privacy. A ten-minute drive from the village, where there was an adequate grocery store, an old-fashioned ice-cream parlor, and an auto repair shop. The air was cool and fresh, fragrant with the scent of summer greenery and flowers. Some of the tension of the day ebbed away as she sat on the porch with Mallie and listened to the night sounds in the woods.

Anne started as the phone rang inside the house, shrill in the country quiet.

"I'll get it, Mallie." Instantly she was on her feet and hurrying into the house. "I hope it doesn't wake the kids—"

The caller was Doug. His voice shook with rage as he talked to Anne.

"Frank Turner is furious, and he has every right to be. He called moments after you'd left for the day. Felicia, of course, was long gone." So Doug knew that Felicia was cutting out shortly after lunch on Fridays. "He'd just returned from a trip to their new project above Los Angeles to find a letter—signed by Felicia—warning him that his next delivery will be delayed anywhere from six to eight weeks." Turner was committed to build twelve hundred houses in three developments, Anne remembered. This kind of a delay would create a devas-

387

tating situation. "I told him we'd sit down with him tomorrow morning and work this thing out."

"Felicia left for a weekend at Puerto Vallarta," Anne said.

"I know. And I have no phone number." A devious habit of Felicia's to avoid any interruptions. "I hate to spoil your weekend, but could you drive down for a ten o'clock meeting with Turner? We should be able to do whatever has to be done within an hour or two, then you can drive back up."

"I'll meet you at the office at nine," she said quickly. "That'll give us time to check through the files."

In the morning she ate a hasty breakfast prepared by Mallie because Olivia was off on weekends.

"I'll be back probably in time for lunch," she promised the children. "Uncle Doug needs me to help with something at the office."

"You drive carefully now," Mallie ordered. "If you're gone an extra hour the kids will survive."

To Anne's frustration the car refused to start. Mallie came out to the garage with keys to her Chevy.

"I'll call down to the village and have somebody come out and have a look at your car," she told Anne. "I just filled up my tank yesterday—you won't have to bother stopping for gas."

Driving into the city Anne tried to reconstruct what might have happened with Frank Turner's next shipment. This should go through their sales office automatically. It was scheduled. Why had Felicia intervened?

Then all at once she understood. Felicia had shipped the logs scheduled to be milled for Turner to Tsuda in Japan—because of the new tax loopholes that allowed them to delay indefinitely on paying federal taxes on 50 percent of their export-related profits. Plus Felicia had probably connived to up the price on an extra shipment to Tsuda, whose mills were hungry for timber.

Anne walked into Doug's office to find him, pale and grim, hunched over office files he'd brought in from the sales department.

"Felicia shipped the logs meant for Turner to Tsuda?" Anne asked.

"You figured it out." He managed a rueful smile.

"I know how Felicia's mind works." Anne dropped into a chair beside Doug's desk. "Strictly bottom line."

"Turner's grandfather was one of our first accounts. His company has been doing business with us since the turn of the century. How could she treat them this way?"

"I'll make us some coffee," Anne soothed. "Then we'll sit down and figure a way out of this mess."

An hour later they both recognized there was no way they could handle Turner's needs without cutting old-growth timber scheduled to remain untouched until the end of the century. It was what Felicia kept screaming at them to do, Anne remembered in silent frustration.

"I don't like this anymore than you do," Doug told her, "but we can't hold up Turner's development. It'd be outrageous. And those trees are fine for rafters and floor joists. We'll replace them at the Forest Service auction next month."

"More trees out of the national forests," she said painfully. Doug knew how angry she was about the way the Nixon administration had just upped the cut in the federal forests.

"Damn it, Anne, when will you understand that timber is renewable? It's not like oil and coal. We can regrow our forests. Private and public."

"But we're not doing that! We're cutting far more in this country that we're replanting." And trees that could be felled in a few minutes couldn't be replaced in less than fifty to a hundred years. The redwoods required a century to reach full growth. "It's morally wrong," she said heatedly, "to destroy our national forests."

"No," Doug said, his face taut. "It's only right that the public lands should help supply the lumber this country needs. What's the point in letting mature trees remain uncut?"

"Because they're a national treasure that should be preserved for future generations," Anne said passionately. "Because . . ."

"Let's not get philosophical." All at once Doug seemed exhausted. "We're here to do what must be done."

"But we should be trying to replace what we take away." She was too emotionally involved not to pursue this further. "I don't even know that it can be done," she said with candor, "but it's time the timber industry paid its dues. We—"

Anne paused at the sound of footsteps down the deserted hall.

"That's Turner now," Doug said crisply. "We've got fences to mend, Annie."

Thirty-three

WATCHING Marsh and Robin on the improvised swing in comfortable view of the kitchen, Mallie prepared lunch for them. They were disappointed that their two friends at the cottage down the road had gone to a family reunion for the weekend. She'd bring out those two new puzzles their father gave them yesterday, she decided. That would keep them occupied for a while after lunch.

She frowned at the flash of lightning that darted across the sky. They'd had lightning all week. What about some rain? She paused, stared up at the sky. She didn't like the children out there under the trees with a dry lightning storm coming up.

She hurried to the kitchen door and called out to them.

"Robin, Marsh—come on inside the house now. Lunch is almost ready."

Drained by their meeting Annie hurried to her car while Doug and Turner went off for lunch. She was impatient to be back at the mountain house. When Turner had gone off to the men's room to wash up for lunch, Doug had twitted her affectionately about allowing Josh to convert her into an environmentalist. But for the first time she felt an ambivalence in him toward the values instilled by his mother. He had been up in arms about the pollution at Lake Tahoe, she remembered. How could a man as sensitive and bright as he not see that killing the forests ranked with killing the lakes?

She had never seen him so angry as today. Felicia would have a rough time winning him over to her side after this insanity. Perhaps now *she* would be able to make some serious inroads. The timber industry must make tremendous changes—and huge investments.

Grandma had seen what needed to be done—and in their own small way they were trying to do this at Lazarus Timber. In the industry at large timber management had to be improved. Wasteful habits abandoned. The new technology utilized fully. The country didn't have to face a lumber crisis every few years. There was room for logging and wildlife and wilderness recreation.

"Can we go out and play now?" Robin asked while Mallie cleared away the remains of lunch.

"Why don't you and Marsh play with your new puzzles?" Mallie coaxed. "When the lightning let's up, then you can play outdoors again."

"Yeah, let's do the puzzles," Marsh said. "Bet I finish before you do," he challenged Robin.

With the children settled down in the living room with their puzzles Mallie decided to watch television. But five minutes into her program the television set went dead.

"I hope we haven't lost our electricity." She rose from her chair and went to switch on the lamp. "It's off. Lightning must have struck somewhere."

"When's Mommie coming home?" Robin asked without removing her eyes from the puzzle on which she was working.

"She ought to be driving up real soon," Mallie told her. "If the electricity doesn't come back on in a few hours, we'll have to drive somewhere for dinner."

"Hamburgers and French fries," Marsh decreed exuberantly. "At that place just past the village. It's cool."

"I hope the electricity doesn't come back on," Robin giggled. "I want hamburgers and French fries. And a chocolate shake."

"I smell smoke." Marsh looked up from his puzzle. "Somebody must be having a barbeque."

All at once Mallie was anxious.

"I'm going out to the kitchen for a glass of water," she told the children.

From the kitchen window she saw smoke spiraling into the sky. The lightning must have started a fire in the forest. And with that gusty wind the fire would spread fast, she realized in alarm. Still, it was quite a distance away.

She'd call the garage and see if the car had been repaired. Ask the mechanic to bring it up—it made her nervous to be here without a car. Fighting off a touch of panic she reached for the kitchen phone. Of course the fire was miles away. They were in no danger.

She waited for a dial tone. Nothing. The phone was dead. Both the electric and phone lines were down in the area. Maybe the phones were working down at the Andrews's house. She'd feel better if the mechanic brought up the car.

"Let's take a little walk down to the Andrews's house," Mallie said casually. "Our phone's out, and I want to call down to the garage."

"I smell smoke—" Robin sniffed curiously.

"There's a fire farther up the mountain," Mallie told them.

"Where?" Marsh jumped to his feet.

"Up toward the north. Not near us. Come on now. Let's go ask Mrs. Andrews if we can use her phone."

The aroma of smoke was drifting toward them. The wind was high. By the time they were out on the road, they could see flames towering into the sky.

"Is our house going to catch on fire?" Robin asked, simultaneously alarmed and fascinated.

"No, Robin." Mallie reached to take one small hand in hers.

"It's awfully windy." Marsh gazed over his shoulder at the sky while they walked down the road in the opposite direction. "How long will it take to put it out?"

Josh left the modest but pleasant little house of the logger who had contacted his group to report that logging debris was causing hazardous conditions in a neighboring stream—and headed for his car. He was barely a fifteen-minute drive from the cottage, he thought wistfully. But Annie would be at the house with the kids. Stu said she drove up every Friday night for the weekend. Shirley had been instructed to get that message to him, he decided, Annie making sure they wouldn't cross paths.

The weekends without Annie and the kids were the worst times, Josh thought as he drove away from the house and turned south. Weekends had always been their special time together. In a sudden need to puncture the silence in the car he reached to switch on the radio.

He frowned as disco music invaded the car. God, he wasn't in the mood for that. He took one hand from the wheel to fiddle with the radio dial. A newscaster was reporting on a forest fire on a mountain slope north of the city. Not uncommon in California in the summer.

All at once he went cold with alarm. The fire was in the vicinity of Annie's summer rental—farther up the mountain, but the winds were high.

"Fed by drought-parched trees the fire is at the moment burning out of control. Extra firemen, helicopters—"

Josh switched off the radio, his mind in turmoil. A fire like that could travel fifteen hundred to two thousand acres an hour. He swung off onto the shoulder of the road, glanced briefly toward the northbound lane, and made a sharp U-turn. *Annie, the kids, and Mallie were right in the line of the fire.*

Mallie rang the doorbell at the Andrews's house again, knowing already they were not at home. The garage door was up. Both cars were gone.

"Maybe the door's open," Marsh said.

"Not if they've gone away." But Mallie reached for the knob. The door was locked. "We'll go back to the house," she told the children with mock cheerfulness. "Mommie will probably be driving up the road any minute now."

She heard the sound of cars on the road. People in houses up above fleeing from the fire, she thought and rushed hopefully from the porch of the Andrews's house to signal for help. But the station wagon and sedan—packed with passengers— rushed past before she could stop them.

"They didn't see us," Robin complained.

"Look how high in the sky the flames go." Marsh looked up at Mallie. "The firemen will stop it before it gets to our house, won't they?"

"Sure they will," Mallie reassured him. But she knew about forest fires. They traveled so fast if they went out of control. She hesitated. The nearest houses were almost three miles below. Too far to walk. They would go back to the house, she decided. The fire was still a good piece above them. It looked worse than it was, she comforted herself.

"We'll go back home and watch for Mommie. If the fire looks like it's getting close, then we'll get into the car when she gets to the house and drive down to San Francisco."

"Suppose Mommie doesn't come soon?" Robin was growing anxious.

"She will," Mallie said with confidence. She mustn't let the kids know how scared she was. "She's coming straight home from the meeting."

Turning off onto a secondary road Anne debated about stopping off for a sandwich. She'd had a headache since mid-morning and now she was hungry. She'd had breakfast—just juice and an English muffin and coffee—hours ago. Okay, stop for a sandwich. Maybe that would clear up her headache. She could be in and out of the diner just ahead in fifteen minutes.

She turned off the road onto the parking area of the diner. A pair of trucks were parked. She remembered how everybody said truckers knew all the best diners. She went into the pleasant air-conditioning. The aroma of fresh coffee was appealing.

Several booths were empty. She slid into the nearest and reached for a menu.

"Grilled swiss on rye and coffee," she said when a waitress approached her booth.

Mallie stood in the backyard and stared up at the thick, dark smoke that shot high into the sky. Overhead she saw a helicopter that was part of the fire-fighting force. The sharp wind driving the flames in their direction.

"Mallie, it's getting near us." She swung around to face Marsh. Robin hanging onto his arm.

"We'll start walking down the road," she told the children. "We'll go to meet Mommie."

"First I have to get Teddy," Robin said, momentarily pugnacious.

"Go get Teddy," Mallie agreed after an instant's hesitation. "Quickly," she said, trying not to show her alarm. "Let's see how far we can get before Mommie arrives."

Mallie took a hand of each child in hers—while Robin clutched the teddy bear that traveled everywhere with her.

"We know Mommie takes this road," Mallie said cheerfully. "She'll be driving toward us any minute now." But the murky gray and red sky was ominous.

Anne bit hungrily into the grilled cheese sandwich, her mind still occupied by the heated meeting with Doug this morning. These were the times, other than the lonely nights of sleeping alone, that she most missed Josh. She needed to talk to him about their cutting in their old-growth redwoods. Not that Josh could change anything but she longed to share her anguish with him.

He must have been as upset as she last month when

396

Nixon—to the cries of the industry about a timber emergency—ordered the Forest Service to offer an additional billion board feet of timber for sale. The Forest Service didn't bother to point out that the annual allowable cut was already too high.

The door opened and a pair of workmen, clearly regulars in the diner, walked inside and straddled stools at the counter.

"Hey, Marie, turn on the TV," one of them ordered. "Let's see if they've got a bulletin on that forest fire near the top of the mountain."

Anne stiffened to attention. *What mountain?*

"It's one of them lightnin' fires again," the other reported. "And movin' like hell."

Anne abandoned her sandwich. Her heart pounding. The regular program was being shown. No bulletin.

"Excuse me," Anne said, reaching into her wallet for a bill and crossing to the counter, her voice strained. "Where's the fire?"

"Straight up this road about fifteen miles," one of the newcomers told her, "and travelin' south. Don't go drivin' up that way now," he joshed. " 'Less you want to be barbecued."

Her face drained of color, Anne handed the bill to the waitress and hurried to the door without waiting for change.

Mallie abandoned trying to make a game of "walking to meet Mommie." The children were frightened, though Marsh was pretending he wasn't. The fire was moving relentlessly forward, traveling at a faster rate than they could walk.

"Mallie, I'm tired," Robin whimpered. "Let's rest."

"I'll carry you," Mallie soothed. They had to keep moving.

"I hear a car!" Marsh's face lighted. "It must be Mommie."

A car came into sight. Not Mallie's.

"It's Daddy!" Robin squealed. "Daddy's come for us!"

The car pulled to a stop and Josh emerged.

"I heard about the fire on my car radio," he explained to

Mallie, scooping both children into his arms simultaneously. "Where's Annie?"

"She had to drive into the city this morning. Some emergency at the office," Mallie explained. "She was driving up later."

"All right, everybody, into the car and let's clear out of here," Josh said briskly.

"We might miss Mommie." Robin was uneasy.

"No, baby," Josh comforted. "This is the road we always take. We'll meet her farther down."

Anne drove with abnormal speed. At intervals her eyes searched the sky. The smoke from the fire—probably visible even in the city, she guessed—stoked her anxiety. Had Mallie been able to reach somebody to drive them away from the house? One of the reasons she'd rented that place was because of its privacy. Just the three houses there and nothing more for three miles down. The northbound road was deserted except for herself. She hadn't seen a car coming down from above in the past three miles. Mallie and the children must have been evacuated earlier, she told herself. But uncertainty wracked her.

Then she spied a car in the distance. Josh's Olds, she realized moments later. She thrust a hand from the car window and waved. *Josh had come up for them.*

They each pulled up at opposite sides of the road, and then the children were darting from the car to her side.

"Mommie, we were so scared," Robin told her.

"She had to bring Teddy with her," Marsh scoffed. "Just like a girl."

"I heard the news on the car radio," Josh told her. His eyes bright with love. "I had to be sure you were all right."

"Oh, Josh—" She held out her arms in silent supplication and Josh pulled her close. "I shouldn't have left them alone without a car. Mine broke down—I had to take Mallie's. They could have been trapped in that fire—"

"Annie, it's all right," he soothed. "Everything's all right."

"Why don't I drive ahead with the kids, and you two follow?" Mallie suggested. "Come on, kids," she ordered without waiting for a reply. "When we get near the city, we'll stop off at that place you like so much for frozen custard."

Josh and Anne followed closely in his car. Her head on his shoulder.

"We won't ever allow anything to separate us again," Josh said. "It's been hell without you and the kids."

"I missed you so much, Josh. The worst time of all was the nights—"

"I know." His voice echoed remembered pain.

"Sometimes I'd wake up in the night and forget that you weren't there. I'd reach out—and realize I was alone. It was awful."

"We'll never let it happen again, Annie," he repeated. "No matter what the future brings, we'll see it through together. I'm only half alive without you."

"I'm walking out on Miller Timber," Anne told him. "I should have been there with the children. That's where I belong."

"No," Josh said and she lifted her head from his shoulder in astonishment. "Annie, you're not a quitter. And you're not depriving the children of anything—you're building for their future." His smile was wry. "I had a lot of empty nights to think about our situation. We're both working for the same thing—"

"Josh, I'm on the other side of the fence," she said passionately. "With a company that's helping to rape our forests!"

"But you're fighting to turn that around," he continued. "And you're privvy to inside information that's useful to our side." His eyes left the road to rest fleetingly on her with love.

This was one of those perfect moments in their marriage, Anne thought tenderly. A reaffirmation of the joy of their finding each other. It was frightening to think that she could have gone through her whole life without meeting Josh. And oddly, it was Naomi Miller who had brought them together.

"Josh, your parents are out in Palm Springs this week." Anne dropped a hand on his thigh. "Do you suppose we could drive up to their place for the rest of the weekend? Just the two of us," she emphasized and sensed his sudden exhilaration. "Mallie won't mind."

"We'll take the kids and Mallie out for dinner, then drive up," he said ebulliently. "We've got a hell of a lot of catching up to do."

Thirty-four

FELICIA willed herself to be silent as she sat in one of the two armchairs before Doug's desk—Anne in the other—while he excoriated her for tampering with Frank Turner's shipments.

"May I say something?" she asked with a condescending smile when he paused.

"You may," Doug said coldly.

"Turner needs us. He'll be angry for a while, but who else will supply him in this tight market?" Felicia shot a swift sidewise glance at Anne. The little bitch had gloated at Doug's tirade. "I ordered the extra shipment to go to Japan when Adrian discovered Takaji Tsuda had people looking around to buy sawmills in Washington and Oregon."

"Adrian's sure about that?" Doug was startled.

"He has the names of four small sawmills being approached." That upset the old boy. "With their own sawmills here they wouldn't renew their contracts with us. I phoned Takaji in Tokyo and convinced him he didn't have to resort to that—we'd keep him supplied. We can't afford not to," she emphasized.

"Tsuda is a fine account," Doug said slowly. "But that doesn't give us the right to shortchange a firm that's been doing business with us since 1903."

"This is 1973!" Felicia's eyes glittered with defiance. "We

can't run Miller Timber the way it was run in 1903. We have to look after our own interests."

"Felicia, I won't tolerate this kind of operation," Doug told her, his indignation resurfacing. "If another incident such as this arises, I'll go to court and have my mother's will invalidated. I'm sorry, Anne," he apologized, "but that would be necessary."

"You can't do that!" Felicia stared in disbelief.

"Oh yes, I can." Doug was emphatic. "I have a copy of the will right here." He reached into a desk drawer, pulled out a sheaf of papers, and tossed it toward Felicia. "Down among the endless small restrictions—which I remember you couldn't bother to read—is a clause that allows me to have the will invalidated if I feel that either you or Anne is acting against the best interests of the company. There's a provision that everything willed to you and Anne will go, instead, to the museum. So you understand, Felicia—we run this company the way my mother wished, or the ball game is over."

For the next few weeks Felicia avoided Doug as much as possible, both at the office and at the house. She toyed with the idea of renting her own apartment. Not to live in full-time, but to be an escape hatch when she was in the mood. A small place that wouldn't make a serious dent in the seventy-five thousand she was currently drawing in salary. She had no intention of abandoning the luxury of living in Naomi's Washington Street mansion.

Why hadn't she ever noticed that crazy clause in the will? Why hadn't Paul told her about it? He was supposed to be such a sharp lawyer. Had Doug meant that—about going to court to invalidate the will? He just might. He followed Naomi's line, but he had that weird sense of ethics that belonged to the last century.

She'd always been sure he leaned toward favoring her, though he put up a great show about being impartial. But he wasn't impartial right now. He leaned toward Anne as the next CEO. Still, he wasn't preparing to step down, she comforted herself. Somehow, she had to turn around his thinking.

Sitting in her office on a mid-September morning, she appraised the situation. What was particularly bugging Doug? He was anxious about the way the preservationists were fighting to save choice timbered areas under the Wilderness Act. God, how could he feel kindly toward Anne when Josh was part of that idiotic preservation scene—and *she* was always crying about the "timber people's responsibilities"?

All right! All at once she knew which way to move. She reached for her phone and dialed Adrian's extension.

"Meet me for lunch at one at Jack's." Adrian would understand it was better that they not leave the office together. "We need to talk."

Over Jack's classic chicken Jerusalem Felicia and Adrian focused on the best way to win approval from Doug. The Forest Service was holding public meetings in the northwestern states to examine and discuss their selections of land to be set aside as protected wilderness areas—meetings where the timber industry was well represented because what remained of the unlogged northwest wilderness was the prize. Felicia was interested in proselytizing at these preservation meetings. They were being overlooked. Show Doug she was waging a successful campaign in that area, and he'd be impressed.

As she discussed this project with Adrian, she was astonished by his knowledge regarding the slew of public meetings being called by the preservation groups.

"I was dating this gorgeous chick who was involved in some local group," he explained with a grin. "We broke up because I didn't want to spend Saturday evening listening to that shit."

"Brace yourself," Felicia drawled. "You're going to those meetings. You're going to warn those people they're trying to drag in that a lot of jobs will be lost if the preservationists tie up all that timberland."

"Okay." Adrian nodded, squinting in thought. "I'll go to these towns and talk with the loggers and the sawmill workers.

And what do you know, some of them will go with me to the meetings. After all, they don't want to be thrown out of work because of some screwy preservationists."

Immediately Adrian focused on his newest assignment. Soon he brought back local newspaper reports about loggers and sawmill workers who were attending preservationist meetings with the intent of frightening off new followers. He allowed himself—"as a young man interested in a future political career"—to be interviewed to express his concern that thousands of jobs were at stake. He was quoted as declaring that "the wilderness areas would be set aside as playgrounds for the rich—they'd be off-limits to working people."

In triumph Felicia presented the newspaper clippings to Doug and explained the campaign she had launched with Adrian.

"Smart," Doug conceded.

"Now I think we ought to do what Weyerhaeuser and Boise Cascade and Georgia-Pacific are doing. Invest in public relations and consumer advertising." She smiled at Doug's lifted eyebrows. "We have to make the general public understand that if they want new homes—or second homes—or for the bleeding hearts, homes for the urban poor—they can't achieve those if Congress locks up millions of acres of timberland."

"We've never gone into consumer advertising or public relations." Doug was hesitant.

"We didn't have to in the past," Felicia pointed out. "We didn't have to cope with insane laws passed by Congress. And at the same time we're spreading Miller Timber's name around the country. When we eventually move into homebuilding—" She ignored Doug's disparaging smile. Like Weyerhaeuser they would eventually move into homebuilding. "Then the public will recognize the name. That's thinking ahead to the future." She softened her contention that they would one day move into homebuilding. "Naomi would go along with this."

"We'll discuss it with the board," Doug said finally.

Felicia suppressed a smile. She had already talked with four board members. They agreed that the company should move into a public relations and advertising campaign.

At Christmas the family was to gather as usual at the Squaw Valley house for a long weekend. Anne was upset that Felicia was sending Timmy and Karen to Squaw Valley with the current governess while she flew off to Las Hadas, the newly opened resort masterpiece on the "Mexican Riviera." Glenn and Norma, whom he had never bothered to marry, were going off to Mexico for the holidays.

Marsh and Robin pleaded to be allowed to fly to Squaw Valley with Timmy and Karen the night before their parents would be going out.

"Please, please, please," Robin begged. "I can sleep with Karen, and Marsh can sleep with Timmy. Aunt Consuelo says she'll look after us," she added triumphantly. "She's going to call you."

It was arranged for the children to fly with the first contingent: Consuelo and Leon—and a reluctant Adrian, Edwina and Bruce, Timmy and Karen, and their governess. Anne suspected that Timmy and Karen would feel less deserted in the company of Marsh and Robin. She was pleased that the four were so close.

The following noon Anne and Doug were joined at the airport by Josh and Todd. It was routine for Todd to avoid his parents wherever possible. When Doug and Josh joined the crew in the cockpit for casual conversation, Todd confided his anger at Felicia.

"Why the hell did she have to run down to Las Hadas over Christmas? She ought to remember what it was like for us on holidays. Our parents were forever leaving us behind. I remember how hurt—and scared—we were when Mother and Dad dashed off somewhere or other everytime there was a school holiday and we were sent home."

"We'll all make a point of being attentive to Timmy and

405

Karen," Anne promised. Not difficult. They were such warm, appealing kids.

"Mother and Dad used to order presents for us over the phone," Todd remembered bitterly. "They couldn't even take time out to shop themselves. I thought there was something wrong with me and Felicia. God, the guilt I felt for so long because I couldn't love them the way I thought I should. Felicia spent a lot of time with Naomi and Uncle Doug—they were both always so conscious of family. I never hit it off with the old lady," he admitted. "Felicia and Adrian knew how to handle her. They could get anything out of her."

"But in the end," Anne said softly, "she knew how to make Felicia toe the line."

"The summer I was fourteen and Adrian was twelve, Naomi decided it would be good for us to spend a summer at the ranch. She bought a foreign sports car for the ranch—because Adrian was too young to get a driver's license and he couldn't wait to drive a car. We could drive on the ranch—private property," Todd pointed out, "without a license. I hated that summer. Felicia was having a ball with some group touring Europe. Adrian acted like he owned the ranch, and nobody dared contradict him. I spent most of the summer in my room. Reading, listening to Chubby Checker or The Drifters, and watching TV reports about the 'sit-ins' by Negro students in the South." All at once he smiled. "I think it's great the way you and Josh bring Timmy and Karen into your house so often."

"We'll make it a great Christmas for them," Anne resolved, and laughed. "They helped make Hanukkah a great holiday for Marsh and Robin. They came over every one of the eight nights to be there for the candle lighting."

"And the presents," Todd remembered. "They enjoyed those nightly Hanukkah presents more than the expensive deals Felicia ships back to them from her jaunts. Because they know," he said softly, "they come to them with love."

Felicia shared a white leather love seat with Jackie on the plane the Tylers had chartered to fly the five of them to Las Hadas—Jackie and Bill, Bill's parents, and herself. The other three, seated in a cluster of lounge chairs at the opposite end of the cabin, were caught up in a lively discussion of the latest developments on Watergate. Felicia seethed at the news Jackie had just confided.

"Why did you wait till now to tell me?" Felicia scolded, her voice too low to carry to the others.

"I figured Las Hadas would be diverting enough so you wouldn't be too upset," Jackie said candidly.

"How did Craig and Hera manage to be so secretive about the divorce?" The rotten bastard. Once he knew she'd divorced Glenn, he was through. He hadn't once called since she told him. "And when did he marry that Eurasian model?" she demanded. That nineteen-year-old Eurasian model.

"Three days ago. It's in all the columns, darling."

Felicia bristled. "I don't have time to read the columns."

"Anyhow, you said you never wanted to see him again after that weekend at his Acapulco house," Jackie reminded her.

"How much longer before we land?" All at once Felicia was restless.

"We reach Manzanillo in twenty minutes. Then it's a ten-mile drive to Las Hadas," Jackie explained. "I hear it's fantastic."

On the brief drive from the new oceanfront international jet airport at Manzanillo, Congressman Tyler, relishing this respite from the Washington rat race, filled the others in on details about Antenor and Beatriz Patiño's new international resort.

"Patiño spent twenty-five million on Las Hadas—the ultimate luxury where there was once only jungle and uninhabited beach. I gather not all the villas and suites are finished just yet, but our accommodations and the swimming pools and the tennis courts are ready. And there's a great marina for guests who arrive on their yachts."

Felicia tensed at the mention of a marina. But Craig's yacht would not be there. Jackie said he and his new bride were honeymooning at Lyford Cay. Craig was pushing fifty and his new wife was nineteen. Did he consider *her* over the hill at thirty-two?

Felicia was impressed as they drove into the green-sloped, all-white wonder-village designed by the great Mexican architect José Luis Esquerra. Bougainvillea, hibiscus, mimosa, palms everywhere. Mosaic-paved roads and walks and steps connected the domed and turreted villas.

She was equally impressed as she settled into her personal villa. The floors were white marble, the walls stucco—and they'd been told that each villa was different, with arches and niches defining its inner design, all rounded and curved, none square. The bedroom and sitting room were colorful with painted bamboo furniture and printed linens and cottons. Each villa opened onto a balcony or verandah or a walled garden.

Inspecting the bathroom Felicia chuckled, remembering Mrs. Tyler's exhortation—not necessary because she was familiar with Mexican plumbing.

"Felicia, remember. The 'C' on the taps means *caliente,*" Spanish for 'hot." She would remember, too, not to walk barefoot on the hot beach—and to wear a hat. The weather here was reminiscent of North Africa.

She had changed into a long, white cotton caftan and flat white sandals by the time Jackie arrived to sweep her off to visit the boutique that flanked the plaza.

"Bill's mother is taking a siesta. Bill and his father are in the gaming rooms, of course. Let's go see what we can buy."

Felicia tried to erase from her mind the news of Craig's marriage, to a girl the age of his older daughter, she tormented herself at unwary moments. Thirteen years younger than she. *Damn him.*

At dinner at the formal Legazpi—designed by Valerian Rybar—Felicia became aware of a handsome young man who stared conspicuously at her. Now and then he averted his gaze to a sleek older woman in a gown by Valentino.

"Jackie, do you know that gorgeous character who keeps staring at us? And who's the woman?"

"That's Don Bertinelli," Jackie said instantly. "The woman with him is his mother. I hear she just had a rump lift by that Brazilian surgeon who's supposed to be so wonderful."

"The Bertinelli Hotel chain?"

"That's the family," Jackie said. "But he's a kid," she warned. "Twenty-two or twenty-three and mad about polo ponies."

"I think he has something else in mind at the moment. Arrange to introduce us, darling."

"Mother dear may want to scratch your eyes out," Jackie cautioned. "She's dying to marry him off to Old Society. Every deb of this season is after him."

"Introduce us," Felicia ordered. Craig might need a nineteen-year-old to excite him, but it was clear she excited this twenty-two-year-old.

Jackie introduced her to Don Bertinelli as their party drifted out of the restaurant. She and Don made a whispered arrangement to meet thirty minutes later at the open-air, black-and-white discotheque designed by famous French decorator François Catroux. They remained only briefly at the discotheque.

"Why haven't we met before?" Don demanded as he followed her into her villa.

"You've been too busy with polo ponies," Felicia drawled.

"They take second place to you." He reached to pull her close.

"Lock the door," she chided. "We don't want visitors."

"Felicia, you're being scandalous," Jackie scolded, just hours before their departure, but her eyes glinted with amusement. "You've been constantly with Don."

"What's scandalous?" she challenged, her smile brilliant. "We're both unattached. He's meeting me at Sun Valley next month for a weekend."

"He's twenty-three," Jackie reminded her.

"So?" Beside Don, she thought with satisfaction, Craig was an old man. "It's not like Eva with guys one-third her age. I don't sag, bulge, or creak. He's mad about me."

"How is he?" Jackie asked curiously.

"Too fast," she admitted. "But I'll teach him." She smiled reminiscently. "I have to say he has a lot of talent."

Despite his mother's efforts to foist him on a twenty-year-old post-deb with the proper credentials, Don cornered Felicia in her villa when the maid who packed for her had left.

"Why can't you stay over till tomorrow?" he coaxed.

"I have a job," she replied. He thought it was a colossal joke that she was working. "I have a date with a desk at nine tomorrow morning."

"When do you leave for the airport?" He pulled her close, his hips nuzzling hers.

"In about twenty minutes." She almost wished she were staying longer. God, he was passionate.

"Not long, but we'll have to make do."

"Don!" She was simultaneously amused and angry when he shoved her onto the sofa and slid a hand beneath her mid-knee skirt. The other hand made its way down the deep cleavage of her blouse.

"Get out of your clothes," he ordered after a moment and rose to his feet.

"We're out of our minds," she complained but she was undressing as swiftly as he.

It made her feel so young, she thought, to grab at sex this way—with only minutes available. She lay back against the sofa while he lowered himself above her, hot and impatient. Young, she thought in a surge of satisfaction as he thrust himself within her and grunted in pleasure. And she pretended to be as excited as he.

"I have to dress," she said after a few moments, while he lay momentarily exhausted above her. How lovely that she didn't have to worry anymore about getting pregnant. Dr.

Bernstein took care of that when Karen was born. "That'll have to do until Sun Valley."

"You are a gorgeous woman," he said, lifting himself from her with obvious reluctance.

"For a polo player you're not bad," she laughed.

"What about a week in Morocco in March?" he asked, reaching for clothes he'd tossed to the floor.

"Let's talk about that in Sun Valley."

Morocco in March with Don Bertinelli might be great.

Thirty-five

THE timber industry and the preservationists continued to battle. To some it appeared that the preservationists were making substantial strides. The Forest Service set up interdisciplinary teams to plan sales that would minimize the impact on environmental qualities. The average size of clear-cuts in the lower forty-eight states had been reduced to forty acres.

"It's not enough!" Josh declared, echoing the feelings of other preservationists and some Forest Service supervisors as well. "They're making too many poor decisions—harmful to the environment. Increased logging in the national forests means thousands of miles of new roads. You know what that means, Annie. Erosion, landslides, heaps of slash that are fire hazards."

"And I know what this does to the soil," Anne said painfully. "All the nutrients that are lost. The flooding. The polluting of the streams. And it's sad and frightening to see what's happening to our wildlife."

Preservationists were pointing out now that old-growth harvesting was threatening the owl. A number of bird species required forest stands that were at least two hundred years old if they were to survive. Elk and deer depended upon old forests for food and shelter in the heart of the winter. The preservationists continued their fight.

In January Felicia spent a ski weekend with Don at Sun Valley. She took off a week in March to fly with him to Morocco. In June she met him in Santa Barbara to spend a day on a nude beach. She knew she still looked sensational in or out of a bikini. In between he flew into San Francisco for twenty-four-hour visits. Felicia rented a small, lush apartment for herself on Russian Hill which she occupied at these intervals. The newspaper columns devoted to jet-set activities followed their affair avidly.

Todd was upset about the Felicia-Don affair. He cornered his mother at a family dinner at the Miller house.

"Talk to Felicia," he urged his mother. "She's behaving like a jerk. Don Bertinelli is ten years younger than she is."

"Nine," Edwina corrected. "And so what? Felicia's only amusing herself."

"Suppose she decides to marry him?" he challenged.

"Todd, darling, Felicia isn't about to throw away sixty million dollars plus fringe benefits because Don looks gorgeous in swimming trunks."

All his mother was thinking about was the money, Todd thought in exasperation. Felicia hadn't walked out on the will when she married Glenn. She wouldn't walk out if she married Don. But that wasn't the point he was trying to make. Don was a playboy—how could he fit into Felicia's life?

In July Felicia was to fly to Venice for a costume ball being given by Don's older sister in a rented eighteenth-century palazzo overlooking the Grand Canal. It was to be one of the most lavish affairs of the year—and she was sure Craig would be there with Valerie, his second wife. She wanted Craig to see her with Don. She knew, also, that Don's parents were irritated by their affair, religiously followed by the columnists. They were still trying to push Don into marriage with the debutante daughter of his mother's longtime friend.

Felicia flew first to Paris, where she was to meet Don—flying in from a polo match in Andalusia. He met her at Orly with a rented Jaguar and drove her to their suite at the Ritz.

"So why did I have to meet you in Paris?" he complained good-humoredly, fondling her knee with one hand as they dawdled in morning traffic.

"I have to be here for the fitting on my costume," she told him. "What about yours?"

"Oh, Carol's taking care of that." Carol, she recalled, was the sister who divorced some Italian count to marry a rising young associate of her father's—being groomed to take over the hotel empire one day. Don had made it clear he'd never been involved in the business. "I'll go for a fitting at the tailor's when we arrive in Venice. It's the same tailor who makes most of my suits. No problem. What are you going as?"

"I thought of going as Lady Godiva," she laughed, "but I was afraid your sister might not appreciate that."

"That's right," he agreed. "The horse might leave a load in the middle of the ballroom. All right," he pushed. "What are you going as?"

"Theda Bara. In slinky black."

"And every woman there will hate you because all the men will be dying to jump you. Why couldn't you come to Andalusia to see me play?" he scolded.

"I've told you. I work for a living." Hadn't he seen that spread on her in last month's *Fortune?*

"If this traffic doesn't start moving, we're going to have to do something about me." He reached for her hand and brought it to his crotch.

"Too bad you don't have venetians on the car windows," she drawled. "Hold on to that till we get to the hotel."

"We're flying down to Venice tomorrow afternoon," he reminded. "We're getting a lift with a couple of Carol's guests."

On the Lear jet that was flying them to Venice Felicia was annoyed by the talk about Craig and Valerie.

"Craig and Valerie are throwing a week of bashes after Carol's ball," their hostess told her. "His yacht's at anchor in the mouth of the Grand Canal. He'd just renamed it the *Valerie.*"

Nineteen Craig could marry, Felicia seethed. He could rename his yacht for that stupid bitch. What had she ever done with her life except pose for a few magazine covers? Let Craig see

that Don—twenty-three and gorgeous—was mad about *her.*
And that she was mad about him.

The costume ball was a spectacular success. Thank God it
was a mob scene, Felicia thought while she danced with Don
to the rock music played by a British group brought over
from London to alternate with the more conventional orches-
tra. She didn't want to come face-to-face with Craig. She just
wanted him to see her with Don. She'd seen him twice across
the room. He must have seen her. He looked *old,* she thought
with vindictive amusement. Old beside Don.

Why was she so bored? Why did her mind keep roaming
back to San Francisco and the business? What did she have
to do to make Doug step down as CEO in favor of her?

"You're not here," Don chided. "You're off in outer space
somewhere."

"Do we have to stay here?" she challenged.

"No." His eyes were deceptively ingenuous. "What would
you like to do?"

"Go back to the hotel and fuck," she said coolly. And forget
that bastard Craig threw her over for a nineteen-year-old
model.

"On one condition," he stipulated, pulling her off the dance
floor. "That first thing in the morning we fly to Cannes and
get married."

"Why?" she demanded, startled by this proposal.

"Because I want to own you," he whispered hotly and a
moment later exchanged giddy conversation—shouting above
the music—with two young women unknown to Felicia. It
was amazing how many people she *didn't* know these days,
she thought.

"Donnie boy," she murmured as they moved away from
the crowd, "nobody owns Felicia Harris."

"Just your body," he soothed. "Your mind belongs to you."

All at once the prospect of marriage to Don Bertinelli was
enticing. She and Don would belong to Valerie's age group—

Craig was an older generation. Nobody who didn't know would guess she was thirty-two. She could pass for twenty-three or twenty-four.

"It would have to be a freestyle marriage," she stipulated, mentally caught up in the possibilities this offered: she and Don photographed at polo matches in Andalusia, Palm Beach, Palermo. Skiing at Sun Valley, St. Moritz, down in Portillo. Splashy magazine stories about the two of them, labeling her as the heiress of Naomi Miller's empire. Doug would bitch, but she could say it was just her p.r. woman being carried away.

"Hmmm." Don pretended to be weighing her stipulation.

"We'd be together as it fits our schedules," Felicia insisted. Stimulating weekends at the new house at Big Sur, quick trips to Paris or Cannes or Rio. Let people in their world—and especially Craig Preston—understand she was young and beautiful and desirable, not just a business machine. "Well?" she demanded.

"Why not?" His smile was movie-star charismatic. "I'll know my baby's there waiting for me." He prodded her against the corridor wall, ignoring passing guests, and kissed her passionately.

Despite seeming obstructions they were married late the following afternoon in Cannes and settled in for the three-day honeymoon Felicia allowed them. From their suite at the Carlton—while Felicia dressed for dinner—Don called his mother in Venice to announce his marriage.

Don held the receiver away from his ear as his mother shrieked into the phone.

"Don, you're out of your mind! She's a divorcée with two children! A dozen years older than you." *Barely ten.* "She'll never give you a family! Don, you have that marriage annulled or your father and I are writing you out of our wills! Forget about your allowance!"

"Cool it, Mother," Don scolded and pantomimed apology to Felicia. "I'll see you at Newport for the races next month."

"Don't bring that woman with you," Celia Bertinelli warned. "She's not welcome in our house."

"Dad'll calm her down," Don said as he put down the phone.

"Who cares?" Felicia shrugged. "Now let me call my mother."

Felicia caught up with Edwina at Bar Harbor, where her parents were houseguests of old friends. She waited for the explosion after a long moment of shocked silence.

"Felicia, you're out of your mind!" *Exactly what Don's mother had said.*

"Don't worry, Mother," she said coolly. "I'm not leaving the company." That was what concerned her. "We'll have a part-time marriage that fits into both our life-styles. Prearranged sex," she laughed. "I do deserve some diversions."

On August 8—in a televised address—President Nixon announced he would resign from office. On the following day Gerald Ford was sworn in as president. Now, with a new president and with congressmen returning to Washington after the long, tension-riddled summer, timber leaders and conservationists were rushing to the Capital to promote their respective interests.

Settled in the kitchen for a late snack, four evenings before Josh was to leave for Washington—both he and Anne too uptight for sleep as yet—they discussed President Ford's leanings regarding the national forests.

"It doesn't look good for us," Josh assessed. "Ford may have been a summer ranger at Yellowstone as a kid and he's still an outdoorsman, but he's voted with Nixon on every important conservation bill. They're both on the side of the timber industry." He squinted in thought for a moment. "I'm not sure I'm the right one to make a pitch for our group, Annie. I'm not a lobbyist."

"We can't afford expensive lobbyists," Anne pointed out. "And everybody agreed you are the logical choice."

417

"I'm not a politician—"

"You're a lawyer who's thoroughly familiar with the particular laws involved. You're articulate about the problem." She and the children were so proud of the articles he managed to get published, his occasional radio and television appearances. Though Artie was uncomfortable that Josh was opposing the timber industry, Tess had confided that both she and Artie followed his every public activity. "And as Stu said, 'all lobbyists are nice guys'—and you're the nicest he knows.'"

"We're such a small group—with so little clout." Josh sighed. "It's damn frustrating."

"With all the groups working together we're finally seeing some headway. Every voice counts, Josh."

"The timber people have all that money behind them. They go out with their high-powered lobbyists, and they distort the facts. Look what they've done with their advertising!" He leaned forward in remembered rage. "Promoting clear-cutting as 'nature's way' of clearing the forests. Claiming there's no ecological damage from tree farms. That all this is great for wildlife."

"I remember that ad in *Time*." Anne shared his rage. "The one showing a beautiful picture of the Clearwater River in Idaho—and the timber company bragging that 'It cost us a bundle but the Clearwater River still runs clear.' The truth came out—the photo was taken fifty miles north of the pulp mill. Below the plant the river was badly polluted."

"People tend to forget that our forests are important sources of life, food, and oxygen. We're killing off what helps provide us with air and water."

"Conservationists must get a bill through Congress to ban clear-cutting," Anne said forcefully.

"But both sides are making it a black-and-white situation," Josh pointed out. "We're insisting clear-cutting has to be banned to save the forests. Timber people claim that'll kill the industry. We know that clear-cutting has some economical advantages."

"Josh!" Annie stared at him in disbelief.

418

"Back up, Annie," he coaxed. "Haven't you always said that your grandmother practiced 'healthy clear-cutting'? One quarter of an acre to ten, you said."

"We're facing a thousand-acre clear-cuts. We know that destroys wildlife habitats. We know that kind of clear-cutting on steep slopes causes rivers to silt up. Look at those terrible floods two years ago in India and Pakistan. The devastation would have been far less if the trees of the Himalyan foothills hadn't all been chopped down. There were no forests to slow down the water, to absorb some of it. We face the same problems right here in this country."

"Annie, I know that. What I'm trying to say is that we must have *controls* on clear-cutting. It'll be a hell of a lot easier to get through controls rather than a total ban."

"Josh, do you expect the Forest Service to do this?" she scoffed.

"Not the Forest Service," he rejected. "We have to prod Congress into putting through legislation with tight controls—and written into law." Josh reached for her hand across the table. "That's what we have to make Congress understand." He smiled ruefully. "I feel so ill-equiped to participate in this lobbying deal. I wish to hell you were going to Washington with me. I could use the moral support."

"How can I go with you to protest wide-scale clear-cutting when I'm very visible in a company that's doing just that?"

"I know," he chuckled. "A lot of people can't figure us out."

"We can," Anne laughed. "And that's what matters."

They were just about to retire for the night when the phone rang. Anne reached for the receiver.

"How would Josh like backup on the Washington jaunt?" Todd demanded ebulliently.

"I'm sure he'd love it. But what brought this on?"

"I was just talking long-distance to this girl who was taking some courses at Berkeley during the summer. You remember I mentioned Chris Jenkins? She lives in Washington. She's doing postgraduate work at Georgetown U."

"Right." Anne gestured to Josh to come to the phone.

"Her father's just got some appointment on President Ford's staff. I don't know for sure it'll do us any good, but it's a lead worth following. She'll manage to introduce us to her old man . . ."

"Hold on, Todd." She turned to Josh. "He's got some contact in the Ford Administration. He wants to fly out to D.C. with you."

The two men talked briefly. Josh appeared elated when he hung up.

"I guess we're full-scale lobbyists—though we don't need to register." Josh grinned. "Todd said to make sure to pack dinner clothes. Chris will take us to some parties."

"I remember staying here at the Mayflower when I was about fourteen," Todd reminisced while he and Josh unpacked in their room in the venerable hotel, where door plaques indicate the rooms where FDR and his family stayed before the Hoovers moved out of the White House, where the likes of General Charles de Gaulle, King Farouk, and Nikita Khrushchev slept. "Naomi kept an apartment here, and she loaned it to my school group when we came to Washington for sightseeing during spring holidays. Not to make me look good," he said humorously, "but because one of the kids was the son of some business associate."

"The company still keeps that apartment," Josh recalled. "It's headquarters for their lobbyist. And occasionally Felicia or Doug stay here when they fly out because some big bill is coming up for voting."

Doug made a point of never bringing Anne into direct negotiations with their lobbyist. He made sure she was knowledgeable about every aspect of company business—except for that.

Todd hung up his dinner jacket, the last item to be unpacked.

"I'll call Chris at her pad and tell her the marines have

landed." He chuckled. "She probably expects us to be staying at a youth hostel considering the state of our budget."

"Annie was right. We need to have an impressive address even for four nights."

"Fine with our budget director as long as you and Annie are paying the tab." Anne insisted this would be their personal contribution.

Off the phone with Chris after a few moments, Todd told Josh they were meeting her for lunch at the Sans Souci.

"Sounds expensive." Josh allowed himself a humorous shudder.

"Chris is putting it on her father's tab." Todd grinned. "Don't fret. In this age of women's lib women pick up checks. She says the Sans Souci is taking over from the Jockey Club as the 'in' place to lunch. It's a block from the White House, and the food isn't outlandishly priced. And we might just encounter some of those wheels we're out to lobby."

Chris was a slim, pretty blonde who talked faster than anybody he knew, Josh thought—except for Annie, whose words had a way of tumbling over one another, too. She was unpretentious, clearly liberal despite conservative Republican parents with old Washington roots. He gathered her father's status had earned them this choice booth beneath the rear balcony at the San Souci, where they could see the entire room.

"We've got a cocktail party this afternoon and an Embassy bash this evening," Chris began.

"Embassy?" Todd lifted an eyebrow.

"Congressmen show up," Josh pointed out. "Hopefully, congressmen we want to pigeon-hole."

"My old man will be useless," Chris confessed, "other than providing us entrée into parties. I tried to talk to him. He owns a chunk of stock in Georgia–Pacific. You can't tell him we're killing our forests."

Each evening Josh called home to talk to Anne. They found an occasional sympathetic ear, he reported. There are members of Congress—like Senators Jackson and Mansfield—who understood and were fighting on their side. But this was an election year, and the timber industry was eager to feed campaign funds in return for favors.

Early on their last night in town Anne phoned Josh.

"I just thought you and Todd would like to know," she told him, "I heard via the office grapevine that Adrian left for Washington yesterday afternoon after a long conference with Doug and Felicia. I wasn't invited so I don't know whom he'll be romancing."

"I assume he'll be staying here in the company apartment?"

"I'm sure of it. Keep an eye out for him. Though I don't suppose there's much chance you'll run into him," she conceded.

"He wouldn't be coming out if he didn't have some special target," Josh said. "Adrian's slick. He must be on to something."

"If you find out whom he's bird-dogging, maybe you can squeeze in some opposition campaigning."

"We'll keep our eyes open. See you tomorrow, Annie. Miss you and the kids like hell."

Ten minutes later, emerging from the elevator, Josh and Todd spied Adrian with a small, pretty brunette clinging to his arm.

"Wouldn't you know Adrian would show up in a brocade dinner jacket?" Todd drawled. Men's attire in Washington remained staid and conservative.

"Who's the girl?" Josh paused, watching Adrian and his companion—unaware of this scrutiny—stroll down the long lobby toward the Connecticut Avenue entrance.

"Here comes Chris," Todd nodded toward the entrance. "She's stopping to talk to them—"

They waited impatiently for Chris to finish with the chit-chat and join them.

"I didn't realize you knew Adrian Harris." Todd made a pretense of scolding her.

"I don't," she said. "I know Melanie."

"Melanie who?" Josh asked.

"Melanie Norton. Her father's Congressman Norton from Oregon."

"So that's it." Josh whistled knowingly. "Adrian is out to insure Norton votes for the timber industry. From what I hear he's been on the fence for months."

"He's powerful, and he's up for reelection," Todd added. "I can just hear all the things Adrian's going to say to him. How so many small Oregon towns depend upon the timber industry for their livelihood—and if Congress ties up the public forests, the state will be hit with massive unemployment."

"Oh shit," Josh murmured softly. "We've just lost Norton."

Thirty-six

ON election eve, 1974 Felicia and Adrian watched the TV returns at her small, chic apartment—decorated in an art deco ambience—on Russian Hill. Both felt some unease about the anti-Republican sentiment that had been generated by Watergate.

"Norton will win," Adrian said with an effort at optimism as he leaned back in the lemon-yellow leather armless sofa and propped his feet atop the low lucite coffee table. "We've been out there talking to every logger, every sawmill worker in the district. They know their jobs are on the line if legislation unfavorable to the timber industry gets through Congress. Norton's vote will be a vote for them."

"How're you doing with Melanie?" Felicia asked.

"Great. I'll probably ask her to marry me when I fly out to Thanksgiving dinner with the family." He smiled smugly. "Her parents are waiting for me to pop the question."

"In another three or four years you'll run for the legislative assembly," Felicia planned. "In an upstate district where we can be sure of the vote. You and Melanie will have to settle there."

"That could be a bitch." Adrian was wary. "Who wants to live in a timber town?"

"You set up residence there. Soon you'll be running for office. You'll spend most of your time in Sacramento. A few

424

terms there and you'll run for Congress," Felicia plotted, and Adrian broke into laughter.

"God, you're a carbon copy of Naomi!"

"When the hell is Doug going to admit that?" He wanted his mother back at the head of Miller Timber. Whatever Naomi could accomplish in the business she could do. The way the company was structured the two of them could call a meeting, sit down and vote her in as CEO. Doug and she controlled 55 percent of Miller Timber stock. "Don't discuss our political plans with him," Felicia cautioned. "He's too limited in his thinking to understand how important it'll be for us to have our own man in Congress."

"Were you in his office today?" Adrian pushed ahead without waiting for a reply. "He has a new painting on one wall," he drawled in sardonic amusement. "Some stupid piece of canvas that Marsh painted and gave to him as a present. He's carrying on about how talented 'Anne's little boy' is."

"Maybe I should have Timmy take art lessons," she mocked. "But seriously, Adrian, the man will be seventy-nine years old in February. Wouldn't you think he'd have enough sense to step down?"

"Hold it, Felicia." Adrian withdrew his feet from the coffee table and leaned forward to focus on the TV set. "This is it! Norton's competition just conceded the election. I'm marrying the daughter of a fourth-term congressman from Oregon!"

The day before Thanksgiving Felicia flew to the Acapulco house to meet Don for the long weekend. They were both disturbed by his parents' continued refusal to pay his bills now that he was married. He struggled to maintain his jet-set lifestyle on the money he received from the trust fund left him by his grandmother. They'd decided on the Acapulco rendezvous since the expense would be minimal.

Already the marriage was dissatisfying to Felicia. In none of her relationships, she realized, had she found any lasting sexual satisfaction. Still, she was proud of Don as a possession. He was her rebuttal to Craig. Other women envied her. She was married to this gorgeous, sexy hunk—and yet she retained her freedom.

On Thanksgiving morning, while they waited for their breakfast trays to arrive, Felicia received a phone call from Adrian. He was spending the holidays, as planned, at the Nortons' magnificent house in Kalorama Heights. Mrs. Norton preferred this exclusive section of impressive houses and embassies to Georgetown, where the wealthy appeared to live in charming but modest circumstances—though Georgetown's Federal or Victorian houses commanded awesome prices.

"The old lady is planning a splashy June wedding," Adrian reported jubilantly. "They're building us a house when we decide where we're going to live."

"You know where you're going to live," Felicia reminded him. Like Naomi she thrived on timetables.

"I do, but they don't. I'll tell them in time—and why. The congressman will understand."

"And spend money to promote his son-in-law's career," Felicia said. "And about your little bride? She's very pretty. How's she in bed?"

"I haven't found out yet."

"Adrian, you're making her wait," Felicia laughed. "Smart strategy."

"Oh, we've done everything but. And she can't wait for that."

"You won't leave the company right away. Stay in place until the wedding."

"I think Doug will be glad to see me out. Despite everything I've done for the company I don't think he really trusts me."

"Stop worrying about Doug. How much longer can he hold off turning the company over to me?"

"Felicia, don't jump the gun." All at once Adrian was serious. "He's really interested in that new report of Anne's. I've heard talk at the office."

"We would be insane to spend all that money on new

426

equipment!" Stirring awake next to her, Don grunted in protest at her strident complaint. She tossed aside the coverlet and left the bed to take the long-corded phone to a window looking out on the Pacific. Why did all the men she knew want to sleep forever? She could do well on four hours a night. "Anne's talking about more money than we've spent on equipment in the last twenty years."

"Some of it makes sense," he cautioned. "She's done a lot of talking with manufacturers. You know that new chipping headsaw? It'll cut lumber from logs that are no more than four inches in diameter—what we're cutting down on our tree farms. She's coming up with a system that will recover up to one hundred percent of mill residues. There's . . ."

"Adrian, forget it." Felicia was brusque. "I want to see that money in housing. And if we don't do that right away, then we should buy up timberland in the south—that's where the action is going to be next."

"Maybe you and I should talk about buying small lots down south ourselves," he said. "Our private corporation— you a silent partner—will sell to Miller Timber at a beautiful profit."

"Let's talk about it when you get back." Adrian was a shrewd one. He knew she could borrow at the banks with no sweat. *Let them buy in the south.* Weyerhaeuser had been doing that for years. "That could work out well for both of us."

Late in January—shortly after Consuelo and Leon returned from their annual jaunt to Rio—Melanie's parents hosted a spectacular engagement party at their mansion in Kalorama. The family was represented by Adrian's parents, and Edwina, Bruce, and Felicia. Only after Doug mentioned his rejection of an invitation on the grounds of "business conflicts" did Anne realize she and Josh had been ignored.

"Do you suppose the invitation was lost in the mail?" she asked Josh uneasily. "Not that we could get away right now."

"It's Adrian's way of reminding us we're not really 'of the

family,' " Josh speculated. "Don't worry that Melanie's parents think we're being rude for not RSVP-ing. We weren't invited." He grinned. "Saves us buying a fancy present for them."

By spring Anne acknowledged to Josh, as they were en route to a Museum benefit, that they were not being invited to the wedding either. It was to be held at the Oregon estate of Congressman and Mrs. Norton. From remarks overheard at Doug's seventy-ninth birthday party in February, Anne knew that a chartered plane was to bring guests from Washington, D.C. and another plane would travel from San Francisco—where Melanie's maternal grandparents were entrenched in "old society."

"I think we'll survive that slight," Josh chuckled. "To Adrian the ultimate insult was that you married Arthur Blumberg's son. In his mixed-up mind Dad's partially responsible for Naomi's will."

"I know Consuelo's upset. She's so tense when we're together."

"She's steeling herself to tell you."

As usual at the Naomi Miller Museum benefits Anne and Josh were seated with Consuelo and Leon. Anne saw Consuelo wince as a table-hopping woman friend paused to inquire about the wedding preparations.

"That's the problem of the mother of the bride," Consuelo said with an effort at indulgent amusement. "I have absolutely no part in the planning."

"We're going down to the Homestead for two weeks," the woman told Consuelo, "but I'll be back in time for Felicia's shower." To which, Anne assumed, she would not be invited.

While Leon and Josh argued good-humoredly about the new baseball season, Consuelo leaned forward to talk to Anne.

"I feel awful, but I have to tell you." She paused, seeming to gear herself for what must be said.

"That Adrian isn't inviting us to his wedding?" Anne smiled in sympathy. "Consuelo, I know you're upset about that, but it's of no consequence to Josh and me. Adrian and

I have just never hit it off." Not since the morning at Lake Tahoe twelve years ago when he'd tried to run her down with his bike. "I don't love you any the less for that."

"There are times I just don't understand Adrian. I don't know whom he takes after," she said in a rare burst of impatience.

"Not you or Leon," Anne said tenderly. *His great-grandmother, Naomi Miller.*

Anne was startled when Doug suggested that she and Josh and the children join him for a weekend at the new house in Big Sur on the second weekend in June.

"That's the weekend of Adrian's wedding," she reminded him.

"Yes," he said quietly. He was showing his disapproval of their not being invited by refusing to attend himself, Anne assumed. To Doug it was an insult to the family.

"Consuelo and Leon will be hurt."

"I'm an old man—they'll forgive me," Doug smiled. "Todd's going, even though he hates the thought. He's a good kid—he doesn't want to hurt Consuelo and Leon. By the way, is there something serious between him and the pretty Jenkins girl?"

"I wouldn't be surprised." She suppressed a chuckle. Doug was anticipating another offshoot in Naomi's dynasty. "She's out here for the summer." Anne refrained from mentioning that Chris was out here to work with Todd and the conservation group. This was one subject that remained off-limits in their conversations with Doug.

"Well," he prodded with pretended brusqueness, "are you and Josh and the kids going to spend the weekend at Big Sur with me?"

"We'd love it," Anne assured him. "From what you tell me the house is magnificent."

Anne pretended to be unaware of the shower Felicia gave for Melanie when the bride-elect came into town to visit her maternal grandparents. She was polite on those occasions when she and Adrian encountered each other at the office. She sensed

Doug was relieved when Adrian announced that he and Melanie would settle in a small town in Oregon after a month-long honeymoon. Adrian would work for his father-in-law at the congressman's Oregon headquarters.

The Friday before the wedding Felicia left the office early. Shirley returned from a trip to the washroom to report she'd collected gossip about a heated confrontation with Doug earlier in the day, when he refused to allow the company plane to be used for family transportation to Oregon. They would travel on the plane chartered by Melanie's parents to transport guests from the San Francisco area.

"Felicia can't wait for Doug to retire," Shirley concluded. "And what makes her so sure he'll retire and put her in charge?"

"She doesn't care anymore about antagonizing Doug," Anne said apprehensively. She'd been outwardly critical of him at the last board meeting because he was spearheading a drive against new construction at Lake Tahoe, on the ground that additional sewage would wreck the lake. "Shirley—" Anne paused, alarm spiraling in her. "After all these years, could Felicia be planning to walk out on the will?" It was a fear that forever hung over both their heads. It was shattering to consider.

Felicia impatiently jiggled one Ferragamo-shod foot while she waited for Paul to finish a long-distance call. He'd bombed out politically, she considered with amusement, despite all of Eleanor's connections and the family money but it must be a consolation to be a full partner in his father's prestigious law firm. He hadn't aged well. He was only thirty-nine, but his jaw was sagging and he had the beginning of a martini paunch.

"I'm sorry, Felicia," he said warily as he put down the receiver. "It was an important call."

"Let's get back to Doug." Was he going to be squeamish about this? "The man is pushing eighty, and he's making bad decisions in the business. I've got three board members who'll back me up in this. Why can't we go into court to have him declared incompetent to head Miller Timber?"

"Every CEO makes bad decisions at one time or another," Paul countered.

"He's going senile!" Felicia's voice was sharp. "For some supposed slight to Anne he's refusing to go to Adrian's wedding. You know how Doug's always been about the family. Now he's making an ass of himself about some pollution drive out at Lake Tahoe."

"Which side is he on?" Paul asked with a faint smile.

"He's carrying on about how they're going to spoil the beauty of his precious lake. They're using a senile old man to promote a ridiculous cause. And that's going to backfire." She leaned forward to stress her point. "Conservationists are going to point out that the CEO of Miller Timber is fighting against pollution at Lake Tahoe, but he's too blind to see what his own company is doing to the forests. You *know* how these people twist everything around to suit their own purposes."

"You need a lot more before any attorney will go into court to try to have Doug declared incompetent."

"What would you suggest?"

"I'd suggest dropping the whole idea," Paul said bluntly. "But knowing you, I'm sure you won't."

"You're saying I have to dig up positive proof"—or what could appear positive—"that Doug could endanger the future of Miller Timber?"

"That's it."

"Okay," she agreed. "I'll do that." She sat motionless for a moment, her mind charging into action. "Paul, may I use your phone for a minute?"

Forty minutes later she was sitting across the table from Glenn at a hastily arranged luncheon appointment. Not at the secluded side street restaurant that Glenn suggested but at a choice table at Trader Vic's.

"Remember that detective you dug up when we were after Ezra Evans's hide?" Felicia probed and Glenn smiled.

"Evans didn't go back to Washington for another four

years after Brick Griffin finished with him," Glenn recalled. "What he dug up was the backbone of the opposition's campaign."

"I need him again," Felicia said.

"Who're you after this time?" Glenn's eyes were bright with curiosity.

"Doug. I want to go into court and have him declared senile. I want him out of Miller Timber."

"What happens if he's dumped?"

"Arthur Blumberg votes his ten percent of the stock. And Blumberg," she said triumphantly, "will vote with me. Because if he doesn't, I'll threaten to walk. And that will leave Anne and Josh with nothing. Now do you suppose a shrewd attorney like Arthur Blumberg is going to let that happen?"

"I'll track down Griffin. I'll explain what we need." Glenn looked uncomfortable. "Yeah, like you said, he's pushing eighty. Why can't he step down on his own?"

"We'll nudge him," Felicia laughed. "I've waited long enough."

Thirty-seven

ANNE attended Gerry's high school graduation with Shirley. Afterward Gerry went off to celebrate with a cluster of graduating friends and Anne took Shirley to lunch at Julius' Castle because both women loved the breathtaking views of bay, ships, bridges, and waterfront that the old wooden restaurant on the slopes of Telegraph Hill provided its diners.

After they'd ordered, they leaned back in their chairs with sighs of satisfaction that this special day was so beautiful.

"I was scared to death she'd never get through high school. I survived Gerry's adolescence." But Anne saw a somber glint in Shirley's eyes.

"Something's bugging you," she said. "Gerry come up with another wild idea?" At twelve Gerry disappeared for a day and night in Haight-Ashbury but had come home chastened and contrite. At fourteen she'd been determined to drop out of school and become a rock star. At sixteen she'd wanted to leave school to be a forest ranger in Alaska.

"Deep down Gerry's a great kid," Shirley said with conviction. "She's steered clear of the drug scene. Except for an occasional flirtation with pot. I can't complain about that. How many times did I go to a party and joints were passed around? Considering what some parents go through—the runaway scene, the hard drugs, the sleeping around—I did all right with Gerry. Oh, we've fought," she chuckled reminiscently. "Remember the battles we had when I bought her jeans on sale and they didn't have Calvin Klein's name on the butt? And now she's going to live in a dorm, and I won't have to listen to her stereo blasting as though she were one step away from total deafness. But you know," she said softly, "I'm going to miss her like hell."

"Shirl, what's bugging you?" Anne repeated.

"I don't think Gerry's sleeping around," Shirley said slowly. "She says she isn't. But she wants to go on the Pill."

"The kids all talk a lot. Gerry thinks it's the 'in' thing to do," Anne said. "I remember the way we used to talk at school—but for most of us it was just talk."

"You're talking about twelve or fifteen years ago. Everything's different now. When we were in college, the girls who slept around were the radicals. Today these kids consider it normal to go off for a weekend with a guy. Sometimes nothing happens but a lot of times it does."

"And you took her to your gynecologist," Anne said, reading Shirley's mind.

"Look, I don't want her coming home pregnant her first year in college." Shirley sighed. "She has an appointment with the gynecologist next week."

"I think you did the right thing," Anne comforted.

"What would be the point of yelling and threatening? I want to be sure she doesn't get caught. Thank God, she's realistic enough to take care of herself." Shirley frowned in thought. "At eighteen they think they're women—but in some ways they're younger than we were at eighteen. They've won a lot of freedom. I just hope they know how to handle it."

"Gerry's going to be fine," Anne said. "Stop worrying about her and let's figure out a real dessert binge."

With the closing of school the two sets of children were settled in the Big Sur house for the summer. Anne and Josh would spend the first two weeks in July there and then commute, along with Doug, via the small company plane. Felicia talked vaguely about coming up for some weekends. She was to meet Don in Portillo in August for two weeks of skiing. It had always been understood that Anne and Felicia would stagger vacation periods.

While Anne was officially on vacation these first two weeks at Big Sur, she spent six or seven hours a day working on Doug's latest requirement of Felicia and herself. Naomi's overall advance schedule for Miller timber—which had been Doug's bible—had expired two years earlier. Now he was foundering. He had instructed Anne and Felicia to work out individually a ten-year program in intense detail. Then he would plot the ten years that lay ahead.

With Doug's approval Anne brought Shirley out to Big Sur to work with her for a week. She undertook this latest project with full comprehension of its importance. She knew Doug would review it with utmost seriousness. It was her opportunity to press for the kind of changes she considered urgent, not only for Miller Timber but for the whole industry. Changes urged by those she considered most knowledgeable about the state of the world's timber supply. She suspected that Felicia would have her private board of directors—Adrian, Glenn, Joe Colton—work out her own presentation.

She had fallen in love with the rugged grandeur of Big Sur at first sight. Like Josh she enjoyed the wildness of the ocean, the sea-beaten rocky coast, the great gorges, and the mountain ranges that reached up into the clouds. The large, rambling house, carefully fenced to protect the unwary, clung to the side of a mountain and overlooked the Pacific. Magnificent redwoods cast their shadows about the house.

Anne was determined to have her father come out for a week or two because she knew that he, too, would fall under Big Sur's spell. "The magic hours," she wrote him, "are sunrise and sunset. The views then are unbelievable." She sent him sketches that Marsh had made for him—one of the windy grasses along the beach and another of a gnarled old cypress.

She enjoyed the closeness between Doug and the four children—her two and Timmy and Karen. Marsh and Robin had three grandfathers, she thought in moments of whimsy—their natural grandfathers plus Doug. In truth, Doug was Timmy and Karen's acting grandfather. Glenn's father was long dead—and Bruce and Edwina might as well be, she thought angrily, considering the erratic affection they bestowed on Timmy and Karen. She felt compassion for the children of jet-setters—who had time to ski in Switzerland and South America, to lie on the sands of Palm Beach, Bar Harbor, and the Riviera, to follow the sun and the snow to suit their moods—but who had no time for their children.

On Shirley's last evening at the Big Sur house she and Anne had a cozy dinner served on the deck overlooking the ocean at sunset. The sky was a magnificent blend of orange and red with the huge ball that was the sun moving majestically down toward the sea. Josh had taken the four children for a day trip to Carmel, and they were expected back shortly.

"This week has been heavenly." Shirley's smile was euphoric.

"But you missed Stu," Anne teased.

"We'll make up for it when I get back to San Francisco. He's been working his tail off this past week, anyhow. Josh is supposed to be on vacation and he's chased into town twice already this week."

"When's Gerry due back from Hawaii?" The trip was Anne and Josh's graduation present.

"The middle of next week. Annie, I can't believe she goes to Berkeley this fall! Where have the years gone?"

"They haven't been uneventful," Anne laughed but her eyes were somber. "So much has happened in the last dozen years." Times were changing, she reflected. She deplored the mood of cynicism that seemed to permeate the country. People distrusted the government, their lawyers, their doctors, the corporate structure.

"The apartment is going to be so empty with Gerry living in a dorm. Of course, she says she'll be home often with Berkeley so close. But it won't be the same."

"Maybe it's time to think about marrying Stu," Anne said, her eyes chiding Shirley.

"I can't do that." Shirley sighed. "I can't put myself into the position of wife again. I know—not every husband is like Hank. But I'm set in my ways. And I'm almost forty, Annie. Stu still looks dreamily at every pregnant woman. I'm not going to have another child at my age. If we got married, Stu and I would live on a perennial battlefield."

"Mommie!" Both women smiled at the sound of Robin's voice in the distance. "We're home!"

Late in the month, when Felicia was demanding more time to finish the new project for Doug, Anne received a call from one of their loggers in Oregon—a man she had met on a field trip and who had invited her into his home for dinner. His wife had sat silently at the table while the two of them lingered over endless cups of coffee and talked about the mismanagement of many of the private forests—including Miller Timber.

"Clear-cutting is a major mistake. We're taking down trees that shouldn't be taken down for another forty to a hundred years. My grandfather worked for Miller Timber, and my father after him. But the way I see it, there won't be any job for me in another fifteen years. The forests will be gone."

"George, you talk too much," his wife had intervened. Anne understood. She was fearful that he would be fired for such open defiance.

"I'm not sure I ought to be calling you this way," he admitted now. "My wife says I'm out of my head. But we've got orders to cut right to the stream's edge at this stand we're taking down. We're dumping the logs and brush right into the stream—and I tell you, it's one of the best spawning streams in the Pacific Northwest. It's like we talked about. We're not logging. We're butchering the stand!"

"Thank you for calling it to my attention, George. I'll look into it and see that it's stopped." She hesitated. "You wouldn't know who's in charge of the project?"

"Yes ma'am, I would. And he's taking his orders right from Felicia Harris."

Anne left her office and went downstairs to confront Felicia.

"What does a stupid logger mean by phoning you this way?" Felicia flared. "This project doesn't concern you. And don't you think it's time you stopped fraternizing with the workers? How do you expect them to have respect for our decisions when you treat them like equals?"

"George Anderson has been with the company for eighteen years!" Anne shot back. "His father and grandfather logged for the company. He . . ."

"He's about to be fired," Felicia told her, scribbling down his name. "I won't tolerate this kind of behavior."

Doug backed up Anne when she ran to report the incident to him. He refused to allow George Anderson to be fired.

"Damn it, Felicia. Somebody could be killed by logs floating downstream!"

"I can't understand what's happening to you, Doug!" Felicia lashed back. "You're going soft in your old age!"

"To cut that close to a stream is more than just greedy," Anne intervened. *How dare Felicia refer to Doug's age in that tone.* "It's dangerous."

"All that logger is worried about is that when he goes fishing he might not have as much luck as he'd like. We don't have to concern ourselves with his recreation habits. Logs have been floating down streams for centuries, and nobody gets hurt."

"That's not true," Anne contradicted. "It's . . ."

"Let's not discuss this any further," Doug broke in, seeming suddenly drained. "You're not to give orders to have Anderson fired, Felicia. And I'm sending out a memo to all our logging superintendents. We've got to stop knocking down everything in sight."

438

Todd waited with Chris at the airport until boarding-time for her flight east.

"Are you going to tell your parents about our spending twenty-four hours in jail for antinuke demonstrations?" he teased her.

"I'll tell them after my sister Lila's wedding," Chris said. "They'll explode, of course."

"Are you going to tell them about us?"

"I'll see how they react to the other bit." She reached for his hand. "I won't—I absolutely won't—go through the splashy wedding they're giving Lila. It's obscene to spend all that money on a party."

"I'll be happy if we have a ceremony in Anne and Josh's living room with a few of our friends there."

"We'll talk about that when I get back." She lifted her face to his. "My flight's boarding now."

Todd remained to see Chris's plane go down the runway, then headed for his vintage Valiant. He never felt entirely comfortable with Doug since he'd become involved with the conservation group, but the prospect of a weekend in town without Chris was gloomy. Doug kept telling him to come up to Big Sur—and Anne and Josh and the kids were up there. What the hell, he'd drive up.

He'd talked about the Doug situation with Josh because Josh was in the same spot as he was, fighting the timber industry—including Miller Timber. Somehow, Doug seemed to manage to blot that knowledge out of his mind. But they could never discuss what was truly most important to the three of them—what was happening with the nation's forests.

Todd arrived at Big Sur in time for dinner. Here the four children always sat down with the grown-ups, something that had rarely happened in his parents' home. He relished the warmth that circulated among those at the table. And it recurrently astonished him to see how Doug responded to the children—with love and genuine interest rather than the irritation his own parents would have displayed.

"Hey, kids," he said ebulliently when they were reluctantly en route to bed, "how would you like to go on a day camping trip at the state park tomorrow? Providing we get permission," he added, meaning from Anne, Mallie, and Tim and Karen's current governess. "We'll hike through the woods, stop when we're hungry and grill hamburgers—"

"And marshmallows," Karen added with a grin that revealed two missing teeth.

"That'll be cool!" Timmy said excitedly and the others echoed his enthusiasm.

"Can we?" Marsh turned to his mother.

"I'm sure it'll be all right."

"Downstairs for breakfast at seven sharp," Todd ordered. "We want to beat the traffic."

By eight o'clock—with the four children exuberantly singing "Puff the Magic Dragon"—Todd was silently cursing the Saturday morning crawl along the approach to Pfeiffer–Big Sur State Park.

"I've got a better idea," he said, interrupting the songfest. "We've got the whole day ahead of us. I know a terrific wooded area where we'll have the place to ourselves. Not a soul in sight." He and Chris had taken a wrong turn several weeks ago and wandered into virgin wilderness that was great. "We can drive there in an hour and a half. Okay?"

"Okay!" the children chorused.

When they arrived at their destination, they climbed out of the car and collected their gear from the trunk. In jubilant spirits they moved into the heavily wooded area, where a footpath had been beaten down for them by earlier hikers. The air was fragrant with varied forest scents; an awesome, cathedrallike quietness was broken at intervals by birdsong.

Todd felt fresh anger as he thought of those who dared to scoff at the need for such recreation areas as this. Most Americans lived in areas where they were jammed into a couple hundred urban acres. They needed the wilderness as an escape hatch from the tensions of everyday life. And the timber barons wanted to destroy all this.

They hiked with healthy curiosity, well beyond what he and Chris had covered, Todd recognized, but he knew they'd be able to backtrack with no problems.

"Look, there's a stream!" Marsh pointed ahead. "Let's set up camp there."

"Great idea," Todd said, but his face tightened as he inspected the stream. There had to be a lumber mill a few miles up, he told himself in unvoiced anger. A mill that dumped foliage, branches, bark into the water. Not only unsightly but polluting.

The five focused on digging a barbecue pit, prepared for their cookout. Todd reminding them at every step of the precautions necessary to avoid a forest fire.

"We know," Robin said solemnly. "We almost got caught in one when I was little."

The team effort to prepare their meal was an experience the four youngsters clearly enjoyed. Todd was pleased. After they'd eaten, he suggested they all nap. "It's a long hike back to the car. Let's rest up for it."

They settled themselves about the banked fire and lapsed into quiet euphoria. Lying on his back, Timmy snored lightly.

"Todd, look!" Marsh's voice punctured the forest stillness.

"Where?" Todd raised himself into a sitting position.

"It's a puppy!" Karen squealed. "Marsh, don't let him drown!"

Marsh was moving gingerly over branches toward the frightened puppy, clinging to a log floating down the stream.

"Marsh, get back here!" Todd ordered and charged toward the stream. "Marsh!" he added in sudden alarm, just as Marsh scooped the tiny beagle into his arms. "Look out!"

A large log was tumbling down the stream, headed toward the branch where Marsh teetered with the puppy. In one swift gesture Todd kicked off his loafers and plunged into the water.

"Marsh!" he yelled again, but an instant later he saw the log thrust Marsh from his feet, then graze his head.

441

"Marsh!" Robin screeched in terror as the children and Todd saw Marsh go limp and fall into the stream, the puppy yapping in terror. Todd was conscious of the children calling encouragement as he clutched at Marsh and pulled him from the water.

"The puppy!" Robin shrieked. "Don't let the puppy drown!"

With Marsh over his shoulder and the puppy under one arm Todd made his way to shore. The children took charge of the puppy. Marsh was unconscious.

"We have to get him to the hospital fast," Todd told the others. "Timmy, make sure the fire is out. Now let's all move!"

Anne stood at a window in the hospital waiting room and stared without seeing at the July sunset. Why was she never with the children when they needed her most?

"Something cold to drink, Annie?" Todd returned from the soda machine with a paper cup.

"No," she said, her voice sharp. "No, Todd," she said, gently this time.

"It was my fault," Todd said, his eyes agonized. "I should have been watching."

"Todd, you can't watch them every minute."

Anne's eyes moved compulsively to the elevator as it stopped at their floor, though she knew it would take a while for Josh to drive the children home and return. But the elevator door slid open and Josh emerged.

"The kids are in the car with the puppy," he said as he walked toward Anne and Todd. "They won't let me drive them home—they insist on staying."

"I'll go down to the coffee shop and get some sandwiches for them," Todd said. "They must be hungry by now."

Too impatient to wait for another elevator Todd headed for the stairs. Josh reached for Anne's hand.

"Stop blaming yourself for not being with him," Josh said,

442

reading Anne's mind. "You can't protect them every moment of their lives."

"Why is it taking so long?" She lifted her face to search his eyes. "Why doesn't the doctor come out and tell us something?"—knowing this was illogical even as she asked.

"Annie, we just have to wait."

Another elevator stopped at their floor. Moments later Doug strode toward them.

"Mallie just told me." He struggled to sound calm but his face was ashen. "How's Marsh doing?"

"We're waiting for word," Josh told him.

"He was hurt trying to save a puppy," Anne said, her voice harsh with pain. "He was hit by a log rushing downstream. From a sawmill, Doug." She saw him recoil in shock.

"Here's the doctor!" Josh dropped an arm about her waist.

"Marsh is going to be fine," the doctor assured them, walking toward them with a smile. "No serious damage. But we'd like to keep him overnight as a precautionary measure."

"May we see him?" Anne asked.

"In a few minutes. He's being moved into a room. The nurse will come and tell you when you can go in to him."

"Thank you, doctor." Josh's face was incandescent with relief.

Anne turned to Doug, her mind churning.

"Doug, I'm sorry," she told him. "I'm leaving Miller Timber. I can't stay on after this. Marsh was almost killed because of careless clear-cutting. We're doing that, too."

"Annie, don't leave," Doug pleaded. "Stay on and we'll make changes. You know the memos I've sent out to all the superintendents. We're not to log to the edge of streams. We . . ."

"We're still clear-cutting in large areas, Doug. Maybe not in the national forests just now," she conceded, "but on our private timberland we are."

"Annie, stay," he urged. "We'll work together and stop this chopping down of everything in sight. If you leave, ninety percent of Miller Timber goes to the museum. Control will be out of my hands. Together we can make changes."

"I don't know, Doug," she wavered, her eyes moving to Josh.

"I want you to listen to me, Annie," he said quietly, seeming to search for words. "I know I've made many mistakes in the company. I've tried to operate as my mother would. I've spent most of my life living according to my mother's dictates." Anne felt a silent rage charge through Doug. "But that's over. Now—when I'm seventy-nine years old—I'm declaring my independence. Stay and we'll fight together for what's right for the forests."

Anne managed a tremulous smile.

"When you put it so eloquently, how can I refuse?"

"Mrs. Blumberg—" A nurse beckoned from the hallway. "Marsh is asking for you."

Thirty-eight

FELICIA hurried into the nondescript but immaculate downtown coffee shop and sat in a rear booth. She was meeting Adrian and Brick Griffin for a seven o'clock breakfast. She had chosen this time and place because they were unlikely to encounter anyone she knew here—and because this would enable her to make her mid-morning flight to New York with ease.

The coffee shop was sparsely populated. Though favored by San Francisco brokers, those regular patrons had already deserted their booths. By six-thirty local brokers were rushing down Montgomery Street—the "Wall Street of the West"—because the New York Stock Exchange was already in operation.

A waitress came over immediately and took Felicia's order while covertly inspecting her exquisitely tailored pantsuit.

"Coffee now," Felicia instructed, watching the door for Adrian's approach.

More than ever she felt pressured to unseat Doug as CEO at Miller Timber. She'd heard him raving to Mrs. Morrison late last night about how Marsh had nearly been killed on account of bad lumbering practices. Doug would cost the company a fortune if he stayed on the job. He was playing games with *her* money.

She glanced at the wall clock. It was a minute past seven. Where the hell was Adrian? She wanted to talk with him before Griffin arrived with his report. Griffin had been noncommittal over the phone about his findings. By now he should have dredged up enough to hang Doug, she thought restlessly.

She saw Adrian approach the door, push it open and walk inside. He and Melanie had come into town the day before to attend a birthday dinner for Melanie's grandmother.

"Did it have to be this early?" Adrian complained good-humoredly while he placed a perfunctory kiss on Felicia's cheek. "I'm hung over."

"I wanted to talk with Griffin before I leave. How're things up your way?"

"I'm the fair-haired boy, working for the congressman and saying all the right things." He grinned smugly. "Don't worry. I'll be ready to run for local office in the next election. Another two years," he predicted, "I'll be running for the legislative assembly." Simultaneously his eyes undressed the pretty young waitress who was walking toward their booth.

"Adrian, behave yourself," Felicia warned and he raised an eyebrow in feigned innocence. "You can't afford to play games," she reminded him when the waitress had taken his order and left. "You live in a fishbowl in politics."

"I'm the perfect young husband," he teased. "Melanie and I are the perfect young couple."

"Make yourself the perfect young father," Felicia told him. "That's the real vote-getter."

"You're in a bitchy mood. Troubles with Doug?"

She told him about Marsh's accident and about Doug's reaction. "Anne's going to be able to lead him around like a pet monkey after this." She churned with frustration. "He was already upset over that son of a bitch calling her about the clear-cutting up in your neck of the woods. He's . . ."

"Here's Griffin." Adrian waved a hand in greeting.

Over a breakfast she hardly tasted, Felicia listened in soaring anger to Griffin's detailed report of Doug's activities for the past weeks.

"You've got nothing there we can use!" she lashed at the investigator.

"Can I help it if the guy's clean?" Griffin flushed in anger. "He's an old man."

"Let's go back over the details again," Adrian said. "There's got to be something we can turn around."

Felicia dozed most of the flight east. At JFK she found Jackie's chauffeur waiting to drive her out to the Southampton house Jackie's parents had bought for her and Bill. They'd chosen Southampton, Jackie had told her, because a lot of national media people summered there and Bill might make some useful contacts for the congressman. They had two congressmen on tap, she congratulated herself with a flicker of good humor: Jackie's father-in-law and Adrian's.

En route to the Hamptons she carefully reread the typed report Griffin had handed over before they separated that morning. Somewhere in Doug's life there had to be something they could utilize to declare him incompetent to run the company.

All that bastard Griffin came up with was what they already knew—plus the fact that Doug kept a studio in North Beach, which he loaned at intervals to starving young artists. So Doug was a frustrated artist—how could they use that to dump him?

Approaching Southampton Felicia told herself to wash business out of her mind. She'd have two great days here with Jackie, and then Don would come out for the Fontaines' dinner party and they'd set off for Rio. He was sulking when they talked on the phone last night. He'd wanted to fly directly to Portillo for the skiing.

It was important to Felicia to meet Consuelo's family. The three times she'd been in Rio before this she had avoided meeting them but they might be helpful in the future. They were influential in Brazil—and she wanted to learn everything she could about the Brazilian rain forest. There were fortunes to be made down there. Naomi would have seen that. Doug was a scared old man.

She looked forward to the two days alone with Jackie, who was pregnant again and anxious this time to carry full term. They would spend most of the daylight hours lounging on chaises on the oceanfront deck, she promised herself. She wouldn't think about business for one minute.

Felicia was pleased that Bill was down in Washington; he wouldn't be back until late the following day. She and Jackie were served dinner on the deck, with a dramatic orange-red sun descending over the ocean. For a little while it was as though she and Jackie were nineteen again and all their lives lay promisingly ahead.

"I told Bill," Jackie said, destroying Felicia's youthful illusion, "this is the last time we try to have a baby. I'm thirty-four and with two miscarriages behind me. The third time's enough. If I carry this time, I'll probably need a tummy tuck afterward. You were young when you had your kids."

"I don't consider thirty-four old," Felicia said sharply. But she'd told the p.r. woman to drop stories about Timmy and Karen. A ten-year-old son and an eight-year-old daughter didn't fit in with the image she nurtured: *"The young and beautiful business tycoon Felicia Harris."* She'd vowed to be CEO of Miller Timber at thirty. She had to make it by thirty-five.

Doug would be eighty in February. There had to be a way to unseat him. *She would find it, and she would do it.*

"I can't believe it, Felicia." Jackie's voice brought her back to the moment. "Bill and I have been married for ten years. How many people do we know—other than our parents— that stay married that long?"

"I think long-distance marriages are the best," Felicia laughed. Belatedly she realized her first wedding anniversary had just passed unrecognized by Don or herself. "Before I have a chance to get bored, Don and I are off in separate directions."

"Don't you ever wonder?" Jackie asked. "I mean, who's he sleeping with when you're not available?"

"I've never thought about that. Maybe once in a while," she conceded. "Most of the time I'm too involved with business." Don was like a possession, she thought. He was on tap

448

when she wanted him. But now unfamiliar doubts assaulted her. "Jackie, are you trying to tell me something?"

"No," she said defensively, "I haven't heard any talk about Don chasing after anyone." She paused, seeming to grapple with an inner conflict. "But he *was* hanging around Paul's sister-in-law Sharon out in Bar Harbor a couple of weekends ago." That houseparty he'd talked about, Felicia recalled. "She's Eleanor's baby sister—starting Vassar in September. Eleanor was really pissed."

"Paul told you," Felicia pinned down.

"I'm sure nothing happened," Jackie emphasized. "Paul's such a gossip. Don and Sharon were just lying around the beach together all weekend. God, does that kid have a body!" She stared wistfully at the slight swell of her belly beneath her St. Laurent caftan.

Were people making remarks about Don and other women? Felicia asked herself in sudden revulsion. She'd let herself think he was so mad about skiing and polo he had no time to fuck around. *That was stupid.*

"Felicia, I shouldn't have mentioned it." Jackie was contrite. "Nothing *happened.*"

"So what if it did?" Felicia shrugged. "Don doesn't ask me who I'm sleeping with when he's not around." Nobody. But he didn't know that. Sex wasn't Number One on her agenda. Still, the possibility that Don might be playing around on the side was unsettling. Not because she was wildly in love with him, she admitted to herself. It was a question of pride. Don was her property. She didn't want him leaving the corral.

Don arrived early Wednesday afternoon, full of talk about fleeing the ghastly New York heat for skiing at Portillo.

"Change into swimming trunks and let's go for a swim before we have to dress for the Fontaines' dinner party," Felicia said. He was gorgeous with that fresh tan he'd picked up in Bar Harbor, she thought with momentary complacency. *Had* he slept with Eleanor's sister? No more than eighteen, Felicia surmised, if she was just starting Vassar. "Or maybe you'll settle for a nap and a shower?"

"Let's shower and nap." He slid an arm about her waist and pulled her close. "I haven't seen you in ages."

"Do as the man says," Jackie drawled.

While Don slouched in a chair on the private deck off their suite and sipped at a margarita, Felicia went in to shower. She'd told herself she wouldn't think about business out here at Southampton or at Portillo, but she was obsessed by the need to oust Doug from the business—before he teamed up with Anne to bring *her* in as CEO.

"Feel like company?" Don's voice filtered into the shower and an instant later his hand reached to slide the glass door ajar.

"You're dressed for it," she drawled while he stood there naked and aroused. He may have been lying around the beach at Bar Harbor with Eleanor's baby sister, she thought smugly, but she could still turn him on. And knowing this, she felt the first stirring of passion. "Hop in, old boy."

Felicia was restless on the overnight 747 Pan Am caviar-and-champagne flight to Rio. Don was still sulking because she wouldn't agree to cut short the Rio stay to twenty-four hours. But he managed to cast furtive glances at the exceptionally pretty stewardess with the gorgeous legs, she noticed in annoyance. And what the hell was that pitch he gave her earlier about losing out on his polo skills because he couldn't afford to play as often as he should? Did he expect her to pick up the tab? *No way.* Right from the beginning they'd agreed to split all expenses—and that was the way it stayed.

Don brightened considerably when they were en route to their hotel at Copacabana. The striking beauty of Rio was seductive: the parkways lined with hibiscus, pyrocanthus, and coleus; the scalloped beach edged with shining white apartment towers and hotels, set shoulder-to-shoulder along the South Atlantic—reminiscent of Nice and Cannes but on a far larger scale.

"I want to stop off at H. Stern before we leave," Felicia told Don. "They have such bargains on gems down here."

"I could understand you wanting to stay here if this was Carnival season," Don returned to his earlier gripe, "but to waste three days when we could be on the slopes."

"Don, I told you." *Did he ever think of anything beside polo, skiing, and fucking?* "The Coronado family is important to me in business." *Why had she agreed to spend two weeks with Don? Three or four days could be amusing.* "You did make our reservations at the Ouro Verde?" she asked in sudden wariness.

"Of course." He lifted an eyebrow. "But I don't know why you insisted on staying there. Ipanema is much more chic than Copacabana."

"The Ouro Verde is small and elegant and very continental. I enjoy it." But already her thoughts were focusing on dinner tomorrow evening at the Coronado mansion.

"Let's have lunch at La Fourchette." His slightly hostile voice told her he expected an objection.

"I love La Fourchette," she said. The restaurant, on the second floor of the Leme Palace, was one of her favorites in Rio.

They registered at the hotel. In their suite, hanging over Copacabana Beach, Felicia went into the beautifully appointed bathroom to shower while Don sprawled in a club chair in the sitting room and tried to decipher the morning newspaper, swearing because Portuguese was incomprehensible to him.

"Wow, would I adore a massage right now," Felicia sighed, emerging from the bathroom in a towel.

"Not one of my talents," Don apologized. His eyes rested appreciatively on her near nudity. "But if you'll wait till I shower, I'll demonstrate a more fascinating one."

"Save it for tonight," Felicia said. "After dinner with the Coronados we'll be in the mood for stimulation."

They lunched at La Fourchette, then walked along the black-and-white marble mosaic sidewalks of the beachside boulevard, stopping when they were tired at a sidewalk cafe for a cafezinho—the strong, thimbleful of black coffee so cherished by the resident cariocas.

"Let's run downtown to the Jockey Club for a drink," Don suggested. "Dinner's going to be late." Earlier Felicia had spoken with Senhora Coronado and confirmed their dinner hour—always late in Rio.

The Coronado limousine arrived at the hotel to drive them to the family mansion.

"Stuffy old house," Don commented as they arrived at the iron-grilled residence that hinted at elegant Old-World roots.

"Portuguese Edwardian," Felicia decided. The chauffeur spoke little English—he wouldn't understand what they were saying, she guessed.

They were welcomed charmingly by Consuelo's patrician mother and father and her sister and brother-in-law. In time, Felicia promised herself, she would guide the conversation into channels that interested her.

After a sumptuous dinner they retired to a drawing room for coffee. To Felicia's irritation the women settled on one side of the exquisitely furnished drawing room and the men on the other. Senhora Coronado and her daughter talked in low, beautifully modulated voices about the Miró collection at the Museum of Modern Art, about the ballet and opera at the Teatro Municipal. The men were engrossed in discussing last month's polo matches in Rio. What else could Don talk about, Felicia thought distainfully. Skiing and polo. Involuntarily she thought of Craig, who commanded such respect. Don was so *unimportant*.

"Tell me about your rain forests." Felicia turned to Senhora Coronado at a momentary lapse in conversation. "We've heard so much about them back in the States." Her smile was charismatic, her voice carrying to the men across the room. "To a timber family this is fascinating."

Immediately the atmosphere became electric. The two Brazilian men, and Don, deserted their corner of the living room to join the women.

"What is happening with our rain forests is criminal," Senhor Coronado said, his genteel voice all at once harsh. "Foreign timber companies are invading the Amazon basin. In most areas no more than eight to ten trees per acre are commercially useful—but these exploiters chop everything in sight. Can't these maniacs understand what they're doing to the world's oxygen supply? The forests provide the oxygen we need to sustain our lives! They recycle carbon dioxide. Our forests and our grasslands absorb half of the carbon dioxide we create each year by burning oil, coal, gasoline."

"And forest plants absorb as much as fifteen percent of the solar energy that touches the earth," his son-in-law picked up. "They help control our climate."

"One of your American scientists has written recently that much of the world's tropical rain forests may be destroyed by the end of this century unless we put a stop to the cutting," Senhor Coronado continued, inspired by Felicia's rapt attention, but unaware of her disinterest in the state of the world's environment. "There are timbermen who see our tropical forests as gold mines. They buy cheap and they sell high."

"Carlos, enough of this talk," his wife scolded. "Our guests are here on holiday. I do wish," she said warmly, her eyes including Don along with Felicia, "that you were not leaving our city so soon."

After an affectionate farewell Felicia and Don climbed into the waiting limousine for the drive back to the Ouro Verde. The lights from the hills glittered against the night sky. The dramatic hundred-foot concrete statue of Christ that stood at twenty-four hundred feet in the clouds on Corcovado Mountain—appearing as a huge floodlighted cross—was visible from every point in the city.

"God, the Coronados are dull," Don said to Felicia when they were in their suite again.

"One of the most powerful families in Brazil," Felicia shot back. Senhor Coronado's words ricocheted in her mind:

453

"They buy cheap and sell high," the time-honored formula for success in business. Damn, Adrian and she couldn't afford to buy down here yet. But if she were appointed CEO, she would be able to raise funds more easily. "I'm bushed—" she kicked off her shoes and began to undress. "Jet lag's catching up with me."

"And here I thought we'd go pub-crawling tonight." But he, too, was suppressing a yawn.

In the morning they ordered breakfast sent up to their suite and ate at a table that provided a magnificent view of the Atlantic. Over coffee Don suggested to Felicia that she go downtown to shop at H. Stern alone.

"I'd like to jog on the beach," he said casually. Because of all those girls in string bikinis, she thought in instant irritation. "I'll meet you downtown later for drinks—at the Jockey Club. We'll come back and have dinner here at the hotel. Real continental posh."

"I'll phone you when I'm all clear," she said, all at once relishing the prospect of a day of shopping on her own in Rio.

Dressing for dinner Felicia decided to wear the aquamarine earrings she'd bought at H. Stern.

"Those must have set you back a bundle," Don said, his eyes appraising the beautiful earrings.

"Not really," Felicia shrugged. "In San Francisco, yes, but the bargains down here are great."

"Sweetie, would you loan me a little walking-around money? I seem to be flat." He grimaced in apology.

"Cash a check downstairs."

"I can't—my balance is down to twenty dollars," he said with a wistful smile. "I'm strapped until my fourth-quarter check comes through." From the trust fund his grandmother left him, Felicia understood.

All at once Felicia was wary. "How do you plan on paying our hotel bill? Your American Express?"

"That's on hold. I didn't realize my checking account was

shot until I sat down this morning and worked out the balance. Wow, was that a shocker!"

Warning signals flashed across her brain. There were community property laws in California. If she and Don split up eight years from now, he could demand half of what she inherited from Naomi.

"Don, I paid for our airline tickets." She was deceptively calm. "It's your responsibility to pay the hotel bill."

"Felicia, I'm broke." Her eyes went opaque as they tangled with his. Now was the time to get out of this mess. Before the inheritance came through. "I'll pay you back October first. You know my check's coming in."

"I'm not paying the hotel bill," she said coldly.

"What'll I say when we go to check out tomorrow?" His face was flushed now.

"That's your problem. This is the end of the line for us."

"What are you talking about?" He gaped in shock.

"This marriage won't work. It was a mistake from the beginning. I'm going back to San Francisco."

"You're flipping out," he yelled at her. "And what the hell am I supposed to do about the hotel bill? You're my wife—you're supposed to see me through in a crisis."

"This is your crisis." Her eyes dared him to contradict her. "Call your parents to wire you money. Tell them you're divorcing me. They'll take you back, pay your bills again. Perhaps you can get an annulment—everybody knows we're usually in different parts of the world."

"I don't believe this!" He was incredulous and scared.

"You'd better believe it, darling." *Let her free herself from Don as soon as possible.* "Within the next hour I'm going to be on my way to the airport. I'm taking the first flight out of Rio that I can get. You take care of the divorce—or the annulment. You can find the time to do that between skiing and polo."

455

On her return from Rio Felicia phoned Paul Emerson. She told him about her breakup with Don and asked him to follow through on her behalf. Don was either to divorce her or arrange for an annulment.

"I don't care which it is," she told him bluntly. "I just want out of that marriage. And no financial settlement," she emphasized. "Don surely can't expect alimony—and all I own at the moment is my car." At the present. He couldn't know, nor could Paul, about her investment in the secret corporation with Adrian. Nobody knew about that except Adrian and herself.

"I don't anticipate any problems," Paul reassured her.

"If there should be—if Don stalls—let him know we'll find a way to pressure him into action." On the flight home she'd worked out a sure-fire threat. "He'd hate to have me circulate a rumor that I asked him to divorce me because he was useless in bed."

"Felicia, you wouldn't," Paul chuckled.

"I would. And Don knows I would."

She remained for two days at her apartment—where she kept a skeleton wardrobe—then returned to the Miller house. When Doug expressed surprise at her unexpected presence at the dinner table, she told him she'd realized her marriage was a mistake and had asked Don to divorce her.

"He has the time to waste—I don't," she shrugged.

"Are you coming back into the office or going off somewhere on vacation?" He was polite but tense.

"I'll be in tomorrow morning," she said. She debated about discussing the Amazon rain forest with him—Senhor Coronado's assessment charging through her mind yet again—but decided to postpone it.

"Then I'll bring you up-to-date on what's been happening with the Monongahela National Forest decision in the few days you've been away," Doug said grimly.

"What's the score?" She knew about the appeal against the decision to ban clear-cutting in West Virginia's Monongahela Forest. *An absurd decision.* "The higher court ruled against it?"

"The higher court upheld it," Doug told her.

"Oh, God! Now those damn preservationists are going to hit other areas."

"It may just be an East Coast deal." Doug tried for an optimistic note, but his eyes betrayed his anxiety.

"You know it'll spread, Doug. If it goes national, we'll have a serious cut-back in production—we'll see a shortage of everything from telephone poles to toilet paper. Can you imagine how many people will be laid off? Well over a hundred thousand," she estimated. That would disturb Doug.

"Felicia, it isn't happening yet."

"We'll know soon enough if it becomes a national situation. Of course, a few outfits like Weyerhaeuser and Georgia-Pacific don't have to worry. They mostly log their own lands." She paused, smiled faintly. "And it doesn't *have* to affect us. We have a huge amount of uncut redwood stands."

"That are not meant for this decade," he reminded her. "Not for this century."

"Time will tell," Felicia said sweetly. "As Naomi used to say, we must adapt to the times."

If Doug put the company in a spot where they were unable to deliver to their accounts, then the company would be in jeopardy. She, and the board, could go to court and have him judged incompetent. *He just might cut his own throat.*

Thirty-nine

ANNE waited impatiently for the long Thanksgiving weekend because her father had finally agreed to fly out to San Francisco for the holiday. She worried that he was becoming obsessed by visions of Lazarus Timber as a major force in the South. Anne suspected they were expanding too fast, and felt guilty that she was unable to take an active part in management. Yet it was the money she fed into the company that kept it enlarging.

On Wednesday afternoon—pausing to remind Doug that he was to have Thanksgiving dinner at her house the following day—Anne left the office to drive to the airport to meet her father. There would be twelve at the table, she thought with pleasureable anticipation while she waited at a traffic light.

Tess and Artie wouldn't be with them this Thanksgiving— they were going to Bert and Janice this year. But there'd be— in addition to herself, Josh, and the children—her father, Doug, Shirley and Stu, Todd and Chris, and Felicia's children. Chris had not returned to Georgetown U after vacation; she had broken off with her parents because of their demands that she abandon her antinuclear activities and had found a job in San Francisco. It would be the kind of gathering Doug enjoyed, she thought affectionately, though he seemed upset that much of his immediate family would be out of town.

At the airport she felt a childish eagerness to see her father.

Thank God for telephones—they spoke once a week—but at intervals she felt a poignant need to see him, to reassure herself that he was faring well.

She felt a rush of love when she saw him walking toward her on the airport concourse—slightly disheveled from the long hours of the flight, she thought tenderly, and remembered how a neighbor had once described her father as always looking as though "he's just stepped from a bandbox."

"Daddy! Oh, Daddy!" She clung to him, and for a moment it seemed as though she were twenty-one again and Naomi Miller had not yet come into her life.

Her father held her off to inspect her. "You look wonderful, Annie. And how are Josh and the kids?" He paused for a moment, as though unsure of their names. "The two of them—" he fumbled self-consciously.

"Josh and the kids are fine. They're waiting anxiously to see you. Marsh wanted to come to the airport, but he was expected at a friend's birthday party, and Robin has a dance class on Wednesday afternoons."

"Robin's old enough for dance class?" Her father seemed startled.

"She was seven in June, Daddy—"

"That seems so young to be going to dance class." Her father shook his head in amusement. But for years he'd talked about watching her dance—just five years old—in Miss Anna's annual soiree. "Let's go pick up my luggage so we can get out of here."

Anne gloried in the joyous welcome the children and Josh showed her father. Even Hannibal—the beagle puppy Marsh had rushed to save and was now a member of the family—joined in the welcoming. It was so wonderful to have Dad here!

Thanksgiving day, with most of those close to her gathered in her house, was a warm, relaxed occasion for Anne, the tensions of business on hold. This was the kind of day to be cherished, she thought sentimentally as the three women gathered in the kitchen to load the dishwasher and to soak the remainder of the dinner dishes in the sink.

"Only on a holiday like this should we let the men ship us off to the kitchen to do 'women's work,' " Shirley decreed, "while they sprawl all over the living room and watch football on TV."

"I'm worried a little about Dad," Anne confided with a sudden need to share her anxiety. "He doesn't seem himself. He—he forgets things," she stumbled, feeling traitorous at this admission.

"Annie, don't you forget things?" Chris scolded. "Don't we all when we're under pressure? You said your father's terribly involved in the business. He probably drives himself the way you do."

"He's a darling man," Shirley told her. "If I wasn't committed to Stu, I'd chase after him even if he is older."

"Chris, you heard her," Anne joshed. "She said she's committed to Stu."

"But not enough to take out a marriage license," Shirley added. "This is 1975. A woman can survive without a man in her life on a full-time basis."

"What are you women plotting out here?" Josh grinned at them from the entrance to the kitchen. "While the four kids are ready to kill each other over gin rummy."

"You taught them to play it," Anne shot back. "Just promise me you'll never take them to Las Vegas."

"We were wondering out there in the living room." He reached to check the temperature of the "party-size" percolator on the range. "What are the chances of refills on coffee and pumpkin pie?"

The weekend passed in poignant swiftness—then Anne was standing with her father in the airport reception area while they waited for his flight to board. It seemed as though he had just arrived. Each time he left after a visit was a fresh wrench. She thought wistfully of her girlhood conviction that she would spend her life in Belleville, Georgia—close to family, involved somehow in her grandmother's business. But Dad

460

was going home in good spirits, she told herself as they clung together for one final moment as his flight was announced.

In December Anne and Josh were caught up in the court decision to ban clear-cutting in a heavily forested area in Alaska, a follow-up to the ban in the Monongahela National Forest. Anne confided to Josh that Felicia was carrying on as though this were a personal disaster.

"She's scared to death it'll expand to the national forests in every state," he said.

"And if that happens, Miller Timber won't be able to buy from the Forest Service and go in and clear-cut. And if we don't clear-cut, our costs double. We lose time. But we can make a very comfortable profit with selective cutting," she said in exasperation. "The figures prove it, Josh."

"The timber chiefs are greedy. They want more." Josh squinted in thought. "I'm uneasy about some of the arguments I hear against the Monongahela decision. Timber lobbyists are pointing to the Monongahela to show how 'healthful' clear-cutting is," he said bitterly. "They talk about how before it became a national forest back in 1920 it had been totally logged over—nothing more than a 'great brush patch'—and now it's a terrific forest again."

"But they don't say it grew back that way because between 1920 and 1964 the Forest Service wasn't clear-cutting!"

"How do we make the timber industry understand that trees are not a crop?" He shook his head tiredly. "Whatever you call it—uneven management, all-age-management, selective cutting—this is the only way to assure a future that'll include our forests."

"Every year more Americans are beginning to understand," she comforted. "We have to keep telling them, Josh."

Then word circulated that the Forest Service, prodded by the timber industry, was seeking relief from Congress.

Senator Humphrey was presenting a bill backed by the timber industry that would direct the Forest Service to set guidelines for timber management in the national forest. Which

461

meant, Josh scoffed, that the Forest Service would have a free hand. "It'll be business as usual," he warned.

Immediately, the preservationists sought support for a bill that would favor their side. Senator Jennings Randolph, a Democrat from West Virginia, prepared to introduce a bill to set controls on timbering, including a limit on clear-cutting in national forests to twenty-five-acre plots. The fight was sure to be bitter.

"We're not fighting against a total ban on clear-cutting," Josh pointed out at a late-night meeting in the family living room. "We're against clear-cutting a thousand acres at a time."

"And against clear-cutting steep slopes," Stu picked up. "We know what havoc that causes."

"We need what my grandmother talked about for as long as I can remember," Anne said. "Sensible forest management."

"Right now we have to concentrate on some intensive fund-raising," Todd emphasized. "The lobbying is going to be fierce."

"I just found out today what some timber people are doing in that respect," Anne reported. "It seems I have a spy in Felicia's office."

"You, Annie?" Todd clucked in amused disbelief.

"Felicia's secretary loathes her. She's getting back at her by feeding information to me via Shirley. Right now—with the need for friends in the Senate and the House—some of our timber leaders are feeding honorariums where it'll win support for a bill in their favor. I gather Felicia is working on Doug to follow suit—though it hasn't come out at any of our meetings as yet."

"Hey, there're rules against honorariums to government officials," Stu protested.

"Members of Congress are exempt," Todd told them. "Even the lowest-level executive-branch employee can't accept an honorarium—but members of Congress can. And honorariums are more welcome than campaign contributions to senators and representatives who're shoo-ins for reelection. These little goodies line their personal pockets."

462

"We've got to win support for Senator Randolph's bill. Once we can do that," Josh said with a messianic glow, "then we'll work to set the same regulations for private timberland."

"We're fighting against terrible odds," a dedicated but pessimistic recruit warned. "You know the money the timber industry is going to throw into this fight?"

"We have to go out there and raise funds. Remember, we're just one of a bunch of preservation groups fighting for Randolph's bill." Todd refused to be awed by the competition. "So it's David and Goliath all over again—you know who won there."

On New Year's day, 1976 Todd and Chris were married in the living room of Anne and Josh's house. Of the family only Doug and Anne were present. Todd had not invited his parents. *"They'd be upset at having to postpone going to Palm Beach."* Chris's parents had not been invited because they refused to talk to her. Consuelo and Leon had left for their annual trip to Rio. Felicia and Todd were on bad terms.

Doug cornered Anne for a few moments in the kitchen when she went out to bring in another tray of finger sandwiches for the guests at the small reception.

"Annie, why isn't Felicia here?" he asked. "Didn't Todd invite her?"

"No," Anne said gently. "She wouldn't have come if he had."

"It's wrong, Annie." He shook his head. "Family should not be split up this way."

"They'll make up in time," Anne said. But she wasn't sure that they would.

In March Anne received a long-distance call at the office from Mary Lou.

"I ain't sure I oughta be callin' this way," Mary Lou said anxiously, talking louder than normal as though to bridge the distance between them. "But I jes' had to tell you that I'm worried about your daddy—"

"Is he sick, Mary Lou?" Anne's throat tightened in alarm.

"He ain't exactly sick—but he ain't himself. Yesterday he went shoppin' at that new mall—and he forgot where he put the car. He called the office to have Mr. Olson come out and find it for him. He pretended to be laughin' about it when he told me last night, but I could tell *he* was worried."

Anne hesitated. "Mary Lou, is there anything else?"

"He ain't my Mr. Kevin sometimes. He'd keep wearin' the same shirt every day if I didn't sneak into his room and throw the one he wore that day into the laundry hamper. And you know how fussy he always was about bein' so neat and clean."

"I'm flying out tomorrow, Mary Lou—"

"Now don't you let on I phoned you, baby."

"I'll say I had to be in Atlanta on business, so of course I came home for a day," Anne improvised. "I'll call him in about an hour." She mentally switched to Eastern time. "He should be home by then, shouldn't he?"

"Yes'um, he'll be here. But don't say I called, you hear?"

"I won't," Anne promised. "He won't suspect a thing."

Doug was sympathetic when she told him about Mary Lou's call.

"It's probably nothing at all," he assured her. "The man works too hard. But you go out there and try to make him understand he shouldn't drive himself the way he does."

Anne phoned her father and talked gaily about a rush business appointment in Atlanta the following day.

"It won't take me much more than two hours of dickering. I should be in Belleville by ten P.M."

"I'll drive up to Hartsfield to pick you up," he said in high spirits. "It'll be a real treat to see you unexpectedly."

"You don't have to do that, Dad. I'll have a car rental waiting at the airport. I'll drive to my appointment, then drive home." He shouldn't be behind the wheel of a car at night, she thought in sudden anxiety—remembering the incident with his car at the shopping mall.

464

At the Atlanta airport she picked up the car and drove directly to the house. Mary Lou was waiting up with fresh coffee and a pecan pie. Anne realized that Mary Lou's hair had gone white. Mary Lou had always seemed ageless, but now Anne remembered she had been fifteen when she came to the Lazarus house as nursemaid. Mary Lou must be seventy-six, she thought with astonishment.

"I declare, I can't believe you're home. When your daddy told me you was comin', I was so surprised," Mary Lou rattled on in an Academy Award performance.

Anne was shocked by her father's disheveled appearance. When Mary Lou went off to her room, Anne tried to talk to him about seeing a doctor. He was indignant at the suggestion that he wasn't well.

"Dad, all I'm saying is that you look run-down. You ought to have a checkup. How long has it been since you've seen Dr. Meadows professionally?"

"When I had the flu four winters ago. There's nothing wrong with me, Annie. Where do you pick up these fool ideas?"

"Humor me, Dad," she cajoled. "Tell Dr. Meadows I'm in town for two days—and I want him to see you while I'm here."

"There's nothing wrong with me." He stared at her with an unnerving hostility. *This was a stranger.* "I don't want to hear another word about this." He glanced at his watch. "It's time to go to bed. I have to be at my desk by eight o'clock."

Anne lay sleepless far into the night. She was shaken by her father's hostility. She knew he was ill. Terrifying possibilities assaulted her. Could he be suffering from a brain tumor? Cancer? How was she to cope? He was a man—she couldn't order him to see a doctor. She'd make a point of talking with Dr. Meadows before she left, she promised herself. He'd tell her what to do.

In the morning she phoned Dr. Meadows and talked with him about her father.

"Anne, it's probably nothing at all," Dr. Meadows comforted in his usual laid-back manner. "Still, I would like to do some tests. I'll talk to him if you like—"

"Would you?" She felt a surge of relief. Dad had known Dr. Meadows for twenty years. He'd listen to him.

"I can't promise you I'll have any better luck than you," he cautioned. "I can't force him into taking the tests. I can't force him to come into the office."

"You'll try?" Anne clung to this.

"I'll try."

Her father was furious—with both her and Dr. Meadows—that they dared to suggest that he was ill. In all her life she never remembered his being angry with her. She felt helpless and afraid. Dr. Meadows's words ricocheted in her mind. *"All we can do, Annie, is play this by ear."* He couldn't in fairness make a diagnosis without tests, he pointed out.

After three days of hostile rejection by her father Anne left for San Francisco. She had talked twice with Josh about her father's condition, but he felt as helpless as she. On the flight back to San Francisco she tried to come to grips with reality. Her father was obviously in no condition to continue running Lazarus Timber, but her one timid effort to discuss this had sent him into a tantrum.

Should she talk to Doug about taking a two-month leave of absence to go back to Belleville to try to work out this situation? No, she rejected that. Dad didn't want her there. He'd made that clear. She wasn't his much-loved Annie anymore. She was the enemy, trying to say he was ill.

Tensions were running high at Miller Timber, as at all timber companies. Nobody knew what would be the ultimate result of the bills regarding clear-cutting that were being sponsored in Congress. Adrian sent Felicia Oregon newspaper clippings that showed loggers holding a mock funeral procession to dramatize what they thought would happen to their industry if Congress passed a bill that would limit clear-cutting in the national forests.

Always in the forefront of Anne's mind was the knowledge that her father was not well. She phoned him at his office as usual once a week, and called Mary Lou at the house in between to ask about his behavior. Twice he went into a tantrum when she questioned a company decision he'd made. He was not functioning normally and it tormented her. Yet how could she tell him that?

In June she received a phone call from Jim Hunt, a longtime friend of her father's, with whom he played chess once a week.

"I don't want to upset you, Anne—it's probably some minor medical problem. But your father isn't well. I've tried to talk to him about seeing a doctor, but he just gets angry." Anne's heart began to pound as she listened. "You know how genteel he's always been. Last night he created an ugly scene at a small dinner party—and he doesn't remember it today. I asked Mary Lou for your phone number out there. Something has to be done for him."

"I'll be in Belleville tomorrow," she said, cold and trembling. "This time Dad will have to listen to me."

Anne waited until she was at the Atlanta airport to call her father. In another half hour or so he should be leaving the office for the day, she estimated.

"Dad, I'm at Hartsfield," she said lightly. "Can Mary Lou hold dinner until I drive down?"

"Of course she'll hold dinner," he said, his voice resonant with pleasure. "Why don't I drive up for you?"

"I have a car waiting for pickup," she told him. "A business expense," she added with an air of levity. "See you in about forty minutes if the traffic isn't too heavy."

She was impatient with traffic delays, relieved when she was on the lesser-traveled highway to Belleville. Thank God, the car was air-conditioned. The area was suffering a typical June heat wave, the grass and the trees passionately green, summer flowers bursting into glorious bloom.

Dad hadn't asked any questions about why she was down here, she noted. She wouldn't lie this time. She was here because she loved him and was worried about him.

467

At the house Mary Lou greeted her with a relieved hug.

"Mr. Kevin came home from the office right after you called from Atlanta," Mary Lou reported. "Mad as a hornet 'cause he figures Mr. Hunt phoned you all the way out in San Francisco." Anne nodded. "But sugar, I knows he's scared. He knows he ain't well."

Anne looked up with a welcoming smile as her father appeared on the stairs. Clearly he was happy to see her, yet she sensed a wariness in him.

"Anne, you look wonderful." He reached to pull her close.

"I'll get dinner right on the table," Mary Lou said and hurried down the hall to the kitchen.

"How're the kids?" Kevin asked. "Marsh and Robin," he added and she felt his satisfaction that he remembered the children's names.

"They're fine, Dad. Of course, they can't wait for school to be out," she laughed. "Then by middle of August they can't wait for it to begin again."

Over dinner Kevin talked with pride about the way Georgia's Jimmy Carter was winning the Democratic presidential primaries.

"Elena and Johnny Amos gave a great party for him down in Columbus," he recalled. "Jim and I drove down there for it. When Elena Amos gives a party, you know it's going to be something special."

Not until they left the dinner table and went to settle themselves in the air-conditioned living room did Anne reveal why she had come to Belleville—though furtive glances from her father at dinner told her he was suspicious.

"Dad, we have to talk," she said gently. "I'm worried about your health."

"Who's been talking to you?" he flared. "Jim Hunt," he accused. "He's a meddling old man! What did he tell you? That crazy story he told me about my acting up at Sam and Esther's dinner party night before last? If it happened, I would have remembered."

"Daddy, there were other people there, too." She tried to

sound calm. "They remember." She was conscious of a sudden reversal in their roles. He was the little boy, she was the parent. "Whatever is wrong, we have to find out and take measures to correct it. It's probably nothing terribly important." She struggled to hide her own anxieties. "But you must have a checkup."

As they argued about his seeing Dr. Meadows, Anne realized he must have known for months that something wasn't right with him—and as Mary Lou said, he was scared. When he finally agreed that he would have a checkup, she called Dr. Meadows at home, explained that she was in town briefly and hoped he could see her father while she was here.

"Bring him in tomorrow morning," Dr. Meadows advised. "I'll do some shuffling of my schedule. Tell him he's not to have any breakfast—and be here by eight-thirty."

Her father was pale but tranquil when she told him he had an appointment with Dr. Meadows in the morning and that he was not to have breakfast.

"All those stupid tests," he said with an air of quiet martyrdom. And then he reached for her hand. "Annie, I don't want to cause you trouble. I'm disrupting your life with these crazy trips home."

"You're not disrupting my life. I love you. I want to help you get well."

For the next three days Anne sat, apprehensive and fighting off panic, in doctors' reception rooms while her father underwent tests. She was grateful that Dr. Meadows had taken complete charge, arranging for the necessary examinations. First the complete physical—"because physical diseases can create the memory problems, the disorientation your father seems to be experiencing," Dr. Meadows explained. The following day a neurological examination in the morning was followed by a psychiatric interview in the afternoon. An electroencephalogram and a CT scan were also done.

At last Dr. Meadows sat down with them to explain what was happening. He had asked if Kevin wished Anne to be present, and was assured that he did.

"We have enough now to make what is probably a correct diagnosis," Dr. Meadows said gently. "There's no absolute way to diagnose Alzheimer's disease."

Anne was suddenly dizzy. This wasn't real. She had suspected a brain tumor, even dreaded cancer—but there was hope there. Alzheimer's disease was irreversible. *Why?* Why did something like this happen to Dad? The finest, sweetest man alive. How could God let this happen to somebody like Dad?

"You're telling me that my brain is dying!" Kevin clutched one hand in the other. "You're saying I'm losing control of myself! God only knows what I might do tomorrow!"

"Kevin, this isn't going to hit you overnight," Meadows said compassionately. "You have years ahead of you. They can be good years if you plan for them."

"What about the business?" His voice was harsh with shock. "Are you telling me I have to give up my business?"

"Go in for an hour a day," Dr. Meadows said, and Anne understood. That was to give him some sense of purpose. "But I don't want you in stressful situations, Kevin." She'd have to go in and reschedule management in the company, Anne told herself. *She would have to run Lazarus Timber from San Francisco.* "Involve yourself in some physical activity every day," he urged. "Take up golf. Everybody takes up golf when they retire."

"I'm not retiring!" Kevin said with savage rage.

"A lot of men take early retirement these days," Dr. Meadows said gently. "They . . ."

"I'll never go out of the house again," Kevin vowed. "I'll stay at home and wait to die."

"Kevin, you mustn't do that," Dr. Meadows said vigorously. "You're going to find that friends care about you. They'll understand. They'll do everything they can to help."

"Maybe Dad should move to San Francisco with me," Anne intervened, her mind in chaos. *How was she to handle this situation?*

"No." Kevin was brusque. "I want to stay here in my own house."

"You can do that," Dr. Meadows said, with a warning glance at Anne. "We'll take tests at intervals and make sure you're as comfortable as possible. But for now—maybe for years yet—you'll be yourself much of the time. I just want you to avoid stress. I don't want you to drive," he cautioned and Kevin reared in rebellion.

"You're going to take away my driver's license?"

"No," Dr. Meadows assured him. "But there must be somebody who can drive you around. Relieve you of all that tension."

"Eustis," Anne suggested. "Our part-time yardman. He's on a small pension and happy for any odd jobs that come along. Dad, you like Eustis." She took a deep breath and plunged ahead. "We love you too much to take a chance of your not feeling just right when you're at the wheel. I'd worry every minute I was away if you insisted on driving."

She'd fly home once a month to see him. She'd phone every day to talk to him, and to Mary Lou, and prepare for the time he'd have to come home. She'd never allow him to go into a nursing home—they'd hire around-the-clock nurses if need be. Thank God, they were financially able to see him through without that.

"I never thought I'd be a burden to my child." Kevin's voice broke. "Annie, I'm sorry. I'm so sorry—"

Forty

ANNE endeavored to juggle the demands of Miller Timber, her family, her father, and Lazarus Timber. It was an exhausting, draining way of life. She was unnerved by the moments when she was sharp with Marsh and Robin. Each time she apologized and made them understand they were not at fault. Thank God for Josh, she told herself repeatedly. Another man would want no part of a wife being torn in so many directions.

She knew the time would come when she would have to bring her father to San Francisco; but as long as he could function in the Belleville setting, she was convinced, and the doctors agreed with her, that it was best to leave him there. Once a month she flew to Belleville for a twenty-four-hour visit with her father. Eustis had become too arthritic to continue as yardman and part-time driver, but Mary Lou's nephew had come in to replace him. Together, Mary Lou reported with pride, her nephew Zeke and Kevin went out each day to the golf course.

"Oh, he enjoys playin' golf with Zeke," Mary Lou said. "Sometimes they comes home for lunch and turns around to go back to play golf all afternoon."

Pleased that her father enjoyed Zeke's company, Anne hired him as a live-in companion. She felt less pressured with Zeke in the house. Friends were supportive, too, she remembered in dark moments. And her father was finding pleasure in following Jimmy Carter's campaign for the presidency.

At last Congress passed the bill introduced by Senator Humphrey and hammered out after much assault by environmentalists. In October President Gerald Ford signed the National Forest Management Act of 1976. The law restored basic control to the Forest Service.

"Damn," Josh railed, "it still allows clear-cutting!"

Still, the Forest Service was subject to guidelines set by the Department of Agriculture. While the act was considered a victory for the Forest Service—and therefore, for the timber industry—Anne reminded Josh that the Service had to operate under more specific guidelines. Environmentalists would constantly be looking over the Forest Service's shoulder. In some measure they had achieved a victory.

On election eve, November 2, 1976 Anne and Josh invited their inner circle to dinner and to watch the returns on television. The polls called Carter and Ford a "virtual tie."

"We'd better pray Carter makes it," Josh said fervently while the gathering settled about the room to watch the numbers that were coming in. "With Carter we'll have a friend in the White House."

"We've had three friends so far," Todd pointed out, an arm about Chris as they sat together on the floor before the TV set. "Theodore Roosevelt, Franklin Roosevelt, and Lyndon Johnson."

"My father has always talked with such pride about how FDR gave the South its second forest," Anne said, her eyes luminous in recall. And as she said this, she felt a fresh surge of anxiety about her running Lazarus Timber from San Francisco. She'd anticipated problems with long-distance management, but some of the day-to-day decisions had to be handled locally and she was unhappy with some of them.

After her grandmother's death her father had become the backbone of Lazarus Timber. She realized now how important he was to its operation. For many years he had been important. Grandma used to say he knew what she was thinking before she said it.

Felicia had already brought up the possibility of Miller

Timber's buying the Lazarus forests in the South. Their trees would not be cut, Anne vowed, except to fill the needs of her grandmother's company. They would not be massacred for Miller Timber—or anybody. Let Felicia look elsewhere with her increasing insistence on their buying southern timber.

As anticipated, the election was close, but after a long night of waiting the word came through. In the morning Anne called her father to talk about the Carter victory.

"Carter?" he said doubtfully. "Isn't FDR running for a third term?"

"How's the weather down there, Dad?" Swiftly she rechanneled the conversation, anguish welling in her as she realized her father's condition was deteriorating. Later she would call Dr. Meadows and talk with him.

"It's beautiful, Annie," he told her. "When are you coming home from school?"

"Soon," she promised. "And I'll phone next week."

Anne talked with Dr. Meadows and then with Mary Lou. For now, it was unanimously agreed, it would be best for her father to remain in familiar surroundings.

On the first night of Hanukkah she phoned her father. He talked with her and then with the children. But she knew from the expression on Marsh and Robin's faces that he was not totally coherent. She had told them about their grandfather's illness and that some time in the future he would come to live with them.

After earnest discussion Anne and Josh brought in contractors and arranged for the attic space in their house to be reconstructed as a comfortable apartment for her father when the time arrived that he must be there.

For the Christmas holidays Anne and the family, along with Todd and Chris and Felicia's children, joined Doug at the Squaw Valley house. She sympathized with his disappointment at not having what he called "Mama's full family" at the house for the traditional long Christmas weekend. She understood he felt he was failing his mother in not bringing the family together for important holidays as had been her unfailing custom.

Bruce and Edwina were in the Bahamas with friends. Leon and Consuelo had gone earlier than usual to Rio because her father was desperately ill. Adrian and Melanie were at the Homestead with Melanie's parents. And Felicia had flown down to Las Hadas for a reunion with Jackie, now the proud mother of twins.

"Why in hell does Felicia have to fly off every Christmas and leave the kids alone?" Todd railed to Anne in a private moment before the fireplace, ablaze with color and lending an air of serenity to the sprawling living room. "And Glenn is no father," he said scathingly. "He sees them once a month because he considers it an obligation."

"Todd, they'll survive," Anne said softly. "You did."

"A governess is not a stand-in for a parent. So Felicia works her butt off—so do you. And you find time to be a mother. A damn fine one," he added. "You're the best thing that ever happened to this family. Give Naomi credit for bringing you into the fold."

In one of the dramatic "Russian" dresses from St. Laurent's fall/winter collection—black velvet off-the-shoulder bodice and fuchsia faille skirt embroidered with jet, comfortable at Las Hadas because the evenings were pleasingly cool—Felicia sat at dinner at Legazpi and fought against boredom. She'd needed to get away from San Francisco in the worst way, she thought; but to listen to Jackie's constant babbling about the twins was more than she could handle.

"I really didn't want to leave the babies back in Georgetown with the nurse," Jackie said with the touch of melodrama that colored much of her conversation since their birth five months ago, "but Mother insisted the change in climate would be bad for them. And we did have to be in San Francisco last week for my cousin Della's wedding."

"Jackie—" Felicia's boredom suddenly evaporated. She

leaned forward so that the others at the table—other than Bill, who sat between them—couldn't hear. "Who is that clone of Paul Newman just being seated over there?" Felicia nodded toward a slim, well-built man with a dark tan and sun-bleached hair—appearing somewhere in his late thirties.

"I haven't the faintest idea." But Jackie registered approval.

"That's Norman Cantrell, the journalist," Bill told them. "He spends a lot of time in Washington and the Middle East."

"Do you know him?" Felicia asked. He was movie-star handsome and with an air of authority that was sexier than good looks.

"We've talked on occasion," Bill replied.

"Introduce us," Felicia ordered.

"Felicia, you picked up Don in this very room," Jackie cautioned.

"Don was wet behind the ears. This one's a man." Felicia's smile was dazzling. She hadn't felt this kind of excitement in years. "I'll never marry again but I'm not ruling out a relationship." That came under the heading of extracurricular activities.

Two hours later Felicia and Norman Cantrell—a favorite of the talk-show hosts because of his good looks, his charisma, and his potent reporting—were in bed in her Las Hadas villa.

"Do you always go after what you want?" Norman asked curiously while they sipped champagne after a sexual romp.

"I have no time to waste." He'd been amused by her blatant invitation to her bed. "I work like the devil—as who doesn't in a career job?" From the glint in his eyes when Bill introduced them, she understood he knew who she was. "And when I manage the time, I play hard. I'm down here for three days. Why should I waste an hour of it?"

"You're something." His eyes were quizzical. "What are you aiming for? Title of the most important woman tycoon in the country?"

"In the world," she drawled, a hand moving to fondle his thigh. "I'll do it before I'm forty." An earlier resolution darted traitorously into her mind. *"I'll be CEO at Miller Timber before*

I'm thirty." Here she was, thirty-six and straining at the bit. "That gives me a lot of leeway." He probably figured her for thirty or thirty-one, the age Eileen—her p.r. woman—managed to imply regularly. The era of the "beautiful young mother" was buried. Timmy was already almost as tall as she.

"You coming to Washington for the inauguration?" he asked, his hand emulating hers. He was hot as a pistol again, she noted with satisfaction. It turned her on to do that to a man.

"I could."

"Do it," he whispered hotly.

"If you promise it'll be as great for us then as it is tonight." Sometimes she was scared she'd never be passionate again.

"Greater," he boasted, lifting himself above her. "You are a fabulous woman. And you deserve a fabulous man," he laughed, thrusting impatiently. "Me."

She would be in Washington for the Carter inauguration, she promised herself, combining business and pleasure. From all the timber industry could learn about Jimmy Carter, he was apt to cause problems with the national forests. She would be there with the Miller lobbying team to line up their people in Congress.

While Felicia was down in Washington attending one of the Carter inaugural balls, Anne received a call from Mary Lou.

"I don't like troublin' you this way, honey, but I figure you have to know. Last night, with Zeke sleepin' right in the next room, your daddy wandered out of the house. The police found him wanderin' around the empty streets at three in the morning. Most ever'body in town knows him, so they brought him home. They knew he wasn't drinkin'," she added quickly. "He jes' wasn't feelin' like himself."

"Lock the front door and the back door with keys tonight, Mary Lou," Anne instructed, "and hide them. I'll fly home tomorrow." What she had dreaded was happening; her father couldn't be left alone for a minute now. She'd bring him home. His apartment was ready except for the final finishing touches.

There was a cardinal rule that either she or Felicia would always be there with Doug. This was an emergency. She was sure Doug would understand that she couldn't delay bringing her father into her own house.

She spoke briefly with Dr. Meadows, whom Mary Lou had already called to report the middle-of-the-night excursion.

"It's time to take him with you," Dr. Meadows agreed. "He's going to require constant supervision." He paused. "And a lot of love and understanding."

"He'll have that," Anne promised. "I'll talk with you in Belleville tomorrow."

As Anne expected, Doug was full of sympathy when she explained the situation.

"You'll fly to Belleville in the company plane," he insisted. "You don't want to put him through the experience of traveling on a commercial airline. Strange faces, an unfamiliar, constricted setting might bring on a bad period. And make sure Josh goes with you. There might be physical problems," he said gently, and Anne remembered that Dr. Meadows warned that frustration could bring on a certain violence in behavior. "Work out your time schedule, and I'll have the plane and crew standing by."

Early the following morning Anne and Josh were aboard the company plane, bound for Belleville. Neither pretended that the years ahead would be easy. They'd read about the lives of families of Alzheimer patients. And Marsh and Robin understood, she comforted herself. Together they would see Dad through the shadowy years.

Sitting alone in the cabin while Josh was visiting with the crew in the cockpit, Anne asked herself, as she had a dozen times since Mary Lou phoned her, if she should give up on her Naomi Miller inheritance and return to Belleville, to care for her father in surroundings familiar to him. She would be able to run the mill herself. Yet how could she ask Josh to turn his own life upside down? How could she disrupt the children's lives?

She wouldn't think about what was to be done with Lazarus Timber, she resolved. Not until Dad was settled in his new home. It wasn't as though he had been active in the mill these last months, she forced herself to admit. The mill would continue to run under her long-distance supervision. For now.

She felt a painful sadness at the prospect of selling the company that Rae Lazarus had spent a lifetime in building. She was failing her grandmother, she tormented herself. Yet she knew that in time she must sell the mill. But not the forests, she silently reiterated. The Lazarus forests would remain uncut for the next fifty years. A monument to Rae Lazarus.

Forty-one

FELICIA waited restlessly for Doug to bring the late-afternoon meeting to an end. Why was he being so damn philosophical about the proposed Redwood National Park Enlargement Bill? They would have valuable timberland condemned. It was a "land grab" that should be halted.

Most of the companies were ignoring the pleas of California Congressman Phillip Burton and the new Secretary of the Interior Cecil Andrus for a six-month moratorium on logging in sensitive areas adjacent to the park while committees ironed out the bill. They were launching full-scale operations in Redwood Creek as scheduled. Why did Doug insist they put their logging in that area on hold? *It would cost them.* She had fought him and Anne, but it had been a futile battle.

Yet in these last months she'd come to believe that Doug would want to see her in control when he stepped down because he could be sure she'd fight to keep the company alive and expanding. She admitted this was an obsession of hers, one she flaunted at every opportunity. Anne would sell her shares and forget about Miller Timber once their twenty-year sentence was over. All Anne thought about these days was her father, sitting in her house and waiting to die.

"I know the heavy lobbying we're doing in Washington," Doug conceded. It was a joint effort by the industry. Public relations people were telling the nation that the best of the redwoods were already off-limits in California state parks and

480

that park expansion would create economic chaos in the region. "I don't think it'll have any affect on the passage of the bill."

"It's sure to pass," Anne agreed. "There's tremendous state and federal support behind it."

"I wouldn't take any bets," Felicia drawled. Josh's group— every stupid environmental group in the northwest—was fighting for park expansion. "The industry has the AFL-CIO on its side. That's a lot of power." She glanced at her watch. "I have to meet Adrian in ten minutes for a drink at The Top of the Mark. He'll give me some feedback on what's happening up in Oregon."

"Adrian's in town?" Doug lifted an eyebrow in mock astonishment. "I thought now that he's a town councilman he'd have no time to run down here." His face softened. "Leon and Consuelo are so proud of him."

"He and Melanie are here for some family affair," Felicia explained. "You don't mind if we break now?" Her smile was cajoling.

"No, we've covered all the ground I had in mind. Run along, Felicia."

Felicia found Adrian waiting for her at The Top of the Mark.

"What's new and exciting?" she asked as she settled herself at his table, ignoring the exquisite April twilight on view. "Melanie pregnant yet?"

"We're working on it," he assured her. "I told her if I'm going to run for Congress next year, I'd like to do it as a father."

"What is this about running for Congress next year?" Felicia's voice crackled with reproof. This was not part of her master plan.

"I've thought this thing through," he said casually. "I want to bypass the State Legislature. I'll run for Congress in my district. Even if I lose, I will have earned terrific exposure. And after the election, if I lose, we'll move down to Humboldt County—where they'll remember that I was the young councilman from a hundred and seventy-five miles away who came down to help fight for the working people in the timber industry in the explosion that's going to happen tomorrow."

"What's going to happen tomorrow?" Felicia demanded.

"There's going to be a hearing in Eureka about the park expansion. Starting at ten in the morning, and it'll go on for hours. You know how public relations people have been telling the nation that Redwood Creek's old-growth and the second-growth it'll produce some day are essential to the timber companies' sustained yield programs—"

"So you heard the screams up your way?" Felicia chuckled. "It'll be a thousand years before those redwoods will have a mature second-growth. But we're not worrying about a hundred years from now."

"Listen, Felicia," he scolded. "All the crying we've been doing about lost jobs if the expansion goes through is finally paying off. At the subcommittee hearings tomorrow several thousand townspeople are going to demonstrate. Remember, they're fighting for their livelihood—and the local newspapers and public officials are prodding them on. A tractor-trailer will carry local leaders to the municipal auditorium."

"Where the field hearings are to be held?" Felicia asked.

"Right. There the mayor will express the anger of the workers." Adrian's face glistened with satisfaction. "And I'll be right there with them, declaiming their right to fight for their survival."

"And you figure that's going to follow you back home?"

"I'll make sure it will. With a little help from me, we'll have a demonstration of our own. Look, these areas are dominated by the timber industry. The future of the people living there is at stake. And if I don't win in my district, then I'll move down to Humboldt County—where they still remember Naomi Miller. They can't scream carpet-bagger. I was born and raised in the state. I'm fourth-generation Californian. I'll win, Felicia."

"No." Felicia was deliberately blunt. "You've had a few

482

months as a small-town councilman. You can't expect to jump into Congress with that little background."

"You're not listening to me," he said accusingly. "I'm going to make headlines in the newspapers in the northwest. The crusading young councilman fighting for the workers—in a county where unemployment already hovers between fourteen and eighteen percent."

"Great for the Oregon Legislature. Not for Congress. You try, Adrian, and you'll screw up the whole blueprint. What does your father-in-law have to say about this?" Felicia challenged.

"He said it's too soon." Adrian was grim.

"The old boy's right. Don't be in such a damn rush. All this business about rushing down to Eureka is a real vote-getter—for the Legislature. Once you're there for two terms, then we work for a seat in Congress. I'll be behind you all the way. Between Melanie's father and the timber industry, you won't have to worry about campaign funds."

"I hate living up in that one-horse town," he grumbled.

"You'll survive. The Legislature in seventy-eight," she told him. "Congress in eighty-two."

"That's what Melanie's old man says," Adrian admitted grudgingly.

"That's the way it'll be. You'll still be one of the youngest men in Congress."

"I won't be a junior Congressman," he warned.

"We don't expect you to be. You're the kind who makes waves."

"I have to run," Adrian said, glancing at his watch.

"Adrian, no playing around," Felicia cautioned. "You can't afford to be found in anybody's bed but Melanie's."

"It's tough," he conceded with an insouciant smile, "but I'm toeing the mark. What's doing with you and the pride of the press?" he asked, eyebrows lifted in question.

"Norman?" Felicia was startled.

"Don't tell me you don't know you two are making the columns."

"I saw him in Washington for the inauguration. We skied one weekend in February at Vail, and then I had dinner with him last month at Trader Vic's when he was in town for some speaking engagement. Then he took off on an assignment in the Mideast." She smiled in amusement. "I don't bother reading the columns these days." The items about Norman and her must have slipped past her mother, or she would have heard about it. "I'm more concerned with profit-and-loss statements."

"Six years to go—roughly—and you'll be a very rich woman," Adrian said, his eyes appraising her.

"And very powerful," Felicia promised. "I'll do whatever it takes to control Miller Timber. The right moment will come along, and I'll seize it. And you, Adrian, will be my voice in Congress." A loud, combative voice fighting for what would make Miller Timber richer and more powerful. "Call me tomorrow night after the hearings in Eureka."

This morning the town of Eureka—county seat of Humboldt County and dominated by the timber industry—reeked with tensions. Congressman Phillip Burton and his three-man park expansion subcommittee were in town for hearings on the financial impact of the bill.

In jeans, plaid shirt, and scruffy jacket, deliberately avoiding his custom-tailored suits, Adrian stood among the hostile townspeople awaiting the arrival of the almost eight thousand angry lumbermen—in a town that boasted a population of around twenty-eight thousand—who were marching here in protest. Headed for the municipal auditorium where the hearings were to be held, the procession was led by a tractor-trailor carrying local bigwigs while three hundred timber rigs, their airhorns shrieking, were bringing up the rear. Local small presses—the Eureka *Times-Standard*, the Healdsburg *Tribune*, and the Willow Creek *Klamity-Kourier*—had been feeding their anxieties for weeks.

When the municipal auditorium doors were opened,

Adrian pushed his way inside along with the close to three thousand people who sought admittance. From the stage Mayor Sacco, using a bullhorn, voiced the lumbermen's fury at those who pushed for park expansion. Onstage behind the mayor loggers pounded on the floor with their axes to emphasize their feelings, swung the wedged blades over their heads.

At 10:00 A.M. Burton and his subcommittee arrived under police escort. For seven hours they sat and listened to complaints and recriminations. Loggers and union officials warned that park expansion would cost thousands of jobs. The older loggers lamented that they would never work again. Public officials pointed out that if more public lands were taken away, the tax base would drop, local children would suffer educationally because schools and colleges would lose tax funding. Thousands of families would go on welfare.

Adrian suppressed his amusement when loggers displayed open switchblades as environmentalists spoke their piece. Those guys were enough to scare the shit out of any witness, he told himself complacently. Maybe after today they'd think twice about supporting this bastardly bill.

Most of those speaking in favor of the bill were students from Humboldt State University. Then an older woman came forward to speak on behalf of the trees, and the crowd respectfully withheld the boos and hisses accorded to others in favor of the park expansion.

"What the fuck is the big stink?" a logger beside Adrian grumbled. "Big deal! You cut down one tallest tree, then you got another tallest somewhere else."

The audience loudly protested claims that the park expansion would have little effect on the local economy, booed reports on how clear-cutting caused soil erosion, polluted streams, adversely altered the temperature of stream water, affected the water tables, fish, and wildlife.

A union leader who mockingly declared the park expansion unnecessary because they were only "play sites for the fashionable rich" received a standing ovation. And at the end of the day, with the loggers' anger undiminished, a caravan of logging trucks headed south to be in San Francisco for the next day's hearings. An overnight drive of 283 miles.

Adrian flew to San Francisco, and holed up for the night at Felicia's occasionally used apartment on Russian Hill. She was pleased to hear about the reactions in Eureka.

"Why are you bothering to attend the hearings tomorrow?" she asked curiously.

"I may want to talk about being there when I run for Congress in eighty-two. Like you're always saying, sweetie, we have to work on that master plan. Besides, I needed a break from the old routine."

"Adrian, don't go bar-hopping," she warned. "You can't afford to mess around when you're in politics."

"Sweetie, I'm so clean-living I can't believe it. I run five miles every morning. If the weather is rotten, I use the stationary bike. And Melanie lectures me regularly on the evils of too much fat, too much sugar, too much salt." He grinned. "We're in training for the White House."

In the morning Adrian was at the San Francisco Federal Building, where hearings were being held, when the seventy-five logging trucks plus twenty-three Greyhound buses chartered by Eureka merchants at a thousand dollars each arrived. While the hearings were carried on inside—where John F. Henning, head of the 1.7-million-member California Labor Federation, declared that to expand the Redwood National Park "would make an economic Death Valley of Humboldt County"—fifteen hundred flag-waving lumbermen demonstrated on the plaza.

Inside at the hearings Adrian was annoyed to see Todd and Josh across the room. The idiot brigade, he thought to himself, and moved out of their line of vision. The two of them still living in the sixties, steeped in that social consciousness crap. Didn't they know that wasn't the scene anymore?

His eyes lingered lustfully on a curvaceous college student cutting classes to attend the hearing. Like President Carter said in the *Playboy* interview, he had "looked on a lot of women with lust." But usually he—Adrian Harris—followed it up with action. But hell, a great piece of tail wasn't worth messing up his political career. Maybe Felicia was right.

"Adrian, what are you doing here?" He swung around to face Todd, with Josh just behind him.

"Slumming," Adrian answered. "Actually I still have an interest in the timber business. Every now and then I buy up some timberland that comes on the market. It's in the blood." His private corporation with Felicia was paying off. "What about you two? Still biting the hand that feeds you?" His eyes moved from Todd to Josh with a hint of contempt.

"The timber industry doesn't feed Josh and me," Todd shot back. "You're still as nasty as ever. And we're here," he continued, "because we have a personal stake in the park. We want to be sure there are redwoods around for our grandchildren to see."

"Is Chris pregnant?" Adrian lifted his eyebrows in surprise.

"We think so, but we're waiting another few days before we post a notice," Todd chuckled. Todd was like Doug—if you were family, you could say almost anything and get away with it, something he and Felicia discovered a long time ago. "I'm not sure my mother will appreciate becoming a grandmother once again."

Adrian didn't remain long at the hearings. He decided to go over to Gump's to pick up a piece of jade for Melanie. Then he'd head home—with a stopover at that gin mill just outside of town. The blonde was a Farrah Fawcett look-alike and quick to hop into bed. So he lied to Felicia, he thought complacently, dismissing earlier reservations. He knew enough to be careful.

The controversy over the Redwood Park Enlargement Bill continued to heat up. Anne listened somberly to countless discussions between Josh and Stu and then to Felicia's arguments with Doug because he dared to support the bill personally even while Miller Timber contributed, along with the other companies, to a fund to fight the bill.

A month after the San Francisco hearings Anne came home from an after-dinner meeting with Doug and Felicia at the Miller house to find Josh, Stu, and Todd holed up in the den in hilarious conversation while Marsh and Robin listened avidly.

"Why aren't you kids doing your homework?" she asked automatically.

"We did it," Marsh beamed while Robin nodded in agreement.

"All right, why are you all so smug?" Anne enjoyed their levity. The three men worked so hard.

"Word just came through from Washington," Josh said with relish. "You know that twenty-three-rig convoy that went across the country to protest the expansion bill?"

"Three hundred Eureka people flew out there to meet them," Anne recalled. "They plan to call on all the congressmen to urge them to vote against it."

"They made one bad mistake," Todd said exuberantly. One truck in the convoy was carrying an eight-and-a-half-ton redwood, carved in the shape of a peanut—a gift to the President. They expected to hit nationwide TV when they presented it to Carter. Well, the President refused to accept it. He wouldn't even come out and meet with the loggers. A White House spokesman came out to report that President Carter felt it was "an inappropriate use of a redwood."

"Hear, hear!" Stu chortled. "That bill will go through when it finally comes up for vote."

"The fight isn't over," Anne warned.

"It was a Carter campaign promise," Marsh said softly and Anne smiled in pride. She was pleased that Marsh and Robin absorbed much of what was discussed in their presence. "And he's going to see it through," he added with conviction.

"What happened at your meeting?" Josh asked Anne, serious now.

"Nothing constructive." She kept telling herself she was bringing Doug over to her side, yet Naomi seemed to be a continuing shadow between them. "Felicia is furious at the charges that the industry is using," she pantomimed quotation marks, " 'delaying tactics to allow them to liquidate the remaining lucrative stands of old-growth.' "

"This country will never again see virgin redwood forests," Todd said, pain in his voice. "Let's save what we can."

"Then I ticked her off with the proposal that we do something about our reforestation plans," Anne told them. "She pointed to our tree farms—which are a joke. Sure, at the turn of the century Naomi Miller focused on reforestation. Not redwoods," she emphasized. "Douglas firs that will be marketable within another ten or fifteen years. If we don't go in and slash them before they should be cut. But she didn't keep up reforestation. And that's one of the cardinal sins in the industry."

"Mommie," Robin asked fearfully, "when the forests are cut down, what happens to the birds and the owls and all the little animals?"

"They have to find another home," Anne said, sympathizing with Robin's fears. "Wildlife suffers when we cut down our old-growth forests. Some species won't survive—they'll become extinct."

"Look what's happened in Germany," Stu said quietly. "There's almost no wildlife in their forests."

"When I grow up," Robin said with the intensity that endeared her to her mother, "I'm going to work to save the trees. I don't want to see the birds and the animals killed off. *I don't want them to die.*"

"We'll all work together, darling." Anne reached to pull her small daughter close for a moment. The children, she thought with a surge of pleasure, were mirrors of Josh and herself. "Now off to bed with you two," she ordered gently. "Tomorrow is a school day."

Forty-two

ANNE watched anxiously over her father, ever mindful of the doctor's exhortation that they must take one day at a time. She hired a pair of companions, plus a relief man who came in over the weekends when the other two were off-duty.

"Mom, does somebody have to be with Grandpa every minute?" Marsh was startled by the sudden enlargement of their domestic staff.

"It's best, darling. But there'll be lots of time when he's the Grandpa you know."

"Will he be all right for my bar mitzvah?" Marsh asked hopefully. He was preparing already for that important occasion.

"I hope so, Marsh. Just let him see that you love him. It's so important that he understands that."

There were precious lucid hours when her father participated in the family life—and the anguished hours when he struggled with what he called a "living death." *I'm a body with a brain that's rotting away. Why? Why does this have to happen to me?* He was encountering increasing difficulty in communicating through speech. Anne was touched by the children's patience with him. Often they were the first to help him find the words to convey what he was trying to say.

But now in the fall of the year he was becoming restless and hostile. After consultation with his doctors Anne arranged for a therapist to come to the house to teach the family to help break these moods. She comprehended the agony of a man who had been so independent and now needed help even to dress himself. Bless Josh for his understanding, she thought repeatedly. Not every family could cope with an Alzheimer's patient at home. Not every family could cope with the financial drain.

A week before Thanksgiving a lighter note was injected into Anne and Josh's lives. Close to midnight Todd phoned to say that Chris was in labor. Immediately Anne and Josh dressed and hurried to the hospital to wait with Todd. He vacilliated between exultation, terror for Chris's ordeal, and humility. Both children of jet-set parents, Todd and Chris vowed to give their own child the love and care denied them.

At dawn the obstetrician emerged to report that Chris had given birth to a daughter.

"When can I see her? Them?" Todd glowed with a heady blend of relief and joy.

"In a few minutes." The obstetrician smiled in understanding. "The nurse will call you."

"How do you like that?" Todd turned to Anne and Josh, his pleasure bringing tears to Anne's eyes. "We're a family now." He hesitated. "I'll wait until six to call Uncle Doug. He'll be awake by then."

He hadn't thought of calling his parents or his sister, Anne realized. Nor would Chris call her family. How wrong for families to be divided.

With the approach of the new year Anne realized that she could not continue to operate Lazarus Timber in absentia. Insurmountable problems were developing.

"Annie, don't torture yourself," Josh pleaded because he knew she felt she was failing her grandmother to consider selling the company. "You're doing the only possible thing. You have to sell."

"Not our forests," she stipulated. "The sawmill."

"Go down to Belleville after New Year's," Josh urged. "Explain to the staff—though surely they must see the handwriting on the wall. Hopefully whoever takes over will keep

491

them on but you can't go on trying to run the business from San Francisco."

"I'll go down early in January," she promised.

In Belleville as planned, Anne arranged for Mary Lou and her nephew to remain in the house as caretakers. Eventually she would sell, she knew, and buy a small cottage for Mary Lou, who would be able to manage with her own house plus her social security checks. She spent a painful day at the office, explaining the situation to the staff.

"A sale won't go through tomorrow," she pointed out. "It may take a year." She prayed it wouldn't. "Until then we'll continue to operate as we have been."

Now Anne braced herself to go to the cabin in the woods that had been her father's private domain, out of bounds to everyone except himself. On a crisp January morning she took the car that had been her father's and drove there, feeling poignantly close to him as she opened the door and walked inside. Whatever was personal and private must be packed away.

She closed the door behind her and gazed about the small wood-paneled room. The sofa and club chair, which she remembered being part of their living room when she was a child, showed signs of the passing years. Above the stone fireplace was a blown-up photograph of a little girl. Herself at eight, she recognized. Three paintings by Marsh hung on one wall. On the time-scarred desk—an old manual Royal at the center—was a collection of snapshots of herself, of Josh and her, of Marsh and Robin.

Fighting tears she crossed to the desk and sat in the chair where her father had sat through the years. This was where Dad had come to escape from her mother's petty tyrannies. Where he'd found cherished peace. The calendar above the desk showed the month of March, 1975. That was when his illness began, she thought in fresh pain. He'd no longer bothered to tear off each passing month. He'd known, hadn't he—and he'd been afraid.

She opened a drawer to discover a cluster of birthday cards that had arrived through the years—from Josh and her, and

492

later from Marsh and Robin as well. Small presents—made by the children themselves—filled two other drawers.

Then she turned to the file that flanked the desk, curious about what might be there. Boxes—the kind in which typewriter paper was sold—were stacked neatly in the top drawer. And then, feeling herself an intruder yet compelled to explore, she discovered the life that her father had kept secret even from her.

All these years, when she'd thought he'd come here to relax, he'd been writing. She read a handful of yellowed rejection slips from New York publishers, dated over a five-year period in the mid-forties and dealing with one title. He'd lacked the self-confidence to pursue other publishers, forgetting how many fine novels receive a dozen or more rejection slips before ultimate publication. But he had continued to write. Five novels sat neatly packed in their boxes.

In the second file drawer, in addition to more boxes containing carbon copies, she discovered his journals. The last entry was made on the day of her third birthday. She read about his ambitions to write and how her mother insisted he go into the family business, that he "take on the responsibilities of a family man."

For hours she sat in the chilly cabin, not bothering to start a fire in the grate, forgetting about lunch, only realizing how long she had been there when dusk settled about the room and it was necessary to turn on a light. With love and reverence she carried the boxes that contained the five novels her father had written through the years to the car. She suspected that only the first had ever been seen by anyone other than her father.

In her bedroom she read far into the night. She knew instantly that her father was a major talent, silenced forever now by his illness. She was assaulted by conflicting emotions—an ecstatic pride in his talent and rage that this had never been recognized. But she would change that! Dad's novels *would* be published, even if she must finance this herself. Dear God, let her in some way make him understand that his talent was at long last being recognized. Let it not be too late for him to know.

In San Francisco she conferred with Josh and Doug about how best to handle her father's manuscripts. The two were impressed by her father's work. Doug was realistic.

"You have a time problem," he reminded her with compassion, knowing her desperate need to place a printed book in her father's hands while he might understand. "And the publishing field operates slowly. Let me arrange for one of the novels to come out through a vanity publisher." And he explained the mechanics of this. For a fee a vanity publisher would take the manuscript and develop it into a printed book.

"Will there be reviews?" Josh pressed.

"I personally can guarantee some reviews," Doug promised. "Through my contacts with certain newspapers."

"I want some recognition for him." Anne's voice broke. "I don't want him to leave this world without knowing others were aware of his talent."

In February the Redwood National Park Enlargement Bill came up for a vote in the House. The bill was passed by both the House and the Senate and signed by Carter, who was being regarded now by many Americans as the fourth great environmentalist president.

The passage of the bill was considered a clear victory for the redwoods. Still, Josh pointed out, the administration had pledged funds to set up an unprecedented jobs program for loggers deprived of work because of the park expansion.

"We're talking about a park of the future," Stu pointed out. "Much of the land in the expansion is a mess—tree stumps, bulldozer gashes in the earth, streambeds loaded with debris."

"But in seventy-five to a hundred years," Anne said reverently, "there'll be a growing redwood forest as far as the eye can see. After our time, perhaps, but future generations will be grateful."

494

Anne was touched by Doug's efforts on behalf of her father's novel. He was determined to have the book in print in record time. By mid-summer, he reported, a thousand copies of the novel she'd chosen for publication would be delivered into her hands. The publication of her father's novel and Marsh's bar mitzvah in December would be the highlights of the year for her. The nadir would be the sale of her grandmother's company. Already she was in negotiations on it.

While they harbored no affection for Adrian, Anne and Josh made a show of approval of his run for the Oregon Legislature because they knew Consuelo and Leon were so eager for him to win.

"Better in Oregon than in California," Josh told Anne with a wry smile after a dinner party at Consuelo and Leon's house, where family had presented a solid front in favor of Adrian's rising political career.

"That's what Doug said to me," Anne laughed in recall. "He's proud of Adrian because he knew Naomi would be— but he says he can't forget what a monstrous brat he was."

"How did a sweet kid like Melanie get mixed up with him?" Josh grimaced in distaste.

"We all can't be lucky," she said but she understood Josh's concern for Melanie, who was depressed since she suffered a miscarriage a few weeks ago. And at a Naomi Miller benefit earlier in the month and at a family dinner party last week she'd clearly drunk too much.

Late in June a dozen copies of her father's novel—*A Time To Be Born*—were sent to Anne's office by messenger. The rest were being held for distribution per her instructions. She sat immobile, a copy of the book in her hands. More than anyone else, except perhaps for Josh, Doug understood what this would mean to her father. Provided Dad could understand, she told herself while her throat tightened in anguish.

In sudden decision she left her office and went to Doug's.

"Is he busy?" she asked Doug's longtime personal secretary, who guarded his privacy with unwavering tenacity.

"Not for you, Anne." The secretary smiled and reached to buzz him.

"You have your father's book!" His face lighted as Anne approached, holding the book aloft with a mixture of triumph, love, and sadness.

"I'm praying he'll be able to understand."

With infinite tenderness Doug reached for the volume. Anne remembered that he, too, had been forced into business and to deny his talent. At intervals he'd made sardonic remarks about his "limited talent," but she suspected Doug had never been convinced he could not have one day become a fine artist. And she remembered—it seemed so long ago—a waiter at the West End Bar across from Columbia, who had mourned that "the world has not used my talents as it should."

"I'll need four copies to give to reviewers I know personally," Doug told her. "At the very least I can guarantee readings."

"If there's any chance at all that it can be as well accepted as I think it should, then we'll try for a sale to a legitimate publisher," Anne said. "We'll spend for promotion and advertising." She wasn't reading it with the closed vision of a daughter. Dad's book was special.

"Take it to him now," Doug urged. "And if he doesn't react, then show it to him later. He has times when he's himself. Wait for one of those times."

The first three times she showed him the book, Kevin reacted vaguely. Polite but bewildered. Then—when Anne almost despaired of reaching through the shadows to her father—she tried yet again.

"Dad, it's your novel," she said softly, offering the beautifully jacketed book to him. "We're so proud of you."

For a moment he seemed puzzled, and she berated herself for trying to pierce the tranquility that mercifully seemed to envelop him in the past weeks. Then a luminiscence radiated from him. His hands trembling, he reached to take the volume from her.

496

"My book?" he whispered. She never remembered seeing him so joyous. "Annie, how did this happen?"

Even before she finished her explanation, she saw him retreat into the shadows again. But for one poignant, exquisite moment he had understood.

In December—following Marsh's bar mitzvah services at the temple—Anne and Josh were hosts at a family dinner that included Stu and Shirley along with Todd and Chris, Doug, Consuelo and Leon, Tess and Artie, and Bert and Janice. There was never a thought of inviting Adrian, now a member of the Oregon Legislative Assembly.

Anne had forced herself to invite Bruce and Edwina, along with Felicia, and was relieved when the three contrived conflicting engagements. Timmy and Karen, of course, were part of the festivities. How fortunate for them, Anne thought, that Felicia had continued to live in the Miller house through the years. Doug and Mrs. Morrison assumed the responsibilities their mother and father abdicated—along with whatever governess was employed at the moment.

Sitting at the elegantly appointed table, surrounded by those dear to her, Anne was at intervals infiltrated by sadness. Dad should be sitting here with them, but his condition was too far advanced to permit it. Still, she found comfort in the knowledge that, at fleeting intervals, he understood that his novel had been published, that a prestigious New York publishing house was about to publish it commercially. A contract had been signed for the publication of the other four novels. She cherished the conviction there were moments when he knew his talents were being recognized.

"Oh, I admit that it's ridiculous for me to become so obsessed about digging into our family background." Doug's voice brought Anne back to the table conversation. "But once I saw *Roots* on television last year I had all these questions in my mind. My mother understood the need for family to stay close generation after generation," Doug pointed out with pride as he turned to Anne. "That's why she was so eager to bring her sister's family back in touch with her own. We're all one family, descended from Annie Sudermann and Willi Sachs. And now I'm digging further into the past."

"Marsh—" Doug called to the other end of the table, where the four young people were debating about the existence of UFOs.

"Yeah, Uncle Doug?" There was a special tie between Doug and Marsh, Anne observed with pleasure, because both had the same love of art.

"Now that you're a teenager," Doug teased, "how would you like to go with me to Evan Barlow's studio next Saturday?" Barlow was a young artist whom Doug was convinced would someday be recognized as one of the finest of the century. Despite the difference in their ages, they had become close friends. Doug often went to dinner at the Barlow house, and Evan and his wife were frequently at the Miller mansion and at the museum's social events.

"Wow, that would be cool!" Marsh glowed in anticipation. "What time can we go?"

"We'll set it up later," Doug promised.

"Did you see Marsh's newest painting of the trees at Big Sur?" Tess asked Doug with grandmotherly pride.

"Uncle Doug was the first one to see it," Marsh told her and was suddenly shy. "He said it wasn't bad."

"I said I thought it showed a lot of talent," Doug corrected, "like everything Marsh paints." He paused, seeming to be in inner debate. "I have an announcement to make," he said slowly. "Actually it should wait until Monday when Felicia is back from Las Hadas, but this seems the perfect occasion to make it. Annie, after the first of the year I'll be coming in to the office only twice a week. The company will be largely in your hands and Felicia's."

"Doug, are you sure?" Anne asked after a moment of startled silence around the table.

"Doug, you're all right?" Artie asked in sudden concern.

"Physically I'm fine," Doug assured them. "Longevity runs

in this family." His smile was whimsical. "But in slightly over five years ninety percent of Miller company stock will be turned over to Anne and Felicia, as you know, Artie. And I feel that for this last quarter of the period set up in the will, Anne and Felicia should be in there making top decisions."

"Of course, if we're wrong you'll set us straight," Anne laughed, but her heart was pounding.

The conflict between Felicia and herself would be painful, she knew, each of them with separate goals for Miller Timber. And in truth, she reminded herself in relief, exchanging a glance with Josh, Doug would continue to hold the decisive vote as long as he was alive. And more and more with each passing year he was voting with her.

She would not allow herself to think what might happen when Doug was gone.

Forty-three

ADRIAN enjoyed staying at his parents' house when they were away. Some day, he remembered complacently while he inspected his reflection in the bedroom-closet mirror, the Hillsborough estate would belong to him. How convenient that Mother and Dad left for Rio before New Year's Eve. The servants were on vacation, but he and Melanie would only be sleeping here.

Reaching to refill his glass from the cocktail shaker that sat on the fireplace mantel, he remembered with relish that a week from Monday he would take his place as a representative in the Oregon Legislative Assembly. Not that they would overwork, he thought good-humoredly. They were paid a daily allowance for the first hundred and twenty days of a session—and somehow, the session usually ended in a hundred and twenty days.

"Melanie?" he called into the dressing room of their suite. "Aren't you ready yet?"

"In a few moments, Adrian," she said apologetically. "I decided to change into another dress."

"What the hell's the difference?" he asked, his voice sharp with exasperation. "It's a New Year's Eve party—nobody will notice what you're wearing. They'll all be bombed."

"Felicia is always so gorgeously dressed," Melanie replied. She appeared at the entrance of the dressing room now, lovely, wraith-thin, in black velvet. "Adrian, you shouldn't be drinking when you have to drive."

"*I* don't have a drinking problem," he shot back in irritation.

"Adrian, I'm not drinking anymore." She stared in poignant hurt.

"Never mind. Get your coat and let's go. The white mink," he ordered. "Let people know we're not hurting financially even if Naomi did cut me out of her will." The white mink was an anniversary gift from Melanie's parents.

"Adrian, Naomi Miller's been dead for over sixteen years," Melanie protested. "Nobody remembers that you didn't inherit what you thought you should."

They left the house and settled themselves in Adrian's red Jaguar for the drive into town.

"Could we stop by my grandmother's house for a few minutes?" Melanie asked. "Just long enough to wish her a Happy New Year."

"Call her tomorrow," Adrian said. "We're already late. You always take so damn long to dress."

"The party's just beginning," Melanie said in soft reproach. "You never like to be the first to arrive."

"Tonight I want to be there before anybody else arrives," he told her. "I have some business to discuss with Felicia." He wanted to talk to her about their buying land down in Brazil. Before prices started rising like crazy.

"I'm sorry—"

"Damn it, you're always sorry."

"Adrian, look out!"

He tried to swerve, but he knew he'd hit whoever it was that had stepped from the curb into the road. Hell, they'd better get out of here fast! He pushed hard on the gas pedal.

"Adrian, you hit somebody!"

"I didn't see in the dark." He felt perspiration beading his forehead.

"You turn around and go back," Melanie ordered with a

strength he'd never seen in her. "We can't leave her lying in the road that way. She could die! It was a girl. I saw her dress."

"Somebody will come out of one of the houses in a minute—"

"Adrian, you go back. You run away, and I'll tell the world what you're really like!"

He hesitated only an instant. "We're going back," he said tersely.

He couldn't trust Melanie not to get hysterical and label him as a hit-and-run-driver. He'd be able to explain the girl just popped into the road out of nowhere.

The injured girl, a teenager, was unconscious but breathing. Melanie hurried to a nearby house to summon an ambulance. Simultaneous with its arrival, a police car appeared. Two men emerged. Right away the interrogating police officer knew he had been drinking, Adrian realized. He saw the suspicion in the cops' eyes. Christ, he could be facing a homicide charge.

"Get hold of Felicia," he ordered Melanie. "Tell her to call Arthur Blumberg and to come down to the police precinct."

Within an hour Adrian was walking out of the police precinct with Felicia and Artie. The teenager, who had been en route to a baby-sitting assignment, was in critical condition. She couldn't be questioned. In a way, as Adrian analyzed it, he'd be in better shape if she died. She couldn't testify against him. As it was, he and Melanie were both insisting she jumped right into the path of the car. There was no way he could avoid hitting her.

At Felicia's orders Adrian and Melanie met on New Year's day with Doug and Artie, at the Miller house. The teenager was in an intensive-care unit.

"There's only one way to handle this," Felicia said when they were settled in the library. "The cops know Adrian had been drinking. Melanie has to come forward to say that she was at the wheel. He can say he was protecting her—he was concerned for her mental condition."

"You're going to tell them I'm—" Melanie broke off in shock.

502

"You're going to tell them that you've been close to a nervous breakdown after your miscarriage. Your husband was trying to protect you," Felicia repeated.

"This might never come to trial," Artie intervened. The old bastard was furious with him, Adrian thought, but for the family he'd help out. "I gather the young girl comes from a low-income family. It's possible we can persuade them not to press charges—" He paused meaningfully. "For a price."

"The family will manage to meet their price," Doug said. "See what you can arrange, Artie."

Learning about the situation via phone, Consuelo and Leon flew back from Rio. Consuelo chastised herself for failing her son. Where had she and Leon gone wrong? she agonized to Anne.

"Consuelo, stop blaming yourself," Anne pleaded. "You've been a fine mother. You're not responsible for Adrian's actions."

Within a few days the teenager was off the critical list. Artie arranged for a financial settlement. The injured girl's parents refused to press charges. Adrian was in the clear. But Anne knew that Doug would never forgive him for possibly exposing the Miller name to ugly charges.

As the new year rolled along Felicia battled with Anne and Doug over their lack of expansion in foreign markets. The timber industry was coming face-to-face with the bitter truth—timber is not infinite. American forests were shockingly over-cut. They weren't growing back as heavily and quickly as predicted; in a frightening number of instances they weren't growing back at all. And environmentalists were fighting to save what remained.

The timber barons were on the move for another "final cut." Eager for American, Japanese, British, and Canadian money, less-developed countries were selling off their forests. Clear-cutting was becoming rampant in virgin forests in Brazil, the Phillipines, Indonesia, and Colombia. In Sri Lanka,

Malaysia, and Indonesia the rain forests were being attacked by American and Japanese timber companies.

At a meeting with Doug and Anne in late spring Felicia warned that Miller Timber would lose its standing as one of the top timber firms in the country if it didn't move out into global forestry.

"Five years ago Weyerhaeuser already owned and controlled cutting rights to more than ten million acres in foreign countries. More than they own here in this country," Felicia emphasized. "U.S. Plywood—Champion is down in Nigeria and . . ."

"So now they're facing global destruction," Anne shot back.

"The tropical rain forests offer us tremendous possibilities. If Naomi were alive today, she'd be buying up land like mad." Felicia turned to Doug, but Anne was already commanding his attention again.

"The world needs the tropical rain forests—the way they are now, not slaughtered," Anne said.

"It's useless to talk to you two," Felicia flared. All Doug cared about these days was Evan Barlow's career—and Evan Barlow's family. "You're both scared to make a move that's new and important. But watch Miller Timber move backward in the next ten years. We won't be able to compete."

Back in her office Felicia analyzed the situation. She'd arrange to stop off to spend a few hours with Adrian when she went up the following week for the auction in Eugene. At least, she thought with satisfaction, she was in charge of the auctions now that Doug came in to the office only twice a week.

At their private meeting Felicia and Adrian agreed to divert all the finances they could raise privately to buying up land in Brazil.

"The old routine," Adrian said. "We'll buy low and sell high."

"In time we'll sell to Miller Timber," Felicia asserted. "At an enormous profit," she chuckled. "You did it before—and now we'll do it again."

In July Felicia, ostensibly on a ski vacation, flew down to Portillo. Timmy was at summer camp, along with Marsh, in Switzerland. Karen was spending the summer with Robin at the Big Sur house. Norman was back from a long assignment in the Mideast and was meeting her at Portillo for four days of skiing before he settled down in Washington to write a series of articles on the Mideast situation. She was impressed by his growing stature as a journalist.

The relationship with Norman was different from what she'd experienced with other men, Felicia acknowledged, lying across the king-size bed with him in the chalet they were sharing on an Andes mountainside. She was never quite sure that Norman was truly with her. Even in bed, she thought with a faint resentment, part of his mind was off in Iran or Bangkok or Johannesburg. He never totally left his work behind him.

But then she was no different, she considered while they dallied between sexual romps. Here she was, relaxed and complacent because Norman was good—no question about that—and her mind was zeroing in on her meeting in two days with a landowner in Sao Paulo.

There was no trouble with the Brazilian government over clear-cutting, she recalled. Brazil was eager for foreign investments. She would buy land and they'd hold it until the right time to sell.

In less than three and a half years she'd have 45 percent of Miller Timber stock in her hands. She would find a way to guide the company as *she* saw fit. By 1985 Miller Timber would be among the timber companies dominating world forestry.

"Ready to go out for lunch?" Shirley hovered in the doorway of Anne's office.

"Just let me call home and talk to Dad," Anne said. Every

day before she went out to lunch she called her father. Sometimes he thought she was a little girl. Sometimes he thought she was away at Barnard. But always, she told herself, she sensed a lilt of pleasure at hearing from her.

Anne talked briefly with her father, then reached into a drawer for her purse.

"All right, let's go. I made reservations at the St. Francis."

"Wow, we are being fancy," Shirley said good-humoredly.

"Your twentieth anniversary with the company calls for something fancy." Anne linked an arm through hers. "What's the latest word from Gerry?" She knew Gerry was in the throes of a heavy summer romance with a graduate student at Berkeley.

"Wait till we're settled at lunch." Shirley's earlier vivacity was ebbing away. "I need to sit down when I talk about my daughter today."

When they were seated at their table in the St. Francis's Mural Room and their orders taken, Shirley leaned forward with an air of bafflement.

"I don't understand these kids," she began. "Now Gerry doesn't want to live in the dorm."

"She wants to take an apartment with some other girls?"

"With a guy," Shirley hissed. "She thinks she's in love with him, but she's not sure. So she wants to shack up with him this term to find out if it's real."

"A lot of kids are living together these days."

"My first instinct was to yell, 'No way am I supporting you while you live with some guy you've known three months.' But I didn't," Shirley admitted. "I was scared she'd just cut out, forget about school, and find a job so she could pay her share. He has an apartment—his roommate just moved out. To move in with a girlfriend," she added dryly.

"It's part of the times, Shirl." Anne tried to sort out her feelings. How would she feel if this were Robin? Shaken. Scared. "Maybe people are right when they say premarital sex is cutting down the divorce rate. But we don't have much

506

to say about it. At twenty-one they're sure they're old enough to make all their own decisions."

"But not to support themselves," Shirley said grimly. "All right, that's the situation with Gerry—which I'll force myself to live with. But you know the old wives' tale about things happening in threes? I've been hit twice. What's going to be Number Three?"

"What's the second thing?" From Shirley's obvious reluctance to come right out with it, Anne knew it was serious.

"It's Stu." Her eyes betrayed her inner pain. "I suppose I knew it would happen sooner or later. I can't be angry with him—or hurt."

"What about Stu?" Anne pressed.

"Last night he told me he was seeing someone else. Some girl in her late twenties." Anguish crept into her voice. "He's said all along he's wanted a home. A family—" Shirley managed a philosophical smile.

"Gerry's moved out," Anne said urgently. "Why can't you marry Stu now? You've had something special all these years."

"Annie, he wants a family. I'm almost forty-five. Even if I could have a baby, I couldn't put myself through raising another child. It's just that both of them hitting me at the same time—" She shook her head in anguish. "It's scary."

"Why don't you talk about this with Stu? If he thinks there's any chance at all that you'll marry him, he'll forget this girl he's seeing."

"He wants a family, Annie. I can't give him that."

"Maybe he'll settle for a home," she said gently.

"But there'll always be doubts in his mind. What had he missed out on by marrying me? No. I'll survive. And you know what?" She contrived a jaunty laugh. "I know what the third thing is. I'm staring right at menopause. But I can deal with that."

Anne was elated when Josh and Todd won a much-headlined case as defense attorneys for a battered wife accused of killing her husband. As he preferred, Josh handled the out-of-court work and Todd tried the case in court. Now they were caught up in another case much in the public eye.

"We're relics of the sixties," Todd derided humorously when he shared a victory dinner with Anne and Josh. "It's not fashionable now to be committed to worthwhile causes."

"The pendulum will swing," Josh chuckled, "and we'll be there when it does."

In the new year there was much anxiety in Anne's household. She and Josh were upset by Stu's hasty marriage to Beatrice Adams, the twenty-eight-year-old school teacher who'd run a high-powered campaign. Stu and Bea were married at City Hall, with only her sister and brother-in-law present. While Josh insisted Stu's marriage was putting no strain on his relationship with them, Anne was aware of Bea's efforts to wean Stu away from his closely knit circle.

While Shirley and Stu insisted they were still good friends, each made a conscious effort to avoid seeing the other. Anne worried about Shirley's reaction to Stu's marriage. Over a late lunch in the company cafeteria Shirley admitted her sense of loss.

"I suppose I thought we'd go along the way we were forever," she said somberly. "I never thought Stu would run off and get married."

"Shirl, he tried a million times to persuade you to marry him."

"I know. It's all this women's lib shit. I was brainwashed. Maybe some women don't need a permanent man in their lives. Felicia doesn't," she said with dark humor, "but she's tried it twice. Me—there's this awful hole in my life without Stu. Here I am, forty-five years old—staring at the big five-oh—and what're my chances of finding a replacement for him?" Her eyes were baffled. "I look ahead, Annie, and I don't like what I see. And you know something," she said frankly. "I don't want a replacement for Stu. I want *Stu* back in my life. I blew it, baby."

On a broader level Anne and Josh worried that Carter was

encountering serious problems in dealing with the Iranian hostage situation—in addition to rising inflation and unemployment. A mood of pessimism was gripping the country. And now it was certain that former governor Ronald Reagan would be a serious contender for the Republican nomination.

"That's the man who sent the National Guard onto the Berkeley campus," Josh scoffed. "The same man who's supposed to have said, 'If you've seen one redwood, you've seen them all.' If Reagan's the Republican candidate and he defeats Carter, we'll see the cut in the national forests escalate like mad. Reagan's always been a front for big business."

Felicia became active in the Reagan campaign, declaring it important that Miller Timber have a friend in the White House and she was convinced the Reagan forces would swing the election in his favor. Dashing about the country in the company plane—insisting this was company business—Felicia was managing frequent trysts with Norman, covering the presidential campaigns for a national magazine.

Her thirty-ninth birthday had been an unexpectedly traumatic experience. Not only because she had promised herself she'd be CEO of Miller Timber by forty, but that brief division of a year was a personal threat to her as a woman. Yet Norman, she told herself, could have almost any woman he chose—girls half her age—but he found *her* fascinating.

They were much alike, she thought, both of them damn good-looking, ambitious, driving. And she offered something those sexpots in "Band-Aid bikinis" couldn't provide: She'd made an important place for herself on the national business front, and her potential was awesome. Norman respected that.

In August, en route to the Democratic convention at Madison Square Garden in New York, Norman called to urge her to fly east for a few days.

"Once the convention's wrapped up, I'm headed for a borrowed house in the Hamptons. Gorgeous place high on a cliff and looking down on the Atlantic. Surrounded by woods. Total privacy. I'm burned out. We'll sleep and eat and make love."

"No working out?" she joshed. Norman was a physicalfitness buff.

"There's a spa nearby. I'll spend an hour in the gym each morning. The rest of the time will be ours. What do you say?"

"I can take off for four or five days," she said after momentary debate.

"The convention winds up on Thursday," he told her, exuding high spirits. "We'll drive out to the house the next morning. I can't wait to get away from the fucking crowds."

Thursday night they holed up in his suite at the Pierre, in the morning ordered an early breakfast, and were in Norman's black Corvette and on the Long Island Expressway before eight o'clock in order to beat the summer weekend traffic.

While they drove toward the borrowed house, in Montauk rather than Southampton as she had assumed, Norman talked nonstop about the two presidential candidates. He figured Reagan had the election in the bag. For the timber industry that would be great. Reagan would appoint a secretary of the interior who would understand their needs.

The Montauk house was a masterpiece of fieldstone and glass, high on a bluff overlooking the Atlantic, as Norman had told her, and surrounded by three acres of woods.

"The staff's on vacation," he told Felicia while he unlocked the massive front door. "We'll be totally alone. Can you cook?" He lifted one eyebrow in question.

"Not at all," she shrugged.

"I'll make breakfasts. We'll have lunch and dinner out, or sent in. Let's unpack the gear and go down to ferret out a supermarket."

Over a sumptuous early dinner at Gurney's, where their table faced the ocean, Felicia arrived at a decision. Despite all she'd said about never marrying again, she meant to marry Norman Cantrell. He had charisma, talent, and success. And he made her feel totally female.

"We'll have breakfast on the deck and watch the sun rise," Norman interrupted her plotting. "Then we'll walk on the beach. When the spa at Gurney's opens, I'll go to the gym.

Why don't you have a massage or one of their fancy treatments?"

"Norman, before you dash off into the wilds again, why don't we get married?" Wow, that shook him up, she thought in amusement.

"Let's talk about it later—in bed," he suggested after a moment. "You hit me out of left field."

Forty-four

DOUG made a show of enjoying the occasion, but inwardly he was furious with Felicia for forgetting Timmy's fifteenth birthday. Thank God he—and Anne—had remembered. Together they'd planned tonight's small birthday party. But he knew that Timmy realized his parents had forgotten, and he was hurt.

"Timmy, let's show Uncle Doug the movies we took at Yellowstone," Marsh urged. The two boys had just returned from a youth-group tour of Yellowstone Park and Grand Canyon.

"Sure," Timmy agreed. "The film's up in my room."

"We'll set up the projector after dinner," Doug announced.

"We've got snapshots from our month at camp," Robin said, faintly defensive. "But they're at home."

"I've got mine here," Karen said. "I'll bring them down after dinner."

Doug glanced up inquiringly as Mrs. Morrison walked into the dining room. She crossed to his chair and bent over to whisper in his ear.

"There's a phone call for you." Mrs. Morrison's eyes glinted with disapproval. "It's Felicia."

"For me?" He was surprised. Felicia should be calling Timmy.

"She wants to talk to *you*," Mrs. Morrison emphasized.

Doug excused himself and hurried out to the library.

"Hello." His voice was testy.

"Doug, I have news," Felicia began but he interrupted her.

"Felicia, don't you know this is Timmy's birthday?"

"Oh, God, I've been so busy. Is he there? Let me talk to him. Oh, but first—" She hesitated and Doug waited warily. "I don't think this is the right time to tell Timmy and Karen, but would you tell them tomorrow morning? Before they hear it on a TV newscast or see it in the newspapers. I've just been married. To Norman Cantrell."

The following morning Doug told Timmy and Karen that their mother had married Norman Cantrell in New York. He flinched before the anger he felt in both children.

"Again?" Karen said disdainfully.

"Is he coming here to live?" Timmy made no effort to conceal his hostility.

"I doubt that." Doug made a point of appearing casual. "He's a famous journalist. Always chasing off to some foreign assignment." He was astonished that Felicia had been attracted to Cantrell. He was a brilliant journalist but a decided liberal. But then, he reminded himself with bitter humor, it wasn't Norman Cantrell's mind that interested Felicia.

"She'll divorce him," Timmy prophesied. "Like she did my father and Don."

In January Felicia and Norman, along with Adrian and Melanie, attended one of the nine Reagan Inaugural Balls in Washington. Felicia was proud of the respect with which major politicians regarded her latest husband. He was an important journalist. She was annoyed when he rejected a ski weekend in Squaw Valley. He was flying off to South Africa on a rush assignment.

In mid-February Norman was back in the States. Using Doug's eighty-fifth birthday as a reason for hosting an elaborate dinner party, she summoned Norman to San Francisco.

"Darling, Doug's getting on in years—I do want you to meet him." The dinner party would make an enormous splash,

513

she promised herself. The newspapers would send photographers. It might even be written up in *Town & Country*.

"I'll come," Norman agreed. "Then we can run down to Acapulco for the weekend."

From the moment the first guests arrived, Felicia, dramatic in gold lamé and black velvet, knew that the party would be a spectacular success. But she was irritated later in the evening when she overheard Norman in absorbed conversation with Doug, Josh, and Anne on the evils of apartheid. That attitude wasn't likely to find favor with the Reagan administration.

The following morning Felicia and Norman flew down to the Acapulco house for a brief reunion. She'd warned him that she couldn't take off for more than two days because of business, but she would be in Washington next month. She was eager to meet and talk with new Secretary of the Interior James Watt.

"You'll have to get in line," Norman chuckled. "Every timber company, every oilman—and woman," he added with mock deference, "will be there. All dying for a chunk of the national wilderness."

"Do some scouting for me," Felicia coaxed. His base of operations was Washington. He knew everybody there.

"I'll be taking off again at the end of the month," he told her. "Back to South Africa."

"You're going to alienate some important people if you keep up this campaign against apartheid," she cautioned. "It's not smart."

"It's necessary," he said brusquely. "Now tell me—" He switched on his potent brand of charm. "What would you like to do this evening? Besides fuck," he added with a charismatic smile. "That comes later."

In April Kevin died in his sleep. Though Anne had known his time left on earth was brief, she was badly shaken. She flew with Josh and the children in the company plane carrying his body to Belleville. The heavy attendance at his funeral touched her. She had not realized how many friends her father had acquired through the years.

It was Josh who chose a real-estate broker to handle the sale of the house, and then went with Mary Lou to choose a cottage that was to be bought for her use.

"I can't believe they's all gone," Mary Lou mourned. "Miz Rae, Miz Denise, Mist' Kevin. But thank the good Lord," she told Anne, "you got Mist' Josh and yo' precious chillen."

"You'll come out to see us, Mary Lou," Anne insisted. "I'll send you the airline tickets and we'll meet you at the airport. In the fall," she decreed, "when you've settled in your own little house."

"I ain't never been on an airplane," Mary Lou objected.

"By plane or train," Anne insisted, "you'll come to us in the fall."

When Josh began to talk about their taking a two-week vacation in Europe, Anne understood he was concerned over her grief for her father. She realized, too, that she was allowing her emotions to erode her efficiency at the company, yet she seemed incapable of controlling this.

With the school year drawing to a close, Josh became more insistent on their going away for two weeks—the longest time either could comfortably be away from business.

"Annie, I know what we're going to do this summer," he said with a lively show of decision as they went upstairs to their room on an early June evening. "You and I and the kids are going to Baden-Baden in July. I know it's late to get reservations but . . ."

"Baden-Baden?" Anne stopped dead on the stairs. Her heart all at once pounding. "Josh, could we? Grandma talked for years about going to Baden-Baden to see the town her mother had loved so much—to walk in Annie Sudermann's beloved Black Forest. But for Grandma there had never been the right time."

"I'll check with the travel agent right away," he promised, and she saw the relief in his eyes that she was excited about the prospective trip. "We'll see a bit of Germany and then fly on to Paris. We can do it all in two weeks. Neither you nor Robin have ever been in Europe." Marsh had spent a summer at camp in Switzerland. He himself had back-packed in Europe the year before he had started at Berkeley and again the summer after his sophomore year. "It'll be a great experience." He chuckled now. "I'll have to resurrect my college German."

Marsh and Robin were ecstatic at the prospect of seeing Germany and France. Just let the travel agent be able to make all the necessary arrangements, Anne prayed. Going to Baden-Baden and the Black Forest was like making a pilgrimage, she told herself. Bless Josh for thinking of it.

There was a rush to acquire passports—only Marsh had a current one—and a frenzied effort to make plane and hotel reservations on such short notice. But early in July the four flew to Frankfurt.

Walking in the Frankfurt Airport Marsh glanced about with youthful curiosity.

"All big airports look alike," he decided while Robin fought off yawns. The flight time from San Francisco to Frankfurt was eleven hours. They had left San Francisco the day before at 2:45 P.M. California time and now it was 10:30 A.M. Frankfurt time. "It's what's outside that's different."

A deep love and pride welled in Anne as she watched her son and daughter move with lithe grace among the rush of tourists just a few steps ahead of their parents, as though unable to restrain their eagerness to embrace the experience that lay ahead. In December Marsh would be sixteen. Robin was thirteen last month. *Where had the years gone?*

She saw occasional admiring glances sent in the direction of her teenagers. Marsh was taller than Josh already, with his father's trim body and intense good looks; Robin lovely with masses of dark hair, expressive blue eyes, and exquisite white skin that she inspected each morning in fear of finding the first outbreak of acne, which thus far Marsh had avoided.

When they had gone through customs in the supermodern Frankfurt Airport, the largest and busiest in Germany, Anne was conscious of an unexpected tension in Josh. She saw it in his face, in the tautness of his shoulders.

"Josh, what's bothering you?" she asked while Marsh and Robin walked ahead toward the taxi area.

"I didn't expect it to hit me this way," he said, almost apologetically. "But all of a sudden I realize we're in the country where six million Jews died at the hands of the Nazis. Annie, six million human beings!" His voice trembled with fresh rage.

"Josh, that was another era," Anne said quickly. "The war's been over for thirty-six years." But for her, too, that era was all at once very much alive.

"I grew up hearing my father's stories about how a whole branch of our family disappeared in the gas chambers." His pain reached out to infect her. She remembered stories told by the handful of refugees who had fled Germany—in time, by the grace of God—to settle in Belleville. "I remember going to that museum in Copenhagen that's dedicated to the holocaust. I remember seeing their re-creation of the concentration camp living quarters. I shouldn't have suggested we stop off in Frankfurt," he reproached himself. "We should have planned to drive directly to Baden-Baden and then fly to Paris."

"We'll be here for only three days," she reminded him. But she understood, and shared, his feelings. For most Jews Germany would be full of ghosts. "Our main objective is Baden-Baden. And the Black Forest," she added, and was all at once suffused with tender anticipation. She would allow nothing, she promised herself, to spoil this pilgrimage.

They left the airport and headed in a taxi for the Frankfurt Inter-Continental Hotel, Marsh and Robin avidly absorbing the passing scenery.

"You'd never guess Frankfurt dates back to pre-Roman times, would you?" Josh asked. "Here's a thoroughly modern city, streets clogged with traffic, tall new office buildings. Of course, Allied bombs reduced much of the city to rubble during World War Two."

"It's not especially attractive," Anne commented. "But I understand there's been an effort in the last few years to restore some of the old landmarks."

"The Romans built the first bridge across the Main about two thousand years ago," Josh said. The children abandoned their sightseeing via the taxi windows to listen. "The first customs house was built in the eleventh century. In 1595 the first Frankfurt Stock Exchange was established."

"You read up on Frankfurt before we left," Marsh teased.

"Marsh, your father has a Ph.D. in European history," Anne reminded him gently. She was always proud of Josh's extensive knowledge.

They settled themselves in their suite in the luxurious Inter-Continental Hotel, a modern highrise overlooking the Main, and debated about what sights to see during their brief stay. With her usual efficiency Anne blocked out their itinerary. As millions of tourists before them, they visited churches, the impressive Frankfurt museums, and because Robin insisted they go to the zoo, the *Tiergarten*. They made their way to the Römerberg, to see what had been reconstructed of the ancient park of Frankfurt. Here was the Römer, a block of re-built fifteenth-century houses that had been the coronation palace for the Holy Roman emperors. They visited the *Goethehaus*—the house where Goethe was born and spent most of his life.

Immediately after breakfast on their fourth morning in Frankfurt they left in a rented Mercedes for the ninety-minute trip via the autobahn to Baden-Baden. Leaving the autobahn to drive into Baden-Baden they were immediately conscious of the aromatic scents of the pines in the legendary Black Forest, of the picturesque countryside, farmhouses with high-pitched thatched roofs, farm people in colorful regional costumes—even in 1981.

In Baden-Baden, with the graceful mountains of the Black Forest a dramatic backdrop, they saw the trout-rich Oos river, bordering the famous tree-shaded Lichentaller Allee where in past centuries had strolled the likes of Queen Victoria, Kaiser

Wilhelm I, Tolstoy, Turgenev, and the leading actors and actresses of London and New York.

They pulled up before the elegant Victorian Brenner's Park Hotel—one of the grand hotels of Europe—and immediately a porter charged forward to take care of their luggage. A doorman manipulated the revolving door for them. Inside the unexpectedly small lobby—where Anne admired the large Isfahan rug—they were welcomed by the concierge, then checked in by a smiling receptionist.

Following their guide from the elevator down the corridor to the tall, white door of their suite, they were impressed by the fine antiques that lined the walls. Their rooms, too, were furnished with beautiful antiques. Down pillows were on the beds, white linen sheets, down comforters for cool evenings. Chilled wine, a bowl of fruit, and local chocolate bonbons were there to welcome them.

"Mom, come look at the bathroom," Robin called and Anne reluctantly left the French-doored balcony that overlooked much of the town. "It's so pretty."

Anne joined Robin in the spacious gray-marble bathroom, its chrome heated towel racks laden with bath sheets and quantities of white terry and linen hand towels.

"Wow, look at the magnifying mirror and the bath scale," Marsh exclaimed. "And there's a bath thermometer."

"They're designed to serve as miniature treatment rooms. Perhaps I'll call down for the masseuse one day while we're here," Anne mused.

Josh phoned downstairs to order a light lunch sent up to their suite. A pair of maids appeared to unpack for them. After lunch Anne insisted that everyone nap for at least a couple of hours.

Late in the afternoon Anne and Josh and the children left the hotel to stroll about the town. Even today, she thought, Baden-Baden had the Old-World aura that Annie Sudermann had known. Everywhere flowers were in bloom. Most of the five-story Edwardian houses that lined the streets offered window boxes of brilliant red geraniums. Huge containers of white roses adorned the squares, pansies bloomed along the walks. The doorways of the attractive shops were flanked by pots of bleeding hearts.

"It's a storybook town," Josh said, reaching for Anne's hand.

Anne glowed with pleasure when Josh led them to the elegant Hotel zum Hirsch—where her great-grandmother had once worked as a chambermaid.

"I asked about it at Brenner's," he explained. "The concierge told me it has been in the same family for five hundred years."

Rather than afternoon tea on the marble hotel terrace, Anne chose to have this served on the balcony off their suite. For their first dinner at Brenner's she chose the rustic, tavern-reminiscent Schwarzwald Grill rather than the somewhat formal dining room.

After a gourmet dinner of succulent slices of Chateaubriand, mixed salad, and wild strawberries with fresh cream, Anne and Josh retired to the grand salon to sip tea from heated cups. Marsh and Robin hurried off to the television room.

In the morning, immediately after breakfast, they left in the Mercedes for the first of a scheduled series of day trips into the Black Forest, the wooded paradise that is the mecca of tourists from all over the world. They turned onto the *Schwarzwald Hochstrasse*—the Black Forest High Road—which begins at Baden-Baden, with the mountain resort town of Freudenstadt their ultimate destination.

"If we decide to stay there for the night," Josh told the children with a tranquil smile, "then we will. Your mother packed for that possibility."

"I can't believe we're really here." Anne's face was luminiscent.

Marsh and Robin expressed their astonishment that the Black Forest was not black but a magnificent display of towering dark-green evergreens that rose from earth surprisingly free of underbrush. Nor was it a forest as they knew back home. The expanse of evergreens was broken at intervals by areas of green slopes.

As they drove through the forest, they were conscious of a beautiful serenity, along with the grandeur of the scenery. The mountain air was crisp and sweet, the sound of waterfalls here and there exquisitely relaxing.

"The ground is so clear and neat," Anne marveled when they'd parked to stroll along one of the myriad paths through the forest, remembering the tangled underbrush of American forests.

Then all at once Anne stopped dead. She reached for Josh's hand in a surge of shock.

"Look at those trees just ahead!" she gasped. As far as the eye could see were trees with yellowed needles, lifeless branches. "Josh, they're dying!"

"There's probably a disease that's attacked some small sections," Josh said soothingly, but she sensed that his dismay matched her own.

"What happened to those trees?" Marsh asked, his voice troubled.

"We don't know," Josh answered gently. "But trees everywhere are hit by disease on occasion. Even in the Black Forest."

"Let's head back to the car and go find a restaurant for lunch," Anne said, touched by Marsh and Robin's obvious anxiety. They had grown up hearing about the storybook Black Forest. At their ages, Anne thought compassionately, it was painful to see a legend reduced to normality.

For the next four days they traveled about the Black Forest, stopping at intervals to explore on foot. They discovered a startling number of dying and dead trees. Returning to Baden-Baden from an overnight trip to Freiburg, where the Black Forest mountains are highest, they stopped for lunch at a village inn.

While they waited to be served, Anne and Josh, with Marsh and Robin listening absorbedly, talked about the devastation they'd encountered in the past four days. Anne became aware

521

of a weatherbeaten old man sipping wine and eavesdropping with a wistful smile.

"Josh," she whispered, "I think that man understands English. Are we upsetting him by talking this way?"

Josh turned to the pair of elderly men at the next table. *"Sprechen sie Englisch?"* he asked with a warm smile.

"I do," the one who had been observing them said. "I lived in Canada thirty-two years. I was a lumberjack in the forests above Vancouver."

"We're in the timber business." Anne felt a joyous kinship with this stranger. "Please, why don't you join us," she asked.

Josh and Marsh rose to their feet to pull the two tables together and the two men, with a disarming shyness, sat down again.

Josh explained Anne's position with Miller Timber—and she noted the quickly veiled glint of disapproval in the eyes of the former Canadian lumberjack. Then Josh talked about his own participation in the burgeoning environmental movement, as the lumberjack translated for his companion, who nodded in vigorous approval.

"It's sad," the lumberjack said, "what's happening here. Not just in the Black Forest but all over Germany. These trees that used to live to be two hundred years old—they die long before their time." He paused to translate. His friend answered in rapid German that seemed to elude Josh.

"What did he say?" Josh asked with a sense of urgency.

"That in ten years there will be no Black Forest," the lumberjack translated and his friend, perhaps picking up a bit of English, burst into a fresh impassioned speech. "He reminds me that this—this disease is attacking trees in East Germany, too. In Bavaria and Czechoslovakia and Poland. And now there are signs of it in France and Scandinavia as well." He shook his head. "We saw the first signs five summers ago, but it was a terrible summer, hot and dry, so we blamed what was happening on that. But each year more trees die. Not just the Norway spruce, which make up half the Black Forest, but all the evergreens. And now we see the signs of trouble in the beeches and oaks and in the younger trees on lower slopes. It'll happen in America one day," he warned. "What will we do when all our trees die?"

"There's trouble already in the United States," Josh acknowledged, "but not to the extent you have here. Some red spruce and Fraser fir at high elevations in the southern Appalachians are dying. And we've known for years that trees in the Adirondacks, the Green Mountains in Vermont, and in the North Carolina Appalachians are growing more slowly than normal."

"Why are the trees dying?" Marsh asked earnestly. "Does anybody know?"

"No one is sure." The old lumberjack's voice trembled with frustration. "But most people blame it on acid rain. Or on the pollution from the cars. Why can't we have laws to cut down the speed limits on the autobahn and the other highways?"

"I was amazed that the German autobahns have no speed limits," Josh said wryly. "When I do seventy-five miles an hour, I feel as though I'm crawling."

"Can't they bring tree doctors into the Black Forest?" Robin asked. "Isn't there some medicine to help the trees?"

"They're trying, *liebchen*," the lumberjack told her, touched by her obvious solicitude. "But only time will tell."

"Back home acid rain has been killing our lakes," Marsh said. "And Lake Erie—one of the Great Lakes—was so polluted fifteen years ago that everyone was sure fish would never live there again."

"I know Lake Erie." The lumberjack nodded with pride. "I visited once in Detroit. Oh, maybe twenty years ago. Before there was trouble."

"People worked to save the lake," Marsh interjected. "They made strict laws about industrial pollution. And state laws banned laundry detergents with phosphates. And Lake Erie is coming back. If everybody works together, maybe the Black Forest—all the trees—can be saved."

"Here the forests are dying." Anne's throat tightened in anguish. "Back home we're slashing far more than we're growing. In South America and Asia and Africa the developing nations are selling their forests to the highest bidder without thinking what havoc they're creating for themselves. They don't want to hear about soil erosion, water-table loss, nutrient depletion—nor about restrictions of cutting or forest management."

"It would be an awful world without trees," Robin said softly. "And where would all the animals and the birds live?"

"The time is growing short," the lumberjack cautioned. "We can't just talk about saving the trees—saving the lakes—saving the earth. We have to *do*. The world has to work together if this planet is to survive."

Forty-five

ANNE found it impossible to erase from her mind the horror of the dead and dying forests in Germany. Along with the threatened destruction of the Pacific Northwest's thousand-year-old coast redwoods, she mourned for the dying Black Forest. Both she and Josh watched with trepidation for reports of disease among the forests in their own country. Not the normal diseases that ravage the forests from time to time, but the plague that was attacking Europe's trees.

Now Marsh began to clip and save items from the San Francisco newspapers and from the national magazines that dealt with the potential ecological disasters that hung over the world. It became a ritual to analyze these problems in those brief but cherished periods when the family was together each day. Even Robin was involved in these discussions.

With both children in their teens Anne decided to include them in some of the social events that evolved around the Naomi Miller Museum. The first occasion was the late October benefit dinner at the museum. Robin was euphoric when she went with her mother and Shirley to shop for a dress to wear to the dinner.

"No, not black," Anne rejected Robin's first choice. "That's too old for you. But it'll be a grown-up evening gown," she promised.

"Kitty Lowe is getting a black evening dress for New Year's Eve," Robin pointed out aggrievedly.

"Kitty Lowe can wear black if she likes," Anne said firmly. "Not my daughter."

While they waited for Doug to pick them up with the limousine on the night of the benefit, Anne lovingly surveyed her two children, Robin in a long dress of delicate peach chiffon and Marsh in his first tux. Her beautiful babies, she thought sentimentally, though Marsh towered above her already and Robin threatened to pass her at any moment.

How proud Dad had been of them. How Grandma would have loved them. And she remembered that next week Mary Lou, still protesting about flying, would arrive to spend a week with them. She would borrow Doug's chauffeured limousine, she anticipated with pleasure, to pick up Mary Lou at the airport. That would be something for her to talk about when she was back home in Belleville.

When they arrived at the museum, a number of guests were already circulating about the brightly illuminated lower floor. Anne saw Robin's face light up at the resplendent sight of her first grown-up social evening outside the family circle. She would be the youngest guest here, and Marsh the second youngest.

"Robin, you look beautiful!" Consuelo walked toward them with outstretched hands. "And Marsh, how handsome you are in your tux."

After a brief exchange of greetings Doug swept Robin and Marsh off for a viewing of a new exhibit, and Anne and Josh listened to Consuelo's effervescent report on Adrian's latest plans.

"He's giving up his seat in the Oregon Legislative Assembly. He and Melanie are moving back to San Francisco. I know this sounds ridiculous, but there's a reason. You know how canny Adrian is. He wants to set up residence here so that nobody starts accusing him of carpetbagging." Consuelo radiated happiness. "He hopes to run for Congress next year."

"Consuelo, how exciting!" Anne managed a show of approval. Inwardly she recoiled from the vision of Adrian as a congressman. How ironic that Consuelo and Leon were so receptive to Adrian's bid for political office, and Edwina and Bruce so cold and disinterested when Todd talked about a possible career in politics. One a selfish conniver, the other warm and giving and eager for public service.

"I assume Adrian will be campaigning for the Republican nomination?" Josh concealed his own distaste, Anne noted gratefully. He loathed Adrian, but he loved Consuelo and Leon.

"Oh yes. And Felicia will be working to help him raise campaign contributions," Consuelo told them. Felicia would put pressure on the timber industry, Anne interpreted. "And of course, Melanie's father will be most helpful."

"Consuelo, darling!" A local socialite approached for the customary exchange of pecks on the cheek. "I haven't seen you in weeks."

Anne and Josh disengaged themselves to talk with a pair of timber industry bigwigs. Ever since their return from Europe they had been trying, thus far unsuccessfully, to promote a foundation to do research on the dying forests in various parts of the world.

"Come on, Anne, you can't believe this is a serious threat here in our country," one of the men scoffed, and the other nodded in agreement.

"Read the reports that are coming in," Josh said somberly. "Spruce and firs at high elevations in the eastern United States are dying—and scientists admit they haven't been able to discover why this is happening. We need to . . ."

"Josh, are you proselytizing again?" Felicia said mockingly as she joined their small group. "Trees are always dying somewhere in the country. Disease and forest fires have always been with us."

Later, talking with Doug and Evan Barlow, Anne and Josh confided their alarm about the possibility of what the Germans called *Waldsterben*—"forest death."

"The world must wake up to the dangers of a balding earth," Anne stressed. "When Josh and I were younger, we were concerned that the trees would be lost forever to the world. But now scientists have made us understand the total consequences of destroying our forests."

"And when the rain forests go," Marsh said, coming to stand beside his mother, "we'll lose the source of about twenty-five percent of our prescription drugs. Plus all the new drugs that might come out of the forests. A lot of medicinals grow nowhere except in the tropical forests."

"Perhaps right now the plant that will someday provide us with a cure for AIDS is growing in the rain forest," Evan said, his face reflecting his sadness for the loss of so many creative people in San Francisco's gay community.

"I've heard the Amazon called a 'huge pharmaceutical factory,'" Josh recalled. "But all our tropical forests are in danger. Over two thirds of those in Latin America are gone, or badly depleted. Africa has cut half of its woodlands. Thailand at least a quarter in the past ten years and the Philippines are rushing to cut like mad."

"Josh, we know the Third World has planted millions of seedlings," Doug protested uneasily. So often of late, Anne remembered, he was upset by the figures she thrust at him. "In Africa, Asia, and Latin America."

"But they're dying," Josh insisted. "Either because of lack of proper care or because they're eaten by cattle—or they're chopped down for firewood long before they're ready. Basically, it's the old story. Reforestation is expensive. What banks will loan a Third World nation the funds to plant trees that will take decades to reach full height?"

"The time may come," Anne said softly, "when the richer nations will have to buy the rainforests from the Third World in order to make sure they're never cut."

By late February Adrian was campaigning heavily for the Republican nomination in his district, the same district where Todd and Chris lived—and both were upset because indications were strong that Adrian would win the Republican pri-

528

mary. He was running a sharp, well-organized, well-heeled campaign. His opposition was weak.

The Democratic candidate who was far out front among the half a dozen who, had announced was equally displeasing to Todd and Chris. He was a conservative, with a poor record in the fields of environmentalism and civil rights.

"The way it looks, it won't matter if a Democrat or Republican wins the seat," Josh railed for the dozenth time. "Assuming that the early polls are right."

"What about some consolidation among the Democrats?" Anne asked, "Some kind of coalition to get behind a Democrat we can believe in?"

"There's not one among the declared candidates who's worth getting behind," Josh said bluntly.

"Then you're saying that another candidate—somebody with clout—should be brought into the primaries?"

"That's about it," Josh admitted.

"What about Todd?" Anne asked. "He's had a lot of favorable exposure lately. Everybody knows where he stands on the important issues."

"He's never held public office," Josh said, but Anne sensed he was intrigued by the challenge.

"Put some feelers out," she urged. "Todd's impressed a lot of people in this area."

"Can you imagine the family if Todd goes after the Democratic nomination?" Josh considered the possibility with candid amusement. "And if both Todd and Adrian win in their primaries and go after the same seat? Wow, the newspapers would have a field day!"

"It's a far-out prospect," Anne admitted. "But I think Todd ought to go for it."

"Todd's been thinking about a niche in public office. Of course, he was considering something local or statewide. Not at the national level."

"You and Todd know where to take this," Anne prodded. 'Go to work on it."

"I'll call Todd right now." Josh squinted in speculation. "Wouldn't it be great to have our own man in Congress?"

"You sound like Felicia." Anne shook her head in pretend dismay. "But go ahead. Call Todd."

With dizzying swiftness a movement was being put together to promote Todd's candidacy. Even before Todd made his official announcement, the group behind him had rented a store to serve as campaign headquarters. Volunteers were being organized. Printing ordered. His inner circle was convinced Todd Harris would be a strong candidate in the Democratic primaries.

In one of the Adolfo suits that were becoming her workaday trademark, Felicia sat down to breakfast alone in the Miller dining room. On the mornings when he didn't go into the office, Doug slept late. Timmy and Karen never came down to breakfast until Felicia had already left. She enjoyed these solitary breakfasts. Times like these she felt herself mistress of Naomi Miller's house.

As customary the morning *Chronicle* was brought to the table with the coffee. For the moment Felicia ignored it. She focused her thoughts on the threatened suit against the Forest Service by an environmental group because of the Service's use of herbicides. Didn't the idiots know that in the Pacific Northwest herbicides were essential? So herbicides killed the maples and oaks—they saved the Douglas firs. The firs brought high prices.

Now Felicia reached for the *Chronicle*. Unfolding it she allowed her eyes to skim the front page. She froze in shock. *What was the matter with her stupid brother?* How dare he go behind the family's back this way! Her instinct was to call their parents, but then she recalled they were still down in Palm Beach. Doug? No. He was always soft on Todd.

She'd have breakfast later, Felicia decided. Right now all she wanted to do was to confront Anne. Anne and Josh were behind this. They were thick as thieves with Todd. And they both hated Adrian.

Twenty minutes later she charged into Anne's office, rage in her eyes.

"Is this insanity true?" Felicia tossed the morning's *Chronicle* on Anne's desk.

"Quite," Anne assured her. "Is there a law against Todd's running in the primaries?"

"You and Josh put him up to this," Felicia hissed. "You've done all his thinking for him for years! Ever since you pushed him into going to Columbia!"

"Todd's not a high-school senior now. He's thirty-six years old," Anne reminded her. "He makes his own decisions."

"I want you to tell him to withdraw from the race. Not that he has a chance," Felicia said arrogantly, "but it's terrible for the family image to have Adrian and Todd fighting on opposite sides politically."

"Todd has a right to follow his own political beliefs."

"Anne, for God's sake, are you so stupid you don't see what the newspapers will make of this? They'll say the family is out to buy that seat—by either a Republican or Democratic victory. That we're playing both sides. And that's going to cost Adrian votes."

"Todd makes his own decisions," Anne reiterated. "Talk to him if you like—but I know he's not pulling out. If he wins the nomination, he'll fight for that seat in Congress. And if the voters in that district have any brains at all, they'll send Todd to Washington."

Adrian and Felicia met nightly with Adrian's campaign crew to work out strategy. Twice Felicia flew with Adrian to Washington for consultations with Melanie's father. It was becoming an obsession with Felicia to see Adrian in Congress.

It was fine that she could call on Jackie's father-in-law when Miller Timber was anxious about a bill——and in most instances Adrian's father-in-law also voted their way, she recognized.

But the two older congressmen had their own axes to grind—what the timber industry wanted would have to take second place to what would buy votes for themselves every two years. With Adrian in office she would feel more confident. Miller Timber would have a loud, persuasive voice that *she* could control.

With time rushing past and primary day approaching, Felicia and Adrian huddled over ways to raise additional funds.

"I've talked to my old man," he said with candid frustration. "He could borrow more against his trust fund." Leon and Consuelo had already borrowed to make a contribution. "Christ, with the way real-estate prices are soaring he could take a loan on the house. But he won't." His mouth became a thin line of anger.

"Did you talk to your mother?" Felicia pressed.

"She's as conservative as he is," Adrian said contemptuously. "If I win the nomination, she says, then they'll take out another loan."

"I'll try talking to Doug again," Felicia decided. Thus far Doug had made only a token contribution to Adrian's campaign fund. "Tonight."

Felicia made a point of being at the house for dinner. When Timmy and Karen had gone up to their rooms to tackle homework, she joined Doug in the library for coffee.

"Adrian's working so hard on this campaign," she said with insidious sweetness. "I've never seen him put up such a fight."

"I gather he's getting plenty of help along the way," Doug remarked. "He's obviously spending like mad."

"Doug, how else do you win a political campaign?" She masked her impatience with a smile. "But I think the family ought to get behind him more. You know how disappointed Naomi was that neither her son nor her two grandsons showed any interest in running for political office. I remember how she yearned to see one of you in the governor's mansion—or in Congress." She paused. "Or even in the White House. With luck and the right support, Adrian might pull that off for her."

"Felicia, I gave equally to Adrian's campaign and to Todd's. They're both Mama's great-grandsons."

"Todd is an ass!" she flared. "He's a disgrace to the family."

It was useless. Doug wouldn't come across with anymore funds. They'd have to appeal for more money from Melanie's father. Hell, he could afford it.

Anne was pleased that Marsh and Robin had insisted on becoming volunteers in Todd's campaign. It was inevitable that Timmy and Karen joined forces with them, though she suspected they kept this secret from their mother. Felicia would have been furious.

As Felicia had anticipated, and it was no surprise to Anne, the local newspapers were playing up the fact that the leading contenders now in both the Republican and Democratic primaries were cousins, both great-grandsons of the formidable Naomi Miller. But the newspapers were playing up its whimsical aspect, with only an occasional hint of dark family divisions. But there were no grim reproaches about jamming through a family candidate, whatever the party. Todd had proved himself his own man.

Anne forced herself to go into the office on primary day, but she left early to hurry to Todd's headquarters.

"Todd's way ahead!" Chris greeted her ebulliently when she arrived at the storefront campaign office. "It's in the bag!"

"What about Adrian?" Anne asked, dreading an affirmative reply.

"Adrian's far out front." Josh came forward and dropped an arm about her waist. "It's going to be Harris against Harris in November."

Forty-six

MANY times in the ensuing weeks Anne remembered what Glenn had said to her when they stood together at the hospital nursery when Timmy was two days old: *"In your own way you're just as ambitious as Felicia. But never forget for one moment, Anne. She's a dirty fighter."*

Felicia and Adrian were fighting dirty in the campaign against Todd. They labeled him a rabble-rouser, dragged out his background as a campus rebel both at Columbia and Berkeley. They flaunted his arrest record, along with Chris's, for demonstrating against nuclear power. They hinted that he was a pariah in his own family.

As Anne and Josh expected, Todd couldn't bring himself to air Adrian's own escapades—including Todd's rescuing him from a bad LSD trip in the Haight-Ashbury years earlier, or more recently Adrian's brush with a drunken-driving charge that almost escalated to manslaughter. Anne understood; Todd couldn't expose Consuelo and Leon to such pain. His parents loved Adrian, though they didn't like him.

On election day Anne and Josh voted early. Then Anne went in to the office, Josh to election headquarters. She was touched when Doug came to her office to tell her that he, too, had voted early.

"I voted for Todd," Doug said quietly. "But I'm afraid the times are against him." As the polls were indicating.

Back in 1980, for the first time in twenty-eight years, the

U.S. Senate had gone Republican. With a Republican president and Senate—and a bull market on Wall Street—Democrats running for office this November of 1982 were running into rough times.

As Anne had feared, Todd lost to Adrian. Late in the evening, after Todd had made his concession speech, Anne and Josh were hosts at a supper party for the disappointed campaign workers.

"This is just the beginning," Josh said with determined optimism at the table of the inner circle. "Todd got his feet wet in this campaign." He turned to Todd. "You'll be in there two years from now again—and next time you'll win!"

"Hear, hear!" Chris chortled and leaned forward to kiss Todd.

"Next time," Anne whispered to Josh, "we'll be able to throw in the kind of funds he needs to win." In just over a year she will have served her term at Miller Timber. She would own 45 percent of the company stock—valued on today's market at around one hundred million dollars. And by 1984, she was convinced, the voters would be disenchanted by Adrian's performance.

Early in December Felicia was en route to Washington with Adrian and Melanie. As usual this was a multipurpose trip. She would help Adrian and Melanie choose a house from among those a Georgetown broker was to show them. She would confer with their lobbyist, who hinted at the possibility of Miller Timber's being the only bidder at a choice Forest Service auction. And she had arranged the timing of this trip to coincide with Norman's return from a lengthy sojourn in South Africa.

Why did Norman insist on writing so often about apartheid? It wasn't chic. Of course, those stupid radicals were always praising him. Even Timmy, she remembered, thought Norman was wonderful.

Lord, she was furious with Timmy last week when he

started talking about how the colleges ought to divest themselves of stock in South African companies! She'd be damn firm about where he went to college. That was a shocker—to realize Timmy would be graduating high school next June.

"We'll be landing in ten minutes," Adrian said ebulliently. "It's like we said, Felicia. This time I'm coming back as a congressman."

Melanie's mother met them at the airport with the family limousine. Melanie and Adrian were to stay with her parents at their Kalorama mansion. Felicia was dropped off at the Mayflower, her customary home in Washington. Tomorrow afternoon Norman would arrive in town after a forty-eight-hour layover in New York to confer with a publisher.

Felicia settled in Miller Timber's Mayflower suite, as usual vacated by the lobbyist and his working staff for the duration of her visit. At the prearranged hour the lobbyist arrived for cocktails and a conference on the possibility of his setting up a "single bidder" auction with the Forest Service. This meant, she realized with enthusiasm, that she would be able to buy from the Forest Service at below-cost prices.

"It won't be the first such auction, Felicia," the lobbyist said meaningfully. "At least ten percent of the auctions this year will be 'single bidder' deals."

When the lobbyist left, Felicia swiftly dressed for dinner with Jackie and Bill at the Jockey Club. Jackie had mentioned an embassy party later, she recalled. But she'd make a point of leaving early. Adrian and Melanie would be here at the hotel with a car at nine sharp the following morning.

"Darling, you look marvelous," Jackie greeted Felicia as she slid into the limousine. "I could never wear anything like that. Not now," she sighed wistfully, inspecting Felicia's short evening dress, completely embroidered with silver and turquoise sequined scales, worn beneath the sable coat willed her by Naomi.

"Jackie, take yourself to the Golden Door for a week," Felicia ordered. "If they have a cancellation, you might get i sometime next month. If they have two, I'll go with you," she laughed.

"How's Norman?" Jackie asked.

"Presumably fine," Felicia told her. She was annoyed that he'd been in South Africa for almost five months. How ridiculous of him to ask her to fly down there for a week or two! "He'll be in town tomorrow afternoon. He's settling in an apartment he's rented at the Watergate. Some major assignment that'll keep him rooted here for at least a year."

"Then you'll be popping into D.C. often," Bill guessed.

"Most likely." All at once she was conscious of sexual arousal. She'd be very sweet to Norman, she promised herself in heady anticipation. God, she hadn't felt this way for months.

By midnight she was back in the suite at the Mayflower. Damn, why hadn't Norman come down a day earlier, she asked herself while she prepared for bed. Tonight could have been sensational for them. *She was so turned on.*

She hesitated for a moment then reached into her makeup box to search for the bottle of sleeping pills. She never took them more than once or twice a month. But she knew that tonight she'd have trouble sleeping.

Moments past 9:00 A.M. Adrian called from the limousine phone.

"We're downstairs waiting for you," he said. "We have orange juice, croissants, and coffee."

They drove directly to the real-estate office. The broker had a dozen houses lined up for them to see. Felicia knew Adrian was annoyed that his father-in-law, who was paying the tab for the house, had set a limit that was below what he had anticipated. Still, they'd have an attractive house, Felicia reasoned, and the old boy was paying for it.

Both Felicia and Adrian made notes on each house they saw. Melanie was leaving the decision up to Adrian. All Melanie cared about these days was getting pregnant again. They left the broker and went for a late lunch at one of the new restaurants that was always opening up in Georgetown. Before dessert arrived they had settled on the house that would be Adrian and Melanie's new residence.

"I really should get back to the hotel," Felicia said with a glance at her watch. "I have some phone calls to make, and then I have to dress to meet Norman for dinner."

"We won't be seeing much of you before flight time," Adrian joshed. "Have fun."

"I mean to," Felicia assured him.

"Say hello to Norman for us." Melanie smiled shyly, and Felicia remembered she'd been much impressed the two times they'd met.

"I will." She rose to her feet and allowed Adrian to help her into her coat.

At the hotel she called San Francisco, spoke with Doug, with Glenn—who would do some research for her re the Forest Service auction, then with her assistant. Now she soaked leisurely in a perfumed tub, visualizing the reunion with Norman, enjoying the erotic feelings that invaded her as she lay back in the caressingly warm water. She dressed, then decided on a different outfit—a different look.

By the time she left the suite and headed for the elevator she was feeling euphoric. She worked so bloody hard she was always tense, she reproached herself. When she was back in San Francisco, she'd arrange for a masseuse to come to the house twice a week. Maybe even go to a gym on a regular schedule.

In a taxi en route to the Watergate she promised herself she'd make a point of coming out to Washington regularly now that Norman would be here for at least a year. As he'd instructed when they talked on the phone yesterday, she'd made a dinner reservation at Jean-Louis.

She smiled whimsically. How like Norman to suggest a restaurant located right beneath the Watergate lobby. He was a man who didn't believe in wasting time. They'd have one of Jean-Louis's perfect dinners, then head upstairs for Norman's apartment. It had been so long since she'd slept with a man, she felt almost like a virgin again.

Norman was already at their table in the monumentally expensive restaurant—its walls and low ceiling faced with dark, shimmering mirrored squares, exquisite floral displays here and there about the room. They were the first diners of the evening, which normally would have irritated her but tonight was different. She was meeting her handsome, journalist husband for a long-overdue reunion.

"Norman, you're so tanned!" she scolded when they'd allowed themselves a warm embrace since the restaurant was all but deserted. "You haven't been working at all—you've been lying somewhere soaking up sun."

"Johannesburg's noted for averaging about eight-point-seven hours of sunshine a day," he admitted. "What basically brought you to D.C.?"

"Darling, you." She made a pretense of being hurt. "Of course, I came in early to check with our lobbyist and to help Adrian and Melanie choose a house. I told you he was elected to Congress, didn't I?"

Their waiter arrived and they focused on ordering dinner. They chose the mussel soup, scented with saffron, because Jackie had insisted it was marvelous, and the chicken in olive sauce.

"Are you pleased with the apartment?" she asked when they were alone. He seemed strangely somber now.

"It's fine," he shrugged. "I'm holing up to finish a book. As long as my typewriter and coffee pot are in working order, I won't complain."

"No word processor?" she asked.

"I haven't got around to that yet."

"What's the book about? South Africa?" she asked. Norman seemed obsessed by the stupid place.

"Apartheid," he told her. "God, there's so much that has to be restructured down there!"

"You and my son!" Her voice was slightly acerbic. "Timmy's dying to change the world."

"What's with Miller Timber and the lady tycoon?" He was striving for a jocular tone, yet she sensed a wall between them.

"I'm a year away from collecting my inheritance." *At long last.* She couldn't wait for this year to pass.

"And then?" he challenged.

"I'll find a way to seize control," she said coolly.

"I don't doubt that." He seemed to be struggling with some inner debate. "Felicia, I had meant to wait till after dinner to talk to you about this, but—I'd like you to divorce me. We're in no position to handle a marriage. You on one coast—me on another."

For an instant she was dizzy with shock. *She* had thrown over Glenn and Don. "No sweat," she said casually, masking a frightening sense of rejection. This was a new experience. Was it because she was forty-one years old and he was jumping into bed with fresh-out-of-college would-be journalists fascinated by his reputation? "You can have a divorce—but at my own time," she stipulated. "When it's convenient for me." *The bastard.* He'd given her no inkling of this.

"Sure. No mad rush." He sounded relieved. Had he expected her to fall on her face with grief? No man was that important to her. Yet she couldn't shake off a sense of humiliation.

"You're right." She smiled, but her eyes were cold chunks of steel. "We're both too occupied with other things." She didn't need Norman Cantrell. There were always men in pursuit of Felicia Harris. "Tell me about New York," she urged with a phoney show of interest. "Did you work out a great deal for this book?"

They might have been two strangers sharing a table in a train's dining car, the conversation polite and impersonal, a way of passing the time while they dined. And she wouldn't be going up to Norman's apartment after dinner, she reminded herself. She'd phone Jackie and they'd have one of their endless "girl-talk" conversations.

He wasn't asking for a divorce because he wanted to marry somebody else, she told herself to bolster her ego. He just liked the concept of being unattached. So when she felt in the mood she'd head down to Mexico for Divorce Number Three.

Forty-seven

AS was becoming a tradition, Doug was at Anne's house for a mid-afternoon New Year's Day dinner. He enjoyed the casual family atmosphere of these occasions. This year he was acutely conscious that in eleven months Anne and Felicia would take possession of ninety percent of Miller Timber stock.

Today he lingered until the other guests had departed. The four youngsters, Tim and Marsh, Robin and Karen, had gone off to meet with friends. He sat with Anne and Josh over fresh cups of coffee and talked about the boys' joint decision to go to school at Stanford after high school graduation in June. He knew Anne was pleased that they would be just thirty miles away.

"You're in the home stretch, Annie," he said quietly, and he knew he didn't have to explain.

"It's been a long time coming," Anne laughed, but her eyes were serious.

"I live in fear that you and Felicia will rush to sell your stock and leave the business," he confessed. "I want to see Miller Timber remain a family business—as my mother dreamed it would. I'm an old man—"

"Doug, you'll still be coming in to the office when you're a hundred," Anne scoffed affectionately.

"I want to live out my life with Miller Timber still 'Naomi's company,'" he went on. "That's *my* dream."

"I have no intention of selling my stock," Anne told him, and he knew she was sincere. "I'm hoping that—with you on my side, Doug—I'll be able to borrow against my own stock and buy out Felicia." Her face was incandescent. "I want to run Miller Timber the way my grandmother would have run it."

"As long as I'm alive, I'll vote with you, Annie," Doug promised. "You've reeducated me through the years. I've learned to think for myself."

"Annie, what about seconds of that good old Georgia pecan pie?" Josh demanded humorously. "You going to let it sit out there in the kitchen all by itself?"

In March—with Felicia flying off to Washington for some personal lobbying, since the Reagan Administration seemed favorable toward the timber industry—Doug gave a small dinner party at the house. He was celebrating a decision he had made to sponsor a major showing of Evan Barlow's work at the Naomi Miller Museum.

"Evan's the son I never had," he said whimsically to Anne and Josh while awaiting the arrival of Evan and his wife. "Or rather, grandson—considering my age."

"He's awfully talented," Anne said with respect. Evan Barlow was the artist Doug would like to have been, she thought compassionately. Naomi had robbed him of that. Leon, too, had wanted to paint. And now there was Marsh with the family talent, she remembered tenderly. Marsh, too, was so special to Doug.

Evan Barlow and his wife arrived twenty minutes after Anne and Josh.

"Doug, we apologize," Evan explained. "Our baby-sitter was caught in traffic." Evan and his wife were parents of a two-year-old who had made Doug his willing slave.

"No problem," Doug assured him, though Mrs. Morrison, somewhat cantankerous in her older years, had appeared twice with reproachful stares because she was fearful dinner might have to be held up. "Now that you're here we'll sit down to dinner."

This was one of those rare warm occasions in this dining room, Anne told herself as they arrived at last at dessert. Family dinners too often were marred by an argument or undercurrents of hostility. Tonight Doug looked relaxed and happy.

When Anne and Josh arrived, they were astonished to find Stu in the living room watching the late news on television.

"Mallie let me in," he explained. "I'd forgot you were having dinner with Doug tonight."

"Something come up?" Josh asked.

"You might say that," he flipped. "My wife's walked out. She wants a divorce."

"Oh, Stu," Anne was stunned.

"Thank God," Stu blurted out. "Marrying her was the major mistake of my life. She didn't want a home and family. She wanted a business executive with a high-six-figure income. That's not me."

"Better now than after you had kids," Josh consoled him.

"Josh, I'm glad she took a walk," Stu reiterated. "The only woman I've ever loved was Shirley. I just got tired of being on the fringe of her life. I was greedy—I wanted her on a full-time basis."

"I'll put up some coffee," Anne said, her mind in high gear.

"That's Annie," Stu laughed. "A coffeepot for every family crisis."

In the kitchen, before putting up coffee, Anne reached for the phone, dialed Shirley's number.

"Hello?" Shirley picked up the phone on the fifth ring.

"Did I wake you?" Anne showed no remorse.

"I was just dozing."

"Splash some cold water on your face, fall into some clothes, and get over here," Anne ordered, the elation in her voice telling Shirley this was not some late-night disaster. "Stu and his wife have just split up—and he's delighted. I gather he wanted out but didn't know quite how to handle it."

"Why do I have to get dressed and come over now?" Shirley stalled.

"Because he just told us you're the only woman he's ever loved. And I figure you're tired of rattling around in that apartment all by yourself."

"I'll dress, put on some makeup, and be right over." Shirley understood this was not a time to be coy.

"Forget the makeup," Anne chuckled. "Stu will love you without it. Just get over here."

Felicia hurried to her luncheon meeting at the Jockey Club with their new lobbyist. She had flown to Washington, aboard the company plane this time, to make sure the new man understood what was expected of him. Doug had hired him after their local lawyers had cleared him, but she suspected Doug had not gone beyond the routine explanations of their requirements.

She wanted more of their lobbyist than the usual campaign. She was determined to know exactly what bills might be coming up that would affect the timber industry—even before word leaked through to the public. It was important to know how the Administration was thinking on all pertinent issues. If this man's qualifications were not strong enough, she'd dump him.

Emerging from the taxi, she spied Norman a dozen feet away. He was absorbed by a fashionably dressed young blonde holding hands with him. He hadn't seen her. Just as well, she told herself grimly. Now she understood why he'd asked for the divorce. He was wary of telling her straight out that he'd lined up a replacement. He was afraid she might nix the divorce out of spite.

Okay, she told herself as she walked to the entrance of the restaurant. She'd phone him as soon as she was back in San Francisco. She'd arrange for an immediate Mexican divorce. She had no desire to see column items about Norman and his new romance.

This was three strikes and out. No more marriages for Felicia Harris, she vowed. She didn't need a husband in her life. There were always men around eager to be her escort—and to take her to bed when she was in the mood. With her forty-second birthday staring her in the face she still felt cheated that she so seldom had a sexual encounter that set off fireworks in her.

But now, she rebuked herself, she needed to focus all her thinking on Miller Timber. What was the sharp way to go—for her personal benefit? The timber industry in the Pacific Northwest was changing—there was all that competition lately from Canada and the southeast. Miller Timber had to expand, as she'd been telling Doug for the past six years. They had to operate on a global scale. And at the same time that they were expanding, she meant to pull millions out of the business for her personal use. There was just one way to handle that.

Felicia sat on the tufted green-silk-upholstered sofa in her recently redecorated Russian Hill apartment and sopped up the words of wisdom being meted out by the pair of investment brokers summoned here for a very private consultation.

"You're interested, we assume, in what will be most advantageous to you," the head of a prominent San Francisco investment banking firm said with a faint smile. "And that usually means a large cash return that can be diverted into other investments."

"Yes, I want a multimillion-dollar cash return," she acknowledged. God, she'd worked twenty years for this! "But I want to retain family control of the company."

"Then you would handle this as we've outlined," the banker summed up. "Offer part of the company stock to the public. You should walk off with twenty million in cash at the very least. You'll be able to diversify your holdings, yet at the same time you can manipulate with careful planning to keep control of Miller Timber."

"Please remember, Miss Harris," the other banker picked up. "Timing is important. You sell when the market is strong—which is this year. We don't know what 1984 will bring."

"The market is strong now," Felicia agreed crisply. Like Doug and Anne, she suspected that by early next year the timber industry would be facing rough times. Which meant that they must be prepared to move immediately once her stock and Anne's came out of escrow.

"Keep in mind," the head of the investment firm urged, "that this looks as though it'll be a record year dollar-wise in the capital markets. And we know Miller Timber is a prime candidate for a changeover."

"I'll discuss this with my uncle and my cousin." For business purposes Felicia could recognize the relationship. "I'll be in touch shortly."

The following morning she sat in Doug's office with him and Anne in the emergency meeting she had called, the atmosphere heavy with rejection as the other two listened to her proposal.

"You're not just proposing selling part of your own stock," Doug said slowly, his face drawn with shock. "You're saying we should go public."

"It's the smart way to go, Doug." Felicia was deliberately playing in a low key. "The advantages are tremendous. You're always complaining about the problems of attracting top-notch personnel. We can do that when we go public because we can offer incentive programs, stock options. We can go international in a big way—which is long past due."

"We lose control of Miller Timber once it goes public," Anne reminded her. "We'll run into situations that require shareholders' approval. We'll . . . "

"It's out of the question," Doug interrupted brusquely. "It was my mother's wish that the company remain in the family. She built it from nothing into an empire. She . . . "

"Naomi has been dead for twenty years." Felicia struggled not to lash out at him. "It's time for this generation to make the decisions. We can't live in the past. We can't run a successful business empire by rules that have gone down the tube!"

"Forget it, Felicia." Doug was terse. "I'll never vote for us to go public."

"Nor I," Anne backed him up.

"You're out of your minds!" Felicia shrieked. "I've talked to the investment bankers. If we sell when the stock comes out of escrow in December, we can walk off with millions in cash and still own enough shares to control the company. The way the market is going, in another year the stock will be worth half of what it is now."

"Stocks go up, and stocks go down." Doug was unmoveable. "We're not playing for the short haul. Felicia, we start paying dividends in December—your income will escalate impressively. You're a rich woman without going to the investment bankers."

"I'm a rich woman on paper," she fumed. "I think you're both insane."

In the weeks ahead the tension between Felicia and Anne was at an almost unbearable pitch. Felicia knew her only resolution was to find a means to force Doug into voting with her. A means that kept eluding her.

Exhausted from frustration, ever conscious of the passing time and her conviction that the value of their stock would sag badly early in 1984, Felicia decided to retreat to the Big Sur house for a weekend in June. Adrian and Melanie were flying out to join her. Adrian was clever—she'd pick his brains.

Adrian was upset that Melanie was drinking heavily again because she was having such difficulty in conceiving since her miscarriage. He hoped Felicia would help him convince her to go into a sanitarium to be dried out.

"Damn it, Felicia," he confided in a phone call from Washington just before the weekend at Big Sur, "I never know what the hell she'll say to people when she's zonked. And I'm up for reelection next year."

"Cool it, Adrian," Felicia told him. "We'll convince her."

Felicia enjoyed being at the Big Sur house. As she had anticipated, she persuaded Melanie their first evening there to go into a private sanitarium near Lausanne, Switzerland. Ostensibly she would be spending the summer with her mother at a rented chalet "because her mother was exhausted from the Washington Scene."

"Felicia, you're sensational," Adrian congratulated her when they sat alone in the evening over cups of espresso. "She wouldn't do it for me, but she thinks you're terrific."

"Why in hell can't I persuade Doug to go along with this 'going public' deal?" she asked in fresh exasperation. "There has to be a way."

"He's a stubborn old bastard," Adrian said. "But I trust you. You'll come up with something. And that brings to mind something that's bothering me. What the hell should my reaction be to this crummy AIDS situation?"

"It's a bitch," Felicia conceded. "It's like a plague hit the city."

"I've got some letters from voters yelling for federal funds to cope with medical care. On the other hand, we've got something close to panic here. People are scared to death they'll catch AIDS just from rubbing shoulders with somebody who has it—and the numbers are creating hysteria."

Felicia tensed in excitement, remembering newspaper items about verbal assaults and beatings meted out to homosexuals, or those just suspected of being gay, and in a city notable for its liberal attitude to the large gay community. *She knew the way to go.*

"Adrian, I may just have the wedge that'll turn Doug around."

"What?" He stared at her in avid anticipation. "What, Felicia?"

"You know how crazy Doug is about Evan Barlow?"

"That artist he's been nursing along for years?"

"That's right. It's insane, the time and money he's spending on promoting Barlow's exhibit at the Museum in November."

She smiled sardonically. "Naomi's museum, whose name must never be besmirched."

"What are you getting at?" Adrian was puzzled.

"You go out and dig up Brick Griffin. I want him to link Evan Barlow to artists who have AIDS. Brick will know how to handle that. Doug is convinced that this exhibit is a crucial point in Evan's career. The exhibit *has* to be a huge success. But with AIDS scaring the hell out of everybody in San Francisco right now we can make that exhibit a real dog. Who'll come?" she challenged triumphantly, "if we circulate reports that Evan's friends—afflicted with AIDS but determined to show their moral support—will be there?"

"You mean to blackmail the old bastard."

"With any luck at all, yes."

Forty-eight

ON an absurdly cold July morning, Felicia waited for Brick
Griffin in the downtown coffee shop that was their usual rendezvous. She was impatient at his slowness in coming up with
the data she needed to confront Doug. Her confidence was
strong that with the right facts she would force Doug to vote
with her to take the company public.

Then she saw Griffin thrust open the door and enter the
coffee shop. His swagger suggested he had come up with hard
facts.

"Well?" she said while he settled himself across from her.

"Got what you're after, I think." He grinned in triumph.
He was thinking of the bonus she'd promised if the evidence
was what she wanted, Felicia surmised. He shuffled through
papers he'd brought out of a manila envelope. A collection
of snapshots. "A few years ago Evan Barlow was living out
at North Beach. He was sharing a cheap studio with another
artist. Now get this." Griffin leaned forward, looking around
to make sure he couldn't be overheard. In truth, they were
the sole occupants except for a pair of men at the counter.
"The other artist runs some AIDS hospital. And Barlow still
sees him. On a daily basis. Well, can you use that?"

"That's possible ammunition," she conceded, hiding her elation. Evan Barlow had become the center of Doug's life for
the past four or five years. "Keep on it. You might come up
with more."

550

Felicia didn't wait for Griffin to come up with more. She approached Doug late that evening after attending a fund-raiser at the Mark Hopkins. He was in the library, watching television.

"Doug, I have to talk to you."

"Must it be now?"

"Now," she insisted, sitting in a chair across from him.

He sighed, reached to switch off the television, and turned to her. "What is it, Felicia?"

"Doug, I want to call a meeting for tomorrow morning. At this meeting," she said with a detached calmness, "you'll vote—along with me—for the company to go public."

"And why," he demanded coolly, "would I do that?"

"Because if you don't, everybody in San Francisco will know that Evan Barlow once lived with Gregory Sutton. You know about Sutton, that homosexual who's set up a hospital for AIDS victims and runs around fighting for funds for it. He even helps to nurse AIDS patients." She saw Doug's face whiten. "Evan still sees him regularly. I have photographs of him going into Gregory's apartment. Not once but day after day."

"Evan isn't gay. Nor does he ask his friends about their sexual preferences! When did San Francisco worry about that?"

"Since the AIDS epidemic!" Felicia shot back. "We all hear the stories about how AIDS can't be contracted through casual contacts—but people are too hysterical to believe that. They know the awful consequences. Do you think people will flock to the Museum—Naomi's museum," she emphasized, "if they're told that even being afflicted with AIDS won't keep Evan's friends from this crucial exhibit?"

"It's not true!" Doug blazed. "You have no right to . . . "

"Evan Barlow's career will never get off the ground," Felicia interrupted, "whether it's true or not."

"There'll be other exhibits," Doug warned. "Evan is a fine artist." He fought futilely for poise.

"It'll be years before he can make another major stab at an

important exhibit," Felicia declared. "Even if you're around to help him."

"You're using Evan to blackmail me," Doug said after an anguished pause.

"You've got it." Her eyes dared him to defy her. "Evan's future is in your hands. Now, do we call an emergency meeting with Anne tomorrow, or do I spread the word about Evan and Gregory Sutton and who'll be attending Evan's exhibit?"

Tense but confident she waited while Doug fought an inner battle.

"We'll meet in my office at nine-thirty tomorrow morning," he said tersely. "I'll notify Anne."

Though it was close to midnight when Doug phoned her, Anne and Josh hurried to the house, both alarmed by the distress she had heard in his voice. Now they sat with Doug in the library while he repeated what had been said in this room half an hour earlier.

"She has those snapshots—" He gestured helplessly.

"Of course, Evan has been going to Gregory Sutton's apartment every day." Anne's mind was in chaos at the impact of what was happening. "He told Josh and me when we were all at his house for dinner last week. Greg's dying of AIDS."

"Oh my God," Doug gasped. "When will this madness end?"

"Greg's family has turned against him. Even his mother. All of his friends are trying to make his last weeks less desolate." Tears filled her eyes, not self-pity for her own situation, grief for the creative people who were dying of this frightening scourge. "Evan, bless him, has been wonderful to Greg."

"He said nothing to me." Doug was shaken. "I've known Greg for years."

"You know Evan. He would say nothing to you that would be disturbing," Josh told him.

"Annie, I have no choice in this matter." Doug's voice betrayed his inner agony. His eyes pleaded for understanding. "I'm sorry. I can't let Felicia do this to Evan."

"What will happen now?" Anne asked after a moment. *Felicia had won.*

"We'll meet with Felicia in the morning. Later we'll have a meeting with the investment bankers. The process of going public takes at least six months. Financial statements have to be prepared. The papers have to be filed with the Securities and Exchange Commission. She's already explained to the bankers that she wants this accomplished by the time the escrow stock is turned over to the two of you." He paused, as though grappling for strength. "Despite its going public the three of us will continue to control the company and . . . "

"*Felicia* will control the company," Anne interrupted, anger and frustration pounding in her. "We'll all dance to her music."

"She'll approach you about buying out your shares." All at once Doug seemed a tired old man. "It would be wise of you to accept."

"If I don't, I'll draw a salary, but I'll have no voice in any major decision," Anne interpreted. "Both of us puppets on a string."

"I can't gamble with Evan's career," Doug said in anguish. "Evan is like a son to me."

"It's funny, really." Anne managed a shaky laugh. "I've thought these last few years that I'd manage to buy out Felicia. I thought that all she wanted was the money."

"Felicia's power-hungry," Doug replied. "She wants to rule my mother's empire."

"And to make that empire global. I knew," Anne admitted. "I just refused to face it."

"At least, Annie," Doug said gently, "you'll walk out of the company a very wealthy woman." She knew that the prospect of her leaving Miller Timber unnerved him. "But nothing's turning out quite the way Mama planned."

For Anne the dragging weeks ahead—while the investment bankers laid the groundwork for Miller Timber's going public—were a period of much soul-searching. She would never be able to turn Miller Timber around into the image that would have pleased her grandmother, but she was determined in some way to give back to the forests what the forests had earned for her.

She decided, and Josh agreed, that most of the funds she would acquire on that landmark day in late November would go into a foundation. The foundation she had hoped to see set up by Miller Timber, dedicated to research that would help in the urgent battle to improve the environment—or as Robin earnestly declared, "to save our planet."

The evening before the landmark meeting in Arthur Blumberg's office—when 90 percent of Miller Timber shares would be turned over to Anne and Felicia—Anne and Josh lingered before their living-room fireplace, where a blazing fire provided them with fleeting solace.

"It's going to feel so strange not to get up in the morning and go to the office to battle with some fresh problem," Anne said wryly.

"You'll be going to the office soon again," he comforted, reaching for her hand. "The Rae Lazarus Foundation."

"I'm not letting her down, am I? What I couldn't do at Miller Timber we'll do together at her foundation."

"People like us—and our numbers are growing—have to alert the world to the disaster that hovers over us," Josh said quietly. "And we must all understand that unless we work together we're lost."

"I like what the new environmentalists are saying." Anne reached for optimism. "That we can't resort just to fighting against all the abuses that are destroying the earth. That we must face up to the fact that behind the raids on our forests and the acid rain and the waste dumps there are genuine social needs—and we have to find environmentally-acceptable solutions."

"Remember in the late seventies when Pacific Gas and Electric wanted to spend twenty billion dollars on huge coal and nuclear plants in California?" Josh asked. "Plants that many people thought were necessary for the state's economic health—and many others thought would wreck our environment. An Environmental Defense Fund team composed of an economist, an attorney, and a computer analyst worked up a package of alternative energy sources and investments that Pacific Gas and Electric accepted. A package," he pointed out zealously, "that not only satisfied the state's electric needs without wrecking the environment, but provided lower prices for consumers and higher profits for PGandE. And consider the cities that have invested in recycling garbage and burning it in ways that are environmentally safe. And at the same time save on garbage disposal."

"I agonized for quite a while over losing Miller Timber," Anne told Josh, and he smiled in acknowledgement. "But I'm sure what we're doing now would please Grandma."

Anne and Josh were the first to arrive at Josh's father's law offices on this typically foggy morning. Tense, trying to cope with reality, Anne sat in Arthur Blumberg's private office while father and son admired the most recent snapshots of Bert and Janice's two youngsters.

Five minutes later Doug arrived. He embraced Anne in silent apology and commiseration. Not until ten minutes past the scheduled appointment did Felicia walk into the office, an exquisite new chinchilla cape over her trademark Adolfo suit. A victory present to herself, Anne knew instinctively.

They gathered in chairs before Arthur Blumberg's desk while he went through the necessary routine of releasing the escrow stock. Felicia seemed almost detached, Anne thought—and she remembered Felicia's rage twenty years earlier when Arthur Blumberg sat behind the desk in the library at the Miller mansion and read the contents of Naomi's will. It seemed a million years ago.

Clinging to Josh's hand, Anne fought against a suffocating

sense of loss. She was leaving Miller Timber forever. She had known it would be a painful experience but she had not visualized the intensity of that pain.

At close to noon the business transactions were finally completed. Anne had relinquished her stock in Miller Timber, and was a hundred million dollars richer for it. Felicia dashed off, her chinchilla cape over one arm, her eyes brilliant in triumph. Anne and Josh, along with Doug, dallied briefly to talk with Blumberg.

"You know I've just lost the Miller Timber account," Artie said with wry humor. "But I think the firm will survive."

A few minutes later, when they were sure Felicia would not be at the elevators, Anne and Josh left with Doug. Their destination, the Mark Hopkins. Todd and Chris had arranged a party to celebrate the occasion. Todd and Chris, Consuelo and Leon, Shirley and Stu would be waiting for them there.

"Shirley says she expects to be fired any day," Anne reported as they rode down in the elevator. "But it doesn't matter," she said quickly because Doug winced. "Shirley will be working with us at the foundation."

The elevator slid to a stop at the lobby. Anne tried for a festive air as they emerged, then stared in astonishment as Marsh, Robin, Timmy, and Karen darted forward to surround her.

"Don't be angry, Mom," Marsh cajoled. "We just had to be with you today."

Robin and Karen had cut classes. Marsh and Timmy had driven down from Stanford.

"Mother didn't even see us," Karen giggled. "She just raced through the lobby with that gorgeous new chinchilla cape about her shoulders."

"Can you imagine how many chinchillas had to be killed to make that cape?" Robin challenged. "They're so little and furry and cute."

In Doug's limousine and a taxi they left in convivial spirits to join the six waiting at the Mark Hopkins. Anne had phoned to advise that their party had been increased by four. They arrived to find their table graced by a magnum of Dom Perignon, which Leon had ordered.

"You're a free woman, Annie," Shirley chortled as the new arrivals settled about the table. But her eyes were sympathetic. She knew it would be a while before Anne would enjoy her new situation. "Congratulations!"

"Come on, Leon," Stu prodded. "Pour the bubbly. We've got some celebrating to do."

They were all so sweet, Anne thought, while tears lent brightness to her eyes. They understood that she would feel a terrifying sense of loss today despite the wealth that was coming into her hands.

"To the Rae Lazarus Foundation." Leon lifted his glass in a toast when champagne had been poured for everyone, including the two youngest, enthralled at being considered sufficiently grown-up to drink champagne.

"It's the beginning of a wonderful new life for Anne and me," Josh said with quiet satisfaction.

"For us, too," Todd reminded them, because he and Chris would be part of the new foundation. In time, Anne told herself with soaring pleasure, her children and Felicia's children would be involved.

"You know, Annie," Doug told her, "you're the real victor in this battle between Felicia and you. You're rich—not only in money but in love and friendship and dedication, in a way that Felicia will never know."

"Oh yes, Doug." Anne's face was luminous as she gazed about the table. In the course of her "thralldom to Naomi Miller" she had brought together as a warm, loving family those of Naomi Miller's descendents who were "Annie Sachs's children." "And the Rae Lazarus Foundation, along with all the other fine environmental groups growing in strength in this country will fight the likes of Felicia to make this world a better place in which to live. And we'll win!"

Forty-nine

FELICIA slid onto the rear seat of her Mercedes and ordered her chauffeur—a recent acquisition, acquired to emphasize her new status as CEO of Miller Timber—to take her to her apartment. She had never felt so totally pleased with herself as she did today. She'd had to take a staggering loan against her shares to make her initial and major payment to Anne but she was confident she could handle it.

"I'll call you on the car phone when you're to pick me up," she told the chauffeur as they approached their destination.

Walking from the car to the entrance to her posh apartment house she glanced at her watch. Lunch from the Mark Hopkins would be delivered in fifteen minutes. Champagne was chilling in the refrigerator. She would celebrate in solitary splendor.

Not until she was at the door of the apartment did she remember that this was her maid's day off. She reached into her elegant gray Judith Leiber bag for the key, let herself into the austere stillness of the foyer. Though Naomi's Washington Street mansion was her official residence, this was her private kingdom. Timmy and Karen had never been here. On two occasions, when it was useful to her, Doug was a guest at a dinner party here.

She walked down the hall to the master bedroom to hang away her cherished chinchilla. Her eyes focused on the night table beside her bed, where a copy of Norman's new book, already a best-seller, awaited her reading. She didn't *want* to read the stupid book, but she enjoyed the vision of herself making some clever, disparaging remarks about it.

All at once the silence in the apartment was oppressive, threatening her exhilaration. She reached to switch on the radio. Music filled the bedroom. Her gaze swung again to the book on the night table. Damn Norman for marrying that little bitch. So *young*—when she felt menopause breathing down her neck.

She frowned at the jarring sound of the phone and reached to unplug it from the wall. It would be her mother, waiting to pounce with a clutch of bills she'd been running up all year, knowing the escrow stock was due for transferral.

She crossed to the closet wall to hang away the chinchilla cape. Pausing before the opened door she began unconsciously to stroke the luxurious fur. All at once she was aware of sexual arousal. And of her aloneness. An unfamiliar, unanticipated fear invaded her.

What was the matter with her? This was absurd, she admonished herself, and turned to gaze at her reflection in the mirrored segment of the closet, anxious for reassurance.

She was still damned attractive, she told herself. And face-lifts—and other lifts—would keep her that way for a lot of years. For a startled, unnerving instant she thought of Eva, her throat tightening as she remembered her grandmother. *No.* She wasn't like Eva.

She lifted her head in defiance. She didn't need anybody. Not Norman. Not a stable of young studs. She was Felicia Harris. One of the richest women in the country—and one of the most powerful. Like Naomi, she would become a legend in her own time.

Contemporary Fiction From Robin St. Thomas

Fortune's Sisters   (2616, $3.95)

It was Pia's destiny to be a Hollywood star. She had complete self-confidence, breathtaking beauty, and the help of her domineering mother. But her younger sister Jeanne began to steal the spotlight meant for Pia, diverting attention away from the ruthlessly ambitious star. When her mother Mathilde started to return the advances of dashing director Wes Guest, Pia's jealousy surfaced. Her passion for Guest and desire to be the brightest star in Hollywood pitted Pia against her own family—sister against sister, mother against daughter. Pia was determined to be the only survivor in the arenas of love and fame. But neither Mathilde nor Jeanne would surrender without a fight. . . .

Lover's Masquerade   (2886, $4.50)

New Orleans. A city of secrets, shrouded in mystery and magic. A city where dreams become obsessions and memories once again become reality. A city where even one trip, like a stop on Claudia Gage's book promotion tour, can lead to a perilous fall. For New Orleans is also the home of Armand Dantine, who knows the secrets that Claudia would conceal and the past she cannot remember. And he will stop at nothing to make her love him, and will not let her go again . . .